Hot Roll

HOT ROLL

Caught Dead in Wyoming, Book 8

Patricia McLinn

Dear Readers: If you encounter typos or errors in this book, please send them to me
at Patricia@patriciamclinn.com. Even with many layers of editing, mistakes can slip
through, alas. But, together, we can eradicate the nasty nuisances. Thank you!
— Patricia McLinn

DAY ONE

FRIDAY

Chapter One

THE MOST EFFECTIVE means of communication for every TV newsroom I've worked in is eavesdropping.

It's faster and far more interesting than any memo. Also more accurate.

But newsroom eavesdropping is specialized.

A good newsroom eavesdropper quickly learns who to eavesdrop on. In other words, the best sources. And then this good newsroom eavesdropper refines the input by tuning in or out according to the nuances of the eavesdropping target's volume (Whisper? Must be something good) and tone (Excitement? Dismay? Listen up.)

It's not bragging to say I'm one of the top TV newsroom eaves-droppers. Colleagues and even the more fair-minded of my rivals will tell you Elizabeth Margaret Danniher is up there with the best.

Not that there's much scope for my skills in the KWMT-TV news-room in Sherman, Wyoming, not even my eavesdropping skills.

I'd begun to wonder if those particular skills will rust, since news is not a daily occurrence here, much less multiple times a day.

Will rust? Who was I kidding? I was worried they *had* rusted.

Only two days ago I'd overheard Jennifer Lawton, someone I considered a mentee, a friend, talking about a breakup with a boyfriend I hadn't even known she had, a roustabout for a local oil company.

I gathered the breakup had come almost two months ago, while their dating had been some time before that.

And I hadn't heard a thing.

Yes, we'd all been involved in solving a murder until a few days ago and I'd been on real estate overload since. Plus, I wasn't entirely unpacked from a trip East that included tying up loose ends with my ex and stopping off to see family.

No excuse for a pro eavesdropper.

It came down to this: If my eavesdropping was only good for retroactive information, I might as well hang it up as KWMT-TV's "Helping Out!" consumer affairs reporter much less as a real newsperson.

Knowing I'd missed the beginning, middle, and end of Jennifer's relationship probably sensitized my eavesdropping now.

That didn't mean listening to every word.

As a production assistant and news aide, Jennifer answered the phone a *lot* at KWMT-TV. Constant eavesdropping on her would be like those people with hyperthymesia who remember every detail of everything.

I first tuned in from across the scramble of old desks that passes for a newsroom when I heard "This is her. She. Her. I'm her. She." She huffed out a breath. "Jennifer Lawton is me."

I made a mental note to suggest, during our next discussion on making a career in journalism, that she go with "This is Jennifer Lawton" to avoid grammatical breakdowns under pressure ... which she seemed to be experiencing at the moment.

"*Who* are you?" Her tone confirmed my *pressure* theory and kicked me into full eavesdropping mode.

"What? ... No. *No.* ... But... That's not possible. There must be some mistake—Oh... Oh, *no.*"

She was typing into her computer. Presumably what the person on the other end said. I knew from experience that she could type as fast as I could talk, which was considerably faster than most people I'd encountered in Wyoming.

"Yes. I will check ... But I don't understand... You have to tell me—No... Yes. Good-bye."

She stood, half turning toward me, phone still in her hand.

I was already out of my chair, picking up speed when I saw her expression.

But instead of coming toward me, she continued pivoting and headed for the door marked Ladies' Room.

I adjusted my path and entered a space so small the sign should have said Lady's Room.

She hadn't reached either of the two stalls, falling to the floor, collapsed against the wall and half under the farther sink, sobbing.

✧ ✧ ✧ ✧

"WHAT IS IT, Jennifer? Tell me what's wrong."

I was on the floor, too, with her head pulled into my shoulder and really wishing I'd kicked off my shoes first.

I'd been celebrating the someday-I-might-be-warm-again promise of the weather by not wearing boots—snow or otherwise—but now the cute little heels were digging into me. One into my derriere as I sat on that foot, the other into my thigh. These kitten heels were fully clawed. Or was it their teeth biting into me?

"She's *dead...*"

My heart clenched. "Who? Who's dead?"

She lived with her parents here in town, would someone have called her at the station if—?

"Calliope."

Not her mother's first name. I didn't recall what it was right now, but I would have remembered Calliope.

"Oh, *God.* I can't believe she's dead." She sobbed harder into my shoulder, but I caught fragments. "...I'm a horrible friend... My best friend..."

I knew she was close to a group of computer whizzes online, though they'd never met in person. One of them—?

"...little kids... into high school... the best. The *best... deserted* her..."

Not an online friend. Someone she'd known in real life.

Her lament of sorrow, guilt, regret continued along with the tears.

I wanted to say something wise. Something consoling.

I had nothing.

Worse than nothing.

Any possibility of inspiration could not get past the pain of these heels stabbing into my flesh.

Holding Jennifer's shoulders to minimize the jolt to her, I shifted to my hip and pulled the heel-in-my-derriere shoe-wearing foot out from under me.

Swallowing a huff of partial relief, I managed, "You were the best friend you could be, Jennifer."

"No, I wasn't. I was a terrible friend. She wanted me to come down to Colorado to visit her. She kept asking. She really wanted me to come and I kept making excuses. Work and my parents—They've never really liked her."

That brought on a renewed bout of sobbing.

I came up partway on my knees and reached around with one hand, working this shoe loose.

"But…" She mumbled directly into my shoulder and I didn't catch it.

"What?" Flexing my foot and tugging at the heel, the first shoe finally came loose. I dropped it to my side.

"I lied to her. It wasn't because of work or my parents."

With the worst pain gone, the second-worst pain—the one in my other hip—shot to the top of the list.

"It was because I didn't want to risk missing out on anything if you and the others … you know."

I knew.

A group of us had pursued a number of investigations and we'd often called on Jennifer's computer skills and other connections to help us figure things out.

"How selfish could I be? I ignored my friend for a little excitement and now she's… Oh, God, now she's *dead*."

With this fresh bout of crying came shudders. I held her tighter.

She sucked in deep, open-mouthed breaths like she'd been under-water. In a way, she had been, with all her tears.

"Easy. Easy," I advised.

Stroking her shoulder and back to encourage her breathing, I reached around with my other hand, trying to get the second heel out of my thigh.

It felt selfish and petty to concern myself with my minor woes at the moment, but as I would tell her—eventually—beating herself up for pursuing her interests didn't do any good and wasn't what a true friend would want. Just as my suffering served no purpose, neither did her self-blame.

Besides, I'd think better post-torture.

But the frame of the stall behind me prevented moving my foot away from my body. The only way to remove the shoe was to press the heel deeper into my flesh.

Jennifer had calmed a bit, even lifting her head. Possibly wondering what I was doing.

"Your friend—Calliope—had she been sick?"

"Sick? No. She's totally healthy, that's what my parents didn't get. She kicked it. She really did. But they couldn't see her any different." She gave a coughing kind of sob. "I'm no better. I couldn't be bothered to go see her or anything."

I bit my lip against the pain of the heel driving deeper.

I could ask Jennifer about not seeing her friend for a long time. I could ask about an apparent rift over this friend with her parents. I could ask what I really wanted to ask—how did she die. Or…

"What did she kick?" When the safest topic is someone's addiction, you are definitely in touchy territory.

"Cocaine."

I made a noncommittal sound. That was an achievement. Not only because of the kitten claw stabbing me. But because the idea of a contemporary of Jennifer's having been addicted and beating it by that age…

I know. A sure sign of aging when law enforcement, athletes, actors, and recovered addicts all look like they're twelve.

"But she's done really, really well," Jennifer continued. "She went to rehab down there, got off the stuff, and she's stayed off. She's gone totally healthy. She does—" She blinked, swallowed, then started again.

"She did all this hiking up in the mountains. She knows—knew her way around."

My heel finally slid free. I unwedged the shoe and almost groaned with the relief. I pushed the shoe to the side.

Jennifer straightened away from me. "Sorry."

I *had* groaned with relief.

"No, no. It's okay." I hugged her.

Lots of people would think this was a natural point to get Jennifer talking about something different. To change the topic. To get her to stop crying.

My experience said this is the time to keep the tears flowing, to let out as many as need to come, so they don't clog up the system later. Possibly forever.

"You said she went to rehab down *there*. Where?"

"North of Denver. She did great. And she stayed because she had support and—" She gulped. "—friends. And she fell in love with hiking and stuff. That's why it doesn't make sense." More tears came and her shoulders shook, like a young tree lashed by rain. "It doesn't… make sense."

A knock—determined, but hesitant—sounded at the door.

"Go away," I told the knocker.

"Elizabeth? It's Mike." Michael Paycik was KWMT-TV's "Eye on Sports."

He also was a former NFL player and a strong prospect for a great TV news career. But that wasn't why he was knocking on the ladies' room door.

Paycik, camerawoman Diana Stendahl, a rancher named Tom Burrell, Jennifer, and I, aided by an assortment of Cottonwood County citizens, had solved a number of crimes together including the oh-so-recent one.

Based on that partnership, I suspected someone or multiple someones in the newsroom enlisted him to get the story of what was going on with Jennifer.

Also, possibly, to clear the ladies' room. But more likely to find out what was going on, since no one could eavesdrop effectively through the door.

Mike being outside the door told me Diana was not in the building. She would have been everyone's first choice for this job, especially Mike's.

"Are you two okay?" he asked.

"No, but there's nothing you can do right now."

"Can I stick my head in?"

I looked at Jennifer. She nodded. She had her back and one shoulder to the door anyway.

"Okay."

The door eased open slowly. Mike's thick head of brown hair came into view first and then his cameras-love-that-bone-structure face. He gave the closet-sized room a quick, curious glance, then zoomed in on us, sitting on the floor.

"I don't want to pry." A fib, but he was a good guy who tried to curb the curiosity at inopportune moments. "But thought you should know Thurston called in from lunch, looking for Jennifer to do something for him. Audrey told him she might be in the archives, so that bought some time, but..."

We all understand what came after the *but*.

...Thurston will call back, brooking no excuses for not getting what he wanted.

Thurston Fine, the station's one and only full-time anchor took lunches long enough to do a bacchanal proud. But between lunch and his afternoon nap, he not only would get irked at not having his work done for him, he might be alert enough to make her pay for thwarting him. If she was here.

"I take it back, Mike. There is something you can do. Get our coats and purses—Jennifer's and mine. We're leaving." She looked up at my executive decision. "No arguing. Mike will tell Thurston and Les that you're sick and I'm taking you home."

"I don't want to go home. My parents... Calliope... No. I don't want to go there."

I understood her not wanting to be with parents who had disapproved of her friend right now. I also could understand her parents' viewpoint, which surely included concern about the friend's cocaine addiction. Was there more they hadn't approved of?

Jennifer's broken off sentences about her friend and her parents might bear digging into at some point, but not now. I stuck with the practical. "We're not going to your house."

"Yours?" Her question held a measure of relief.

My house?

The phrase felt odd. Unnatural. Yet it was true. Sort of.

I was about to move to a house in town. I planned to rent it until legalities concerning a will and probate were sorted out. Then I'd buy it in an already done deal. But that wasn't where we'd be going.

"The Bunkhouse," I said of the efficiency apartment on Diana's ranch I'd been renting.

"Aren't you packing?" In response to my head shake, Mike added, "Shouldn't you be?"

"Not much to pack, but come to think of it, the Bunkhouse isn't the best place. I have clothes all over to sort." On my trip East, I'd shopped in Washington, D.C., plus picked up items from a wardrobe stash my parents were storing. "It's a mess. We'll go to Diana's. She won't mind."

"I could—" Mike was about to volunteer to come with.

"No, you can't. You have to work."

We exchanged a look. I hoped my side conveyed—tactfully—that it wasn't only his professional duties keeping him from joining us.

Jennifer needed to let her emotions out. She didn't hang on Mike the way most females did around here. Most men, as a matter of fact. Still, sobbing unreservedly was easier to do without a good-looking, hometown hero, and former pro football player around.

His nod confirmed *message received*. He let the door close slowly behind him.

"C'mon. Let's get up. This is going to take some planning. I'll go first." I pulled my legs back from their stretch into the stall, got them under me and, by grabbing the edge of the sink with both hands, stood without encountering those heels that could double as an ice pick.

A knock, followed immediately by Mike's voice. "Ready."

I opened the door. He handed over the purses first. What is it with men not wanting to touch a woman's purse? You'd think they were radioactive the way they hold them gingerly and unload them with more speed than grace. It frequently leaves the female to struggle to get her arms into the coat while encumbered with a purse strap.

Maybe I'd maligned Mike, however. Because, while he handed me my coat, he held up Jennifer's. To get into the coat, she had to turn away from the curious eyes in the newsroom. It also put the coat and Mike's taller and wider body between the curiosity and Jennifer.

He truly was a good guy.

"Call me after the Five," I said quietly to him in passing. Waiting until after he did the sports segment on the evening news should give Jennifer time to regain her footing.

I whisked her out of the building and to my SUV.

All the while, hearing her words from just before Mike knocked pricking at me.

It doesn't make sense…

What was that quote from Shakespeare about by the pricking of my thumbs, knowing evil this way comes?

It doesn't make sense…

Chapter Two

JENNIFER DOZED ON the drive to the ranch Diana took over when an accident left her a young widow with two children. She'd gone to work for KWMT-TV to support her family and leased out the grazing land to support the ranch while keeping it intact for her kids.

It doesn't make sense...

Does the death of a young person *ever* make sense?

For that matter of a middle-aged or old person. Heck, I think the whole system of death stinks.

She lived a good, long life.

No good life is long enough.

He lived the full measure of his days.

Then top off the measure with some more days.

But I didn't think Jennifer's words had to do with my objections to mortality.

Instead, the words and her tone pinged my journalist radar.

It doesn't make sense...

But this was not the time to be a journalist. Certainly not yet. Maybe not ever in this case.

At Diana's house, I settled Jennifer on the couch by the big rock fireplace, tucking an afghan around her.

Sometimes the only possible follow-up to a storm of tears was to close your eyes and hope sleep knit up what Shakespeare called the *ravell'd sleave of care.*

Poor Jennifer's sleeve of care needed a lot of knitting.

While I made hot tea in the kitchen on the other end of the open front half of the house, my dog, a multi-breed named Shadow, sat pressed against her knees. She bent over and hugged him, her chin on the top of his head. And he let her.

He truly was becoming a social creature.

When I brought the two mugs of tea and fixings, Shadow dropped down to lie on her feet. I knew he beat any afghan for comforting and warmth.

Her downcast gaze fixed on the mug.

Sitting beside her, I felt like an amateur trying to lance an abscess.

On a family camping trip, one of my brothers broke down and admitted to one just before bedtime. The choice was pack us all up and drive eighty miles or DIY. Dad heated a sharp knife, and held my brother. Mom did the deed.

He howled, but felt much better by the next day, with the help of antibiotic from Mom's traveling pharmacy.

I wish Mom were the one wielding the knife now. There was only me.

"How long have you and Calliope been friends?"

She made a noise that reverberated with self-recrimination.

I hastily added, "How did you meet?"

"We always sort of knew each other. But then in middle school she drew my name to do this project on a day in the life of somebody from another country. Then I drew the country and we got Brazil. And it was great, because I had friends there already—from the internet—and all we had to do was like ask them about their daily lives and we had all the information we needed. Then she wrote it up—she was a really good writer—and we got a great grade."

We got the information? I'd bet that was all Jennifer, with her computer skills and connections. Yet she shared that credit while giving Calliope solo credit for the writing.

"Sounds like you were a good team, with complementary skills. You found the information and she presented it."

She continued looking down at the mug of tea between her hands. "Yeah. We got to be friends and by high school we were together all the time."

"Best friends?"

She hitched one shoulder. "In real life, she was. I should have been there for Calliope. I shouldn't have—"

"How could you have done anything? Did she…? Was it drugs?"

"*No*. She was *clean*. And it sucks people will think that."

I had to quit wimping out. Time to lance the abscess. "How did she die?"

"He said she was hiking in a national park and fell."

"How awful. But you couldn't possibly have done anything, Jennifer. An accident, in another state—"

"He said incident. And it's all wrong. He said she fell… But she *wouldn't*."

It doesn't make sense…

She didn't say the words this time, yet I heard their echo.

"She was so coordinated. You know how some people are born knowing how to move? That was Calliope. She never was clumsy. She never even bumped into things. First time she ever tried she did a perfect back flip. And *reactions*? God, I remember being with her when she was driving and we couldn't have been more than sixteen or seventeen and this pronghorn came out of nowhere. And she never hesitated—I was screaming—she steered behind it as it ran across the road, then came back into our lane and never dropped a word she was saying.

"So how could he say she just *fell*. How could she?"

"Who said she just fell? Who was it on the phone?"

"I… I don't know. I don't *know*. Oh, my God. I didn't ask him. I didn't ask *anything*. I forgot everything you ever taught me. The most important time in my whole life to be like a journalist and I totally failed. I didn't even—"

"Whoa, whoa, whoa. Hold up there. Quit self-flagellating and—"

"Self-*what*?" Very faintly, surprise showed in her eyes. At least it was something other than misery.

"Flagellating. It's whipping, flogging as punishment. And when you throw in self-, you're doing it to yourself, which is entirely uncalled for. So stop."

"But—"

"No buts. Forget what you didn't find out. Tell me what he said."

"He said she fell. There was an incident and—" She sucked in a sob, trying to stifle it and hiccupping in the process. "—I don't remember anything else. It's blank. She was hiking at Rocky Mountain National Park near—"

"Another detail. Where she was hiking."

"Oh. Right."

"And you were typing while you were on the call, so you have more information on your computer at the station. When you go in tomorrow—"

She gave a scoffing *pfft*. "Tomorrow? I can retrieve everything from work remotely."

She had her device out before I could blink. In about the same amount of time, she sighed deeply and tossed it down to the cushion on her other side.

"Not who called. Or when it happened. Or how. Or any of that."

"We'll find out. We'll find out as much as we can of what you want to know. But first—"

First, she needed to feel more. Not *get it out,* because grief wasn't kept in neat compartments, so you could drain the container once and be done with it. But to feel what she needed to feel.

Who, what, when, where, how, and why formed a sturdy framework for a news story. They also could create a screen to hide your feelings behind. Temporarily.

"—I'm going to get you more tea."

I was nearly done making the second round of tea when my phone vibrated.

"It's Diana," I called to Jennifer. "If you don't want me to tell her anything—"

"No, you should tell her. It's her house. Besides…"

She didn't add to that *besides* and the phone vibrated a second time, so I answered.

Diana cut off my greeting. "Mike told me. Someone died?"

"Uh-huh."

"Not family." She said it with certainty. She'd checked somehow and, knowing Diana, it had not been a clumsy phone call to the Lawton household asking if all its members were still shuffling along on this mortal coil. (What was with my Shakespeare-quoting today?) "Friend?"

"Uh-huh."

"How is Jennifer?"

"Middling."

"You're at my place?"

"With the upheaval at the Bunkhouse—"

"Not criticizing or complaining, just confirming. You did the right thing. The kids won't be home until after dinner. But I was going to be there soon. I started before dawn for a weather shoot. What do you think?"

"See you soon."

"You sure she wants to see any more people?"

"It'll be fine."

"Okay. See you soon."

Jennifer was staring glassy-eyed at the wall.

"Diana's coming home soon."

"Okay."

"You don't have to talk about things if you don't want to…"

"I do. I'm going to need to, aren't I?"

I murmured not-entirely truthful agreement. Telling her some of us were pretty darned good at mashing down things we needed to talk about until they exploded out at the most inopportune moment didn't seem like a good plan.

Her thoughts apparently followed a different path. She said, "But… For right now, can I tell you about when we were kids, Calliope and me? Before… Before everything."

"Of course."

I handed her a mug of tea, sat beside her, and drew a larger afghan up over both our laps. Then I listened.

Chapter Three

"...CALLIOPE WASN'T BIG into outdoors when she lived here."

I'd heard about their growing friendship—true BFF. When Calliope started dating a boy named Lance, the three of them formed a unit.

That spoke well of Calliope to me. Of Lance, too.

Jennifer muttered darkly about someone not approving *for no good reason*.

About Lance joining the friends? And who didn't approve? Her parents? Calliope's? His?

I stilled my questions. Those details didn't matter. Letting Jennifer talk did.

At the start of college at Colorado State in Fort Collins, Calliope began abusing opioids.

"She said if she'd been like most people, she'd have gotten addicted to those," Jennifer said. "Instead, she told me it gave her the feeling she could use anything without getting addicted. Cocaine said otherwise. She said she thought she became addicted the first time she used. I didn't think that could happen, but I researched and it can because of how it changes the brain."

As Jennifer talked, a picture emerged of Calliope as a high functioning addict who could have gone on for years without seeking help. She'd even gotten decent grades.

But then Lance broke up with her over her drug use and returned to Sherman to take classes at Cottonwood County Community College.

Calliope's drug use multiplied.

A month later, she went to the ER thinking she was going to die after a binge.

It scared her enough that when her parents arrived, she asked to go into rehab. She tried to back out later and even ran away from the facility once, but gradually the program took hold with her—or she took hold of the program, aided greatly by the outdoor living components preached and practiced.

"Hiking and stuff was part of rehab. She said it was something to get through at the beginning. Then she told me that one day she was out there, plodding along, one foot after another, when she suddenly took this breath, like it was her first really deep breath ever and she looked around and *saw* things. And she's loved it ever since. The way she talks about it…"

"Made you want to try it, too?"

She cut me an are-you-crazy? look. "No. It's how I felt when I first found computers as a kid, though. But it might have hit her even harder because she was so much older when she found it. She wanted to move up to Estes Park, this town right at the entrance to Rocky Mountain National Park. She said almost everybody there did hiking and nature stuff all year round. We talked about how she could do that, get a job to support her up there and stuff. She could be outdoors practically all the time. Lots of people have that idea, so jobs can be hard to find. I sent her listings a few months ago I'd found online." Her lips trembled. "She knew as much about computers as I do about the outdoors."

I patted her arm. "You were a good friend, Jennifer. The two of you connected as people, not just what you like to do. That's important."

Shadow's head came up. Then he stood. But he was relaxed, expectant.

A moment or two later we heard a vehicle.

I opened the door to Diana. Good thing, because her arms held a full load of grocery bags.

She deposited them on the top of the counter, patted Shadow in greeting, then went immediately to the sofa, sat beside Jennifer, and hugged her wordlessly.

Over Diana's shoulder, I saw tears well up in Jennifer's eyes again.

"Word about Calliope has reached Penny." Diana accompanied the words with a significant look over her opposite shoulder to me.

Message received.

Penny Czylinski was a checker at the Sherman Supermarket.

Which was like saying Michael Jordan played a little basketball.

It was the truth while totally missing the point.

From her spot at the checkout register, Penny gathered and disseminated information about Cottonwood County and its residents with enough breadth, depth, speed, and accuracy to turn any search engine green with envy. Also like those search engines, she frequently presented results, connections and sequences leaving the beholder thinking *Huh?*

I said to Jennifer, "That means your folks will hear about Calliope any minute, if they haven't heard already. You should call them."

She grimaced.

"I can't imagine they won't be sad about Calliope and concerned about you, no matter how much they disapproved and worried about her drug use." When Jennifer said nothing, I became more direct. "Is something else going on between you and your parents?"

She sighed. "Maybe. I guess."

I used one of the journalist's strongest weapons—silence.

I'd told her about its power. Told her it would draw people to speak even when they didn't intend to. Told her to wait. And wait. And wait.

"I was dating a guy and they didn't approve of us."

Someday I'd remind her about this as proof that silence and waiting worked. Not anytime soon.

"*Was* dating?"

"We broke up."

"Because of your parents?"

"Not really." That wasn't convincing.

"Why didn't they approve of him?"

Her shoulder jerked. "He works for the oil company, I guess. But you're wrong about them and Calliope. She's dead and they won't even ca—"

"No, don't say they won't care, Jennifer," Diana said. "They care. Even if they care only because you do, but I bet they care because of Calliope, too, with the two of you being friends for so long. And they'll worry about you."

The moment drew out.

Jennifer looked down. "Guess I should let them know where I am."

"Use my room," Diana suggested. "Down the hall to the right."

As Diana and I put away groceries, I recapped from the moment my eavesdropping kicked into gear.

She filled in one gap. Calliope's last name was Grandisher.

"Poor kid," she murmured. "Make that kids. Plural. Calliope and Jennifer. Always together. Opposites complementing each other. What a shame."

"Do you know the family?" As soon as it was out, I knew it was a useless question. "How well do you know them?"

"I wouldn't say well. A little. He's the top guy for Sedick Oil here. The company first sent him here earlier in his career, when Calliope was maybe in elementary school. He spent some time at headquarters in Houston before coming back as the top guy here. Most of those oil execs and engineers move up and out fast or go to another company— either way, they don't put down roots here.

"Even when the Grandishers came back, with him in charge, nobody thought they'd stick. But they have, even after Calliope left for college, then stayed down in Colorado for rehab."

"What are you frowning about?"

"After saying that about the oil people not putting down roots, I realized the Grandishers have and so has another family. He started with Sedick here out of grad school. Moved up quickly, then spent a spell at headquarters, too. Everybody thought that was the last we'd see of them, but they came back. Understandable, I guess, since he'd married a local girl. Probably explains why he didn't leave the company when Owen Grandisher—Calliope's father—remained in the top job here everybody thought would go to Brady Joudrey."

"Let me guess. Lance's father?"

"Yes. How did you—? Jennifer told you?"

"Some of the story. Enough to get a star-crossed lovers vibe. Was it a true Romeo and Juliet story, with the rival fathers driving them apart after high school?"

Romeo and Juliet? More Shakespeare. I should try someone different. Though his tragedies did fit the mood.

To Diana, I added, "Along with little things like going to different colleges and Calliope's drug use?"

"I really don't know. From what I've heard, the two couples, the Grandishers and the Joudreys, are part of the country club crowd and spend a lot of time in Jackson when execs from the company are there. The social set, I guess you'd call them. Not old Cottonwood County like Linda."

Linda Caswell was one of the leading citizens of the county. She'd also become a friend.

She might not know the Grandishers well, but she'd know some. If I could get her to talk. A big *if*.

"So Leona would know the Grandishers?" I asked Diana of Leona D'Amato, the part-time "society" reporter for KWMT-TV.

"Oh, yeah. She'll know all about everything. But why do you want to know?"

"It's probably the shock, but Jennifer seems to feel something's weird about this. Background never hurts."

"There's always Penny," Diana suggested.

I snorted. "With the amount you bought, no one's going to need to go back to the supermarket any time soon. Why *did* you buy so much? Thought you said Gary and his pals weren't going to be here tonight— Oh, are you thinking Mike is coming? He's supposed to call or—"

A knock at her door interrupted.

"He did call. He called me. I said he should come," she said.

Since Diana had her hands full with a tub of guacamole and a bowl, I went to the door.

And opened it—not to Mike, but to Tom Burrell, the rancher

who'd helped with those inquiries I mentioned.

But this wasn't an inquiry.

"What are you doing—?"

"Heard about Calliope. Mike said you all were here. How's Jenny?" As a long-time friend of her family, he enjoyed exemption from her mandate that she was now Jennifer. At least a partial exemption from instantaneous reprimands when he slipped and used Jenny. "Where is she?"

"She's in my room. Calling her parents," Diana said. "Close the door, Elizabeth. It's not summer yet."

Couldn't argue that. No matter what the calendar said, the air said *brrr.*

Tom had already walked in, detouring toward the living area to hook his cowboy hat on the back of a chair. "Glad she's calling. They're worried about her. Called the station when they got the word and they said you'd brought her here. Told them I'd swing by and see about Jenny."

"That's nice of you." I closed the door and returned to the kitchen. "But I'm not sure she's going to want a lot of people around. It's a rough time and she might want privacy. To be alone to—"

I was interrupted by another knock.

This one was followed quickly by the door opening from the out-side—no need for me to respond, because Mike was letting himself in, talking as he came.

"How's she doing?"

Under Mike's questioning about Jennifer, then Diana's answer, Tom said quietly to me, "That's you, Elizabeth."

"What's me?"

"Not wanting people around when you're hurting. That's you. Not Jenny."

Before I could respond, he joined Diana and Mike by the sink. He took the guacamole tub, bowl, and a spoon from Diana to finish the transfer while she lined a basket with paper towel for chips. Mike took out glasses and I began adding ice.

"Oh."

We all turned to Jennifer, standing in the doorway from the hall. Her eyes went bright with more tears, but the smallest smile trembled to life.

"You're all here."

I stepped toward her. "If it's too much. If you want—"

"No. It's good. We have to talk anyway."

I didn't quite get that, but before I could question her, Diana said, "What we have to do first is eat. Start with chips and guacamole while I make sandwiches. Did you talk to your parents?"

"Yes. They were... They were nice. I said one of you would drive me home. If that's a problem—"

"No," came from four voices. Mike added, "I'll take you home when I go in for the Five, Jen—Jennifer."

For the five o'clock news, he'd deliver local, state, national, and international sports in a time block he continually fought to keep Thurston from whittling. Later, he'd update his report for an even shorter segment at ten.

"Thanks, but..."

"But right now," Diana said, "we eat. Have any of us had lunch? I didn't think so. We'll talk about something else for a little. Tom, I heard Tamantha's in Cheyenne this weekend."

His Abraham Lincoln-esque face—though from the better-looking side of the family—softened, as always, at mention or thought of his daughter, a third-grader to be reckoned with.

"She was picked for a school program about government called Future Governors of Wyoming."

I snort-laughed, choking on a bit of lettuce in my sandwich. "Future? The current occupant better lock, bar, and bolt the office door or she'll take over today."

"Nah. Told her no political office until she's legal to drive."

✧　✧　✧　✧

"YOU SIT, JENNIFER. You, too, Diana. You made the sandwiches." Mike paused long enough from his putting away leftovers to gesture them toward the seating by the fireplace. "We'll clean up."

"And then we'll talk," I said.

Tom deposited plates next to the sink where I was rinsing and loading into the dishwasher. "*Now* you want her to talk."

The lines at the corners of his eyes folded into a *gotcha* grin.

We finished in the kitchen and brought a plate of my cookies into the sitting area.

Sort of my cookies.

Pepperidge Farm Double Dark Chocolate Milano cookies are my favorite store-bought cookies. Since I rarely bake these days and my mom's cookies, as well as their like baked by family members, are 1,200 miles east of here in Illinois, that makes Pepperidge Farm Double Dark Chocolate Milano pretty much my favorite cookies, period.

Being a cautious kind of person, I keep a supply on hand for cookie emergencies.

Being a kind person, Diana keeps a separate supply on hand in her kitchen for cookie emergencies when I don't want to make the three-minute commute to the Bunkhouse. Would she still do that when I moved into town?

Was I feeling sentimental about her backup cookie stash?

Yes.

When Mike, Tom, and I joined Diana and Jennifer by the big rock fireplace, we saw neither was resting.

Diana was folding laundry fresh from the dryer. Jennifer—of course—was on her phone.

"What are you doing?" Mike sat beside Jennifer with two of my—okay, Diana's—cookies in one hand. At his rate of consumption, her backup stash would be gone before he left for the station.

"Nothing. My phone's acting up. Even if Diana's service isn't working—"

"It is," she said.

"—I should be getting out. But I'm not. It wasn't great when I called my parents, but now..." She released a long sigh. "I was trying to get the word out. Should have done it right away."

"Do you know the arrangements already?" Diana folded the last of her son's t-shirts, nested the full basket into the empty one and pushed them behind her chair.

I took the matching chair, while Tom sat at the narrow end of our rectangle, facing the fireplace.

"Arrangements? Oh. That." Jennifer's voice flattened on the final word. "No. I was trying to get the word out to start people working on background so we can investigate."

Chapter Four

DIANA BROKE A momentary silence I assumed was brought on by surprise.

That was certainly the cause of my silence.

"Investigate?" she asked. "You mean Calliope's death? But it was an accident."

"He didn't say accident. He said incident." Jennifer tapped her screen, apparently futilely trying to get it to respond. Then she put it down. Not gently. "And besides—"

"Jennifer," I tried.

"—Calliope would not just have fallen. She wouldn't. She—"

"*Who* said?" Mike interrupted. "Who called you? What did he say? Why did he call you?"

"Mike." Diana reproved him mildly.

"It's okay. I know you've all got to know the details to investigate like you always do. I can't be all emotional…" Jennifer swallowed. "I have to face it. To know, I have to… I have to…"

"Jennifer." Tom's voice was soft.

"Don't. I'm not a kid. I know about what an investigation means. I've seen what you all do. I've *helped* do it. I do know. I know it means getting answers." She picked up her phone again. "I took notes during the call. Not much. Not everything, like I should have, but he didn't say much. And I didn't ask *anything.*"

She clicked through to what she wanted. "It's so slow… At least I can see my notes. He said he was calling from Colorado. Asked if I was Jennifer Lawton in Sherman, Wyoming. I said yes. He said he regretted to inform me—like the movies—there'd been an incident and Calliope Grandisher had died in a fall today in Rocky Mountain National Park.

"That's all he said. Or all I wrote down. I should've—"

I cut her off. "Wait a minute, Jennifer. You asked who he was. What did he say?"

"I…" She looked at her notes again. "I don't have anything. I don't remember… I don't think he answered, but… I totally fell apart. The one time I should have—"

Diana stretched a hand to her across the coffee table. "Don't. A call like that? Out of the blue? It knocks everything else out of your head."

But what seemed to dry her tears the most was Mike's "Hey. You're human."

"There are always other ways to find information," I said. "A death from falling in a national park, that's sure to be reported. So, we'll get the basics from local news reports."

"Not KWMT's news reports," Mike said bitterly. "Not unless someone hit Thurston over the head with the news release. He sure didn't have it when I left the station, so you know he won't be putting it on the Five. Heck, he's practically locked in stone for his blocks for the Ten already. He won't even look at news releases for fear he'd have to read cold copy."

I ate a cookie—another cookie—thoughtfully.

"Elizabeth?" Diana said. "What's that expression about?"

"Thurston doesn't pay attention to incoming news, but I know someone who does. Excuse me."

With a cookie as sustenance, I took myself and my phone into the back of the house, finding my way to the guest room, so the others could keep talking without interrupting my call.

"Needham? It's Elizabeth. Did you get anything from the National Park Service about a Cottonwood County native dying in a fall?"

Needham Bender, editor and publisher of the *Sherman Independence*, briskly questioned, "Who? When? Which national park? Accident? Suicide?"

Suicide.

"Elizabeth?"

I heard him pounding keys. Probably checking the wire services in case it slipped past him somehow.

"Sorry, Needham. I don't have any answers to your questions. I was hoping for answers from you. If there was a news release or a wire report—?"

"None. How'd you know about it? Who is it?"

"Sorry," I said for the second time, and I meant it.

At least partially.

Needham Bender was a good journalist. I respected him and the newspaper he produced. If he'd had the story, I would have been mostly happy for him. And I would have begged for every bit of information for Jennifer's sake—not KWMT's. Even though that meant leaving Thurston and Les to rework Needham's concise copy into gobbledygook.

But since he didn't have the story, I wasn't going to share unsubstantiated information that had come to Jennifer personally.

"A lot of good you are." He hung up on me.

I frowned at the phone. Not because of Needham's reaction.

That I understood totally. He didn't want to waste any more time with me if I wasn't going to give him more information.

Still, something *was* strange.

As I returned to the group around the coffee table, Diana immediately asked, "Why are you frowning, Elizabeth?"

"Needham doesn't have anything on the—" I stopped myself from saying *story*. "—news. I thought he might be running ahead of Thurston."

"Dinosaurs run ahead of Thurston," Mike said. "So, no news release yet?"

"Is it unusual not to have a news release? Would the park service contact media in Calliope's hometown?" Tom asked.

"Directly? I wouldn't think so. But AP—Associated Press—would pick up a release immediately and put it on the state wire."

"But that would be Colorado's state wire, wouldn't it?"

Jennifer answered Tom this time. "The station gets surrounding state wires. The *Independence* does, too. Besides, the guy on the phone said Sherman. He knew that connection, so it could be on the Wyoming wire, too."

She'd skirted what had me frowning, but before I spilled that, I wanted to check a few more things.

More accurately, I wanted Jennifer to check a few more things.

Before I could make a request, though, Mike said, "I'll look at the state wires when I get to the station. Maybe Needham missed it." He stopped himself. "Yeah. Never mind. Needham wouldn't miss it."

"In other words, there's no confirmation this happened other than a phone call to Jennifer," Tom said.

"You're thinking a hoax? Why on earth would anyone—?"

Jennifer cut across Diana's horrified question. "It's not a hoax. I called Calliope's parents, before you came in the ladies' room, Elizabeth."

It must have been a very quick call, because crossing the newsroom was no marathon.

"Her mother answered. She thought it was Calliope's dad. She was... She was hysterical." Her already pale face lost more color. "She screamed that Calliope was dead, then the phone cut out."

A very quick call.

Just long enough to hear a mother's heartbreak.

So, unless it was an incredibly cruel hoax perpetrated on the parents and the best friend...

And to what purpose? A hoaxed kidnapping to try to get money would be a possibility, especially if she'd fallen back into drugs. But no kidnapper, fake or otherwise, would say the victim was dead. That removed all leverage.

Yeah, I wasn't sharing any of those thoughts.

"Jennifer, how about searching to see what you can find on fatal falls at Rocky Mountain National Park?" I asked.

Her face brightened for a flash with the call to use her skills. Immediately it fell, no doubt anticipating what she might find. Then it fell further. "My phone's not getting anything."

Diana handed over a device and Jennifer quickly put it to good use.

In seconds she said, "There's nothing on Calliope."

"How about other fatal falls?"

Tom's brows lowered. Presumably at the idea of sending Jennifer on the quest for information mirroring her friend's death.

Diana tilted her head and raised her fingers at him in a *let it lie gesture.*

Jennifer was already scrolling, so it would have taken more than that to distract her.

"Here's one." She read aloud a spare news release of a man falling while trying to take a photograph. Then a couple caught in an avalanche. Another fall.

She started one about slipping on ice, stopped, and said, "That's Yosemite."

"That's okay, keep reading."

She read several from Yosemite, stretching back several years. "Yellowstone—No, wait, that's somebody dying in a thermal feature. Okay, Grand Canyon. A photographer again. Sounds like they have a hard time getting to people there after they fall. Here's another from the Grand Canyon. It's two days later." Her features squeezed tight. "They had to find the body."

"That's enough. Thank you, Jennifer." I asked everyone, "Notice anything about these?"

Mike thought he had it. I saw it in his face. But instead of saying it, he looked around at Tom, then Diana. She gave a small shrug.

"Most of the people who fell aren't obeying the rules?" Jennifer offered. "But we don't know Calliope broke any rules, because we don't know *anything.* Actually, we don't know much about these others, either. These releases hardly say *anything.* So even if we found a news release about her we wouldn't know more."

"You're right, they don't say much. They're very cautious," Diana said.

"They each said when the incident happened or when the rangers were notified, sometimes both." Mike *did* have it. And still, he didn't say it outright.

So, I did.

"None of those releases came out the day of the accident. They were at least one day after the fatality, some two days after, as Jennifer said."

Mike said, "So, why'd this guy call Jennifer today?"

Exactly.

The others frowned.

"To get more information, a friend's view...?" Diana suggested half-heartedly.

I shook my head. "That's from a journalist's point of view. This is a governmental organization and one with aspects of law enforcement. Would they want human interest angles? Reactions or remembrances from friends?"

"They didn't include anything like that in those releases Jennifer read," Tom said.

I leaned forward. "True. Also, they'd likely call the family before the news was released. But a friend? No. Bad policy. And, as you said, Why? Not for a release that's not even out yet and one that wouldn't include that sort of information anyway."

"What about media? Maybe somebody from AP called her, for the state wire, like you said," Tom said.

"But the caller didn't get a quote. From what I heard of Jennifer's end he didn't even try. Reporters will *always* press for information in the moment over a vague possibility of something later. And he didn't even leave a callback number." I turned to her. "Did he?"

"You're right. He didn't. Because I type those automatically. All the time. *Every* time. Even with the shock, I would have typed it in if he'd given it to me."

"That means this caller didn't hit the most basic reporting elements. You try your darnedest to get information *now*. If you absolutely can't, you get a blood oath the person will call back, then you leave name, organization you're reporting for, and multiple means of getting back to you—phone, email, text, telegram, cave painting."

"That *is* weird. That's *really* weird," Jennifer said. "I don't think— I'm positive I'd remember if he said he was from AP. I talk to those guys, you know?"

"What about if he'd said he was from the National Park Service?"

She didn't answer immediately, thinking it through, reviewing. "I think I would remember, so I'm pretty sure he didn't. Not like AP, but pretty sure." She looked around at us, challenging. "*Now* do you agree we should investigate?"

"Before we agree or don't agree this is something to investigate—"

"It is. You just showed it is. So—"

"Wait. Two things. There are some … odd circumstances around the park people—or someone—calling you. But there's also the death of your friend. If you get us started, you have to be prepared that we won't stop until we know everything we need to know to explain what happened."

"Of course. That's what I want. That's—"

"Hold up, Jenny. Don't answer on the fly. Listen to what Elizabeth's saying. Think about it."

Tom's words stopped her momentarily. But only momentarily.

"You think I'm wrong about Calliope not having an accident? You think I'm wrong about how she wouldn't ever do something dangerous or stupid hiking? She wouldn't go to the edge to take a picture or go on a closed trail or step back without looking like those people in the news releases. She wouldn't."

Yet she'd done drugs. Talk about dangerous and stupid…

More thoughts I wouldn't share.

"However strong your faith in your friend is, those are possibilities we have to consider. Along with other aspects."

I couldn't tell if she'd picked up on the unvoiced word *suicide* before she retorted with another challenge. "You think there's something about Calliope I won't want to hear?"

"I have no way of knowing, Jennifer. But the odds are yes. Because that's the way it is with most human beings."

"You think she was back on drugs and that's why this happened?"

"Again, I have no way of knowing, but that's a possibility." Time to be explicit. I breathed in deeply. "Beyond whatever else we might find, you need to consider that Calliope might have committed suicide."

"No. She wouldn't. She—"

"Several of those falls you read about were ruled suicide," Diana said.

"Calliope wouldn't kill herself."

To that stubbornness, I said, "Sometimes it's worse than being ruled suicide. Sometimes suicide remains the most probable cause, but it's impossible to know for sure."

She didn't say anything, but didn't mask that she didn't accept the possibility.

After a pause, I said, "Before you commit yourself to going after the truth, you have to recognize it might not be a truth you like. And you have to commit to the truth anyway—all the truth."

Without speaking, she looked from me to Tom. Then to Diana and, finally, Mike.

She stood. "I'll be back."

At the hallway, she turned toward Diana's room. We heard the door close behind her. Then the faintest *thunk* of a second door closing.

"I guess you gotta go when you gotta go," Mike said with a tight smile. "Poor kid."

"Not a kid. Not in this. Give her credit for wanting to consider it thoroughly. You live alone, so you don't understand," Diana said. "She lives with her parents and brother. Bathroom's the best thinking spot in the house."

Into the silence that followed, Tom said, "Okay, not a kid. But an investigation? Investigating what?"

"Well, there *are* questions," I said. "Weird things. Gaps. We can look into those."

"You could look into anything."

"That's true," Diana muttered, just before I would have denied it.

"And would that be enough for her?" Tom concluded.

"We can't decide that for her."

He wanted to argue. To give him credit, he didn't.

Then I glanced at Mike.

Good grief, he wanted to argue, too.

He was usually the most gung-ho to investigate, so if he had arguments against this…

Instead, he stood. "I need to get to the station to prep for the Five."

Impulsively, I said, "I'm going, too. See what—if anything—I can find out from there." Away from Jennifer's hopes and fears and sorrow.

"What about Jennifer? Maybe one of you should take her to her parents. Or I will," Tom said.

"She needs more time," Diana said. "She can stay here. Take a nap. I'll drive her home if she wants. But…"

"She's going to want to tell us what she decides," Mike said. "We'll come back after the Five. Then I'll drive her home when I go back for the Ten."

"That's a plan," I said.

Tom looked at Diana. "Okay with you if I swing back here, too? I've got to check in about the grazing association, but the timing should be about right."

"Of course, it's okay," Diana said. "I'm sure Jennifer will be glad to hear you're all coming back after the Five."

"I'll pick up something to eat on the way," Mike said.

"Thank heavens. Because I can't afford to keep a teenage son *and* you fed."

Chapter Five

AT MY DENTED, gray desk in the KWMT-TV bullpen, I took a jolt of liquid caffeine in the form of the universally awful newsroom coffee. I needed it to start churning through a list of phone calls strung down a document only I could decipher.

To an outside observer, the calls might appear to be for my official job at KWMT as the "Helping Out!" consumer affairs reporter.

They weren't.

But I wasn't leaving KWMT in the lurch. I had enough "Helping Out!" segments done to loll in Tahiti until Wyoming truly warmed up, which in my limited experience coincided with the Fourth of July.

Instead, I was fruitlessly pursuing information on the tragic death of a young Sherman native.

Doubly fruitless, in fact.

Even if my information pursuit magically turned into a story, I wouldn't get on-air with it. Thurston Fine claimed his contract guaranteed him all the big stories. News Director Les Haeburn didn't deny it.

Mike, Diana, and I, with others helping, had done a few special reports around our inquiries, but always with the weight of a major scoop behind us. This time, we didn't have any muscle to hold onto the story—if it *was* a story.

First, I tried the office of public affairs at Rocky Mountain National Park.

I spoke with a very pleasant person who would neither confirm nor deny that there had been a fatal fall at the park that day, because all such information needed to come through the media liaison office.

She then gave me unpleasant news. The head of the media liaison area was on vacation, out of the country. The second-in-command was sick with pneumonia. The third person had gone into early labor.

That left two backups brought in to temporarily handle media liaison from two different departments. The senior of those two was named Peter Bray.

She would put me through to him.

After six rings, a female voice answered, "Ranger Bray's phone."

"Ranger Peter Bray, please."

"He is not available." I interpreted a mini-pause before *available* as meaning the female voice didn't know where the hell he was and wished he'd get back because she was darned tired of answering his phone.

"Perhaps you can help me. I'm sorry. I didn't get your name."

The female voice identified herself briskly. "Ranger Attleboro."

I suspected Ranger Attleboro was the second backup brought over to media liaison, wasn't happy about it, but was doing her job. She did *not* think Peter Bray was doing his job.

I know that's reading a lot into a tone, particularly a brisk, professional tone. But I've talked to a whole lot of people over the phone, especially in my pre-Cottonwood County career when I was top tier reporter.

"I'm Elizabeth Margaret Danniher of KWMT-TV in Sherman, Wyoming, and I'd like to talk about a potential story."

It was a judgment call not to tell her what I really wanted. Was she irked enough at Bray to tell me, yes, there had been a fatal fall and give me the victim's name? Even before a news release? That brisk, professionalism said no.

"The best person to talk to will be back in ten days. The name is—"

"Oh, no. We can't wait ten days. This is very time sensitive. When might I be able to talk to Peter Bray?"

"I will take a message and do my best to see that he gets it."

I settled for that.

For now.

Law enforcement—Estes Park, county, and state level—were even less helpful, each referring me to the media liaison at the park.

The local newspaper wasn't forthcoming, but asked if I'd like to subscribe.

I talked to someone at a radio station who said the "news guys" were busy.

I had a connection at the *Denver Post*. He gave me the name of their reporter who tracked the national parks. She wasn't available.

I considered Denver's TV stations.

Possibility one. They knew nothing.

Possibility two. Hypothetically, one of them had compelling footage, say from an onlooker's cell phone. If they did, it would be on-air for their local news coming up soon. The footage would hit the wires moments later, even if there was no official news release.

But even if such footage existed, they weren't going to tell me all about it before they went on air with it.

There was yet another factor that made them unlikely sources of help. Even if compelling footage existed, this would likely be a one-shot tragic-fall story, with the second day being a reworking of the news release. Beyond that, unless hot angles developed, the TV stations not only wouldn't share, they'd have nothing to share.

I filled in gaps while on hold by looking up the Grandishers, finding articles relating to his job and her charity works. I tracked down their contact information.

Next to the entries on my list notations now showed. MSG (for message, as in I left one) beside more than half and WCB (for will call back, as in someone promised that the person I wanted would) beside the rest.

It was surprising how fast you got through a lot of calls when nobody gave you anything helpful.

My list represented the direct approach. With no dividends there, it would soon be time to start thinking indirect.

Calliope's parents, perhaps? Not fun to approach bereaved parents, but maybe.

Had she been living with anyone in—where *had* she lived?

I jotted a note to find out.

I checked the park's website and the state wires again—no news release.

In a way, that was good news. Sort of.

When the news found its way to Thurston, whether through a news release or if he or—more likely—Haeburn read an account in the *Independence* it would become a mashup of a rewrite on-air.

Yes, it raised my journalistic hackles to see stories abused. But I'd discovered since arriving in Sherman that living in a state of constantly raised hackles isn't comfortable.

In other words, I tried to pick my battles.

This time my focus was Jennifer's peace of mind. Not the news quotient.

Let Thurston have it.

In the meantime, I found and reread those news releases on fatal falls at national parks to see if I'd missed anything before another pass through my list, starting with the ranger's office.

A few minutes later, I had the outline of the news release's format set in my mind. And, perhaps, a lever to try to get more out of my friend Ranger Attleboro.

"He's still not in, Ms. Danniher, and I haven't heard from him," she said. "I have your message for him right here."

"Thank you. In the meantime, can you tell me, is a news release coming out tomorrow?"

"How—?"

She bit it off, but I had my answer.

A lot of their releases had nothing to do with fatalities, of course. My heart thudded harder, anyway.

First, what were the chances of a coincidence that a benign release about, say, the population of elk, was coming out tomorrow? Especially with none of the media section's experts on hand.

I'd bet my office stash of Pepperidge Farm Double Dark Chocolate Milano cookies that a news release that couldn't be delayed until the first-stringers returned was scheduled for tomorrow.

"Did Peter Bray write the news release? Is he writing it now? Is there someone else I could talk to about that?"

"Ranger Bray is the person you need to—"

"Perhaps I could talk to whoever's leading the investigation?"

That was a shot in the semi-dark. Not every release I'd read used the phrase "an investigation is ongoing," but a good percentage did.

No sound this time, but she hesitated a beat too long. "The person you need to talk to is Ranger Bray."

"Is he leading the investigation?" I pressed.

But she was ready this time. "You need to talk to Ranger Bray."

It's tempting to be snide—*I would if I could*—but it would alienate the gatekeeper. Not a good idea.

I thanked her, promised—or threatened—to call again, and ended the call.

I doodled on my pad, considering the faint hope that Bray hadn't written the news release or wasn't leading the investigation or both. That might give me a couple other possible people to pursue.

Whoever wrote the release. Unless that was Ranger Attleboro, because if she'd been prepared to tell me, she would have.

Whoever was leading the investigation. Ditto.

But how to find out either/both? Clearly it would require an end-around Ranger Attleboro, with the attendant risk of alienating the gatekeeper to Bray. On the other hand, if he hadn't written the release and/or wasn't leading the investigation, did I need him and thus her?

I'd ordinarily try to work from the top down, by seeing if I could find a connection at National Park Service headquarters, but the workday had already ended on the East Coast and it was Friday, to boot.

With a news release coming tomorrow, how much could I gain by pressing to get it now? And would I burn bridges that might carry me farther if I kept them intact for later?

Being lost in those thoughts is my excuse for not immediately noticing News Director Les Haeburn lurking by my desk with Thurston in the background, grinning malevolently.

A sudden shiver went through me. Like the shiver the idiot girl in baby doll pajamas has before she opens the closet door in a teenage slasher movie.

I looked up.

Haeburn wasted no time.

"I have an assignment for you."

IT WASN'T SO much an assignment as a ticket to purgatory.

After months of doing his best to pretend I wasn't part of the staff, Haeburn declared I should become more familiar with the coverage area by spending time apprenticed to Leona D'Amato. Leona covered the social happenings of Cottonwood County, such as they were, and other "soft" news on a part-time basis.

For me, that was a ticket straight to hell, if it weren't for Leona. I liked the woman.

Technically, I could have argued with Haeburn that my contract, negotiated by my attorney/agent/relative-by-marriage Mel Welch directly with KWMT's never-seen-by-me-or-most owner (Val Heatherton) and General Manager (her son-in-law, Craig Morningside), said I did "Helping Out!" and "special projects."

But, as I said, I like Leona.

Also, Diana had said Calliope's parents were involved in the social set. This might give me an opportunity to find out more about them from Leona.

And—best of all—my cheerful, "Okay," deflated Thurston and Les like pin-popped balloons.

That was fun.

"But first, I have an appointment at the sheriff's office."

Ever since Sheriff Russ Conrad physically separated Thurston from his anchor chair during the commercial break of a broadcast and told him a few home truths, Thurston—and by extension—Les had steered clear of the man, as well as any hint of interfering with him.

Even to the point of not interfering with his supposed appointments, as demonstrated by Thurston backing up two steps, shutting his mouth, and leaving Les to gabble, "Right after that then. Right after," while swallowing hard enough to bob his Adam's apple.

So, I needed to come up with a reason to visit the sheriff's office.

As the mighty pair retreated, the outer doors opened and Leona breezed in.

Bad timing. I had no opportunity to warn her.

Les snapped, "I need to talk to you in my office immediately, Leona."

Thurston, importantly, added, "Right away." Because *immediately* left a lot of doubt.

As Leona dropped her mailbag carrier tote and raincoat, she shot a raised-eyebrow question to her newsroom allies, including me, but none of us were in a position to fill her in, with Les holding his office door open in a pose of impatient authority.

When Haeburn, Thurston, and Leona were behind the closed door, the buzzing ensued.

"She's not going to like it. No offense, Elizabeth." Was the chorus from the half dozen other souls in the bullpen.

That took some of the shine off my cheer. I didn't want her to suffer for my little fun.

When Leona came out of Les' office, looking far more unthrilled than I felt, she came directly to my desk. "Who's he punishing? You or me?"

That perked me right back up.

I always appreciated that she, unlike her stories, was not unadulterated sweetness. It also intrigued me she might have done things Les Haeburn would want to punish her for. And I might be able to find them out.

"I suspect he's trying to keep me occupied in case anything resembling news happens while Thurston's off this weekend. You know how Thurston gets and then he takes it out on Les."

"And now taking it out on me. Idiot," she muttered. I hoped she meant Les or Thurston, not me. "I have no time for this. Nothing against you, Elizabeth, but not this weekend of all weekends. It was already going to be nearly impossible, with Thurston insisting I anchor Saturday and Sunday nights because he wants to go on some jaunt."

Thurston lived in constant fear—with good reason—of someone

showing him up while substituting for him. Leona was one of the few people he was comfortable letting sit in his anchor chair.

Not because she wasn't competent—she was—but because she patently did not want his job. She loathed that job, in fact, along with hard news in general.

"And Les knows this is a terrible weekend. At least I told him about it. Who knows what penetrates what passes for his brain."

"What's wrong with this weekend?"

"You don't pay attention, either? I expect it of Les, but you? It's the biggest charity party of the spring, that's all. And for the first time, it was going to be hosted by the Grandishers. Then this horrible, horrible news about their daughter and of course everyone is devastated, but the charities are counting on those funds. What—"

"The Grandishers have had confirmation of their daughter's death?"

"The news is all over town."

"But from park officials or someone else official who would serve as a source to get the story on-air?"

"Oh, I don't know about that." And clearly didn't care.

I tried to calm journalistic instincts twitching with the urge to jump up and demand the story be properly reported.

Picking my battles.

Not this one.

Jennifer's peace of mind.

"What I need to know," Leona went on, "is what on earth are they going to do about tomorrow night's party? I have to find out. I don't have time to *show you the ropes* as our dear leader ordered, not even after I pin that down."

"No problem. I have to go by the sheriff's office now. I'll see you tomorrow. I could make calls for you then."

"Are you kidding? We have two assignments *tonight*. And, hell, yes, I have calls you can make. Tonight. Not tomorrow. Even though they won't tell you anything. Oh, maybe caterers or staff will talk to you, but not the ones who consider themselves important."

Chapter Six

DALE, THE NEWS aide still covering for Jennifer, delivered an order from Hamburger Heaven to the KWMT library.

Mike and I weren't researching, but the library offered privacy because few people used it anymore, favoring online sources. Ranks of old file cabinets provided the always-dusty décor. But the table near the door wasn't bad after a wipe with paper towels.

Mike had declared he had to eat before his segment because he might not have time after, with going back to Diana's then dropping off Jennifer.

"How's Jennifer?" Dale asked.

"She'll be okay. It's really nice of you to fill in for her."

Mike ignored all that touchy-feely stuff and homed in on the important issue. "What did you get?"

"Burgers, one with bacon, one without, fries, onion rings, cole-slaw—"

I stopped his artery-clogging recitation, while marveling Mike could eat, much less like this, so shortly before going on-air.

"He got exactly what you ordered, Paycik. I think you like to hear about it before you see it, before you taste it—your version of a three-course meal."

He grinned, confirming my guess, as he followed Dale to the door. He got his change back, tipped the kid for his trouble, and locked the door.

We called Diana on Mike's phone set to speaker. Tom wasn't back yet, she said.

Impatient with preliminaries, Jennifer's voice demanded, "What did you find out?"

"You go first," Mike said to me. "Give me a few minutes."

That was so he could eat, of course.

A solitary minute was all it took to report my lack of progress between bites of my salad.

"So Leona confirms the Grandishers were told Calliope died in a fall," Diana said.

"What do you mean confirms? I told you what that guy said and how Mrs. Grandisher reacted."

I didn't back down from Jennifer's bristling. "Minimum two independent sources," I reminded her from our journalism lessons.

"Me and them. Plus, you said that ranger woman's reaction—"

"Conjecture on my part. Not firm. I'll try again tomorrow, but, realistically, Monday's a better bet when more people are in their offices."

"*Monday?* Wait until *Monday?*"

Diana redirected the conversation. "Jennifer's been in touch with her friends."

"People who knew Calliope?" They might be a source for background information. Or—with more luck—information about what she'd been doing recently.

"No—"

So much for luck.

"—my online friends. There's one—DaisyDukes, my best friend—who's spearheading the whole thing. She's got some others working on a complete search and report on fatal falls at national parks, especially Rocky Mountain, and some other stuff, then she'll funnel the information to me."

"I'm not sure about involving people we don't know."

"I know them. They're my friends. And they're doing everything they can for me. On top of that, my phone's acting like crap and I can barely look up a phone number, much less everything we're going to need for this."

The final words were damp enough to stop my protest. It was

habit to let as few people as possible know what I'm working on until it's done or, better yet, on air. But was it necessary when this was solely for Jennifer's peace of mind?

"Mike, what did you find out?" That was Diana again.

Good time for another bite of salad. At least I was eating well. Mike's double bacon burger, fries, and onion rings made no such claim.

But at this moment, his health and well-being were in greater jeopardy from Jennifer. He not only hadn't found anything, he hadn't looked.

"I was working." He should have left it there. But he added, "Besides, what was I supposed to look for?"

"Anything. Anything that will help."

"But we don't know what will help. Without basic information—"

"You know basic information. We—"

"Mike's right, Jennifer. We need more. And, unfortunately, I'm not going to have much time to work on it."

I told them about Haeburn's surprise assignment.

"How could he? Of all times?" Jennifer demanded.

It took Diana's considerable persuasive abilities to remove confronting Haeburn from Jennifer's immediate agenda.

"It's not so bad," I added. "While I'm working with Leona more information might come in, giving us something to really look at. Besides, Leona says the party Saturday night might give me insight into the Grandishers." A rough paraphrase. A very rough paraphrase.

Jennifer didn't buy that. "They won't be there."

"True, but that can make it easier for other people to talk about them."

"What does that matter? Calliope died in Colorado. Not here. Her parents don't have anything to do with it."

"Jennifer, you know how often something from the past leads us in the right direction. But if you don't want us to investigate—"

Diana said firmly, "Jennifer said she wasn't making a final decision until later, which I think is smart. We'll stick with that. When Elizabeth and Mike get here. And Tom should be here by then."

"About that—I have assignments with Leona tonight."

Jennifer groaned.

Diana smoothed it over again. "That's okay, get here when you can. If anything changes on this end, we'll call you."

In other words, if Jennifer gave up the idea of investigating.

I didn't mention my projected trip to the sheriff's department. I didn't want false hopes that they'd help to sway her thinking.

But I did have a question.

"Jennifer, where was Calliope living?"

"An apartment in Loveland."

"Loveland?"

"It's south of Fort Collins, off I-25," Mike said.

Jennifer uh-huhed. "It's closer to the national park and she found a less expensive place there than she'd had in Fort Collins. After she finished classes at Colorado State, being close to campus didn't matter and she didn't want to rely so much on her parents."

"Did she have a roommate?"

"No." She paused, then said, "Not that I know of."

"See if you can confirm that. Also see if you can connect with any of her friends down there."

"Easy. Already have a few names. There's a memorial page for her and people are posting. I've been in contact. I could ask if they know if she'd been threatened or worried or—"

"No, don't. Gather any information that's offered there, but we don't want to pop off in all directions and miss the best direction."

"Okay. We'll all be here when you finish that nonsense with Leona."

"I don't know how late—"

"We'll all be here."

THE SHERIFF'S DEPARTMENT is on the back end of Courthouse Square, a leisurely ten-minute drive into downtown Sherman from KWMT, which is on the eastern edge of town.

From the front, the symmetrical, impressive courthouse that can claim nineteenth-century origins by the skin of its teeth, is set off by a neat lawn with evergreens supplemented by seasonal plantings that make benches dotted along the central walkway inviting.

Still neat, but not so inviting in the back.

The Cottonwood County Sheriff's Department, the much smaller Sherman Police Department, and the Fire Department shared an unremarkable building shaped like a staple at the bottom of the block. Parking lots and utility areas mostly filled the gaps between this building and the backs of additions plastered on the courthouse's behind.

Still, I appreciated the parking over esthetics at the moment, because this was the rare area in Sherman where street parking could be an issue. Historic residences, including those now used by businesses, hadn't made allowances for off-street parking.

What I didn't appreciate was the presence of Deputy Ferrante behind the front desk.

A stranger wouldn't have known that from the big smile and warm hello I gave him. But he might have known it.

The smile and hello certainly didn't move him.

"I'll go in back for a word with—"

"No, ma'am. No one's allowed in back without escort by a member of the department."

The organizational chart probably listed his sole official duty as "Block Elizabeth Margaret Danniher at every turn."

Today's manifestation of that was saying, "He's not available," in answer to my inquiries after Sergeant Wayne Shelton, Deputy Richard Alvaro, and even Deputy Lloyd Sampson.

Things certainly had tightened up under Sheriff Russ Conrad. Did that make me miss the previous administration, despite its tippy-toeing along the line between ineptitude and malfeasance? Maybe a little.

What the heck, might as well have a complete set, so I also asked for Sheriff Conrad.

"He's not available."

Ferrante's stoic responses did not mask that he was getting a kick out of foiling me.

But Ferrante was foiled in his attempt to foil me when Wayne Shelton came down the hallway from where the offices were and strode into the waiting area before he spotted me.

Shelton is short, but fast, so he was well into the public area before his spotting of me occurred. And, I'd already beat him at the spotting game.

"Sergeant Shelton," I greeted him cheerfully. But not before I'd latched onto his arm. "Just who I wanted to see."

He gave Ferrante a dirty look across the front desk, which was entirely unjustified. But it wasn't my place to sort out departmental tiffs. If Ferrante nursed a bit of pique at Shelton's injustice, resulting, at some future time, in the desk officer closing his eyes to me going in back unescorted, who was I to complain?

"What do you want?" Shelton demanded.

"To ask a few questions on behalf of the citizens of Cottonwood County."

Shelton flicked a look at three of those citizens, who were listening avidly from seats against the wall. Either my charm or their presence persuaded him to backtrack into the hallway, where we wouldn't be overheard ... if we kept our voices down.

I naturally came along, since I still had that grip on his arm.

"What?" he asked ungraciously.

He also jerked his arm free. I helped by releasing it. His resting irked-rate was high enough when dealing with me. No sense elevating it.

Yes, he could flee into one of the offices, but that wasn't Shelton's style.

He also could bowl me over and continue out the door. That *was* his style. But I figured those citizen-witnesses trimmed the chances of that.

"You've heard about the death of a young woman from here down in Colorado?"

"Calliope Grandisher. Shame. Everything I heard said she'd turned her life around."

I tipped my head for a different angle on him. "You knew her?"

"Yeah."

Ah. "She got in trouble?"

"Some." He was his usual fount of information.

"Jennifer, too?"

"Nah. Too busy with her computers."

He sounded as if he considered that an innocent occupation. Little did he know.

He angled a look at me. "Lance wasn't ever in trouble, either."

Jennifer had said Lance Joudrey had been Calliope's boyfriend. But that ended not long after they'd started college, and he'd come back to Sherman. Was Shelton trying to tell me something significant?

Not likely. He rarely told me anything, much less of significance.

I returned to the main point. "I'm trying to find out more about Calliope's death."

"Fell," said Sergeant Helpful.

"You should volunteer to write news releases for the park service. There must be more to it than that."

"Ask 'em."

"I've been trying. I've also been trying to contact law enforcement down there."

"Don't want to talk to you, huh?" His empathy was all for them, none for me.

"They'd talk to you."

"Maybe. If I called them."

"C'mon, Shelton. You said yourself it was a shame, that she'd turned her life around. Don't you want to know what happened?"

"She fell."

If I hadn't been in the sheriff's department where I would be immediately arrested, I might have committed a crime at that moment.

I held onto my patience with both hands. "You know there's more to it than that with any death."

He didn't respond directly. "What I know is if law enforcement doesn't want to talk to you, they're not going to."

"You have contacts at Yellowstone and they're sure to have contacts at Rocky Mountain. They're practically neighbors."

"Why should I work my contacts for you?"

"Not for me. For a citizen of this county. And for her parents."

"What citizen?"

That wasn't Wayne Shelton suddenly pretending he didn't know what he'd already acknowledged he knew. It was the sheriff of Cottonwood County.

Shelton's boss. Diana's honey. My ... hmm. Not enemy. Not nemesis. ... Perhaps mutually prickly acquaintance. Sometimes stabbing a thorn in each other's sides. Sometimes not.

I turned to Russ Conrad. "Calliope Grandisher, the daughter of India and Owen Grandisher." I'd found that out during my internet searches. "Do you know them?"

"No."

"He's in oil. Boss of the Sedick outfit," Shelton said briefly.

He and Conrad didn't look at each other. But there was something in their stillness and silence.

The sheriff might not have met the Grandishers, so he could say he didn't know them. But I bet he knew *of* them.

Also, I'd wager he and Shelton had already talked about Calliope's death.

Could Jennifer's insistence that Calliope's death wasn't an accident possibly...? But what could the Cottonwood County Sheriff's Department know about her dying from a fall in Colorado?

"Are you talking to nearby law enforcement or the park rangers about what happened that led to her death?"

Death was a carefully open-ended term that didn't try to pin down accident, suicide, or murder.

It was half a beat, but an important half a beat before Sheriff Conrad said, "No."

"Will you?"

No beat at all. "No."

Chapter Seven

I DIDN'T LEAVE it at that. Big surprise. But I didn't budge the sheriff in the minute and a half before he excused himself—curtly—went in his office, and closed the door.

Shelton didn't bother excusing himself. He walked out.

I stood there a moment longer, listening, on the off chance one of the other deputies might say something loudly from one of the rooms back here or wander by and be overcome by the urge to tell me everything he knew about Conrad and Shelton's discussion about Calliope Grandisher's death, which for some reason they'd held in public, in direct opposition to their usual overly secretive behavior.

It was a short moment, since there was no chance.

✧ ✧ ✧ ✧

AT THE STATION, Leona gave me a new list of calls to make, not connected to Calliope Grandisher.

It consisted of people associated with the practicalities of tomorrow night's charity event—in other words, those lowly types she'd said might deign to talk to me.

She'd been overly optimistic.

The few who got past "no comment" or its variants, wanted to know why Leona wasn't calling. They weren't happy with a substitute.

I persevered.

Finally, I got a caterer's assistant to spill where the party was being moved to by pretending to stumble over the address.

When the boss caterer heard the assistant filling in details of the

address, she apparently grabbed the phone. Just before it was disconnected, I heard, "I don't care how much my sister and mother beg, I'm
going to fire your—"

I would have felt bad for the assistant, but I had a pretty good idea
the caterer didn't stand a chance against her mother and sister.

Also, I was busy feeling good about getting the address. Particularly since it was an address I knew—Linda Caswell's ranch.

But when I reported that to Leona, as proud as a kid with her first
scoop-ette, Leona already knew ... from Linda.

"I got you an invitation, too," she added.

"*Me?*"

"Yes. I've thought of how you can make yourself actually useful
with Thurston away Saturday night during the biggest party of the
season."

"If you think I'm going to anchor while he's gone, you're going to
be stuck covering a hard news story, because he's either going to try to
kill me or die of apoplexy."

"Tempting, but no. You're going to stay at the party and work the
room while I'm off doing the Ten. To make sure nothing major
happens that I miss."

Before I could object to being held responsible for nothing happening, she gave me something else to think about.

"You do have something decent to wear, don't you?"

That wasn't as insulting as it might sound. A fire had wiped out my
wardrobe last year and attire beyond jeans and comfort clothes was not
Sherman's forte. Remembering my recent shopping in D.C. and the
haul I'd brought from Illinois, I said with solid confidence, "I'll figure
out something."

"Good. The other thing is you can tell me all about getting that
cute little house over by the courthouse."

"Not for a story," I said immediately.

"You think I'd do that?" she said with mock hurt.

"Yes."

"Takes one to know one. But you're not high enough up the social
ladder to make your house-moving worth a story. Not even a mention

in the *Independence*."

Yes, in addition to reporting the society news for KWMT-TV, she wrote follow-ups for the *Independence*. Newsroom scuttlebutt was that the news director before Haeburn tried to put a stop to the practice.

Leona and the practice remained. The news director was long gone.

"It is pretty interesting," she said, "what with the woman murdered and you solving it and all. But your situation's moving so fast it'll be old news before I have a spot on-air or in the paper that needs filling."

And *that* was the primary reason I believed she wouldn't use the strange solution to my house-hunting journey as a news item.

She was right about one thing. It was moving very fast.

The Undlins—Iris and Zeb—had learned a little over a week ago that they'd inherited the house.

They'd inherited it from the woman who'd been my brand new real estate agent until she was murdered.

Seven days ago, the Undlins told me they wanted me to buy the house and had offered a very good deal, saying Renata would have liked making one last match of house and client, and also it was fitting because my friends and I had found her killer.

For the next three days, I swear every soul I'd ever met in Cottonwood County told me I'd be nuts if I didn't accept this generous offer, as well as ungrateful to some of the finest people Cottonwood County had ever known. Some of them said it multiple times.

Four days ago, I'd looked at the house again.

Three days ago, I'd talked with James Longbaugh, a lawyer in town, about if there were any pitfalls I might be missing.

He gave me the finest people Cottonwood County had ever known lecture. Then he said he couldn't say much, because he was handling Renata's estate, but he'd already approved the Undlins' request to have me rent the house until a sale could be finalized.

News to me.

I gave James the contact information for Mel Welch in Chicago as my "family lawyer."

Actually, he was such a top-notch lawyer he wouldn't have touched something as mundane as a temporary lease agreement. Except he was family—by the Danniher definition of that word, which ensnared the whole of a wide-spreading family tree, the numerous in-laws, the in-laws' relatives, a few favored exes, and a spattering of neighbors, former neighbors, and close friends. In other words, don't stand too long next to a member of my family or you might become one.

My parents woke me up before work yesterday morning congratulating me on finding a perfect little house. Because, of course, Mel blabbed to them before calling me at work and telling me he and James had "settled everything" to their mutual satisfaction. He'd also called the storage company in Virginia holding my furnishings and told them to deliver to my new address as soon as possible.

I'd never been involved in a real estate transaction like this.

There'd always been unpleasant surprises, hiccups, and outright disasters. Buying the apartment in Manhattan probably would have cracked our marriage if Wes, my now ex, and I hadn't already been on opposite sides of the San Andreas fault.

Heck, I'd rarely had *any* transaction like this. Pumping gas into my SUV and paying for it was more fraught with frustration and delays than this.

Was there a variant of the phrase *bum's rush* when you were being pushed at breakneck speed toward where you were pretty sure you wanted to go?

"Pretty sure my ass," Diana had said when I'd asked that question at lunch yesterday. "If you didn't want the house or even if you weren't totally sure, you'd have slammed on the brakes."

Hmmm.

"You just can't wait to leave me and the kids," she continued, in a half-kidding tone.

"I'm going to miss you all horribly. At least I'll see you at work, but Gary and Jessica…" I sighed.

"I can send them to stay with you if there's bad weather brewing so they can get to school. You know Mrs. P said families used to do that—have their kids live with relatives or friends in town during winter and—Oh! Better yet, I'll have the kids spend weekends with you here in town."

"So you can spend them on the ranch with Sheriff Conrad in blissful sin?"

"Exactly." No guilt at all.

"You could go off on a luxurious weekend, but I suppose it would be wasted. You're still in the phase where peanut butter sandwiches while sitting—or doing other things—on a rock is the most romantic thing ever."

"Peanut butter sandwiches, sure. But I'm too old for a rock. Or for hay. That stuff itches."

"Hay? You didn't. You *did?*"

"I have an assignment. See you later, Elizabeth."

That was yesterday. Now, I told Leona the pertinent facts— nothing about Diana's sex life.

"Darn. It would make a nice item. But the timing's all wrong. Okay, then. Let's get to it."

That was the beginning of learning more about the softer side of Cottonwood County and the sharper side of Leona D'Amato.

I did not learn what Haeburn might want to punish her for. The woman was wily. She'd worked for the station since it opened, so I should have expected that.

I did learn she must have the metabolism of a hummingbird.

What? You didn't know they have the fastest metabolism around?

You must not know my friend and long-time source Dex of the FBI lab, who gathers and disseminates factoids at about the same rate as hummingbirds—and Leona—metabolize.

My witnessing of Leona's hummingbird-like metabolism started that evening.

We attended a fish fry at a local church to raise funds for needy kids. I really wished I hadn't eaten that salad.

Leona ate a hearty dinner and insisted I sample some of everything. "Don't want to insult the cooks."

Then a cocktail, hors d'oeuvres, and dessert gathering at the country club to plan their summer festival, presumably to raise funds for needy golfers. They involved Leona at this stage to ensure good coverage.

Again, the sampling, no insulting.

By the time she excused me, I was ready to pack it in for the night in a food stupor while planning to skip my next dozen meals.

Chapter Eight

MAYBE FOR A minute, possibly as long as two, I considered ignoring the lights in Diana's house and the familiar vehicles parked in front, including Mike's who'd done the Ten and still beat me back here.

I could have gone directly to the Bunkhouse, removed the spread of clothes on the bed and blissfully fallen asleep.

Except for two things.

My dog was waiting in the main house. I'd miss him. He might even miss me.

Jennifer was waiting in the main house. I'd feel guilty. She'd never forgive me.

Seven familiar faces turned toward me as I entered. In addition to Diana, Jennifer, Mike, and Tom by the fireplace, Diana's kids Jessica and Gary Jr. were on stools at the kitchen counter. The seventh was Shadow, lying between the two groups, facing the door.

"It's about time."

The words fit the dog's expression so well it took half a beat to realize they came from Jennifer.

"Long night." I shrugged off my coat.

"Want something to eat?" Diana asked from the chair by the fireplace.

"*Definitely* no thank you."

Both of Diana's kids stood.

"Don't leave on my account." Shadow had come to me and I stopped to ruffle his ears and stroke his head and back.

They grinned. But Jessica's faded fast. "And listen to all that murder stuff? No thanks." She'd provided us important information not so long ago and appeared to have remaining issues reconciling a teenager's general reluctance to help adults and a strong moral compass operating under her hormones.

Gary was more succinct. "Guacamole's gone. See you later."

"Your charms rate lower than guacamole," Diana said, in case I'd missed that point.

"The guacamole's gone?" Mike's disappointment made the rest of us chuckle ... except Jennifer.

"What did you find out since we talked?" she asked me.

"Nothing about Calliope. And far more than I ever wanted to know about a fish fry."

Mike sniffed as I passed on the way to the chair next to Diana's. "I thought I recognized that aroma."

"Weren't you banned because your all-you-can-eat threatened the economic viability of every local fish fry?" Diana asked.

"Not just me. The whole football team. And we weren't banned. We were asked to limit ourselves to one serving each." His dignified response fell apart. "Which hardly made it worthwhile, because we had to eat before we went."

"Such a sacrifice for charity. That's why I won't let Gary go. Though it is tempting to let someone else try to fill his bottomless pit."

"There's a place in Cody—"

"*Hey.* Forget food. We have important things to talk about." Jennifer faced me. "I do have news. Important news. Calliope's parents have been told someone else fell at the exact same spot—a man—and the park rangers thought Calliope tried to help him. That's why she fell."

"How awful," Diana said. "The poor man. And then for Calliope to try to help and... Just awful."

I asked Jennifer, "You talked to her parents?"

"No. But that's what they told Ursula's parents. Ursula is Calliope's cousin—" What was with this family and names? "—and she posted online. I *knew* it wasn't suicide. She'd *never* commit suicide. You can say I didn't know her anymore because I was a terrible friend, not answering emails or…"

If the report was confirmed that someone else fell and Calliope tried to help her, Jennifer was right about it eliminating suicide. Unless…

Diana's voice pulled me out of thoughts that had gone their own way while Jennifer talked.

"People come in and out of our lives, Jennifer. We're happy to have them come in and hardly ever think about how it happens. It's when they go out that we feel the loss of what we might not have fully appreciated. What's most important now is that you did have Calliope in your life. And you were great friends."

"I guess." Jennifer sighed, then glanced at me.

I took that as permission to ask a question that returned us to the previous topic. "How do the officials who talked to Calliope's parents know who fell first, Calliope or this man?"

Her face fell and I wanted to kick myself. "I don't know. Ursula didn't say. I can see if she knows, but I'll have to call her, because she's not reliable about checking online. Or I could go—"

I patted her arm. "We can check later."

I supposed I should be grateful Jennifer hadn't said the m-word out loud. What she might not have recognized yet was how Ursula's report pointed more strongly toward accident.

Easy to envision the scenario.

Calliope hiking on the trail, sees or hears something indicating another hiker has fallen. She reacts instinctively to try to help, but not with enough caution, and tragically dies, too.

As if she'd heard my thoughts, Jennifer said, "You said I'm not going to like what we find out by investigating. That there'll be things about Calliope … I know you meant suicide. Now we know for sure it wasn't. But you're still thinking about other stuff I might not like. Secrets. I thought about that earlier. I thought about whether it would be better to keep my memories of Calliope as they are, to not risk them… And I know you all want to protect me." She looked at each of us in turn. "But Calliope was my friend. My *friend*. I need to do this for her.

"Maybe I won't like some things we find. But the truth... I've decided. We're going for the truth."

Diana was right.

She had thought it through. And not as a kid.

"Okay. We'll look into it."

Diana frowned at me. Not as deeply, though, as Tom did.

I added, "For starters, we'll pry loose what park officials and law enforcement down there are saying."

"But you have to be prepared, Jenny—" Judging by her frown at him, Tom's period of calling her that with impunity had expired. "—that if law enforcement says it's an accident, it was. It sounds like an accident, so—"

"It wasn't. I *know* it wasn't. Calliope would keep her head in an emergency. She always did."

She turned to me. "Don't you just get a feeling sometimes?"

She had me. Because I did get feelings. Possibly—probably—born from shreds of observation, experience, and puzzle-solving. But they still came through as *feelings* well before facts explained them. And every person in this room knew it.

But her emotions were too closely tied to this situation to discern if her *feeling* was a refusal to accept that a stupid accident or a suicidal moment might have taken her friend or maybe, possibly, a burgeoning journalistic instinct for something being off.

We were going to investigate this for her anyway.

Into the silence, Tom asked, "How'd this guy get your name and number to call you in the first place?"

That was one way of acknowledging he was in on this inquiry.

And it was a good question.

Jennifer had a different response. "Easy—Calliope's phone. Her starred contacts."

She began scrolling her phone at top speed. "Stupid thing. What a crappy time to act up. I can't even find anything on here from her or that I sent her. Nothing. Like we never knew each other. But I must have been on hers... God, I've been such an awful friend."

"She clearly didn't feel that way or you wouldn't be one of her starred contacts."

Either that line worked better than I could have hoped or her own resiliency kicked in.

Jennifer said, "What should we look into first? We could start right now and—"

"No." I was decisive. I was firm. I was tired and had a pile of stuff on my bed to box up for the move before I could sleep. "We rest tonight. Nothing's going to be released now. Tomorrow morning, Jennifer, call around and see about a release from the park service. Then we'll see where we are."

Which I suspected would be just about where we were now.

DAY TWO

SATURDAY

Chapter Nine

MORNING IS NOT my best time. Especially with a fish fry-country club food hangover.

So, it was fortunate Jennifer waved her arms at me before I'd pulled my SUV all the way into the parking spot in KWMT-TV's less than manicured lot—because Jennifer was standing in the spot.

That ended any speculation that she might have changed her mind overnight about looking into Calliope's death.

Had I hoped she might?

Maybe.

For her sake. Because getting past the manner of Calliope's death would also help her get past the fact of it.

But there *was* the weirdness…

"What are you doing?" I demanded peevishly, once my brakes and heartrate recovered.

"Waiting for you. Diana's come and gone already."

Defending myself against the fault-finding in her tone, I pointed out, "She left the ranch before I did."

Clearly unimpressed, she said, "*Ages* ago. I've been out here *forever.*"

That might explain the blue tinge to her lips.

"You should have a jacket on." I grabbed my insulated winter jacket from the passenger seat as I emerged from the car.

"Why? It's spring."

Her befuddlement appeared genuine, so the blue might have been a new lipstick color. But claiming this as spring was laughable.

I laughed.

"Spring is daffodils and tulips blooming, soft blue skies and warm sun. Not frigid gales shaking buildings, not to mention trees showing no signs of budding."

"Well, it's not winter, so—" The phone she held rang. She gave the screen a quick look that turned to a scowl. She hesitated, then declined the call.

One of her parents?

"Your phone's working now?"

"No. This is Dale's."

"You declined a call for him?" This might test how smitten he was with her. "Isn't that kind of—"

"It wasn't for him. It was for me."

"How could you know that without—?"

"Because I knew who it was and why he was calling and he knows I might have Dale's phone, because he was always stupid jealous about Dale for no reason at all."

"Ah. The guy you used to date?"

"Yeah."

"He probably wants to offer his condolences about Calliope. That's very—"

"It's complicated. And I don't want to talk to him. I don't want to be reminded—how we were, when it was all three of us and how it can't ever be all three of us again."

Her voice dropped to nearly inaudible on the last phrase, but an earlier one had hooked me.

"Wait a minute. Wait. The guy you were dating, the one your parents didn't approve of was *Lance Joudrey?*"

"Yeah. But it wasn't that they didn't like him. They were just weird about it. So were his parents, especially his mom. But none of that matters. We broke up."

My head spun. The boyfriend I hadn't known she had until after the breakup—some investigative journalist I was—turned out to be the guy who used to be the boyfriend of her long-time best friend. A best friend who'd just died.

Jennifer, though, was moving on. "What were we—? Oh. Weather. Let Warren worry about the weather—"

WKMT-TV's weather man, Warren Fisk, worried about more than getting the forecast right—he had that covered as long as he said variable skies and windy. He worried about whether Thurston would encroach even more on his time. If Thurston did, about all Warren would get to say was "Variable skies and windy tomorrow."

"—I have news."

She wasn't going to open up more about Lance. Certainly not when she believed she had something important to tell me.

She waited so expectantly that I overcame both my curiosity about Lance and my morning and cold wind crankiness to supply, "About Calliope's death?"

"Yes. Another person definitely died. A man named Felix Robertson. It's in the news release. The official one from the park service. We got that a little while ago. It also said exactly what I said last night. He fell first and Calliope tried to help him, then she fell."

I released a deep, slow breath.

A double tragic accident.

"Okay. So, now you can concentrate on being with your friends and remembering the good—"

"What? *No.* That's not the end of it. Don't you *see?* This means there was somebody else *there.* Somebody who could have killed her."

"But the news release confirmed the man fell first. If they weren't sure, they wouldn't—"

"Not the person who fell. The person who knew she'd tried to help. We have to find out who that was and what he or she had to do with Calliope. We have to do all of it, question all of it, find out what *really* happened, like you always do."

Boy, it *was* still morning. How had I missed that?

For the park service to release an account of this Robertson man falling, then Calliope trying to help and also falling, they needed a source they'd believed.

A source was someone we could find.

"Okay, okay. But we have to do it inside. Before I freeze solid."

For the first time my eyes really focused on her. "What happened to you, Jennifer?"

Her jeans had scuff marks on the knees and dust from there down the fronts to the hems.

"I stopped to pick up eye drops—" Ah. I'd thought her reddened eyes were from crying, but that might be only part of the issue. Had she stayed up last night on her computer, looking for information on Calliope's death? Or—more likely since there'd been little to nothing to find—enlisting online cohorts to help with the search? "—on the way here. Some idiot pickup driver wasn't watching where he was going. I had to jump out of the way, then I tripped and fell."

"Did it hit you? Are you hurt?"

"No, no, I told you. I jumped out of the way. But then my foot caught on something and I went down on the street. I'm fine. Except my hands." She held them up, palms to me, showing abrasions on the heels, apparently from catching herself from going down hard on her face. Grit remained embedded in them.

She hadn't taken time to tend them before searching for, then printing out the news release.

"You need to wash those areas thoroughly, get all that junk out, then wash them again, before you put on ointment. Do you want help or—"

"No. I can do it."

"You need first aid ointment. If no one has—"

"There's a first aid kit in the cabinet in the break area." I'd thought all that cabinet held were sad salt and pepper shakers and an overflowing basket of plastic packets of condiments. "You get busy finding out stuff the way you always do."

AN HOUR LATER, I hadn't advanced much past what I knew in the parking lot.

The four-paragraph news release used only a few more words to convey what Jennifer had already relayed and added nothing new, except that rangers were informed of the accident shortly after eleven a.m. yesterday.

Jennifer had been called just before twelve-thirty.

So, if the authorities recovered Calliope's phone and started calling right away... That was possible.

Barely.

Though there was still the major peculiarity of them calling a friend. As well as the string of oddities about the call itself.

The news release confirmed Calliope Grandisher of Loveland, Colorado, had fallen to her death at Rocky Mountain National Park the previous day. As had another victim, a 51-year-old man named Felix Robertson.

It also said an investigation was ongoing.

Then, in the usual format for news releases, it said to contact Peter Bray for more information, with the same phone number I'd been using.

With my expectations low, I called again.

My friend Ranger Attleboro confirmed precisely what the news release said, not a word more.

She also said Bray wasn't in and she would tell him to call when she saw him. Again.

"Who's your source that Felix Robertson fell, then Calliope Grandisher tried to help him?"

"You'd have to ask Ranger Bray."

In an excess of optimism, I wrote another WCB beside his name.

Then I tried the TV stations.

I know, I said they weren't worth trying the night before. But having the identity of the second victim might open a tiny window.

Because the only way they'd pursue the story was if a victim was from Denver, if the deaths were part of a trend, and/or if there'd been fraud that made the path unsafe or some similar potential scandal.

While I was on hold with various calls, I noodled around search engines seeing if Felix Robertson showed up. He did. Including a high-winning professional gambler and a Confederate Civil War brigadier general.

Yes, I believed in searching outside the box, but confederate brigadier generals might be a little too far out of the box.

Especially since neither he nor any of the other Felix Robertsons I found were both from the Denver area and near the right age.

Calls to all the TV stations, then a second pass at print media in Denver and closer to Rocky Mountain National Park confirmed none of them saw an angle for pursuing the story.

Or they weren't sharing it with me. But if they had something, they were darned good liars.

I started another swing through law enforcement.

"C'mon, Elizabeth. We're burning daylight."

Leona sounded like a cross between a drill sergeant and a trail boss.

"Wait," Jennifer called from her chair. "What have you found out? What should I research?"

"First, let the others know about the other victim."

"Jennifer, you're working for me, not Elizabeth," Audrey protested.

Even if I'd been tempted to correct Audrey—in this instance Jennifer definitely wasn't working for me, more like I was working for her—there was no time with Leona's grip on me.

Jennifer didn't even look toward Audrey. "I'll do both. What should I—?"

"The other victim. Get whatever you can on him. Felix Robertson. Not the Civil War general."

"What?"

Chapter Ten

AT THAT POINT Leona tugged me through the first set of exterior glass doors. Looking back, I held one hand to my ear, extending my thumb and little finger in the old call-me gesture. Did people Jennifer's age still use that? Was there a text-me gesture?

"I'll drive," Leona said, still tugging. The woman was strong. "You look like you're asleep."

It *was* still morning, I'd made a slew of phone calls, had little to show for them, and had imbibed awful coffee. Four strikes in a row.

On top of all that, I soon realized Leona's eat-athon was continuing after an all-too-brief overnight cease fire.

We started at a pancake breakfast to raise money for band uniforms. Thank heavens they had fortissimo coffee.

Back to the country club for a brunch honoring the top fundraiser for the county animal shelter.

Noon was a sampler for the upcoming Taste of Sherman to earn money to give underprivileged kids free admission to the rodeo. It was heavy on beef, light on variety.

Then a swing past a cookout—burgers, of course—at the park district's athletic fields to support the sheriff's department's support of kid's teams.

Did nobody in this county eat at home?

As we walked toward the crowd, I said to Leona, "I'm surprised we haven't seen Linda at some of these events—Linda Caswell."

"Only reason she hasn't been is the scramble to move tonight's party to her place. Quite a feat. I'm doing a piece for Needham on the behind-the-scenes of the switch for Tuesday's edition." She shot me a look. "And the reason Tom Burrell hasn't been at several of them is he's leading the effort to catch up on spring ranch work for a fella who broke his leg in a wreck."

"I heard," I fibbed.

Even without Linda or Tom, there were plenty of familiar faces at the cookout.

Not only law enforcement, but Mike, his Aunt Gee, and her next-door neighbor, Mrs. Parens. Both women lived in the second-largest town in the county—in other words a hamlet—called O'Hara Hill. Which was, in fact, in a valley.

I spotted them talking with Sheriff Conrad. I did not join their group.

Sheriff Conrad and I had plenty of other opportunities to rub each other wrong. No need to inflict it on the others.

Besides, there was the slimmest chance they might be talking sheriff's department business. Mike might have an opportunity to quietly listen. But they'd stop for sure if I showed up.

Gisella Decker, in addition to being Mike's aunt, was chief dispatcher for O'Hara Hill. She could have been chief dispatcher for the entire county, but did not want to live "in town" or deal with the commute.

I also suspected she did not want to be subject to the sheriff's daily observation, if not direct supervision. She approved of this sheriff, unlike his predecessor, but she didn't cede any of her kingdom to him.

That kingdom being the entirety of Cottonwood County.

The tricky part was the kingdom also was ruled by Emmaline Parens, a retired teacher and principal who knew every soul who'd grown up in the county.

They were rivals to the core who never acknowledged that and often united for the benefit of the county.

And I further suspected that another reason Mike's Aunt Gee continued to live in tiny O'Hara Hill was to provide essential transportation for Mrs. Parens, who did not drive.

It was a complex relationship.

I circulated a bit, getting quotes for Leona from two of the grill masters and Ferrante's wife, who'd organized the volunteers bringing side dishes and was as friendly as her husband wasn't.

Looking around, I saw Mike and the two empresses of Cottonwood County again, this time unencumbered by the sheriff. I started their way.

Aunt Gee spotted me first. "Elizabeth. Mike said that Haeburn fella harnessed you to Leona for a couple days."

I said hellos all around, but before I could respond to Aunt Gee, Mrs. Parens said, "How are you enjoying your introduction to many of our county's leading citizens through your association with Leona?"

She was being exceedingly modest. She, Linda, and Tom had to be among the top of any list of the county's leading citizens, with Aunt Gee trailing a bit only because she held a full-time job, and I already knew them.

"Spending time with Leona's always enjoyable. I could use a little more excitement and a lot less food, though."

"You don't find raising funds for worthy causes exciting?" Mrs. Parens' expression qualified as stern, yet a twinkle deep in her eyes alerted the observant.

"Worthy? Yes. Exciting? No. And good works are all these folks seem to do aside from eating. Society people should consume conspicuously. They should have feuds among themselves. They should cause scandals."

"There's not much of that around here. Don't expect any *Real Housewives of Cottonwood County* to go into production soon. As if any of *them* are real," concluded Aunt Gee.

"No *Real Housewives of Cottonwood County* even among the oil company set at the country club? Rivalries? Scandals?"

"Ah."

I leaned forward at that promising syllable from Aunt Gee.

Then Mrs. Parens spoke.

"Scandal is not pervasive in this vicinity. Indeed, the greatest scandal connected to Wyoming as a whole had little to do with our state. Michael?"

I knew precisely what Mrs. P was doing—topic-changing to thwart gossip. When gossip was precisely what I craved.

But challenging her avoidance of gossip rarely succeeded. I might as well enjoy watching Mike, who had the haunted look of a game contestant who knew he was in danger of losing all he'd won to this point, but had no choice but to play the game.

"The Teapot Dome Scandal," he said in a rush.

Congratulating him for not making it a question would have been tactless.

"Very good, Michael." Mrs. Parens turned to me. Darn. I should have kept her attention on Mike somehow. "What do you know of the Teapot Dome Scandal, Elizabeth?"

Hazy memories of something I hadn't known well in the first place misted through my brain. The scandal that rocked Ulysses S Grant's presidency? No, wait … Later than that, wasn't it?

Rocked… That rang a bell. Something about rocks … Geology? That would make sense with a connection to Wyoming, but…

"Oil," I pulled from about as many feet deep in my memory as they drill down to find the stuff. "Drilling for oil."

Mrs. Parens' small, precise nod put me on the right side of failing, but not much above that. Her abrupt pivot caught Mike grinning at me, both sympathetic and smug. "Michael, share with Elizabeth the precis of the Teapot Dome Scandal."

Aunt Gee humphed.

Mike could not summon up such rebelliousness.

"Uh, a guy in Washington—he'd been a senator from New Mexico—took bribes to let big oil guys drill where they weren't supposed to in a field called Teapot Dome. North of Casper. Named after a rock formation that looked like a teapot. The guy got caught, lost his job, and went to prison."

"His name was Albert B. Fall. He was Secretary of the Interior under President Warren G. Harding and the first member of any president's cabinet to be imprisoned."

Mike brightened. "Yeah. He was convicted of taking bribes, but the two oil guys—Sinclair and … uh…"

"Edward L. Doheny."

"Sinclair and Doheny were found not guilty of bribing him. Fall was convicted of taking bribes that nobody was ever convicted of giving him. Neat trick, huh?"

"Mrs. Parens, may we borrow you for a moment?" Mrs. Ferrante approached with a smile. "There's a question of how these fields came to be used for these purposes. Quite the dispute. I was certain you would know and could stop it before ... well, you know."

"Of course. Excuse me."

She didn't quite toss a look at Aunt Gee in triumph at her expertise being requested, but she might as well have.

Gisella Decker drew up her formidable self. "Excuse me as well. I need to speak with a co-worker."

With both women out of earshot, Mike leaned in and said, "All that political stuff? That's the least interesting part of Albert Fall. Did you know his middle name was Bacon? Perfect for a guy involved with government pork."

"Is that the most interesting part?"

"No. You know who Sheriff Pat Garrett was, right?"

"Killed Billy the Kid." I wasn't a total heathen.

"Yeah. Well, after Billy the Kid was dead and well before the Teapot Dome Scandal, a New Mexico lawyer named Fountain was special prosecutor against a group charged with cattle rustling, including a guy named Lee, who was a neighbor and ally of Fall, who at that point was a big-shot lawyer and judge who was getting more and more powerful.

"Fountain and his eight-year-old son leave town to go home and are never seen again. Not even their horses are seen again. The suspects in the *disappearance* are Lee and other allies of Fall's.

"Pat Garrett gets put in as sheriff, investigates, and gets indictments against those suspects. But they run, shoot a deputy during the pursuit, eventually surrender, and go on trial. Guess who represents them?"

"From your expression, our friend Fall."

"Yup. And they're acquitted. Special prosecutor, eight-year-old kid, deputy, all dead, and Fall gets them all off. And then, a guy who works for the brother-in-law of one of those acquitted shoots Garrett dead in let's call them interesting circumstances."

My head was whirling. "You remember all this but don't remember much about the Teapot Dome Scandal?"

"Oh, *this* is interesting. And *then* Fall defends the guy who shot Garrett and gets *him* off, too."

"Albert Fall then changed political parties and secured election as a senator from New Mexico." Mrs. Parens' voice spun Mike around to her. Proving she'd been listening, even though I'd seen her conversing with Mrs. Ferrante and her group, she continued, "That, in turn, led to his appointment as Secretary of the Interior. However, I disagree with you, Michael, that his earlier history, as—" She paused delicately. "—colorful as it was, was the most interesting part."

Must have been handy during her teaching and principalling days to carry on one conversation while taking in every word of another.

"That is," Mrs. Parens continued, "the more *lurid* aspect, certainly. However, the antecedents of the Teapot Dome Scandal are compelling in their potential effect on national security."

"Because of the navy, right?" Mike jumped in, blatantly currying favor.

"What does the navy have to do with Wyoming?" Sometimes I can't stop myself from asking questions, even about a hundred-year-old scandal.

"Shortly before the scandal, the navy converted from coal to oil to fuel its ships," Mrs. P said. "To ensure the navy had access to oil in times of need, oilfields were set aside in numerous locales as reserves, including the Teapot Dome. They were initially under the control of the Secretary of the Navy."

"Initially?"

"Control of the reserves were transferred from the navy to the Secretary of the Interior, Albert Bacon Fall."

"How did *that* happen? The navy just gave them up?"

"There are varying opinions about whether Fall persuaded the Secretary of the Navy or President Harding to transfer control or if there existed another arrangement."

A delicate way to intimate fraud.

But Harding hadn't been impeached—I'd remember that. "What was Harding's role?"

"It is generally held that he was not aware or involved. He had little experience and is purported to have told an aide he was not equipped for the office of president and never should have held it.

"Perhaps more tellingly, a newspaper editor reported Harding as saying, 'I have no trouble with my enemies. But my friends … they're the ones who keep me walking the floor nights.' Whether it was apocryphal or not, it was decidedly apt."

Mike shook his head. "How do you remember all this?"

"I have trained my mind. As for that specific quote, I consider it well worth remembering in the course of day-to-day life."

Was she talking about Aunt Gee? Which camp did she put her neighbor in?

"This Secretary of the Navy handed over the oil reserves to Fall and the Interior Department out of the goodness of his heart? Did they investigate him?"

"Amid the scandal, Edwin Denby resigned as Secretary of the Navy, the same week Albert Fall resigned his cabinet post. That was six months after Calvin Coolidge succeeded to the presidency following Warren Harding's abrupt death. Denby died in 1929 as the trials began."

"Not guilty by death."

Mrs. P ignored Mike's mutter. "Both oilmen were acquitted, although Sinclair served six months for contempt of court involving charges of tampering with the jury. They both died very wealthy men. In contrast, Albert Fall served a one-year term for conspiracy and bribery. Further, Doheny's company foreclosed on Fall's New Mexico home based on his failure to repay the loan, which most would consider was, in fact, the bribe."

"I'd forgotten that. Pretty slick," Mike said. "Doheny's acquitted for bribing Fall, then takes his house for failing to repay the 'loan.' These guys deserved each other. And their getting caught started with a guy in Wyoming noticing Sinclair trucks going in and out of the

Teapot Dome fields, where they didn't belong. In fact—" He turned to Mrs. P. "—wasn't it the Wyoming governor who spotted them?"

A governor as the source who broke open a scandal? That was good.

A source ... My mind went back to the news release. There had to be a witness...

How could I find—?

"One account maintains that Leslie Miller, then an independent oilman and later Wyoming's governor, saw the trucks. Another account is that several people saw them, reported to Leslie Miller, who in turn asked John Kendrick, then a U.S. Senator for Wyoming, to look into it. It is verifiable that the Wall Street Journal reported on the story and the next day Senator Kendrick introduced a resolution in the Senate to begin an investigation."

"Hah! Journalists ahead of the politicians once again."

Mrs. P allowed no sign of hearing me. "That began the unravelling of what was viewed as the greatest presidential scandal in the history of the United States until Watergate in the 1970s."

As if coordinated with Mrs. P's final pronouncement, Leona popped up. "C'mon. We have a wedding to get to."

"No rest for the wicked," Mike said cheerfully.

Chapter Eleven

BACK IN LEONA'S pickup, I loosened the seat belt, rested my head, and closed my eyes.

Then re-opened them.

My phone was ringing ... or ring-toning. It was Jennifer.

"I don't have much time. Audrey's been trying to catch me working on the investigation. What's wrong with her? She used to be so nice."

Frustration was what was wrong with her. She wanted to move up and out of KWMT-TV. Audrey was good. She'd get a chance. Someday. As long as she didn't let all the days until someday get to her.

"But I have something on Felix Robertson. Not a full report. I'll send you his ex-wife's phone number and information on their marriage and divorce."

I didn't say anything, but she must have heard the question in my mind.

"I've been really busy. I'll get to the rest this afternoon. Dale and some of the production staff said they'll fill in for me a bit."

"That's nice of them."

"Uh-huh. I've heard back from people I know online. I didn't think my messages got out last night, but at least two got through and they've spread the word." I heard emotion in her voice. "They're being so great. They jumped on it right away. One's volunteered to organize everyone's findings."

"That's good, isn't it?" I said cautiously. From some of her comments, as well as material she'd unearthed in our inquiries, these pals of hers likely used means that would turn me gray overnight.

"Yeah, yeah, it's good. It's just … they're being the kind of friends to me I should have been to Calliope the past year."

"You're being a friend to her now and—"

"I know, I know. You don't have to say it. Do what I can and that's giving you this information. Felix and Angela Robertson were married seventeen years, until divorcing two years ago. His first marriage, her second. One son, Quincy, and her daughter from the previous marriage, Nessa. They—Angela and Quincy—live in Pennsylvania, outside Philadelphia. The daughter's grown up and not living there. I've sent you the address and phone number. There was a big fight about alimony. Felix said he was broke. Angela said that was his fault for spending it all and she wanted the court to protect her alimony. Oh, shoot. Gotta go. I'll keep working."

During the brief wait for Jennifer's text, I considered my choices.

I could wait for a complete background check or I could make use of this chunk of time while Leona drove us to this high-profile wedding.

Since this was an ex-wife, there was a chance the authorities had not yet reached her and I'd be breaking the news of Felix Robertson's death.

Not my favorite task, but I'd done it before.

In compensation, I would get first crack at covering the same ground as the authorities and might get fresh, less guarded reactions.

I called the phone number Jennifer had sent for Angela Robertson.

A smoker's voice answered. Deep enough to make "Angela Robertson?" a full-blown question, not a courtesy.

"Who's asking?" That truculent response delivered a yes along with the attitude.

I identified myself, tentatively eased toward the topic of Felix Robertson, received a grunt of confirmation that she knew he was dead. I extended brief condolences—they were exes, after all, and her tone was brisk.

Then, without explaining why, I said we were reporting a story about the deaths, and earnestly added, "Of course we want to talk to you, because who would know him better than his wife of seventeen years."

"Ex-wife. And in Felix's case, his bookie would know him better. But it's still the craziest thing I ever heard. I can't believe it."

That sounded like a variant of what people had been saying about Calliope's death. Minus the warmth and sorrow.

In fact, *I can't believe it* qualified as the most common reaction about a victim. Sometimes combined with *such a nice person*, sometimes not.

"They said he was in a *park*? But not like a ballpark?" Angela might live outside the city, but her accent was pure Philadelphia.

"Not a ballpark. Rocky Mountain National Park near Estes Park, Colorado. It's beautiful. Mountains, lakes, nature, wilderness, hiking trails, wildlife."

She made a sound like *pfft*. "Makes no sense."

"There's still some snow and iciness on the trails, but if Felix were an experienced hiker…?"

"Felix never hiked a day in his life. Never walked to the refrigerator for a beer if he could get somebody else to bring it to him. He'd spend twenty dollars we didn't have to get a delivery we didn't need. Must've been something mighty interesting to get him to hike up some path. And mountains? No way."

"What do you think would have interested him enough to hike up a trail?"

"Money. Or sex. No. Forget that. Money, only money. Because that's how he got women. Something real profitable to him, that's what would get him up a mountain. It was always easy go for him, never easy come. Spent it all on himself, of course. Never his family. His son—and his daughter—no matter what he said later. He promised when we married he'd raise her like his own. The bastard."

An accurate portrait of Felix Robertson? Or bitter ex bias?

I found myself hoping it was the latter. Calliope dying trying to help the man Angela sketched added another layer to this tragedy.

"What business was he in?"

Mistake.

I knew it as soon as I asked the question. If I'd been thinking about this interview instead of the death of a young woman, I would have eased into it, not revealing I didn't know what he did. Not knowing had flipped Angela Robertson's switch to wary.

"He never talked to me about business." That was a lie. "He never talked to me about anything. That's what drove us apart. Married to the man for seventeen years and still didn't know a thing about him."

At this point, I might as well swing for the fences. "A man with a lot of deep secrets, huh?"

"More like a lot of shallow blanks," she said immediately. "Just nothing there but boring. But with him traveling so much, it took me all those years to realize it."

He might have been shallow and a blank, but I didn't believe for a second that he didn't have secrets or that his wife didn't know at least some of them and suspect a whole lot more.

My chances of finding out what she knew might have always been negligible, but I'd messed up by not waiting for more background on him. With no desk in sight, I was sorely tempted to thunk my head on the dashboard.

That had to wait. Keep trying and I might still get something.

"Traveling? To where?"

"West Coast, Vegas mostly, like I told the cops who came to my door to tell me he was dead." In other words, if she'd trust it to the cops it was innocuous enough to tell me, too.

Vegas…?

The professional gambler named Felix Robertson? Could there be a connection?

Could that be why she wouldn't share about his "business"?

"Had he visited Colorado before?"

"No idea." No interest, either, from her tone.

"Have you?" I was throwing spitballs.

"Took my daughter there to start college. Got their elevation disease. Never again."

Altitude sickness didn't seem like it would lead us anywhere. I needed to hold onto her or this would be over before I got anything.

"Huh. I guess they must have met elsewhere then."

Her interest made a comeback. "What do you mean?" She knew what I meant.

"The rumors… Didn't you hear there was another victim? A young woman. Very pretty. Fit."

I hoped one of those—young, pretty, fit—would hit one of Angela's buttons.

"I thought the woman—the *girl*—" She twisted it into something distasteful. "—tried to help him. Some good Samaritan who got killed for her trouble."

"Oh, if that's what you heard … I just know she was young, pretty, and fit."

"Fit? You mean one of those skinny girls? No meat, no curves, no cleavage. Not his kind at all. That's where he's different from Woody Allen. You think a girl like that—all sinew—could get him to go walking up a mountain? Never. I knew him too well to ever think *that*. But I guarantee there was a female in it somewhere. A female he was spending gobs on, because that's the only way he got them. And then the jerk had the nerve to claim he didn't have money for alimony or to support his son while he was off screwing—"

She must still use a landline, because she slammed the phone down in a way no cell could imitate.

Chapter Twelve

AFTER CHECKING THERE were no updates from Jennifer or anyone else, I messaged her to specifically look at the professional gambler Felix Robertson. Better a long-shot than no shot.

Then I settled back.

"How do you do it, Leona?"

"Report on all these stories? That's not hard. Every one of 'em's a worthwhile cause. Least I can do is give them a mention on TV. Frustrating thing is, the only time I can really report on them is when Thurston's gone. Otherwise, he doesn't allow me enough on-air time. But when he's gone all that other stuff cuts into my time."

All that other stuff being the news of the world.

"I meant the eating."

Between slitted eyelids, I saw her shrug thin shoulders. "Wouldn't want to hurt anybody's feelings. Besides, I'm hungry."

The earlier non-stop noshing left me in a near-stupor throughout the afternoon wedding and reception—yes, more food—of a Sherman widow to a Cody widower who had invented some gizmo Millennials required for altering photos before sharing them so everyone on the planet knew their "real" life. He'd been trying to invent something else entirely—something to do with phone security—when he stumbled on it and made his fortune.

I learned that at the reception by talking to his second-in-command, a shy, bespectacled young man who reminded me of the stereotypical dude from old western movies.

I also talked with an older woman Leona introduced as Yvette.

After sharing pleasant comments about the ceremony, I addressed the elephant that wasn't just in the room, but standing in front of me, dressed all in black, including a black lace handkerchief. Envision a post-Prince Albert's death Queen Victoria in a shorter skirt.

Yvette certainly stood out among the wedding-attired guests, though no one paid her special attention.

Could it be related to Calliope's death? Leona had said the Grandishers had been invited, so the happy couple clearly knew the family.

"I'm sure the newlyweds appreciate your sharing their day despite your loss." My voiced edged that close to a question.

"I've learned to see the joy, while carrying with me, always, the recognition of the monumental loss of the King."

"The King?" Had I missed a royal death? Even if I had, why would someone in Wyoming go into deep mourning?

"Elvis, of course, my dear."

"Yes. Of course. His death was quite a shock." Decades ago.

"Oh, he's not dead."

"Then why the mourning?" came out before I could stop it.

"Because I drove him to it."

Suicide? But she'd declared him not dead. "It?"

"Faking his death and living in isolation, never able to acknowledge his true self again."

"You drove him to that?" I asked automatically while my mind switched to another possibility.

Could the victim identified as Felix Robertson not be Felix Robertson? Would a man go so far as to fake his death—and provide a body to support the fake—to get out of alimony? Or could he be hiding from something else?

Somebody must have seen what happened or how did the park service know?

"Yes, by my excessive devotion. Until he could go nowhere and could live no life."

Gently, I pointed out, "You were not alone."

"No," Her backbone straightened. "But I was the most to blame, for I was the most devoted. I must take responsibility. Must set a good example for the young people."

She nodded toward the bride and groom, who were knocking on Medicare's door.

✧ ✧ ✧ ✧

WE LEFT CODY later than planned, so Leona floored it back to Sherman to prep for the Five.

She did not let attention to her driving distract her from telling me about the now newlyweds, their families, their guests, and all their histories.

I had my eyes closed. Partly because of the driving—were all the women in this county clones of Diana behind the wheel?—partly from the ongoing food stupor, partly thinking about how to find the park service's source for what happened on that hiking trail.

I could wait until Monday, then work my connections in—

"...except Jackson."

I recognized the lull in her account on a half-second delay and asked, "Who's Jackson?"

"Not who. Where. Jackson. In Teton County."

"Oh. Jackson Hole."

She snorted. "Jackson Hole's the valley. Jackson's the town. It was named after the valley and has no right to usurp its name. Not that it's all that glorious a name. David Jackson. Ever heard of him?" Had Mrs. P deputized Leona for this interrogation?

Unsure of whether not knowing would put me on her good side or her bad side, I opted for a noncommittal sound.

"No, and no reason you should have. Only reason he's remembered is he was the uncle of that Confederate general, Stonewall Jackson, and his name got left on a valley and a lake that a hundred and fifty years later got discovered by a bunch of people with more money than sense."

If there was one thing that united Wyomingites it was not thinking highly of the rich-and-famous who swarmed Jackson Hole. Did that extend to the local Sedick execs who spent time there?

"David Jackson came out here from St. Louis with hundreds of other men, trapped some beaver, went to a few rendezvous, then scooted back East with his money. *Humph*. Like all those billionaires piling into Jackson now, chasing a safe haven for their money."

"Why would Jackson Ho—Jackson be a safe haven for their money?"

"Not just Jackson. Wyoming doesn't meddle in folks' affairs as much as most. There're ways to keep holdings concentrated in the family's hands better here than other places. Course that concentration means that if their one holding goes poof, so does their money, but Wyoming figures it's their right to be fools."

"I understand the Grandishers and other executives from Sedick Oil spend time in Jackson, especially when top executives come from Houston."

"I suppose," she sniffed. "They're not really Cottonwood County people."

I couldn't resist. "But Yvette, who drove Elvis into faking his death, is?"

"Pure Cottonwood County," she said with zest. "Comes by it honestly, too. Her mother went to her grave declaring she drove Jimmy Dean to fake *his* death. Gotta admit they don't shirk responsibility."

I chuckled, but returned to the previous topic. "The time the Sedick Oil people spend at Jackson is purely recreational or something to do with a safe haven for money?"

"Must be because they like it. They could go other places in Wyoming to be left alone to handle their money."

"What are you not telling me?"

She barked out a laugh. "A whole lot."

"About the Grandishers?"

I didn't know how their stays in Jackson Hole—or Jackson—could help Jennifer accept the death of her friend, but I believe in encouraging conversation.

Leona side-eyed me. "You know Sedick Oil is a subsidiary?"

"No. In fact, I don't know much about them. There's not much conversation or coverage about the company. Real coverage. In other words, coverage by Needham." Another bark of laughter from her.

"That's surprising if they employ county residents."

"They hire some local labor, but the top folk they bring in from outside, then ship back out."

Returning to her earlier point, I added, "What's Sedick Oil a subsidiary of?"

If it wasn't Exxon, Chevron, Shell, or the biggies from China or Russia, it probably wouldn't mean anything to me. But I believed in picking up facts where you can and storing them for future use. Or simply for the pleasure of their company.

"Faison-Clafton."

It meant something to me.

It meant something to anyone who followed international or business news.

About a decade ago a handful of its executives were convicted of a scheme to bribe foreign officials in three South American countries. To have not just one, but several executives tried and convicted drew a lot of attention.

Many, many more executives and middle managers were fired. The company nearly went under. Some said it didn't because of its wide-sweeping firings.

So wide-sweeping that there'd been backlash stories about innocent people being fired. Then follow-up stories about how working at Faison-Clafton had become an exercise in walking on eggshells.

"The wake from the Faison-Clafton trials reached Sedick Oil in Cottonwood County?" I asked.

"Not overtly. Us being a backwater probably helped the head guys here. But there have been interesting developments. More accurately, non-developments."

"Explain, please."

"When Owen Grandisher first came here, he was on the super fast-track from what I heard, though Needham could tell you more. Not my bailiwick. What everybody expected was he'd move up and out, then his Number Two would move into the top spot here. Grandisher is still here and this other guy is still Number Two. That's the non-development."

We pulled into the station's parking lot and I could see her mentally shifting gears for the newscast ahead.

"Is there more to this?" I asked. I wouldn't get it from her now, probably not at tonight's party, either, but at least I'd know to track her down later.

"Not that I know of. But, then, I've never been interested enough to ask. Too close to hard news. C'mon. I gotta get in. Damn Thurston Fine's hide."

AUDREY HANDED LEONA a script as we walked in.

Jennifer was on dinner break during her double shift, so I'd report on the call with Angela Robertson later.

With Leona as anchor, Audrey was living the dream of many behind the camera—to keep the folks in front of the camera out of the newsgathering process completely. Let the talking heads speak the words someone else wrote and unplug them after the broadcast.

I could see the appeal with Thurston Fine as the talking head.

Me? They'll pry my rigor-mortised fingers off the keyboard.

Leona steamed back into the bullpen with her makeup done and a towel protecting her on-air top.

"What are you doing here?" she demanded of me.

"Looking over the stories Audrey gave you. Wanted to see if there's been a development in Spain on—"

"Don't get bogged down in that stuff," she said. "You need to get home and change, then meet me here after the Five. The news aide can get us something to eat and we'll discuss the party tonight."

"Eat?"

"Sure. We won't get any dinner otherwise."

I didn't argue.

I did adjust my wardrobe choice for the evening to a looser fitting outfit.

"NICE," LEONA SAID with a discerning look when I returned.

Jennifer looked up from her computer, but Audrey said something to her and she returned to work.

I wasn't going to make things worse for Jennifer—or Audrey—by intruding. Especially not after Jennifer's small head-shake, which I interpreted as meaning no progress on the thinnest of threads I'd given her about Felix Robertson the gambler.

Sharp-eyed gala attenders from a few events in Washington and New York would have recognized my long, narrow black skirt with a slit that showed enough leg, but not too much. No one wanted to witness a journalist's wardrobe malfunction. Coverage was essential—pun intended.

I topped it with a deep, dusty rose top with an asymmetrical neckline, which gave the impression of plunging without actually plunging, and bell sleeves—the better to hide things up.

Both pieces shimmered subtly when I moved.

I wouldn't grab attention by being the belle of the ball or by being drably underdressed.

"Thanks." But I had another matter on my mind. "Have you seen those clouds out there? Looks like a rainstorm."

"Snow."

"What?"

"Don't you listen to Warren?" Well, no, I didn't. There are only so many times you can hear *Windy and variable skies* before you tune out. "We're supposed to have up to a foot of snow starting tonight."

My mind whimpered, *But it's spring.* What I started to say was, "Won't they cancel—?"

Her laughter said no.

It also said that if I tried to beg off this assignment because of a snowstorm coming in I would lose all—well, it wasn't *street cred* in Wyoming, maybe *range cred?*

Leona calmly filled me in on the major players while she actually did eat more. I memorized names and positions, but in a portion of my brain reserved for short-term memory.

She took a power nap and freshened up, while Audrey and I talked

about a possible different angle on the lead international story for the
Ten. Leona would never notice the difference when she read Audrey's
script.

We headed out for Linda's ranch in separate vehicles in case I
needed mine while she was doing the half-hour broadcast at ten.

It started snowing on the way.

Chapter Thirteen

I'D BEEN TO Linda Caswell's ranch house before, but usually to a sunny, book-filled room with a comfortable sitting area in a bay window, perfect for tea and cookies. This was an entirely different atmosphere.

The sunny, book-filled room's door was closed. The house's usual polished comfort had stepped up several notches of formality, including flower arrangements and staff everywhere.

Yet it was different from what I'd known, especially in Washington and New York.

No tuxes in sight. The men arrived in cowboy hats and many wore boots—polished, but still boots—with their suits. Few coifs or up-dos showed among the women. They'd dressed up but hadn't overindulged in bling or dazzle.

And I hadn't seen a single air kiss while making a subtle circuit of the room.

I had found a strategic angle by the drapes beside French doors to the stone patio rapidly being covered in white.

"This must be old hat for you."

The voice from a spot even better hidden by the drapes was that of our hostess. She'd completed greeting arrivals and clearly found this quiet spot for recovery.

"Not at all." The closest I'd come to covering charity events were a kids' lemonade stand raising money to help a classmate with cancer early in my career and, more recently, running down the director of a major organization who thought charity began at home—by diverting a million plus to his new mansion.

Demonstrating far more tact than some people give me credit for, I mentioned the former and not the latter.

"...and they got a generous contribution from me for the worst lemonade I've ever had. I swear they used sand instead of sugar. Since this is no lemonade stand and this—" I lifted my champagne glass. "—definitely has no sand in it, I am out of my depth. I'm here to learn at Leona's knee."

Linda smiled. Her smile doesn't startle me as much now. I'm more accustomed to how it changes her face from plain to lovely.

"You have to tell Grayson that," she said of her significant other. "He was sure guests would want beer or whiskey. I held out to add champagne. To his credit, he wanted *good* beer and *good* whiskey."

I chuckled. "Wouldn't it have been a little easier to donate directly and skip all this?"

"A little? It would be *vastly* easier to donate directly. Given the choice of writing a check while wearing my slippers and bathrobe or putting on one of these functions? No contest. However, the charities remind us over and over that there is a multiplier effect in these fundraisers, because people who might otherwise skip contributing, donate in the spirit of the event.

"But I shouldn't monopolize you, Elizabeth. I'm sure there are lots of people here you'd like to meet and I know there are even more who'd like to meet you. I'd be happy to introduce you around."

I lowered my voice slightly—not to a whisper, because that draws attention—but enough to foil the casual eavesdropper. "I'd most like to meet my employers."

I didn't say the names Val Heatherton, owner of KWMT-TV, or her son-in-law, Craig Morningside, because I knew from being on the eavesdropping side of conversations how names snag a listener.

"Sorry. She's not here. She *can* afford to simply write the check, no matter what the multiplier effect, and that's what she usually does. But, perhaps—Ah." She touched the back of the arm of a woman walking past. "Krista?"

The younger woman stopped. When she saw me, Krista Seger's

smile dipped, then regained power, like a candle flame in a wind.

"Hi, Elizabeth."

"Hi, Krista."

"Oh, you two know each oth—Of course. That situation last fall."

Yes, another *situation*. It wasn't our fault people kept killing other people. And it sure wasn't *my* fault, contrary to what a few people intimated. Or said outright.

My stance was there weren't more deaths since I arrived in Cottonwood County. There were fewer free murderers.

Linda's attention strayed.

Rodeo cowboy Grayson Zane was tall enough to look over a lot of the party guests and he was using that advantage to make eye contact with Linda. He was also good-looking enough to catch the attention of the majority of females in the room. The only one he had eyes for was Linda.

That brought her face-changing smile. A small, private one.

"Excuse me, I have to…" She floated away.

Over my shoulder, I saw them meet in the middle, his arm going around her, the two of them somehow completely and happily alone for a beat before the party flow enveloped them.

"That's the way it should be, right?" Krista's voice drew me back around to her. I took it from her wistfulness that her marriage wasn't as idyllic as she'd like.

"They've both paid plenty of dues."

"I know, I know, and if there's anyone in the world I would hope could land a good-looking, sweet, rodeo star it would be Linda. Really."

I believed her. But the wistfulness remained.

We chatted about the bed and breakfast she and her husband owned.

"Bookings are picking up. We have a group coming in tomorrow, as a matter of fact. They were supposed to come in today, but got held up by the weather. Naturally, winter was quiet, but that gave me time to pick up side work."

"VisageTome?"

Before returning to Cottonwood County to open the B&B, she'd worked for VisageTome. Yes, *that* VisageTome. The one where you keep up with friends and family while VisageTome keeps up with every aspect of your life and sells the data that is you to high bidders.

"God, no. That reminds me, I wanted to say, uh, thank you for keeping us—the B&B—out of the follow-up reports on what happened last fall."

I hadn't kept it out, I just hadn't put it in. A big difference. Before I could explain that, though, she continued.

"And please tell Jennifer how sorry I am about Calliope. I know they were close."

My eyebrows hiked.

They shouldn't have. Everybody in Cottonwood County seemed to know everybody else, with the exception of me.

And then my eyebrows dropped under the weight of an idea.

"Thank you. I know she'll appreciate that." The niceties done, I said, "Do you know Calliope's family?" She nodded. "I understand they would normally be at a function like this. But what about the Joudreys? Are they here? Do you know them?"

"I do," she said slowly, "but…"

I took her arm. "An introduction would be so helpful."

"Of course, but—Oh, they're right there." She took one step forward then stopped. "There's something—"

But a couple was already advancing on us. He had a square face under short gray hair. She might have looked less strained if she'd let the gray come, too, instead of using a dark color.

Their friendliness to Krista tempered some as she introduced Lance's parents, Holly and Brady Joudrey, to me, including my connection to KWMT-TV.

I amped up my friendliness. Some people don't like the media.

Including people accumulating a lot of money by drawing oil out of the ground, moving it here and there across the land, sometimes into the hands of foreign officials in the form of bribes, then making regular people pay more than they'd like to stay warm or drive their cars.

I extended a hand to each in turn and shook with smiling eye-contact, her first, him second.

He sent a look in his wife's direction as we shook. That confirmed my instinct that she was the driver.

"This is a wonderful gathering Linda's put on, isn't it?" I asked her.

"It always is when Linda Caswell is the hostess." The implication that she was an insider and I was an outsider might not have resonated until later if her husband's look hadn't alerted me. And if I'd cared. "And such a worthy cause."

"It is," I agreed enthusiastically, not remembering which cause tonight was. "It's such a shame, though, that she had to step in, that the Grandishers couldn't carry on as planned. Absolutely tragic."

"Damned shame," he said. "Especially after all they went through with that girl. Finally turns around and then this."

Holly Joudrey turned partway toward her husband. He shut up.

"They are understandably devastated." Precise and cool, her words carried no emotion.

"Understandably," I echoed, "Calliope's death is a tragedy for them, as well as for her friends, including my co-worker Jennifer Lawton, who—"

"Excuse us."

Holly hooked a hand in Brady's arm, pivoted and was gone, with him shuffling fast to keep up.

It startled me into saying aloud, "What was that?"

"Jennifer was dating their son," Krista said.

"I know the parents weren't thrilled, but she's *that* angry after he broke up and—"

"But *he* didn't. She's angry Jennifer dumped him."

"JENNIFER DUMPED LANCE?"

As I scanned the room, I saw Needham Bender. He lifted his glass to me, ironically toasting my being snubbed by the Joudreys.

I grimaced back, then focused on Krista.

She nodded. "His mama was *not* happy about them dating. Even less happy that Jennifer broke up with him."

Since it was already clear to both of us Jennifer hadn't told me any of this, I might as well ask outright, "What's he like?"

"Lance? Not the worst guy around. That's an uphill battle with a doting and ambitious mother. She never wanted him to get his hands dirty. To his credit, he ignored her and got real work in the company. Not coasting on his daddy."

Was his mother upset on principle that Jennifer initiated the breakup. Or upset because he was upset. How upset was he?

Why had Jennifer broken up with him?

If Lance hadn't wanted to be broken up with and thought the shadow of Calliope was the cause, could he possibly...?

Krista ended my cogitations. "You know Lance and Calliope dated in high school? Broke up not long before she went to rehab."

"Did he contribute to her addiction?"

"Not that I ever heard."

We both became aware of a male form bearing down on us.

"We should get together for coffee or something," I proposed. After all, she was related to the station owner and might be a source for information on that mysterious figure. Not to mention staying in good with the owner of the town's only B&B.

"That sounds great. As long as we don't talk about murder."

GRAYSON ZANE CUPPED my elbow. "Hi, there, Krista. I'm going to borrow Elizabeth here for a bit."

As we moved off, he said to me, "Linda asks if you'd come upstairs for a moment."

His mild grip and friendly smile didn't fool me.

Linda had requested and that meant he wouldn't hesitate to drop me, hogtie me, and deliver me trussed to his fair lady's feet.

I chose to walk beside him.

We chatted a bit about his recent pro rodeo successes, that he thought he'd slow down a bit, look for a spread nearby, and spend more time in the county.

I wondered if a wedding might figure into that agenda.

We arrived at a door on the second floor too soon for me to work in that question.

He knocked, then opened the door.

Linda was there with Leona, who was brushing snow out of her hair onto a towel.

"Do you want a hairdryer?" Linda asked her, while smiling at me.

"No. That's why I cut this mop short. Should've had my hat on. That'll teach me to be vain about hat hair."

"One of the valets should have—"

"No, no. Stop fussing, Linda. I'm fine. You and Grayson go do your duty. I'll have a word with Elizabeth here, then we'll be back down, mingling, too."

They obeyed.

"How'd the Ten go?"

"Fine," she said with little interest. She carried the towel to an attached bathroom, deftly shook melting snow into the sink, then used the driest end to ruffle her short hair. "I hear you were busy while I was gone. *Networking* all over."

"Word spreads fast."

"Wasn't Linda. But you know it does in this county. Then multiply it by ten for this crowd."

"What do you know about the Joudreys?"

She blinked. "I know they're not happy with Jennifer."

"She broke the heart of mommy's little boy? Is that the story?"

"Something like that. At least you didn't ask them about the Lawtons."

"Jennifer's parents? They have something against Jennifer's parents?"

"There's no love lost there."

"Why?"

She didn't bother to try to make her shrug convincing. "You could say there's some history."

"Spill."

"You know Holly Joudrey—Lance's mother—is from here."

I remembered Diana saying something… "Brady Joudrey married a local girl."

"That's Holly. Well, she'd dated Kent Lawton in high school."

"Of course, she did. I should have guessed they either dated or were related."

"But not both. That's where we draw the line." Her perfectly solemn expression didn't crack. "Knowing about cattle bloodlines we know that's big trouble. Even though there's not a whole lot of dating stock around here. In this case, Holly and Kent were still dating when people who knew her said she saw this nice young oil company guy arrive. Single, good-looking, couple of degrees, holding a good job, and even better prospects. She went after him like a fly on a cow pie. Brady never knew what hit him. The second she had him tied up, she threw over Kent Lawton."

I expelled a slow breath. "But not until she had the new one tied up? That's rough."

"Not until," she confirmed. "But if he'd been properly destroyed, everything would've been okay. Instead, he rebounded in record time to Faith, now Mrs. Lawton."

"Showing Holly he was fine without her? Or for real?"

"Not sure it matters. Either way, he's had the gall to be happy with Faith and their family all these years. Can't forgive that, even if she seems happy enough with her own choice."

"And then their daughter broke up with her son."

"Now you're starting to see the Cottonwood County tangles. Now, other than Holly Joudrey snubbing you, what did I miss while I was doing the Ten?"

It was a short report.

Chapter Fourteen

WITH LEONA BACK on duty and the party winding toward its end, I felt free to roam. Actually, I had before, too, but now with less guilt.

One of the pairs of polished cowboy boots in attendance belonged to Tom Burrell.

No surprise there. He and Linda were good friends. Not to mention his involvement in about every civic endeavor.

We'd said hello in passing earlier, but now those polished boots were beside me in my favorite quiet corner, watching the mingling. The Joudreys demonstrated strong mingle skills. Krista Seger left early.

He looked almost handsome in his dark, dress jeans, crisp white shirt, and charcoal gray sport coat. I squinted, trying to imagine Abraham Lincoln in this wardrobe.

"Heard you had a ruckus with the Joudreys," he said.

I *pshawed* that away. "Barely a ripple. No voices raised. No drinks thrown. Maybe a toe or two stepped on. That's all. Besides, how was I to know it was a touchy subject. I was left out of the loop on Jennifer's dating life."

Not only did I not get sympathy, his silence nurtured a suspicion.

I turned to his profile. "You knew Jennifer was dating Lance Joudrey all along."

"Not all along. To start, I only knew she was dating an oil guy."

A lot more than I'd known. But something else in the way he answered caught my attention. "That worried you? Because he wasn't a ranch guy?"

"There are other occupations than ranching."

"*I* know there are. Wasn't so sure about you. You don't want a nice cowboy for her?"

He didn't answer directly. "Jennifer's been real sharp with computers since she was a little thing. She knows and does things on the computer her folks don't understand, maybe things none of us around here understand."

I thought of my concerns about her hacking and getting in trouble over it. Never having been a parent myself, I still felt a kinship with hers, who knew less of what she did than I did.

"I get it. She goes off into a world they don't know about, where there could be dangers she might or might not be up to handling because they don't have anything to do with the actual computing."

"Computers are part of it. Goes wider."

"Ah. Not just the computer world, but real life, too?"

"Yep."

Jennifer did have a certain naivete about the world along with her superior computer skills. It was why I bugged her about not hacking. To be sure she kept consequences in mind.

"She's learning. And she's grown up a lot in the past year."

"She has." Burrell's perfectly straight face did not fool me. He was chuckling on the inside. At me. Just because I was a little protective of the kid? "Told her folks as much. Told them it was your influence."

"Mine? Hey, don't go thinking I'm some sort of mentor or—"

"Not some sort. You are. Mentor. Role model. Whatever you want to call it. You're it."

"That's … That's—"

He rested a hand on my shoulder. "Be quiet and take your medicine, Elizabeth. You have a lot of influence over her. Understand it's why her folks are wary of you." He started to walk away.

"Me? Wary of me? Why on earth—?"

"They haven't met you. Only heard about you. And that's no accident. Jennifer's seen to it."

"I don't—Why? Why would she…?"

He looked back at me. He wouldn't spell it out.

"Okay. Forget that. Tell me something else." He stopped, but didn't return. "What's the issue with the Joudreys?"

"You got into a ruckus with them and didn't even know what it was about?"

"Like I told you, no ruckussing on my part. But I'm guessing it was over their son and Jennifer dating."

He rumbled a confirmation.

"Why so upset about it now when they broke up a couple months back? They didn't like that they were dating, so even if she broke up with him…"

"Neither set of parents liked it."

Not an answer to my question, but an interesting detour. "Why?"

Tom side-eyed me, then turned to face me. "I see that mind of yours working. Lance came along a couple years after Holly broke up with Kent Lawton to marry Brady Joudrey."

"That's good to know." Though it sure would have explained both sets of parents being against the relationship if they were half-siblings.

Tom turned another ninety degrees to face the French doors, taking me with him by clasping my elbow.

"Is this change of scenery so I quit asking you about people?"

"It's because it's a beautiful night." And the not-so-subtle end of the previous topic.

"If you like white curtains."

One side of his mouth lifted. "Want me to drive you to Diana's?"

"And leave my SUV in town? Thanks, but no. I'll be fine. The road's not *that* bad to her ranch."

Now, if I'd been headed to his ranch, up into the mountains, with an entry that wound and rose and twisted and rose more, I'd've said yes.

Not that he'd be driving me to his place after a party with a snowstorm promising to close the occupants in for a long night, maybe more.

"Why don't you stay?" He left an extra beat before adding, "In town. At your house."

My house.

Oh.

Yeah.

Right.

My house. Not his.

Made total sense. Mine was close. His was way out on his ranch, mostly on the side of a mountain for heaven's sake, where the snow would surely be deeper. Absolutely no sense my staying *there*.

"It's not—I haven't moved in yet."

"There's plenty there to get you through a night. Iris and Zeb will take care of you if you need anything."

"You know the Undlins—?" I bit it off. "Of course, you know them."

"I do. They're real glad you're moving in."

"Did you have something to do with their deciding I should get that house?"

He raised innocent hands. I had doubts about the innocence of those hands. "Me? It was all their idea. But gotta say it's convenient for you on a night like tonight."

I expelled a breath. It did beat the idea of driving out to Diana's through wind-blown blasts of white.

"I've got to let Diana know."

"Use that room." He nodded to the closed door to the room with the sunny bay window. "Linda won't mind."

Diana approved of my staying in town tonight and admitted they'd gotten Shadow from the Bunkhouse around noon and he'd been in the main house since.

I suspected he'd end up beside Jessica's bed as he had a time or two before. She wouldn't admit it, but I suspected she was trying to lure him onto her bed.

"Anything interesting tonight," she asked.

I told her about the encounter with the Joudreys.

"It must be a pretty raw wound to make a potential scene in that setting."

"Um-hmm. Diana, what would your county friends know about the Grandishers' and Joudreys' financial situations? I know you're not close with the oil people, but there must be intersections, some connections…"

"Why do I get these assignments? Poking into people's personal lives."

"We all do when we get into these things."

Her non-response radiated skepticism.

"We do," I insisted. "It's just that Jennifer usually does the heavy lifting with backgrounds, but this time I can't ask her to. She's not in a good state to—"

"Stop. Just stop. Enough guilt. I was going to do it anyway."

"Darn. I should have saved the guilt for another time."

When I came out, Tom was nowhere in sight.

Could he be staying here because of the snow? There'd been a time when I thought he and Linda… But Linda and Grayson were far too close to allow even the consideration of another attachment.

As a long-time friend, though, it would make sense for Tom to spend a night like this here.

I joined the dwindling stream of guests waiting for valets to bring their vehicles around to the porte-cochère on the side of the house. With a final hug from Linda—and without raising the topic of Tom's overnight accommodations—I got into my fast-warming SUV and joined the line of departing vehicles.

At the end of the ranch road, the vehicles scattered into the snowy landscape. It struck me that with the exception of the oil company executives who favored the development around the country club— along with a certain TV anchor—Cottonwood County's social leaders spread wide across its thousands of square miles.

I went slowly and steadily. I could drive in snow. It was snow in mountains that pushed my buttons. Also snow in the wrong season.

Inside the town limits, the snow stayed in one place long enough to reach half a foot and was still coming.

And I realized I had a tail.

At a four-way stop, I recognized Tom's pickup. He acknowledged I'd recognized him with a laconic raising of his index finger from the top of the steering wheel.

I shook my head and eased away from the stop sign. His pickup followed at a safe interval. Someday the guy was going to realize I was not a delicate flower. But not tonight.

I pulled into the drive that had been shoveled tonight but not in the past hour or so. I didn't go all the way to the garage because I wasn't sure if the keys I had included its door.

I got out of the vehicle quickly, so I could wave as Tom drove by.

He didn't drive by. He pulled in behind my SUV.

He got out of his truck and started toward me.

My phone rang.

The screen said Jennifer.

Temptation hovered my finger over the screen, then accepted the call.

He walked up as she said, "You're staying in town tonight."

"How did you—?" What was the point of asking? Cottonwood County. "Yes.

"Can I come stay with you?"

"It's no closer to the station than your parents' house."

"What difference does that make? Oh. The *snow*? I don't care about that. It's... We can discuss the investigation. Can I stay?"

Looking into Tom's eyes looking into me, I said, "Yes, you can come stay with me."

"Great. I'll be there in about an hour when my shift is over."

"Okay. See you then." She'd already disconnected. I clicked off, too, never looking away from him.

One side of his mouth hitched up. If Abraham Lincoln ever produced a wry half-smile, none of the photographers of his day caught it. It was pretty darn appealing.

"You could still come in," I pointed out to that half-smile.

"I could. If you invited me."

"I could invite you." Then I added. "But..."

He lowered his head, deepening the shadow from the brim of his hat. "Jennifer needs you now."

"You mean she needs a place to stay away from her parents."

"I said what I mean."

"She won't be here for an hour."

"Not enough time. Not nearly enough time."

Chapter Fifteen

I STOOD INSIDE the front door.

My front door.

Where I stood was a small enclosed porch. Pegs for coats, a bench for putting on or taking off boots, and a tray for storing them defined a mud room, without indicating the room ever saw wet dirt.

Beyond the archway came the living room, dining room, and kitchen, in quick succession. The rooms were not large, but the openness helped and so did the perfectly proportioned and simple furniture.

And there we had the first issue.

The house was fully and tastefully—if impersonally—furnished. As Tom pointed out, it was ready to be occupied.

Which meant my new home was going to get awfully crowded when my things arrived from storage.

My new home.

Or was it? Wasn't it still Renata's?

Now I was going to replace some of hers with some of mine, moving what remained of hers around, making changes, making decisions.

All by myself.

After Wes and I married, we both worked ambition-fueled schedules, leaving wedding gifts boxed and apartments bare in a succession of early stops. That started to change in St. Louis. Wes took an interest in where we should live, what our home should look like, whom we should socialize with.

By the time we were in Washington, D.C., Wes' views on what we *should* like clashed with my family pieces. I fought to use them until we moved to New York. Then they were shunted into storage and I gave Wes full rein with the apartment he loved and I tolerated.

But those family pieces and other possessions were breaking free from storage and would be here soon.

What on earth was I going to do with them? Or with Renata's belongings? Or half of each?

No way did I remember dimensions. How could I—

A knock at the front door made me jump.

I'd barely made it past the threshold. In fact, had stayed so close to the door I practically felt reverberations of the knock in my backbone.

I spun around. Nothing showed in the horizontal window at the top. Tom would have. So would a recognizable portion of Jennifer's head.

I hesitated, listening.

Nothing.

I opened the door, to discover the nearly matching white-haired heads of Zeb and Iris Undlin, my soon-to-be neighbors and temporary landlords, standing well below the level of the door's window.

"There. I told you she was here," Iris said.

Zeb *huh*ed his apparent disbelief that I was, in fact, here.

"Makes sense you staying over tonight after that big party at the Caswell place." Iris patted my arm as she breezed past me. "Shouldn't keep your coat on indoors, dear. Though it is a bit chilly. Zeb?"

"Got it." He'd breezed right behind her and was at the thermostat. Now I knew where the thing was located—on the wall, next to another archway, leading to a small hallway that opened to a bedroom to the right, bathroom straight ahead, and stairway up to another bed and bath.

"We brought you a few things." She was unloading a grocery bag on the counter.

The furnace kicked on in response to Zeb's ministrations to the thermostat.

"You didn't have to—"

"Knew you hadn't bought basic supplies for here yet. Penny," she added in explanation. "So helpful."

Sometimes the Sherman Supermarket clerk was helpful, but only after careful detangling of her comments.

Apparently, Iris had detangled Penny's comments enough to know I didn't have eggs, bacon, butter, bread, or hot sauce.

I shed my coat, dropping it on a stool, to put the items in the fridge.

"We left what wouldn't spoil, so you have salt and pepper and such. Pots and pans and plates, too. Though with your furnishings coming…"

"A few things." I heard apology in my voice for my belongings pushing out Renata's.

"You keep what you need and we'll add the rest to the neighborhood yard sale. She would have liked that."

"Yard sale?"

"Whole neighborhood gets together for one each summer. Everybody on the same days. Draws quite a crowd. Zeb runs the cotton candy machine and what we make on that and a few other things, earns enough for a neighborhood cookout the last night."

"Nothing fancy. Not like your party tonight," Zeb grumbled.

"It was fancy. Though I was there as a working stiff—on assignment for the TV station."

He grunted, apparently letting me back into the proletariat.

She patted my arm again and said, "How nice. Now, the beds were all made with fresh sheets yesterday and—"

"Oh, Iris, you shouldn't have—"

"You and an army couldn't have stopped her," Zeb said with pride.

"Couldn't have you moving in with unwashed sheets. Towels are fresh, too. Soap in both bathrooms. There's a good supply of new toothbrushes and toothpaste in the medicine cabinets."

A flashback of the Hovel—the listless and listing rental I'd lived in when I first moved to Sherman—brought tears to my eyes. Tears of one kind at remembering the place and tears of another kind at the contrast.

A knock sounded from the front door.

I intercepted a look between Iris and Zeb.

They clearly thought—

"A co-worker's going to stay here with me tonight."

Their second look changed one player but kept the same script.

As I walked toward the door, I emphasized, "*She* needs a quiet place to stay. Just for tonight. Hi, Jennifer. I didn't hear your vehicle."

"Dale dropped me off. I didn't want to borrow my parents'."

"Ah. Come in and meet my neighbors, Iris and Zeb Undlin. This is Jennifer Lawton."

"Oh." Jennifer was surprised.

"Oh." I swear Iris was disappointed.

"Huh." Zeb was uninterested.

"We know your parents—"

"And grandparents," came from Zeb.

"—of course," Iris said, "but I don't believe we've passed the time of day since you were a little thing. One Halloween, I recall. You were a chameleon. Made it yourself so the lights glowed different colors depending on what you pressed from inside the costume. So clever."

"Oh, yeah. I remember that." The memory pleased her, but only for an instant. Then her mouth drooped. Did that memory connect to Calliope?

Iris applied her arm-patting to Jennifer. "Such a shame about your friend. So young and full of life.

Zeb's rumble might have been words or just sounds of condolence.

Jennifer looked down at each of them and said with mature solidity, "Thank you."

"We'll go now." Iris bustled toward the door with Zeb there first to open it. She looked back. "Hot cocoa. Cabinet next to the fridge. Top shelf."

✧ ✧ ✧ ✧

THE HOT COCOA was a winner.

Though how Iris had known where the cocoa package was kept when it was stored well above the top of her head, I couldn't imagine.

Preparing the cocoa gave Jennifer and me something to do, work-ing together, yet with gaps allowing us to freshen up one at a time.

With no discussion, we sat on stools at the countertop. It felt more casual than the sitting area in front of the modest brick fireplace. More casual and less committed to a *serious talk.*

We were just drinking hot cocoa, then heading to bed.

"I didn't have time to do much more work on Felix Robertson, not with Audrey staying on me."

"She's putting herself under a lot of pressure, Jennifer, and—"

"I know, I know. She apologized for being short with me. Said she's trying real hard to have top-notch broadcasts to put in her reel. And with Leona letting her make all the decisions, do most of the writing, it was a hard day. I understand. But it still was a pain when I needed to track things down to do with Calliope. The good thing is a bunch of people are pitching in."

"I know Dale filled in for you—"

"Yeah, but I mean my online friends. Not that they're having a lot of success, either." Her frown turned fearsome. "It's like there's a wall or something. Even with DaisyDukes volunteering to be point person to help me out and she's the best. But it seems like folks are spinning their wheels on Felix Robertson. And everything that can go wrong is going wrong. A couple people got hit with attacks today and even Daisy was offline for hours."

She turned to me with an air of misery soliciting company. "Find out anything at the party?"

I skipped the Joudreys' reaction to her name, and said, "A little background you probably already know. Nothing vital. There's something else, though, I'd like you to look into."

"What?"

Remembering Shelton's and Conrad's faces yesterday, showing absolutely nothing when—if there'd truly been nothing, they wouldn't have needed to bother to show nothing—I considered how wide a net to ask Jennifer to cast.

Everything she could possibly find?

No, I could narrow it a bit. Whatever they were not showing probably wasn't about Calliope and the trouble she'd gotten into. Shelton had been an open book—by his standards—about that.

If we were still stuck in a day or two, I might ask her to go back over Calliope's records. But for now…

"See what you can find out about interactions between the sheriff's department and Sedick Oil, would you? Public records, the *Independence.*"

"What's that got to do with Calliope?"

"Possibly nothing." But there were strong emotions and streams of money flowing around and through Sedick Oil. A powerful combination. "Sometimes a back window's open when the front door's blocked."

She looked unimpressed. "Fine." She took another sip from her mug. "Anything else?"

"Yes. Why'd you break up with Lance Joudrey?"

Her eyes went round for a moment, then she slowly nodded. "Shouldn't be surprised you know about that. Not the way you find out things and *know* things. I can find out things, but I'm not good with knowing about people. If I were, I'd've known something was wrong with Cal."

"You couldn't predict this or—"

"I could have—should have—responded faster to her messages and emails and stuff. But I meant earlier. When she got into drugs. When things went sour with Lance and her. But I didn't. Didn't see any of it until it was over."

"That was well before you and Lance started dating?"

"Um-hm."

"Did Calliope know you were dating?"

"Yeah. Told him I wouldn't go out with him if she wasn't okay with it. But she was. Said she was."

"He was the guy they didn't approve of?"

"Yeah. But it wasn't like they ordered me not to see him or something ancient like that."

"Why did they disapprove of him?"

She lifted one shoulder. "They didn't spell it out. They just *wondered* to me all the time about if I'd be happier dating somebody else. Or if it was hard to keep up with work and all while dating him. Or if I wasn't moving on from high school because I kept seeing my friends from then."

Had she listened to that part? Was that an element of her guilt over pulling away from Calliope? Or was it because she'd dated Calliope's ex, even with Calliope's okay?

"But you broke up?"

"Yeah. He probably wouldn't have, but…"

"But what?"

"It wasn't working out."

I've received more forthcoming answers during interviews with Russian politicians.

"I got the impression Lance's mother didn't want you two dating."

"She didn't."

"One of those mothers who thinks no one's good enough for their son?"

"Nah. She's not like that. Not really. It was something else. And it wasn't just his mom. I told you, it was my parents, too. It was like when we were in high school the parents got all weird about each other. We talked about it some—Lance and Calliope and me—but we never figured it out."

"What are Calliope's parents like?"

She shrugged. "They were nice enough to me. Lance, too. But my parents don't hang out with oil people and her dad's Lance's dad's boss. You think any of this will help figure out what happened to Calliope?"

"You know how these things work, Jennifer. We pull in a lot of information, looking for something—anything—to follow up."

"But Lance and me? We're broken up. Why're you interested in that?"

Because she and he and Calliope had been a pack as teens and now there was a death and a breakup that had stirred high emotions—at least in Lance's parents. Would be interesting to know how he felt about it now.

I sidestepped all that.

"I didn't even know you'd dated Lance until I heard you'd broken up—no, not even then because I didn't know it was Lance. Just that you'd previously dated someone and then, at that point, you'd been broken up for a while. But other people knew you were dating someone—dating Lance?" I asked. "I mean in the newsroom."

"Uh-huh. Diana, Audrey, a few others." So, preserving a professional reticence was not an explanation for not telling me. "But I didn't think you'd be interested."

"Why?" I asked in surprise.

She swirled her mug around, mixing chocolate sediment back into the cooling milk. "You don't talk about those things yourself."

Most of my professional life I'd been married to a co-worker. Talking about our relationship at work had never seemed professional ... or wise. Especially as our careers diverged, with mine remaining in the newsroom and his going into the network hierarchy. Even more so as our marriage splintered.

Jennifer added, "Anybody brings up Mike or Tom in that way and you shut it down."

"I'm not dating either of them."

"I know that. *Everybody* knows that. But why not?"

Absorbing that *everybody*, I stumbled out, "It's complicated."

"See?"

I pulled in a long breath. "Jennifer, it's not that I'm trying to shut anybody out." Though Diana had accused me of that a time or two. "But with my former marriage and working with Mike—working with both him and Tom, really, with these inquiries—it *is* complicated."

"They don't think it's too complicated."

"I don't know about that." A thought struck me and came right out of my mouth. "Because, come to think of it, neither has actually asked me out on date. But that—"

"They haven't? What a couple of idiots."

"—doesn't mean I'm not interested in your life or your feelings. Not that you're obligated to tell me, well, anything. And I'd never want to intrude, but I do want you to know I'm not *not* interested. In you, in your life."

She took all that convoluted gobbledygook, absorbed it in a milli-second and replied, "Okay."

I let out a breath.

Too soon.

Because then she said, "You know what you're going to have to do, since you haven't given either of them enough encouragement, is pick one and ask *him* out."

DAY THREE

SUNDAY

Chapter Sixteen

"YOU LOOK WELL-RESTED after your first night in your new home," Diana said as we met at the door into the Sherman Café.

I had slept well in Renata's bed. "Hot cocoa before bed. It's the answer to the world's problems. Also a wi-fi connection."

The world dazzled with blue sky bouncing off sparkling land. Mostly sparkling land. The wind periodically scoured the snow from one spot and rearranged it playfully under your feet.

Despite the dazzle, I saw her brows rise. "Wi-fi?"

"For Jennifer. I had no idea if it existed, if it had been disconnected, the password… Jennifer found the information on a card in the bedside table of the guest room. Renata was *really* organized."

"So Jennifer was happy and let you sleep."

"Well, only until you arranged this crack of dawn brunch. Let me point out that it's a lot closer to a B-R time than the more humane U-N-C-H."

"Me? I didn't arrange this. I thought you did. I was surprised about the time, but…"

Together, we said, "Jennifer."

"What?" she answered from in front of us.

"Just saying how nice it was of you to arrange this," Diana said.

"Yeah. Well, we have to check in. See where we are."

Jennifer had also arranged for us to have a table in an alcove. With two of us on one side, two on the other, and her at the head, we filled that alcove, while also being cut off from other patrons.

While the waitress worked around the table taking orders, I said to Jennifer, "I hope you didn't stay up all night using Renata's wi-fi."

"First chance I had all day to really get into the records." She barely waited for the waitress to turn away from the table to ask. "What has everybody discovered?"

She skimmed right past Tom, who'd raised his hands to show they were empty, and caught Diana giving me a look.

"What?"

"I asked Diana to check on some things, which we will not discuss in a public place."

As Jennifer opened her mouth, clearly preparing to protest, Diana added, "Nothing to report yet, anyway. Elizabeth only asked last night."

Jennifer focused on Mike. His shrug drew a glare.

"Hey, I'm not the only one," he protested.

"You're not doing *anything*. You're usually all on fire to investigate. Not this time because you don't care. Because…"

Diana put a hand over Jennifer's.

"I care," Mike protested. "There hasn't been anything for me to look into."

With a bit of a huff, Jennifer said to the rest of us, "I have a report for you on what Elizabeth asked about—" She sent a quick look in Diana's direction and added a mild dig. "—last night."

I felt curiosity from the others, but was more interested in satisfying my own. "Already? How on earth—Did you get any sleep last night?"

"Yeah. I had my guys running a lot of the other stuff, so all I had to do was read their reports. But I thought I better do the Cottonwood County Sheriff's Department myself."

Good thinking.

"Most of the reports concerning employees of Sedick Oil involve bar fights," she said. "Some at the Kicking Cowboy—" A bar, not quite a dive, in the southeast part of town. "—some at places I'd never even heard of. Did you know there's a bar behind Easley's garage?"

The answer came from Tom. "Yes, and you are not to go there. Any of you." His look took in all the females.

Dive bars didn't call to me, but I made no promises. You went where the story led.

"Anyway," Jennifer resumed, showing no sign of taking Tom as seriously as he'd sounded, "the most recent report was different. Another fight, but this one was out at a rig, during daylight hours, and no mention of alcohol. The sheriff's department responded. But apparently there wasn't much to it. They didn't even bother to categorize it right. It was marked as a domestic." She clicked her tongue in disapproval of such slipshod work.

That sounded even less interesting than she seemed to think it was.

"What about the reports from your online friends?" I asked. "Anything?"

Her mouth turned down. "So far, there's not much in the way of hard information. But they'll keep working. It's coming from so many people, I don't know what I'd do without Daisy collecting and organizing it. Nothing will get by us."

I closed my eyes.

Us. Not the royal *we*, I feared, but the hacking *we*.

I opened my eyes to find Diana, Mike, and Tom staring at me. Probably waiting for my usual anti-hacking direction to Jennifer.

I didn't have the heart for it.

First, I doubted she'd listen if she thought it had any chance of digging up information about Calliope's death.

Second, she'd already moved on, saying, "They don't even know Calliope and they're doing all this."

"They know you," Tom said.

"From online. That's not really knowing somebody." Mike kept digging himself in deeper.

"I've known them longer than I've known *you*. And they're—"

"Well, I have a report," I said cheerfully. "I talked to Angela Robertson yesterday."

Jennifer turned to me, so she didn't see Mike's mouth forming "Who?" At least he didn't give it any sound.

That might have been because the food arrived then.

Around my omelet, tomato juice, and coffee, I recounted my conversation with Angela Robertson. I ended with the possible connection of a professional gambler named Felix Robertson and Angela's mention of Vegas.

"So far, that's another stone wall," Jennifer grumbled.

I considered bringing in the connection of Felix Robertson the Civil War general, along with her mentioning a stone wall, as in Stonewall Jackson, the nephew of the Jackson of Leona's riff... I didn't think Jennifer's mood could take it, however.

"Elizabeth, I know you just tossed it out to the ex-wife, but could Calliope have known this man?" Diana asked.

"It's something to consider. Coincidences happen, but not as much as some people try to pretend. The other hikers said they hadn't been hiking together, but if she knew him, did they agree to meet there? Was there a reason for them to meet?"

Questions that raised possibilities. Could their meeting have been the reason for their deaths? Or had someone needed to prevent their meeting?

"I should have had a complete background on him by now," Jennifer said.

"We just found out his name yesterday morning and—"

"You should've had complete information yesterday and I *still* don't have it."

"—I decided to call without waiting for the full background. That's on me. Besides, you've had a lot on your mind and weighing on your heart. Give yourself a break. ... But continue research on Robertson's background. Especially with an eye to answering if his ex-wife is right about him, what *did* get him to go for a walk up a mountain?"

Mike leaned forward, elbows on the table, index fingers pointing forward. "I've got another question. Why did the authorities notify his *ex*-wife? It's not like they just got divorced."

"Good question, Mike. Jennifer—?"

"Got it."

"Do we take Angela's word for what he was like?" Diana asked me.

"Not at all. In fact… While I was on hold yesterday, I started searching Felix Robertson and found this Civil War general."

"Ancestor war hero for our guy?" Mike interrupted.

"No reason to think they're related. As for the war hero part, I'm coming to that. He was actually sort of a general. You know how, during the war, they promoted people on the spot because so many were killed?"

"Brevet," Tom said.

"Right. To go from brevet to official it had to be confirmed, but the Confederate Senate rejected Robertson's nomination. That came after Robert E. Lee wanted him brought up on charges for a massacre of wounded black soldiers captured in the Battle of Saltville. One historian called Robertson the worst man to wear a general's uniform in either army."

"Is this to get back at me about Albert Bacon Fall and Pat Garrett?" Mike asked.

"No." Though I should have thought of that.

"What does this Civil War guy have to do with Calliope?" Jennifer asked.

"Our attitude toward Robertson. You hear Civil War general and maybe you think of a statue of a guy on a horse. But there were all kinds. We don't take Angela's account as gospel. But we need to be careful about our assumptions about Felix Robertson. We've been calling him a victim. We've been thinking Calliope died trying to help someone good on that trail. Which brings up something else … I'm going to Colorado."

Creases at the corners of Tom's eyes gave him away before he spoke. "You're a day late if you think going south's the answer to a little snow."

"I wouldn't stop at Colorado if that were my goal." I looked at Diana. "Will you look after Shadow?"

"Of course. But why go to Colorado?" she asked.

"Trying to work back to the primary source by finding out who gave the guy who wrote the news release the information. He won't answer phone calls? Show up in person. That's harder to ignore."

"When?" Mike asked.

"Today." I'd awakened with this plan already formed. "Delaying doesn't work. I'm off the next couple days. Plus, I'll have to be here when my stuff arrives, probably next week. So, now's the time."

"I'm going with," Jennifer said immediately. "I'll message Calliope's friends down there, see if we can have dinner with them."

"That's a good idea, but only if your parents—"

"Me, too," Mike said. "Good plan leaving now. We'll be in place to see people Monday instead of spending most of a work day driving. And I'll drive. Serves them right to have a little reverse invasion, anyway."

He'd lost me. "Serves who right?"

"Coloradans. Wyomingites aren't fond of greenies pouring in." In response to my look, he added, "Greenies. For the green Colorado license plates. We don't get as many of them in Cottonwood County, but for southern Wyoming it's a real issue. Crowding."

"Crowding? Wyoming is the least populated state in the country and second only to Alaska on space-per-resident."

"We want to keep it that way. Won't with all those greenies arriving. Not to mention they want to change things." His expression shifted to something more cheerful. "Only good thing is they're starting to feel the hurt they've been putting on us with all the Californians rolling into Colorado."

I waved away that topic. "I accept your offer to drive—"

"But they're not even sure about more snow coming."

Whatever else Jennifer might have said was lost in the others' shushing.

Too late.

"More snow?"

Mike said, "Just a little. Like one of those little aftershocks with an earthquake."

"Thanks. I've been in earthquakes and the aftershocks can still be major. If we get stuck in snow, I am holding you totally accountable."

Tom clapped him on the back in a consoling way.

"And when we come back, I'll stay at your place," Jennifer said, following her own train of thought to a conclusion that satisfied her.

For half a second I thought she was looking at Mike. Nope. Me. "The Bunkhouse is too small. The one bed and—"

"Not the Bunkhouse. Your house."

"*I'm* not even staying there yet."

"You did last night. *We* did."

"Well, yeah, but sort of camping out. Until my things arrive and I actually move—"

"If you don't want to, I still can. It's got everything I need. I won't make a mess."

"Jennifer, you are not staying there without me or—"

"You don't know what it's like at home. It's awful, totally and completely awful. They wrote her off when she had trouble with drugs. I swear, they're not sad one bit she's dead—*murdered*—and I can't stand being around them. Every second is like I'm betraying her again, like she's dying again."

There it was. The m-word.

"That's not—"

I started a gesture toward Tom as his protest began, but Diana was there first, her hand on his wrist.

Part of his protectiveness of Jennifer came from being lifelong friends with her father and knowing her mother nearly as long. Although that was icing on the cake of his take-care-of-the-county and most-of-the-people-in-it protectiveness.

To everyone's surprise—possibly even his own, judging by his expression—Mike made the next protest. "You're not staying in that house or anywhere else alone."

"Why not? I'm a grown up."

"You're upset, that's why. Besides—" Craftiness slid across his face. "—we don't know what's going on. What if it involves you? What if someone finds out you're living alone? What if—?"

"Oh, c'mon." She heaped on world-weary scorn.

"—you're the one person who knows a clue, without even knowing it, and because you insist on being alone, the gang behind killing

Calliope catches you, too, and then we never know that clue and both murders go unsolved. Forever."

My turn for a world-weary, *Oh, c'mon*, though I kept it to myself. Good thing, because Mike's argument clearly swayed Jennifer.

I was not above adopting a winning tactic.

It clearly didn't faze her that we were talking about danger to her, so I focused it in terms of the inquiry. "If Mike's right and something happened to you, how would we ever find out about Calliope?"

She chewed on her lip for half a second.

Lip-chewing complete, she said, "That's easy to fix. Elizabeth stays there, too."

I noticed, but did not protest, her plunking me in the middle of danger. "I'm not moving until—"

"Might be a good idea for you both to stay there." We all turned to Tom, the surprising speaker. "If you're right about something going on, it might be better for Jennifer."

If *I* was right about something going on? How did this become *my* theory?

On the other hand, would I be going to Colorado if I hadn't started to—at least—wonder?

The giveaway lines deepened around Tom's eyes. "It might be better for you, too, having company. First nights staying in a place new to you and all."

"I am not spooked by staying in a new place."

"Even one that isn't new and belonged to a dead woman?" Mike asked.

I flicked my napkin at him and said, just for that, he was doing all the driving.

AS MIKE AND I walked out to our vehicles after agreeing on a departure time from my not-new new house, I said, "Good thinking on that concoction you sold Jennifer on."

"What concoction?"

"About her having the vital clue but not knowing it."

"It could be true."

I finally got to use my "Oh, c'mon."

"It could," he insisted.

MIKE PICKED US up at Renata's house—my house—in a different SUV.

· I'd dropped Jennifer off to pack a few things, went to the Bunkhouse for my bag, then brought her back to the house with more luggage than a couple days in Colorado would need.

She confirmed that by leaving the biggest suitcase in the house. I pretended not to notice.

If that battle needed fighting later, the suitcase could come out as easily as it went in. Probably.

"What happened to your SUV?" I asked Mike. He'd had it at the café.

"Nothing. I have a standing deal to rent this one for trips."

"Why?"

"Long trips around here can be tough. Better to take that out on a rental." I wasn't complaining. It was nearly as cushy as his.

Chapter Seventeen

WHAT WOKE ME were flashes created by mountains cutting off, then revealing the sun.

Having grown up in Illinois, I don't take mountains for granted.

Mountains on the East Coast warm up their act with rolling ground rising into foothills before clearing their throats with small mountains, then completing the crescendo with their high notes.

Not in Wyoming. Going from east to west, the state hums along in what those not into subtle consider a monotone, shouts out for the Big Horns before dropping back to that hum in the Big Horn Basin, then—with no warm up—belts out the "Hallelujahs" from Handel's *Messiah* as it hits the Rockies.

For those who only know this region from skimming maps, Wyoming and Colorado are the big square states, with Wyoming offset to the west atop Colorado.

The Rocky Mountains don't follow straight lines or right turns. Between that and the offset, we angled southeast through the Big Horn Basin with the Big Horns to the east, the Rockies to the west.

Once out of the Big Horn Basin, we'd select one of three routes: west to pick up I-80 to Laramie, east to I-25 to Cheyenne, or down the middle through Medicine Bow to Laramie. Then from Laramie or Cheyenne south to the Fort Collins-Loveland area.

"Have a preference?" Mike asked.

"Driver's choice."

Jennifer grunted from the back seat.

"We should get you down here to really see Laramie, the UW campus. When we have a few days to look around." Mike slanted a look at me.

For a second, I thought he meant … but there was more mischief than heat in that look.

Wasn't there?

Between humming a few Hallelujahs under my breath, I took advantage of having connection—not a sure thing in many areas of Wyoming's mountains—to call Peter Bray's office.

Guess what?

He wasn't there.

So said Ranger Attleboro.

"You must work seven days a week." Her confirming sound also conveyed disgruntlement. "We'll be at the park in the morning."

"Will you?" She sounded intrigued.

"Yes. And I'd like to make an appointment to talk to Peter Bray."

Long pause.

I had to force myself to keep quiet to let the pause reach full ripeness.

For that forbearance I got "Just a minute" and being put on hold.

That let me hear Jennifer muttering curses at her phone from the back seat. Mike glanced over, our eyes met.

"Trouble?" he asked, pitching his voice so she could hear over engine noise. "Did you check for viruses?"

"Give me a break," she said with utter disgust. "Of course I did. But it's getting worse. There must be connection, since Elizabeth's calling, but I get nothing. At this rate I won't reach any of Calliope's friends down there until after dinner."

"Keep trying," I said. "I'm on hold but—"

"Ms. Danniher?"

"Yes, I'm here, Ranger Attleboro."

"Good. You have a nine a.m. appointment. Under your name."

In other words, no mention of the station. Because she wanted to spring it on him or because he'd skedaddle? Either way, it was fine with me. If she wanted the pleasure of springing it on him, she deserved it. If she suspected he'd skedaddle, I appreciated her effort to prevent that.

I was suitably thankful. She wrapped up the call with brisk efficiency.

"Nine a.m. with Bray," I announced as I handed my phone to Jennifer. "See if you have better luck with mine."

She did.

I settled back to sounds of her thumbs tapping and the drone of the road.

A Civil War general, Pat Garrett, Albert Bacon Fall, and various oilmen rode through my thoughts ... then my dreams.

THE ROAD DIPPED and curved, making it seem as if mountains frosted by the winter's snow—and more recently the spring's—circled, weaved, and teased around us.

It wasn't until I was squinting at one particularly graceful slow-motion dancer that I realized I was fully awake.

And hungry.

I straightened.

Without taking his eyes from the road, Mike said, "Good timing. Hour and a half to Casper or about a half hour to Riverton. I know a café there—"

"Riverton," I said with an echo. The back seat was hungry, too.

Yes, we'd technically had brunch, but Jennifer's impatience had made it breakfast.

Before any of us fainted of hunger, we'd reached that café Mike knew. I spotted the pie choices on the menu, so restrained myself with a salad, while the other two tucked into generous portions.

I drove the next leg, making very good time.

Open road, no traffic to speak of, and the distraction of mountains now generally more in the background, allowed me to think about other things as I drove.

Like how to approach Calliope's friends tonight. And Peter Bray tomorrow.

✧ ✧ ✧ ✧

WE ROLLED INTO Fort Collins right on time to meet Calliope's friends at a funky taco restaurant near the Colorado State campus.

Mike persuaded the hostess to let us have one of the larger rectangular tables instead of breaking us up at small, round soda-shop style tables. By pre-arrangement, he, Jennifer, and I spread out among Calliope's five friends.

Considering we'd contacted them only a few hours ago, that was an impressive turnout. Yet they shared apologies from more who couldn't make it.

"Order the special plate," one of them instructed.

After ordering, we started by introducing ourselves. Jennifer teared up when a couple said Calliope had talked about her a lot.

Mike practically beamed when they brought out plates packed with tacos until it looked like a taco-y cake with none of the slices yet removed.

I asked how they each became friends with Calliope. That brought rounds of good memories and happier times, which went well with the tacos. Their memories supported the image of a young woman who'd slipped badly, but with help and a great deal of her own strength had found her way back.

As if Calliope were here as the bridge, I could see Jennifer connecting with a couple of them.

With the food mostly consumed, the conversation turned.

"There's this horrible rumor going around she was using again," said a young woman with a pixie cut. "She *wasn't.* She absolutely wasn't. But people are saying if she was such a great hiker like all of us claim, how could she fall like that?"

"It's my fault," a second friend said. "I never should have said how I couldn't believe she would fall like that because she was so good. It's the truth, but it opened the way for small-minded trolls who know nothing about anything to spout off."

"Oh?" A militant glint in Jennifer's eyes concerned me. Especially when she added, "Where have people been saying things like that?"

"But you're all sure she was staying clean?" I asked gently. "No relapse?"

"Absolutely."

"For sure."

"I was at her place two nights before she died. Everything was in order. She was happy and calm." This speaker had introduced herself as Zara. She was about the same age as the others, but carried herself with a serious confidence they didn't. She looked directly at me. "I was her... I guess you'd call it sponsor. I know the signs. None of them were there. None."

"And I've hiked that trail with her," said a blonde down the table near Jennifer. "Up at the top, especially with spring's snow and iciness—" Did she not know that spring was not supposed to have snow and iciness? "—it can be real treacherous. A fall up there? Maybe, just maybe. But down where she was? And *off* the trail? No way. She wouldn't do that."

Jennifer shot me a told-you-so look as the pixie haircut backed up that assessment.

"It's so strange," the young woman next to me murmured. "I mean, *how* could it have happened?"

Mike and Jennifer both looked at me.

I cleared my throat. "You haven't heard the latest, then? The authorities believe another hiker—someone inexperienced—fell first and Calliope tried to help him, causing her to fall."

From their astonished reactions, they clearly hadn't consumed any news reports today.

"Oh, my God. She saved—"

"No, he died, too."

"But she tried," said the blonde, with tears in her eyes. "Of course, she did. To try to help somebody... Yeah, that makes more sense. That I can believe."

"*That's* what he couldn't tell us. I told you, Suzanne, there was something." The one named Zara, the one who'd said she'd been Calliope's sponsor, said that to the blonde.

Bray? Had he talked to these friends of Calliope? If he had, that raised the likelihood that he could have been Jennifer's mystery caller. "Who couldn't tell you?"

"The EMT who found her."

"When did he talk to you about Calliope?"

They looked at each other, waiting for one to talk. Again, it was the sponsor, Zara. "We went up yesterday morning. Suzanne and Heidi—" She nodded to the two who'd commented about Calliope's hiking. "—went all the way up the trail. The rest of us met them at ... at the site. That's where we talked with the EMT. Ivan something. Then we all completed the hike to the trailhead together. For Calliope."

I held my tongue long enough not to step on the pause after that, then asked, "You'd never talked to him before? Maybe seen him? Or Calliope mentioned him?"

They looked around at each other, puzzled, and gave back all negatives—by word or gesture or look.

"Why would we have talked to him before?" asked Zara.

I smiled winningly. "Just wanted to keep the timeline straight. What did he say?"

Looks flashed around. Suzanne, the blonde, finally said, "He told us he was the first one called after... And he was with her where she fell until they could take her out. Not much else, really."

"Do any of you have contact information for him?"

More looks. The sponsor spoke this time. "I might have a phone number for him at home. I didn't bring it with."

Fib, definitely fib. She wasn't sure she was ready to share.

Why? Did she think she might be protecting a guy they said they'd met for the first time yesterday morning?

Or did she think she was somehow protecting Calliope?

"Good. Maybe we can get that from you later. Speaking of guys..." Not the best segue, but I had the sense this was winding down and needed to get in more questions. "Have any of you heard of Felix Robertson?"

Universal negatives.

"Who's that?" pixie haircut asked.

"It's the name of the man who fell."

"You think Calliope knew him?" Zara asked sharply.

"Think? No. Asking? Yes. Was Calliope involved in gambling in any way?"

Another round of negatives, this time with an inclination to think the idea somewhere between ludicrous and amusing.

"Was Calliope involved with someone? Dating anyone?"

"She'd had a long-time guy from home—"

"Lance," several voices said.

"—and she's dated guys, but nobody lately," Suzanne said. "Except lately…"

"Uh-huh," two others murmured.

Then nobody said more.

"Except lately what?" I nudged.

With her head lowered, Suzanne shot a look at Zara. I didn't see the sponsor respond in any way, but the blonde said, "Nothing. Really, nothing."

That pretty much broke up the dinner and the questioning.

They each shook hands with Mike and me. Jennifer hugged a couple of them. The sponsor said, "If you learn anything…"

"We'll let you know," Jennifer promised.

"If it's confirmed," I caveated.

The sponsor gave me another clear, hard look. Then she looked at Jennifer. "Some of us thought we'd come up to—Sherman, isn't it?— when there's a service. If you let us know when and where online."

"I will."

I didn't miss that she'd left me out of that promise.

Didn't stop me from saying, "And if any of you think of anything, no matter how small it might seem, let us know."

"JENNIFER, YOU DID really well," I said as we walked back to Mike's rented SUV for the drive to Loveland, where we had three rooms guaranteed in a chain hotel far enough from the interstate to not dream of driving all night. Jennifer's room and mine connected. "I know it was hard and I'm proud of you."

"I'm proud of me, too."

"When you're working an investigation like this—" I usually insisted we were pursuing stories not investigations, but this wasn't a story to Jennifer. "—you have to take a step back, make sure you don't do anything out of emotion—understandable emotion—that might jeopardize the final outcome."

"Like what?" she asked with clear-eyed innocence.

"Like squashing those trolls who are spreading rumors about Calliope not being clean."

"Oh, that. I'm not doing that." I started to breathe. "Other people are. They're already on it. I messaged them from the restroom using your phone. I don't have time to stomp them out with all this going on. Besides, they can do a better job with their main setups than I can on the road with my light set-up, iffy connections."

I drew in a breath to expostulate—not about the *light set-up*, though that boggled my mind. Mike's subtle head shake told me to give it up.

He had a point. There were only so many battles to fight.

"Why did you ask if the EMT had asked them about Calliope before she…" Mike flicked a look toward Jennifer. "Before she fell?"

Before I could answer, she gave a *duh* tongue click. "In case he was obsessed with Calliope. That would make him a prime suspect."

"Hey, pretty smart."

It wasn't clear if Mike meant Jennifer or me. I figured we both deserved it.

"Even if he wasn't fully obsessed, if he'd met Calliope beforehand, that would sure be worth looking into. At the very least, it would skew his emotions, his reactions, and therefore his observations."

"Yeah, I get it," Jennifer said. "That applies to me, too."

Very smart.

"It does. On the other hand, you have helpful insights because you knew her well."

She sighed. "Used to know her well."

"No friendship's perfect. They certainly don't even out day to day. But now you're doing something for her and for her family that none of her other friends could possibly do."

"Only because of you guys."

Mike came between us, slinging one arm around her shoulders and one around mine. "Because of you, too. Couldn't do it without you, Jenn—Jennifer."

"True," I agreed. Then held out one hand. "But you're going to have to do your part without my phone, Jennifer. Hand it over."

"That's okay. The hotel has wi-fi. But look, Mike, the green license plates are everywhere. The greenies really are invading."

"Real funny, kid."

DAY FOUR

MONDAY

Chapter Eighteen

"YOU'RE REPORTING ON this?" Peter Bray sounded slightly surprised, also guarded with no *slightly* about that.

We'd had an hour's drive to be at his office for our nine o'clock appointment. I prioritized sleep over food, but Mike and Jennifer met for breakfast, even though I'd seen the light under our connecting door until I fell asleep.

They brought me a coffee for the road—the winding and climbing road that started with the Rockies ahead of us, then surrounding us.

Saturday's snow had deposited a fresh coating up their sides. Yet all the signs in front of stores referred to spring.

Outside Bray's closed door, Ranger Attleboro greeted us with low-key briskness. She had her hair pulled back with a clip, wore no makeup, which allowed the effects of outdoor life to show clearly, and exuded quiet vitality.

The deviltry deep, deep in her eyes helped, too. That hadn't come through on the phone, but I suspect it's why we were here now.

She ushered us in. "Your nine o'clock appointment."

"Wha—" He put down a coffee cup with ill grace. "Me? Attleboro?"

I nudged Mike to move faster to get into the room before Bray could foist the job of getting rid of us onto Attleboro. She cooperated by immediately ducking out.

I introduced the three of us and said we were here about Friday morning's fatal falls, particularly Calliope's, since she was a native of Sherman. That's when he asked about whether we really were reporting.

"We are," I fibbed.

Or, maybe not a fib.

We could rationalize my statement by saying we *were* reporting the story, though not for on-air.

Nah, it was fib.

"She grew up in Sherman, as I said. A young woman who'd turned her life around only to die in this tragic way at one of our national parks where people expect—"

"I understand the angle, but it was an accident." He had an odd way of talking. It reminded me of something I couldn't immediately pin down. "Merely an accident."

Jennifer made an unfriendly sound.

He glanced toward her. "A tragic accident, but an accident. It's a sad fact. There's no story."

Ah. I had it. What his vocal style reminded me of. A cow mooing.

Each sentence started with one tone, then slid into that long, drawn-out note through to the end.

I responded to his attempt to divert us with a smile. "We could also see it as our civic duty to report on the dangers of vacationing in Colorado and national parks. I'm sure you get a significant number of visitors from Wyoming and we wouldn't want them to come here not knowing death can await them on even seemingly benign hikes like the one Calliope Grandisher started but tragically never had the chance to finish."

If he gathered from my comments that KWMT reached all the residents of Wyoming, that was his leap to take.

He glowered at me, then swept it to Mike and Jennifer. They must have withstood it well, because he came back to me. "It was an accident. An inexperienced hiker went off the trail despite all the warnings and signage not to—" Of course he slipped that in. "—and, uh, the young woman from your town presumably tried to help him and tragically also fell."

"How do you know that?"

"What?"

"Who is the source for your account of what happened?"

"I… I, uh, am not giving my source."

Have you ever seen a dog quiver when it catches a certain scent? That's what I felt like. On the inside only. No quivering allowed on the outside.

"Does that mean you don't have one?" Because that's what it sounded like to me.

"I… I'm not going to answer."

Quiver times two. "Of course. So when we report the story, we'll quote you as the source for the account in the official and publicly disseminated news release."

"Quote me?"

"Yes. You know, Ranger Peter Bray said, etcetera. But, you're right. Far better to get you on camera. Including calling her death an accident on camera. The *tragically* helps, too. We'll do that when we get a cameraperson here."

His eyes dilated. There exists among government employees a subset who would rather do almost anything other than state something on the record for a member of media. Multiply that by ten for doing it on camera.

He scrambled into deflect mode.

"The person you should talk to is Ivan. That's where you'll get your information. Ivan Quentel. He was the EMT, first on the scene."

EMT? The same one Zara and the others mentioned last night? I supposed there could have been more than one. But there was that *first on the scene.*

"Is he the source for what the news release said?"

"In essence."

A weaselly choice of words. I asked directly. "Did he witness what led to these two deaths?"

"Uh, not exactly. But you should talk to him."

"We prefer to talk to his source. Or we could talk to whoever's investigating the matter."

"Investigating? Nobody's investigating. There's no reason to investigate. It was obviously an accident." Something like craftiness muddied the brown of his eyes. "There's really only one person who'd talk to you about this on camera. Ivan Quentel. Ivan is definitely your best bet. He was the first official on scene. Right there. He knows whatever there is to know. He can tell you about any witness."

Ivan Quentel represented a step closer to what actually happened. Progress. But I wasn't ready to let Bray off the hook.

"I don't know. It's so much better to have the top official on camera and—"

"No, no. Not when I was never near the place. Nowhere near. You're far better off talking to Ivan. He can meet you at the site. I'll call and tell him to do that."

"Well... I'd also need his contact information."

"I'll get that for you right now."

"And your personal cell number in case we need to follow up."

"I don't give that... Fine."

Bray found, then shared a contact number for Ivan Quentel, adding it to another number he'd written down.

He looked so pleased with himself to be getting rid of us, I said over my shoulder, "We'll get back to you if we have any questions."

"Enjoy that?" Mike asked in a low voice as he held the door for us.

"The chain-yank never gets old."

From the deviltry lurking a little closer to the surface in Ranger Attleboro's eyes, she'd enjoyed it, too. "Finished already?"

"For now. Can you tell me if this is Ranger Bray's personal cell phone number?" I held out the paper.

"It is."

"Thank you. Just checking."

"Come back any time."

✧   ✧   ✧   ✧

AS SOON AS we were in the rented SUV, I swiveled in the passenger seat to Jennifer. "Was that the voice of the man who called you Saturday?"

"No."

"Sure? It was on the phone and not very long—"

"I'm sure. That weird way he had of talking? No way I'd miss that. It wasn't him."

I nodded and faced forward again. I wasn't leaving it to Bray to make the call, but tried the EMT's number myself as Mike drove us into the park. Two calls were better than none.

But Ivan Quentel didn't answer.

On cold calls like this, I often don't leave messages, but if Bray did call him—assuming Bray told us the truth, the EMT told Calliope's friends the truth, and they accurately reported to us, about Ivan Quentel being on the scene—maybe he'd be intrigued enough to get back to us fast.

Plus, even if Peter Bray was one hundred percent right about the EMT being the best person to talk to, we didn't have time to chase around after this EMT. We needed to start back to Sherman tomorrow. So, we needed to reach him as soon as possible.

I left a message.

I included my name, the station, and the tantalizing, "I would like to talk to you for a story that you were involved with."

If he was a mountain hermit that might scare him off. But I took the gamble.

I told him we were heading for the trailhead and expected to be there for at least an hour.

We needed to see the scene, so even if he didn't show, it wouldn't be lost time.

Chapter Nineteen

WE HADN'T SCARED him off.

In fact, he was waiting at the roadside parking for the trailhead.

We'd passed areas with actual parking lots and wood signs pointing various directions. Here one wooden sign pointed toward a path curling out of sight around an outcropping.

Other vehicles dotted the right side of the road.

The only human in sight was this man in his late twenties. He made being incredibly fit and good-looking seem natural. Sort of like the national parks made it seem as if yet another spectacular view was perfectly ordinary.

He also had a load of worries behind his brown eyes and resting on his broad shoulders.

He strode toward us without hesitation as we exited the SUV.

"E.M. Danniher?"

I admitted it and introduced him to Mike and Jennifer.

"I'm Ivan Quentel." He shook hands all around. "Mike Paycik? UW? The Chicago Bears?"

Oh, come on. We were in *Colorado* for Pete's sake.

But it turned out Ivan Quentel was a Cowboys fan—that's the University of Wyoming Cowboys, not that little NFL team down in Texas—and had followed Mike's football career.

That also let us hear him talk. I took the opportunity to silently question Jennifer with a lift of an eyebrow if he'd been the one to call her.

She shook her head.

Paycik not only handled it well—he gets enough practice—but also segued smoothly into Jennifer having known Calliope.

"I'm real sorry for your loss." Ivan looked her in the eyes as he said it.

"Thank you. I need to know what happened to Calliope."

"All her friends and family back in Wyoming want to know what happened. That's why we're here," I said. "Can you start from the beginning and—"

"Here." He handed me a tablet already running. "This is the report."

He waited while I read with Mike over one shoulder and Jennifer over the other. I made it through first, and handed the tablet to Mike. Jennifer scooted around to Mike's other side, telling him to back up a couple screens.

Her finger jabbed the screen.

"These people who *say* they heard something and rushed to try to help, but Calliope had already fallen—" Jennifer's suspicion should have dripped on the ground all around her, that's how thick it was. "—who are they?"

"The Valentines. Real nice older couple." Ivan apparently didn't pick up on Jennifer's clear belief that the people who reported Calliope's fall were prime candidates to have caused it.

My reading hadn't brought me to that conclusion. The Valentines read like innocent bystanders who tried to do the right thing.

Of course, that needed checking.

In the meantime, reading the report brought me to one big conclusion and one big question.

It read like an accident. That was the big conclusion.

So why hadn't the news release announce it was an accident and closed the case? That was the big question.

Because, despite Bray's indications otherwise, the report said it remained open. Bray certainly wasn't the reason the case wasn't closed.

I looked at Ivan Quentel. He looked back for a long moment, then away.

Was *he* the reason it hadn't been officially declared an accident?

Did that explain the undercurrent with Bray when he'd told us to talk to Quentel?

Did Bray think he'd get rid of two annoyances at once?

It might also explain Ivan's willingness—if not eagerness—to see us and to let us read the report. I tried to imagine Shelton or Conrad handing over a report. My imagination didn't stretch that far.

But Ivan's look away said he wasn't willing to come right out with it. Not to us. Not yet.

"This is an amazing place. Amazing." I looked around and felt disappointed in my understatement—my compounded understatement. "Everyone knows about rangers working in the national parks, but EMT at a national park's not something I would have thought of. How did you come into this?"

"A lot of the rangers have EMS training. During the summer, on some trails, we could post rangers with training every hundred feet and not have any get bored." He was watching me closely for all his assumed casualness. My wry smile must have passed muster, because his shoulders lowered and his hips leveled. Maybe it was his waiting patiently until the next tourist injured him/herself posture.

"As for me, did my EMS education down the mountain and a buddy who was working here said I should apply. They signed me on and from there I sort of specialized. As I said, lots of rangers have some training, but I have more."

"And you love it."

"Yes." That held both conviction and evasion. "You can get every season in one day, if you're willing to do the climb. No elevators to get you to the top here."

"What about Emergency Services work?"

"Challenging and rewarding when it's mostly you and some basic supplies trying to help somebody in trouble."

"Is that what happened in this case?"

"Not really. Wasn't anything I could do. Not for either of them. Nothing anybody could do. They were both dead."

Mike handed the tablet back to him, then shot me a look. I gave a tiny nod.

Maybe Mike could loosen the guy up again.

"But they didn't die at the same time?" he asked.

"They didn't fall at the same time," Ivan corrected. "Some of the material from Calliope's fall was on but not under Felix Robertson. But nothing was on her from his fall. As for when they died… It's about impossible to pin down TOD that precisely. Either of them might have lived for a short time from their injuries. Or they could have died immediately."

I was aware of rough edges in Jennifer's breathing. She controlled it, though, and the EMT, likely accustomed to lowlanders' reacting to the altitude didn't appear to notice.

"What can you tell us about the man who fell first?"

"Felix Robertson. White male, fifty-one. Not in good shape. Wasn't a hiker."

The description agreed with what Angela said. "How do you know he wasn't a hiker?"

"His shoes were wrong."

"Could he have slipped? The report said it had rained shortly before."

"Sleeted. The trail runs inside some boulders. If he'd slipped on the trail, he wouldn't have gone over the edge. He'd have to purposely go around the boulders to get to the edge before a slip could have sent him over the edge."

"Did you see any sign of a slip?"

"No. But you don't always. Especially… Well, you don't always."

Mike got it first. "With suicides? People kill themselves by jumping? Is that when you don't see a slip?"

Ivan sidestepped. "We get heart attacks, lightning strikes, accidental falls, and suicides. We get them all. With suicides, a lot of times there's a note, but not always. And when you get somebody like him, not in good shape, not a hiker, you've got to wonder. Didn't have much gear—a bottle of water and that's it. You can sort of understand somebody like that going off the trail—making a mistake or making a bad decision. Although…"

"But not Calliope?" Jennifer asked.

"I didn't know her personally," he hedged.

A lot of times in interviewing, it's not the question, it's the follow-up that matters most. "From your experience and what you observed of the scene, what did you gather about the circumstances of Calliope's death?"

"Her gear was right."

"Gear? Her shoes?"

"It's more. Her shoes were good, but showed some wear. She had equipment, supplies, but not too much, the way new hikers carry. She looked fit. Everything together said she was right for the trail. Plus, she was coming down. That meant she knew to start off early to have the trail mostly to herself. When I asked around, people confirmed she was experienced and had a good head on her shoulders. Not only that, she'd hiked this trail before."

That reminded me how interesting it was that he'd been here and talked to her friends Saturday morning—as interesting as his talking to us now—and had asked around to supplement his observations about her hiking experience.

He still hadn't come close to answering the question in my head—what wasn't sitting right with him about Calliope's fall?

And it did seem to be Calliope's fall that bothered him.

He'd passed over the death of Felix Robertson with no problem.

"The report said—No. Forget that. Let's try a different approach. You were the first one here, right?"

"Except for the witnesses."

We'd get to them in a moment. "Okay, take us through what you did and saw when you got here."

"The woman witness, Kassandra Valentine, was waiting for me here at the trailhead. Waved me down. I hiked up to where her husband had stayed and—"

"How far?"

"Not even a half mile. We'll go up later."

A half mile *up*? I wasn't going to think about that. "Okay, so you and the woman hiked up to join her husband."

He shook his head. "She stayed here, waiting for the next ranger to arrive. I went ahead. When I got there and he pointed out where they were... It was a hard fall. I was pretty sure from the start, then checking with binoculars, they were both dead. We're supposed to wait for a second ranger at least, but sometimes, well, some of us have pushed it in certain situations. This time I waited. Talked with the husband, got his story. Got set up so when the next guy came, I could get down right away."

He paused, his gaze hazing as if focusing on memories. Couldn't have been easy seeing the two fallen hikers—probably dead, but not certainly—while waiting for the necessary backup.

"As soon as he did, I was the first one over the edge. It was on the way down, getting closer, that I started taking pictures. Don't know why. But I was snapping them a mile a minute."

"Can we see them?"

He shook his head. "Higher ups have them. Deleted them off my phone, too."

Darn. If he'd had a Jennifer in his life he would have gotten a copy to her before the official types commandeered them.

"And I can't honestly say there was anything about the scene that screamed out something was wrong. If there had been, the other guys would have caught on. They know their jobs. They're good. Look, maybe I got spooked about her or the two of them."

He was torn. He wanted to be wrong about what he'd sensed. He was sure he wasn't.

"I doubt it."

His head snapped up at my brisk words.

"Back up a second," I continued. "You said you talked to the husband. The other witness. What did he say?"

"Pretty much what's in the report. They were going up the trail—"

"Wait a minute, let me get something straight. You said before that Calliope coming down the trail meant she'd started early and that showed her experience. But how could you know she was coming down? Maybe she was going up?"

"For starters, the husband and wife hadn't seen her. And—"

"Had they seen Felix Robertson?"

"They weren't sure. They thought they saw someone starting up the trail as they arrived, but they couldn't swear it was him. They were certain it wasn't Calliope."

"Why?"

"They saw something red. He had on a red shirt. She didn't. Besides, we canvassed people as they came down the trail. Several had seen Calliope coming back as they went out. None of them saw Felix Robertson."

"None?"

"That's not so surprising. Like I said, there'd been sleet not too long before all this happened. That won't stop a serious hiker from starting, but it can clear out a section of a trail for a while—people hold off starting to see how bad it is, that kind of thing. And people coming back in might take shelter. It tends to bunch up the traffic on the trail and that leaves gaps."

He wasn't surprised or bothered by nobody seeing Felix Robertson. But something was contracting his frown muscles.

To restart him, I said, "So, the husband and wife had started on the trail." A half mile *up*, I hadn't forgotten that.

"Right. They heard sounds. Someone shout out. They thought male, but wouldn't swear to it. And no words. Then a pause and a female cry—they were certain it was a woman. Like maybe she'd spotted him down below. Then almost on top of that cry, a scream and the sound of falling."

"Sound of falling?"

"Through the brush. They kept emphasizing how fast it all happened. Boom, boom, boom, one right after the other."

"Could Calliope and this Robertson have been hiking together?"

"Wouldn't think so. Nobody who saw her coming down the trail saw him at all. In fact, nobody saw him going up, either."

I considered him. "What bothers you so much about this?"

He pushed his hair back with one hand, the motion dropping his head forward so he didn't need to meet my eyes.

"I can't tell you exactly. I mean, it's rare we have two falls like that, the same place, the same time. Maybe that's what's stuck in my craw.

"Still … it could have happened that she went to try to help him and forgot her training. That would explain what those witnesses said." He tipped his head to the tablet.

The poor guy was arguing with himself.

From the shadows in his eyes he'd been doing that right along. Doubts bubbling, while everyone else told him he was nuts, to forget it, to let it go. I'd been there a time or two in my career.

"If that's not what's bothering you, what is?"

His head came up and he looked directly at me.

"The witness who took off."

Chapter Twenty

"**WHAT** WITNESS WHO took off? You said the husband stayed at the spot and the wife hiked down to get reception and wait for officials."

"Yeah. They did. But according to them there was another witness."

"Kassandra and Ralph Valentine, the couple in the report, weren't the only witnesses?" I knew I was being repetitious, but I wanted to make sure I understood.

"If you're being technical, they weren't witnesses. I mean, yeah, they heard something, called it in, tried to help, and stayed here, like I told you, but they didn't witness anything actually happen. They came after."

Not only wasn't Ivan Quentel a primary source, but his sources weren't primary sources.

We were going backward.

"They told you there was another witness?"

"Yes. Or at least there was somebody else there. They didn't know if he saw anything or not. They said when they reached the site, he appeared to be trying to call out on his phone. They know the trail and know there's no reception, so they told him he wasn't going to have any luck. They said he immediately said he'd go down to find a spot where he could get reception and—"

"But you said the woman went down to call." Jennifer objected. She had not given up on the Valentines as prime suspects.

"She did." He held up a hand, asking for patience. "They said they listened as he went down and they would swear he took an offshoot of the main trail. It comes out at an old trailhead. It's not used officially anymore, but some long-time hikers still use it. The Valentines said they knew the reception was even worse down that trail. They talked back and forth a bit, then decided Kassandra should go down the main trail and call, like I told you."

Silence settled deeper as we each considered the implications.   •

"Did they get his name…"

He was shaking his head.

"Description?"

He stifled what might otherwise have become a wince. "Young, medium height, lightish hair. Couldn't tell build with his loose clothes. Only helpful thing was, he was wearing a cowboy hat. That's not common for hikers."

But not all that helpful, because it was easy to take off.

"Other than that," Quentel continued, "a loose, puffy jacket. Navy? Black? Gray? Green? Something dark. The only thing they were firm on was he was wearing a loose sweatshirt—green and gold."

Mike snorted.

"The Green Bay Packers?" My dad was a diehard Bears fans. From earliest childhood, I knew better than to ever wear the Packers' colors.

Mike, whose whole NFL career was with the Bears, said, "We'd have a better chance of finding the guy if it were, because Packers gear would stand out around here."

Ivan rubbed his chin. "Oh, yeah, Packers are green and gold, too."

Too?

Taking pity on my confusion or noting Jennifer's brewing impatience, Mike explained. "Colorado State's colors are green and gold. Their gear's all over around here."

"About every other person on these trails is wearing a Rams t-shirt, sweatshirt, jacket, cap, or all four," Ivan added.

"So not a detailed description. But do you think they'd be willing to talk to us?"

"Yeah, I think they would. I've got their contact information." While Jennifer typed that into my phone, he added, "Seemed like people who'd do anything to help. Asked to be kept updated."

Now that was interesting. Criminals often liked to try to get into an investigation. Then again, so did reporters.

"Why wasn't any of what these people—the Valentines—said about the other witness in the news release?"

"The, uh, temporary supervisor—" That had to be Bray. "—made the call that the Valentines couldn't be considered reliable witnesses because they're pushing eighty or so—"

I had a fleeting but satisfying vision of Mrs. Parens dealing with Bray's ageism.

"—and even if they were right and they'd really seen someone it was immaterial to what happened—two tragic accidents."

"But he accepted their account of the two falls being separate?"

"Uh-huh."

I eyed him. He returned the look.

"I didn't see anything in the report about these Valentines saying they'd witnessed Calliope trying to help Robertson."

He said nothing.

My urge to find out the truth warred with the question of whether it really mattered if Calliope hadn't tried to help. I resolved to let it go unless the answer to that question became yes, it mattered.

Mike asked Ivan, "What do you think about these witnesses?"

"The Valentines have been hiking these trails for decades. Hope I'm like them at that age. They know what's what. No question. If they said there was another guy, then there was."

"And the two tragic accidents?" Mike followed up.

"I don't know." Then, more strongly, Ivan said, "Nobody knows because a real investigation hasn't been done. I tried to get him to call in the ISB, but—"

"Who?" Jennifer asked.

"Investigative branch for the park service. But he wouldn't even consider contacting them. I was trying to decide about contacting them myself when you called."

He looked up, seeming to assess the sky.

"You folks want to go up? We better do it now, so we're back in time for me to start my shift."

✧ ✧ ✧ ✧

THE SITE WAS the way it had been described.

A twisting trail. Well-marked. Fabulous views. Requiring skills somewhat short of a mountain goat.

Seeing it added weight to the contention that neither Calliope nor any experienced hiker would have gone outside the trail accidentally. Even I recognized the clear intent of the boulders, knee-high and more, at the outside edge of the trail, and most of my hiking has been from chasing news stories.

Mike and I took photos with our phones. Jennifer surreptitiously wiped away tears as she slowly moved around.

Ivan stood back, his expression closed, even when he took us a little farther up the trail to a curve where we could see down to the outcropping where Calliope and Felix Robertson died.

The hike up had been silent—for my part because I was occupied with breathing. The hike down was silent because we were all occupied with emotions.

Back at the trailhead, we gravitated to the spot where we'd stood earlier.

"You've been so helpful, Ivan. Far more than we could have hoped for." I smiled, hoping he heard and responded—unconsciously would do—to the question behind the smile.

"Why?" Jennifer demanded.

"Excuse me?"

"Why have you been so helpful?" Jennifer clarified. "Why are you so interested in Calliope? Did you know her before? Was there something going on between you? Or—?"

"No. Nothing. I'd never met her until—"

"Until what? Until that day? Until—?"

"Until she was dead."

That answer stopped Jennifer. Did the same to me. Mike, though, asked, "What do you mean you never met her until she was dead?"

Ivan looked toward Mike without quite meeting his eyes, glanced toward Jennifer and me, then settled his focus on a boulder used to keep vehicles from trying to drive up the trail or do so without vital low-lying parts.

"I haven't… I'm not a real church-goer. But out here it's hard not to think there's something…" He cleared his throat. "Like I told you, like I said in the report, she was dead when I got to the trail. I confirmed it when I got down to her—them. But there was a feeling— I felt—" He squared his shoulders, shifting whatever he was about to say from the realm of the vaguely unspecified to firmly on him. "—her. I felt *her*. There. With me. I'm not saying she talked to me. She didn't. Not words. But I knew something wasn't right. I *knew*."

He looked up, directly at Jennifer.

After a long, long moment, she released a breath through parted lips. "Sounds like her. I'm surprised she didn't get you to make a blood oath that you'd fix it."

The left side of his mouth lifted. "Looks like she's got you on that task."

Following another train of thought, I asked, "Ivan, what would happen if it came out that you shared the report with us or if you went on camera about this?"

"Nothing good." He grimaced. "But if it's the only way to get answers…"

I touched his shoulder. "It's good to know. But let's see what we can find without putting your job in jeopardy. In the meantime, watch your back." He looked surprised, then confused. "Peter Bray. He thought having you talk to us would get rid of his problem of you putting pressure on him to investigate. Because—"

"How did you know—?"

"—then you'd be shown—at best—as someone coloring outside the lines for no good reason or—far worse—as someone who's a crackpot with a conspiracy theory who aired it to outsiders. You'd be discredited and that would make his life easier and your career harder."

"I don't know how you know—"

"Experience, Ivan. Hard experience."

"She worked for a network. Corporation," Jennifer said wisely.

True. Though the hard experience on that kind of deviousness came from watching my ex-husband operate.

"We might get back to you with more questions, but in the mean-time, don't go any farther out on your limb," I told him.

"Okay. And thanks."

"No," Jennifer said strongly, "thank you. Thank you for trying to help Calliope and being there with her."

We started off, but after three steps, I turned back to him. "Ivan, before we went up the trail, when you were talking about wondering if Felix Robertson might have committed suicide, you said people don't always leave a note. Then you said *although*. Although what?"

He frowned. Then it cleared.

"Oh, right. Sometimes if people leave a note, they leave it in their vehicle. But no vehicle's been found for Felix Robertson, not at the trailhead or anywhere in the park."

THE VALENTINES WOULD be delighted to see us as soon as we could get there.

We grabbed fast food—hey, we'd worked off all those calories with that hike—and ate in the SUV as we drove south to keep our appointment.

I called Needham Bender on the way.

He skipped his usually genial response. "Deadline," he half roared.

"I know. Sorry. I want to ask you something."

"What?" No half measures about *that* roar. And no diminishment as he added, "Do you have anything for me on Calliope Grandisher's death?"

"No. You think I'm your stringer or something?"

He hmphed. "It would be a step up from that consumer stuff you do on the idiot box."

He was trying to distract me from noticing a few facts.

He wouldn't ask me if he'd had a story pinned down for the dead-line for his Tuesday edition.

After tomorrow's edition, he wouldn't have another shot until the Friday paper, which meant that if there *were* a story, KWMT still had a chance of getting it before the *Independence*. Even with our Thurston Fine-Les Haeburn handicap.

Could we secure both Jennifer's peace of mind and a story?

If there was a story, I reminded myself.

"I'll have you know we had two calls and an email in the past month thanking the station for carrying 'Helping Out!' "

"An avalanche of support."

"Relatively."

"What did you want to ask?" He was back to deadline voice, though tempered.

"I want to know about Sedick Oil."

He snorted. "Don't have time now. Call me tomorrow. Unless you find something...?"

"I'll share when I can." Which meant I'd share what I wasn't protecting for one reason or another. Which was precisely how much he'd share with me. "In the meantime, try a guy named Peter Bray." I gave him the phone number. "He was in his office earlier today. You might get something before press time."

"Right," he said bitterly. *"Government."*

He hung up on me.

I smiled at the phone. Not gloating. Honest.

First, I was smiling at remembering the gruff old newspaperman I'd worked part-time for in my hometown as a kid. He and Needham had the same ink running in their veins.

Second, I was smiling at imagining Peter Bray trying to tap dance around Needham.

I heard the echo of Needham's disgusted *government* in my head. Not all government, for sure, but there was a tilt toward inaction in preference to an action that could possibly be criticized. Could all of Bray's actions be attributed to that tilt?

Mike's voice interrupted my thoughts. He and Jennifer had been going back and forth for a while, but nothing had pinged my reporter radar until now.

"I want to come." Jennifer said. "I want to see these people."

"You already think they're guilty. Of something," he protested.

"All the more reason I should see them."

I said, "No."

I thought Mike would appreciate the support, but I saw him weakening, preparing to say maybe.

Looking at her, but speaking to his melting resolve, I said, "First, Mike's right. Having you suspicioning all over will not encourage them to talk."

"I won't—"

I turned in the seat. "Jennifer, you have a lot of skills, but a poker face is not among them. Besides, look at it from the journalistic side. The witnesses will feel constrained, edit what they say because Calliope was your friend and—"

"We won't tell them."

"—because of your age. That's not something that can be disguised. Most people—especially older people—hold back on bad stuff when they're talking to younger people. If these witnesses were teenagers, then, maybe. Under these circumstances, no."

"But—"

"It's about getting the information. As much and as true as we can. It's about finding out what happened. What really happened. Right?"

She dodged with, "What if they say things that I would pick up on that you guys won't because you don't—didn't—know Calliope?"

I regarded her for a long moment before slowly nodding. "We will report to you in full. If you pick up on something that needs pursuing, we'll immediately go back and ask them about it."

Mike's face tilted up to look at her in the rear-view mirror.

"Okay," she agreed. "If you let me use your phone while I'm dumped off, Elizabeth."

✧ ✧ ✧ ✧

WE DROPPED JENNIFER at a coffee shop across the street from the local sheriff's department. Uniform-wearing men and women represented half the clientele.

Mike and I were pleased. She rolled her eyes.

"Remember—"

"If you tell me again to go to a deputy if I sense anything wrong, Paycik, I'm going to hack your computer the minute we get home," she muttered between clenched teeth. She had her impressive device, a couple other gizmos, and my phone already deployed on the table.

That threat shut him up.

And then she swung on me—entirely innocent me. "And, yes, I have his number on speed dial and added the sheriff's department to your phone since you spotted this place. I'm surprised you didn't dump me in the sheriff's department waiting room."

She wasn't a child, but there was something about feeling responsible for taking her out of state like this... Not that Tom was right about that mentor stuff.

So, we left her there, assuring each other it was better than leaving her alone in Loveland or Fort Collins or Estes Park and better than leaving her in the vehicle parked in front of the witnesses' house.

"She might have knocked on the door to join the interview," Mike said as we pulled up in front of the neat one-story house. "And there were all those reasons you said to not have her in on this interview."

"Yup. Okay. Here we go. Let's see what we get."

Chapter Twenty-One

EVERY INTERVIEW IS the same.

It's a dance, sometimes in partnership with the interviewee, sometimes in opposition.

Every interview is different.

The dancers create the dance, the music, the mood from scratch each time. The interviewer tries to mold it, but it all depends on the interaction with the interviewee.

Along with if the interviewer has nice hard facts up her sleeve that the interviewee doesn't know the interviewer has.

But in this case, the other dancers were willing partners who not only welcomed us into their home with smiles on glowing-with-health faces that could grace AARP publications, but offered us chocolate chip cookies that rivaled my mother's.

The Valentines lived up to their names.

We'd all settled in their living room, them on the couch, Mike and I in chairs facing them across the coffee table with the now-depleted cookie plate.

Past the introductions, we'd worked through their backgrounds as people and as hikers, particularly of that trail at Rocky Mountain National Park. With casual confidence they confirmed what Ivan Quentel had said about their hiking that trail for decades.

I felt like a slug. A prematurely aged slug.

They'd been away for a month, visiting their first great-granddaughter—granddaughter and grandson-in-law, too, but they clearly were secondary players to the star attraction. They'd made returning to that trail their first hike since their return.

"It's a great time to go to the park," Kassandra said. "It's gorgeous when there's fresh snow—"

Mike shot me a look. I did not meet it.

"—and we love to snowshoe there. Even if there's not enough snow for that, it's beautiful and that trail weathers well. And the wildlife, oh, my. They haven't moved up the mountains yet. Bighorns can be around any curve. Deer. Elk."

Ralph picked it up smoothly. "Though we got a later start than usual Friday, because we needed to check over our gear and supplies more thoroughly after being in low country for the month."

That brought us to the start of their hike.

"It started like usual, getting into the rhythm. Finding our stride." Kassandra's smile came quickly, then faded. "We heard something up the trail. It's twisting there. You can't see up or down, but you can hear. And we did."

"Trouble is," Ralph said dryly. "We heard different things."

"*No*," Kassandra said.

"*Go*," he disputed. "But we definitely heard ... distress."

She nodded. "Followed by the sounds. Something breaking through vegetation. Going down—we both thought that—falling down through the undergrowth. Then a slight pause."

"Not complete silence, but muffled." Husband and wife nodded together.

"Then a sort of cry. Definitely female." She looked toward her husband. "I'll tell you it wasn't like anything else I've ever heard. Not even an animal in pain. That poor girl. That poor, poor girl. She knew what was happening. She knew what was coming."

Tears stood in her eyes. I felt the same way. Along with thanking heavens we'd kept Jennifer from this interview.

"We hurried up to the spot fast as we could, me a little in front," Ralph said. "And this young guy was there, trying to get his cell to work. Punching at the keys in frustration. Jumped a mile when I said he'd never get service. He'd been so focused he hadn't even heard us coming."

"Can you describe this man."

Kassandra answered. "Like we told Ivan, he seemed young. Upset, of course. Kind of raspy voice. Medium height, I'd say. Hard to tell his build with that big puffy jacket and that loose sweatshirt. Not what most hikers wear. Other than that and the cowboy hat, nothing really stood out about him. To tell you the truth, we were probably so shocked we didn't pay as much attention as we should have. No scars or tattoos or piercings or anything like that. Just an unremarkable youngster and with everything else happening…"

"What color was his hair?"

"Light, I'd say." Not exactly pinpoint.

"How was it styled?" She went blank. I tried jogging her back to the topic with a more specific question. "Did it look like Mike's here? Or like Ralph's? Or—"

"You know, I was realizing I don't believe I ever noticed. I suppose the cowboy hat covered it. But I would recognize him if I saw him again. I'm quite sure of that."

"What about you, Ralph? Sometimes men see things about other men—"

"Oh, dear, no, don't ask Ralph to tell you what he looked like," Kassandra said with a warm chuckle. "He can spot the difference between a metaphoric rock—"

"Metamorphic, not metaphoric."

"—and an ignominious rock—"

"Igneous, dear, not ignominious. After all these years…"

"—at a glance, but people are mostly a blur to him."

"That's true," he said, clearly untroubled by that defect. "Except for Kassandra."

"Did the man have an accent?" They didn't recall visual details, but perhaps sounds…

"Oh." Kassandra sounded startled. "He did a little. He didn't say very much. Just a few words. Like we said, raspy, like maybe his throat hurt. But he didn't sound like he was from around here. Somewhere on the East Coast?"

Felix Robertson had been from the East Coast. Could there be a tie there?

"Would you recognize an accent from Philadelphia?"

"Perhaps," Kassandra said doubtfully.

"Anything else about him?"

"He kept tugging at the brim of his hat. A good one."

I had an immediate image of how the brim of a cowboy hat could shade the wearer's face. Tugging it down would contribute to that. But from Ralph's significance-laden tone there was more.

I waited.

Ralph Valentine waited back, his expectant gaze on me.

I had nothing.

After maybe half a minute, he looked at Mike, who nodded that he got it.

"Tell her, Ralph," Kassandra ordered. "Don't just wait like she's going to hatch. Or no more cookies for you."

Clearly viewing that as no idle threat, he immediately said, "See, tugging the brim is for a quick greeting, same as tipping your hat." He pantomimed those motions. Then he spread his palm wide and moved it higher and back over his crown. "Now, if you need to resettle it, say, you take hold of it at the break—where the brim and crown come together—or take it off completely and put it back on."

I must have looked a little blank, because a tip of his head invited Mike to explain to the Easterner.

"You don't do a lot of adjusting with the brim because it'll lose shape. Nobody with a brain treats a good hat that way. You might tug your brim once, but not keep at it."

The older man nodded approval. "But that young guy was tugging his brim every other second. 'Specially if he was talking or being asked a question."

"Huh." Mike's syllable held both understanding and suspicion.

The others looked at me expectantly.

I looked back at them.

Mike got up, retrieved his hat, sat down again to put it on. He held my gaze as he reached up and slowly put his fingers to the brim and tugged.

I was right that the brim shaded his face. And the tug, bringing it a bit lower, covered a bit more, too, but—

"His arm," I blurted.

"That's it," Kassandra said approvingly. "You got it."

The hat did cover a bit more when it was tugged down, but what really masked Mike's face was his hand and forearm coming across his face to grab that rim.

"He spent most of his time like that." The man jerked his head toward Mike.

"You said he did that every time you asked him a question or talked to him?"

"Near enough. Kept his head down, too. Sort of mumbled into his chest. Made it harder to catch his words."

His wife nodded repeatedly. "He did. He surely did. I remember thinking maybe he had a real bad scar or something he didn't want anyone to see. Made me feel sorry for him."

"This woman could feel sorry for a rock," her husband grumbled, but with that edge of fondness that said he admired her for it. He topped the fondness and admiration with a dollop of pride. "Didn't stop her from realizing about his taking the wrong path down, though."

I leaned forward. "Yes, tell us about that."

Kassandra said, "Like Ralph said, when we came up on him, the man was hitting at his phone, trying to get it to work. Over and over, like that would make a difference. Even after Ralph said there wasn't any service, so he might as well give up. Course that was all after we asked what happened."

"Strange thing," Ralph picked up, "was at first he said he didn't know what happened, or if anything *had* happened. We said we'd heard a cry. He said he'd heard the same thing coming down the trail."

"Ralph pointed out where this little evergreen was fresh broken just past the boulders."

He nodded solemnly. "And the dirt was stirred up. Like somebody scrambling with their feet. I climbed up on the tallest boulder. Gave me a view down without risking standing in that same spot where it might not have been stable, causing their falls. I could see patches of color through the branches with the leaves not out yet and a couple branches broken off from the trail to where that color was. Nothing moving. No answer when we called out. Nothing."

In the silence that followed, I ran back through my head what they'd said. "Ralph, why did you say it was strange that the man said he didn't see anything?"

His forehead creased into a frown for a second then cleared. "Strange because he was trying to call for help. Why call for help if he didn't see anything?"

Also, if he was a killer, why would he be trying to call? Who would he be trying to call?

Ralph continued, "Even after he said he heard a cry, it could have been somebody who twisted an ankle. Could have been folks playing around. Could have been an animal. You can shake your head at me—" Precisely what his wife was doing. "—and I agree the sound we heard wasn't any of those things. Still, it's just possible somebody heard it different and might think those things. But he couldn't have it both ways. If he heard that cry and thought somebody needed help, then he'd have looked around for the person in trouble before trying to call on his phone."

"That's what would be natural for *you*. But lots of people don't know anything to do except try to call. They're not like you." She turned to us. "After the young man left and we realized he was taking the wrong trail, I had to make Ralph swear he wouldn't attempt to get down to those people while I went to call. Or he'd have tried for sure when he was alone and there'd have been three lost that day."

He shook his head. "There wasn't a sound, not a breath of movement from those poor folks. I knew… Listened and listened while I was waiting and there was nothing."

"How did you come to the decision that Kassandra should go down to the trailhead to call?" Sure, I'd heard Ivan Quentel's account of their account, but getting the person you were interviewing to start from scratch often clarified your understanding of what happened and sometimes produced surprises.

They looked at each other.

There was something they weren't going to tell us.

Even if we didn't find out what it was at the moment, knowing there *was* something already made the repeat worthwhile.

"Well," Kassandra said, "as we told you, we'd agreed we'd stay while the young man went down the trail for help. Now, when I say we agreed, there wasn't discussion or back-and-forth. We were shocked, deeply shocked, and I think we didn't produce much more than a few half sentences."

"That's sure right. Like we said, he kept trying his phone. Kassandra said flat out he'd never get reception where we were. You either had to go up a steep mile and a half or back down to the trailhead. That's when he said he'd go down to the trailhead. Barely took a breath before he started down fast, his phone still in his hand."

"We stood there, not moving. Probably the shock," Kassandra said. "And in the stillness, we could hear him thudding down the trail, sliding a bit here and there. Then came another sound. Branches being pushed back out of the way. Not bare branches. Not sure we'd have heard those. But evergreens. Sort of soft, quick whooshes. We know that sound. And the sound of him on the trail changed. Still fast, but not making time as good. Tightening his stride because of what was in front of him."

They nodded at each other.

She continued, "I looked at Ralph and he looked at me and we said, '*The old trail.*' Just like that. Together. I said why, but Ralph—rightly—said it didn't matter why the young man took the old trail. What mattered was he wasn't going to have the least bit of luck calling out even at the trailhead, because of where it is, tucked in against rock."

"Then she said right off, '*I need to go down to call.*' And I said I was staying with—staying there. Then she said what she told you before about making me promise not to try to go down to them alone. Stayed there until that nice young EMT came along. Another fifteen, twenty minutes and more and more came and they shifted us back to the trailhead to get out of their way and answer questions over and over."

"Was there anything else you can tell us? Observations or impressions?"

Another looked passed between them. One of those looks long-time happily married couples use to encrypt and transmit gobs of information right in front of outsiders.

"Not a thing, I'm afraid," Kassandra said. "One more cookie before you go?"

Chapter Twenty-Two

WHILE MIKE DROVE, I called Ivan. "You said nobody saw Robertson on the trail. How about this other witness the Valentines saw? Did anybody see him on the trail or at his vehicle?"

I realized that asking him the question meant I believed them about this other witness. At least more than I'd believed it when Ivan told us, or I would have asked him this question at the time.

"Nobody but the Valentines saw him."

"What do you think that means?"

He said nothing for several beats. "It's not surprising no one would see him if he went down the old trail to the old trailhead. The new one was created six, seven years back because the old one was so rough, eroded. Nobody would have reason to notice a vehicle at the old trailhead because it's tucked in tight around an outcropping—another reason it was replaced."

"He told the Valentines he was coming down the trail. Wouldn't he have met people who were going up?"

"All I can say is nobody we questioned saw him. We tried to catch everybody coming down, but... Plus, some hikers will go off the trail to avoid seeing other people. They like the feeling nobody else is out there with them. If he was one of those, wouldn't matter if we did get a hundred percent of the folks on that trail. They wouldn't have seen him."

"So you can't say he absolutely wasn't coming down the trail?"

"No."

"Or he could have been lying to the Valentines."

"That's a possibility, too. I will say, there wasn't any call to 911 or anywhere else for help except their call."

I heard the alternative scenario in his voice, but he wasn't going to spell it out. Instead, he was going to make me say it about that nice couple who'd fed me chocolate chip cookies.

I got it over with, suppressing my bitterness because that would only contribute to the ruination of chocolate chip cookie afterglow. "Or the Valentines could have made him up."

"And that's another possibility."

"Why would the Valentines make him up?" Mike asked the instant I clicked off the phone.

Without answering, I recapped Ivan's answers.

At the end, Mike repeated, "Why would the Valentines make him up?"

"I don't know. But it's a possibility we can't forget."

"Now you're siding with Bray."

"Which side of Bray? Based on that news release, he believed what the Valentines said the mystery witness told them, but didn't believe he existed."

JENNIFER SAT IN the same spot as we'd left her. She started to gather her things together the instant we walked in, but we gestured for her to stay put.

Despite the cookies, Mike was ready for something more substantial and there were salads and sandwiches on offer here.

Jennifer wanted to leave immediately. Not because of the fare but because she clearly wanted to hear what we'd learned.

Mike predicted immediate famishment if he didn't eat and, since he held the keys, he exercised driver's choice. I benefited from the choice without receiving any of Jennifer's glares.

She delivered those glares while eating a mixed greens, cranberries, and walnuts salad. I also had a small one of those. Mike had a ginormous burger and fries. It would catch up with him someday. I keep saying that, because if there is any justice in the universe, it will catch up with him someday.

I didn't finish reporting on the interview until we were nearly back to Loveland.

If she'd said we had to go back to the Valentines' house, we'd have been in big trouble, because we had eight-plus hours of driving ahead of us.

"Why would those people make up the guy?" Jennifer asked. And she hadn't even met them.

Mike approved. "Exactly what I said."

I repeated what I'd said to him. Then added, "And the major point that argues against them making up the witness is that they didn't find Felix Robertson's vehicle at the trailhead."

"Why?" Jennifer asked.

But Mike was nodding slowly. "Because that's the most likely explanation for how Robertson got to the trail. The witness drove them there. They hiked up together. The witness becomes the killer, goes down the old trail and drives off."

"Exactly. Unfortunately, we don't have anything to go on to try to find this guy. But, Jennifer, can you check the hotels, starting close to the park and working your way out, to see if Robertson stayed there and if anybody was with him? If we can get a record of park entries without hacking…"

"Got it. I'll get my guys started on it as soon as I can use your phone again. In the meantime, I finally made some progress on Felix Robertson."

"Terrific. Your friends came through?"

"I found it, actually. There's been so much glitchiness with my systems and my friends', it was actually nice at that café, working and getting someplace. I tried Colorado media first for anything on Felix Robertson, thinking maybe they'd picked up the story since yesterday, but nothing advanced where we are. But then I tried Vegas. And, boom. A hit."

"The gambler? Really?"

"Yeah. Vegas TV had it on last night and a full story in today's paper."

"He was that important?" Mike asked.

"Not most of his life. According to the paper, he'd been an accountant who decided to turn pro gambler. He was getting by, but not much more. Until he won this big poker tournament, really unexpectedly, at the start of the year. He won more than two *million* dollars. Can you believe that? And then he wins all sorts of money on the NCAA basketball tournament."

This year's college tournament bracket had sprouted upset after upset, including in the finale, which had been played the first week of April.

"This guy raked in another huge pot of money for that. There were earlier stories about him, talking about rags to riches or at least an ordinary guy to rolling in it. He bought a new house and a big car in just a few days. All that was in the papers.

"So, today's story was how shocking it was that after all that, he dies in a tragic accident when he was out enjoying nature. They hardly even mentioned Calliope."

"You know how it works, Jennifer. He was local, she wasn't. Good work."

"I'll dig more and, in the meantime, the crew is working. Oh. And there's a photo of him. I downloaded it."

She held up the screen to me. I had to slide around in the seat to get a good angle, but then there he was.

Felix Robertson.

Not a Civil War general.

"Huh. He's not what I expected from what Ivan and his ex-wife said."

I wasn't expecting James Bond—neither Sean Connery nor Daniel Craig. Instead, I'd envisioned someone completely out of shape and sloppy. I might have been swayed by ex-bias and athletic-EMT-bias in forming that vision.

This guy had a definite paunch and the particular pallor of spending a lot of time under artificial lights. But his brown beard was perfectly trimmed, his head smoothly shaved, his dark glasses professorial, and his smile pleasant.

"Let me see." Our driver tried to crane his neck around for a look.

I turned the screen away.

"No way, Paycik. Keep your eyes on the road."

"I know this road. I've driven it in ground blizzards and had no trouble."

"Including one in May," Jennifer contributed. "He told me all about that at breakfast. Almost died multiple times driving this stretch of road."

I gave him a look.

"That's why I didn't tell you, Elizabeth. Besides, it's not snowing now."

"I don't care. You're not seeing the guy's photo until this vehicle is in a suitable parking spot and stationary."

May.

Blizzards.

I regarded even the smallest, fluffiest cloud with deep suspicion until the sun went down.

✧   ✧   ✧   ✧

WE'D STOPPED AT the same place in Riverton, among the last there for dinner.

Back in the car, Jennifer fell asleep again. Who knew how much, if any sleep, she'd gotten last night. In her priority system, wi-fi came before sleep.

The vehicle's brights cut through the dark, but as soon as the shaft of light shifted, the dark reconsumed what had been illuminated a millisecond before.

The light of the stars—each a pinprick compared to the cannon shot of the headlights—endured.

Those stars, which I'd watched ever so slowly edge across the Wyoming night sky more than once, oddly seemed to advance on us now. As if they were the ones in transit and we remained still.

Mike tilted the rear-view mirror and looked into it.

No worries about traffic, so I suspected he was checking on Jennifer.

With the mirror returned to its proper angle, he said, "What do you think of what that EMT said? We never really discussed it."

"Generally helpful. He gave us some good information, especially the lead to the Valentines. But we have to be careful. It's the same issue as with the Valentines. No substantiation."

His disbelieving *huh* rejected my interpretation of his question. "About Calliope. About him sensing her. He didn't come out and say it, but that's gotta be why he's sure it wasn't an accident."

"He had facts to back that opinion. Sometimes witnesses pick up information subconsciously. They put it together without their conscious mind ever getting in on the act. Then they think it's a hunch, or an intuition, or the spirit of the victim guiding them. It's really their own experience and intellect operating below the surface. But it doesn't matter how they interpret it, as long as they share the information with us and it helps us with our inquiry."

"Uh-huh."

He drove a mile, a second one, then a third. Under those advancing stars.

Then he spoke.

"So, you believe she was there with him, too."

✧ ✧ ✧ ✧

AN HOUR LATER, I shifted around, nudging my purse with my foot, and was startled by a light.

Leaning over, I saw the inside of my purse glowing like a swath of the stars above had taken up residence there.

A reflection through the windshield or moon roof?

I was tired and, unlike the daytime drive yesterday, I was trying to stay awake to keep Mike company. I'd driven an earlier stretch today, but he'd done the majority of the driving over these two long days.

So, it took a second to realize the source of the glow was not celestial.

It was my phone.

Before I dug it out, the glow stopped. But checking the screen, I saw it had been Tom calling. And he'd tried several times before.

Jennifer had used it at dinner and must have silenced it before handing it back.

I tipped the screen toward Mike by way of explanation. Adding, as I clicked the call button, "Tom."

He answered on the second ring.

"How'd it go down there, Elizabeth?"

"Nothing definitive, but some interesting aspects."

"Very interesting," Mike amended. He had good hearing, since I didn't have it on speaker.

"Did Mike say very interesting?"

"Yes. He one-upped me because he's going beyond the hard and fast facts. You know Paycik. All woo-woo."

I had male chuckles in stereo. "You can explain the woo-woo to Diana and me when you get back. She says she's up for a gathering at her place tomorrow night if you three are up for it and have things to tell us. Said she made the kids stay home tonight and last night for family time and she's almost as ready for them to get back to their friends as they are."

"Diana's? Tomorrow night?" I asked Mike.

"Sure."

"Hear that, too?"

Tom said, "I heard. Jennifer?"

"Sleeping. I'll ask, but I'd be shocked if it's not a definite yes."

He grunted in acknowledgement. "There's something else. There've been a number of calls for Jennifer starting yesterday evening and since they got home from work today. Hang-ups. No caller ID. Kent—Kent Lawton—called me about them."

"What kind of calls?"

"Male voices asking for Jennifer, then hanging up when they say she's not there. Last few, they've hung up when Kent or Faith answers."

"What?" Mike demanded.

I held up a be-patient hand, though I didn't feel that way myself.

"Have they called the sheriff's department?"

Mike's attention snapped to me. I pointed toward the road. Reluctantly, he followed that directive.

"Not much they or the police can do. No threats made. It's the number of calls, all from strangers, presumably. None of them have name ID, though a couple show area codes—none of them 307." The area code for all of Wyoming.

"The sheriff's department should know anyway. Shelton, maybe Conrad."

"They know." Probably from Tom directly, judging by that tone. "It's bothered Kent and Faith more because they haven't been able to get in touch with Jennifer. They said she's got her phone set to Do Not Disturb. Hasn't answered messages or called back."

"Something's wrong with her phone. It's been worse and worse. Also we *have* been pretty busy." She'd been free during all that time we talked to the Valentines when she'd had my phone. But if her phone wasn't notifying her of calls...

"For now, Kent and Faith hope Jennifer can keep staying with you at the house."

"Oh."

"If you're worried about safety, maybe Mike could stay with you. I would, but Tamantha came home tonight—"

"No, No. It just caught me by surprise. It's a good idea. And I'm sure we won't need Mike."

"Need me for what?"

I repeated the be-patient hand.

"Good. I'll tell Kent and Faith. They'll be relieved."

"I'll have Jennifer call when we get in."

"They'd appreciate that. No matter how late."

"Okay."

"Me, too. Text me, let me know you two are settled in."

Abraham Lincoln's good-looking cousin as a mother hen—now there was an image.

DAY FIVE

TUESDAY

Chapter Twenty-Three

MIKE STAYED THE night.

His decision to do so—without being invited—set off a dispute between Jennifer, who declared all concerns or precautions ridiculous, and Mike, who talked like we were in for a siege.

I landed in the middle, irking both. But irking Jennifer even more when I insisted she keep my promise about calling her parents.

She was wily enough, though, to use the call as an excuse to avoid the bedding switch Mike and I handled, putting the guestroom sheets Jennifer had used the night before we left onto a pull-out sofa bed in the sitting area of the master suite, so she could join me upstairs, while Mike would occupy the ground-floor guest room ... with fresh sheets.

"More strategic having me where I can stop anyone trying to get in," he said.

I'd have to remember to mention that to my parents when they visited and I put them in the more vulnerable-to-attack guest room.

I also was tempted to comment that he was on the same strategic level as Shadow, since the dog consistently occupied the spot between me and the door. But I didn't want it to sound like I was dissing Shadow.

Mike wasn't half bad at making beds, though.

Jennifer meandered in as we finished.

"How are your parents?"

"Fine. Mom's going to bring a few things I need to the station tomorrow."

More? In addition to the large suitcase? It sounded like she was moving in ... before I did.

If Mike started talking about bringing a few things, this could get out of hand fast.

"Oh, I almost forgot." Jennifer's nonchalance rocketed my suspicion from zero to a hundred and ten. "When I was using your phone, you had a few calls. I turned off the notifications to keep doing what I had to do."

That confirmed why the eerie glow had been the only clue to Tom's calls.

I pulled out the phone and headed toward the kitchen for water while Jennifer explained to Tom the intricacies of the downstairs shower—which as far as I could tell involved turning on the faucet and not aiming the showerhead out of the bathtub.

Caught by the number of times Tom had called, I hadn't scrolled farther back until now. I was scrolling back and deleting, when I spotted one and immediately listened to the message...

"*Agggghhhhh.*"

Mike plunged around the corner from the hallway into the kitchen. And since I hadn't advanced past that point, he also plunged into me.

He kept me from going down by wrapping his arms around me and staggering us both into the wall. "What? What's wrong? Is somebody—?"

"No. Nobody's breaking in. No masked intruders. It's—*Jennifer!*"

"What?" She came around the corner sounding and looking aggrieved. "What are you yelling for?"

"You have got to get a replacement phone. You are not using mine anymore. Do you know what came in while you had my phone today?"

She ignored the question and replied to the statements. "That's okay. Mom's bringing me one of my backup phones tomorrow."

"That is *not* the point. That is—"

"What came in?" Mike interrupted.

For a millisecond I flashed to a long-ago scenario with my parents, with Mike in the role of my dad, Jennifer as the younger me, and me as my mom. It was the first time I'd sympathized with my mother's point of view.

"The storage company called. The truck with my furniture is on the way. It should be here Thursday or Friday."

"That's good news, isn't it?" Mike asked. "They hardly ever come on time anyway."

"I'm not ready. I don't have room. I don't have time—"

Jennifer talked over me. "You definitely don't have time, because we're investigating. What difference does it make when that stuff comes?"

I felt my jaw throb.

I don't know if Mike saw it or sensed it, but he turned Jennifer around by the shoulders and gave her a push toward the stairs. "Go to bed. Now."

"But—"

"Go."

She went.

He turned back to me. "C'mon." He prepared me a glass of ice water. "Drink. You'll feel better."

He didn't know it, but I already felt better after watching him use the icemaker and water dispenser in the refrigerator door. My refrigerator door. My icemaker. The little comforts in life.

I drank half of it at once.

"You know she's not thinking straight," he said when I came up for air.

"I do know that. My worry is that our looking into the circumstances of Calliope's death might be making it worse for her instead of better."

He considered that. "Are you more or less confident now that it was a tragic accident."

"Less." It came immediately.

We looked at each other for a long moment before he nodded. "Then we keep going. She'll be better off in the end with the truth."

I put my hand to his cheek, feeling the bristles of the long hours since he'd shaved. He covered my hand with his, surrounding it with warmth. Then he turned and kissed my palm.

When he turned back to me, his eyes were darker, but his expression light.

"C'mon. We're all beat. Drink up and go to bed."

I did.

Upstairs, the sound of Jennifer's breathing announced she was already asleep.

I texted Tom the all-clear and the furniture arriving news in the two minutes between hitting my sheets—Renata's sheets—and falling asleep.

It felt like I didn't stir until the aromas of coffee, bacon, and eggs seduced me awake.

I DRAGGED ON leggings under and a hoodie over my nightshirt and stumbled downstairs.

My nose had not deceived me.

Mike was cooking. With great enthusiasm. As I arrived, a piece of bacon flew off the end of his fork as he removed it from a baking pan.

"Shadow will be happy," I said.

They turned to me, apparently temporarily unified in surprise.

They thought I'd sleep through that triple whammy of scents?

"Only if you leave that piece of bacon there a long time," Jennifer said.

I blinked.

Oh.

Right

Shadow was with Diana and the kids, being spoiled at the ranch. They probably served him breakfast in bed.

With no dog to patrol the floor, that left me to pick up the piece of bacon.

"The thirty-second rule works for me. But waiting for Shadow to be here might be a little too long," I muttered and started toward it.

Mike beat me to it. "You go sit down at the counter and get coffee. I'll make you a plate right away."

Either I looked really tired or he was indulging my non-morning-person status.

Either way worked for me.

I ate, I drank coffee, I propped my elbows on the counter, and they left me in peace. It was a great way to start the day.

MY CONFIDENCE IN the day took a dip on the way to the station.

"I could go for a walk," Jennifer said abruptly from the passenger seat of my SUV.

We'd left Mike at the house, cleaning up. Cooking and cleaning. This, I could get used to.

I looked over at her. "A walk? When?"

"You know, when we're at your house. With me staying there. Daisy takes long walks every day. She says it clears her mind. Says she returns to work renewed. I never knew that about her until all this."

Feeling my way, I asked, "You want to go for a walk?"

"I said I could."

Could, not want to. That turned the proposed walk from something desirable to a chore. So why volunteer?

"You could. Doesn't sound like you love walks." Despite the recent endorsement from her online friend. "So why would you?"

"To give you some, you know, privacy."

"If I want to be alone, I'll go in my room. And you can do the same in the guest room." Assuming Mike left, of course.

"But if you want privacy but you don't want to be *alone*, I can take a walk."

I must have looked as blank as I felt, because she emitted an exasperated breath.

"You know," she insisted. "If you and Mike want to be together." She hesitated a beat while I tried to absorb her words. "Or you and Tom, I suppose, because that's what people say, but I'd think Mike … But it's none of my business who you want to, you know, be with. I don't want to be in your way."

"It's not—We're not—You're not in my way." A blithering start, but a decent finish.

She regarded me for a long moment. I thought I spotted the instant she accepted the truthfulness of my statement. A beat later, she said, "Geez, why not?"

I have never before viewed the squat KWMT-TV building as a savior.

Chapter Twenty-Four

MY CONFIDENCE IN this day took another hit when I looked up to see a woman approaching through the obstacle course of dented desks in the bullpen of the KWMT-TV newsroom. A disapproving mother. Just what I needed.

I'd never met her, but from the resemblance, I was confident of her identity before she stopped.

"Elizabeth Danniher? I'm Faith Lawton."

She had lost some of the roundness in her face that made Jennifer often seem younger than her years, but the coloring was the same, and so were the direct eyes.

I stood and extended my hand. She shook it firmly, but briefly. "I'm afraid Jennifer's in a production meeting right now, Mrs. Lawton."

"I thought she might be. I'd been in a work meeting myself and thought I'd swing by here on my way home. I told her I'd bring this."

She placed a phone on my desk. Only slightly less next-century than the one that had been causing Jennifer trouble.

"She had a spare phone at home?"

"My daughter has as many spare phones as most of us have underwear."

"Of course she does. Stupid question."

She smiled slightly.

I smiled back.

Both our smiles faded quickly.

"I won't beat around the bush, Ms. Danniher—"

"Elizabeth."

"Elizabeth. Faith," she reciprocated. Without a transition, she resumed, "I have been concerned about Jen—Jennifer spending so much time with you."

I was more taken by the fact that Jennifer was inflicting the name-change edict even on her parents than insulted that I wasn't considered a person Mrs. Lawton—Faith—wanted her daughter to spend time with.

After all, a lot of that time had been spent investigating—

"These murders," Faith said with a tinge of dismay and completing my thought. "She doesn't tell us anything. Confidentiality of sources, is all she'll say. But we know because she's not only on the computer, she's also suddenly on the phone all the time and never home, but when she is, it's like she's been plugged into a current that lights her up."

She grimaced.

Then she added wryly, "My own words make it sound like it's a good thing for her. Ever since she discovered computers, it's like we'd have to crawl inside the thing to connect with her."

I held my tongue.

"Her father and I have become more concerned. We do know you've been talking to her about journalism and educating her on what's right, which is good."

Our erratic talks accounted for the sum of Jennifer's journalist training. Sadly, I frequently wished KWMT-TV's news director and anchor were as advanced as the news aide.

Other than a passing grind of my teeth, I didn't dwell on the ineptitude of Les Haeburn and Thurston Fine, because Faith Lawton wasn't done.

"I know she's interested in all that. Though whether it's a profession to hang your hat on these days..."

No arguing with that.

I could have said I wasn't trying to steer her daughter one way or another and certainly not away from her parents. I could have said Jennifer was enough of an adult to choose her associates. And certainly not enough of a child to have decisions on those matters made by her mother and me.

I held my tongue.

Maybe discretion. More likely the sense that the woman was talking herself toward making up her own mind, so why butt in?

"But I want to be very clear how much her father and I appreciate your having her to stay with you while things are ... unsettled."

I admired that choice of words. It gave a nod toward the friction between parents and daughter without spelling out anything from inside the family to an outsider.

"It's my pleasure." A little strong, maybe, but it would do.

"We're grateful to know she's somewhere safe. That someone's keeping an eye out for her."

I felt a twinge at the *safe*.

I couldn't guarantee any of us were entirely safe investigating things people didn't want investigated. But, again, that struck me as between parents and offspring. Not resting on me.

As for keeping an eye out...

"We all do that for each other," I said. Maybe a little extra for Jennifer.

"Yes, I know. But the way she sees you..." She let that die, hitched her purse strap high on her shoulder, and said, "Tom Burrell speaks highly of you."

"You can get him to talk?"

She smiled. Quick and genuine.

I smiled back.

This time they stuck.

It was a start.

"...AND THEN JENNIFER said, *Geez, why not?*"

Diana and I were sitting in the Newsmobile in the station parking lot. It wasn't the most elegant of surroundings but it had several advantages—privacy away from newsroom eavesdroppers, out of the wind, and decent cups of coffee she'd brought from Hamburger

Heaven.

I'd already caught her up on the phone calls, last night's sleepover, and Faith Lawton's visit, skipping what we'd learned in Colorado, because we'd fill her in tonight, along with Tom.

She told me she'd picked up some information on the Grandishers and Joudreys, but if I was holding out until tonight, so was she.

That's when I recounted Jennifer's take-a-walk offer. I had not told Diana about Jennifer's pick-one-and-ask-him-out advice. Didn't want to hear what Diana said about that. But this should raise a chuckle.

I waited.

She finished her coffee, then said, "She's got a point."

"You're biased because you and Sheriff Conrad are burning up the sheets."

"We are," she said with satisfaction. "Burning up the sheets and more. You could be, too. You should be."

"Oh, for heaven's sake—"

"No, don't dismiss it. You worked out a lot of your demons with that trip back East and—"

"I've barely returned and we were chasing who killed Renata and now being pitched right into this—"

"—you're ready. But you're also scared. And you're worried which one."

"—there's hardly been time to—"

"Make time. Before it's gone. Now, go back inside. I have to go shoot the seasonal switch from snowmobiles to ATVs at the dealership on the other side of town. Sure sign of spring."

THURSTON WAS LURKING at the edge of the bullpen when I returned.

That alone was odd.

Then he started in a way silent movie stars would have considered overacting.

"Oh, Elizabeth. Didn't see you yesterday. I hope you had a nice weekend. I had a grand one. Couldn't have been better. But, then, I'm not one to talk about my personal life. Ah, but what am I saying? You spent all weekend working with Leona, didn't you?"

Smirk. Smirk. Smirk.

"Not all weekend. I was off Sunday."

"Ah, you must have needed to rest after those long hours Friday and Saturday." He should write Fake Sympathy cards.

"Yes, though I had a great time with Leona. She sure knows where all the skeletons are buried."

"Oh?"

My probe had landed. I tucked away for a future day that he had at least one skeleton and worried Leona knew it.

"Meeting so many of the county's *important* people in a relaxed, positive atmosphere was wonderful, too. I made great contacts thanks to that assignment."

I pivoted toward my desk, able to track Thurston's reaction by the expressions of my co-workers.

When his retreat reached the hallway to his office, several pounded their desks in a thudding round of applause.

"Cut it out," Bruce, one of the producers, shouted. "On the phone here."

Without making a sound, I grinned my appreciation to them.

Then I settled in for a burst of work for KWMT.

I debriefed with Leona about my venture into Cottonwood County's social life. Among other things, I gave her the name and contact information for the second-in-command to the groom from Saturday.

She was not impressed.

She gave me nothing.

I tried, again, to pump her on the Grandishers and Joudreys, as well as Sedick Oil. Nothing.

She definitely came out the winner on that go-round.

Her lack of cooperation might have been my own fault.

At the start of our conversation, she asked what the heck I'd said to Thurston, because he was hinting about wanting to accompany her on her assignments—a selected few of her assignments—next weekend.

Uh-oh.

Jennifer had returned from the meeting while I was with Leona and was working away next to the producer, Bruce, not one of my fans in the newsroom.

I took her the phone Faith had left.

"Not *this* one. I told her the smooth gray one," she grumbled. "I can't even use this because it's dead. And she didn't bring the charger."

Not getting in the middle of *that* mother-daughter tug-of-war.

I called Needham and fenced for several fun minutes about which of us knew what and who wouldn't share a word. Then we agreed to meet this afternoon for coffee.

After that, I filled in routine research on Calliope's friends from Colorado and the EMT, Ivan Quentel. No red flags for any of the young women. Ivan's unusual name showed up in sports results, graduation lists, and a commendation.

I was debating alerting the park service's investigators when I became aware of Jennifer half standing and turning toward me from her desk, with her phone headset still on.

A flashback to Friday.

I must have been paying attention without realizing it because I was halfway to her before we made eye contact.

"Is it him? The caller?" Why would he call back? Was he threatening Jennifer or—

"It's my parents."

My stomach flipped. The calls last night. Could they possibly have—

"The house—our house was broken into."

Chapter Twenty-Five

TWO LAW ENFORCEMENT vehicles stood outside the neat frame house not far from where I'd lived when I first moved to Sherman.

This wasn't one of the original houses from more than a hundred years ago, but those workers' cottages still dotted the neighborhood, earning it a historic designation. The majority of the elaborate homes the employers built around the same time on the other side of town hadn't fared as well.

That seemed like some kind of comeuppance for the once high and mighty. Except I did love the few examples of those big, old houses that survived.

The Lawtons' house was white with a porch and dormers promising cozy bedrooms upstairs.

"Hollister," Jennifer muttered from the passenger seat of my SUV, as we pulled in behind the Sherman Police Department vehicle in the driveway. Officer Randy Hollister of the tiny Sherman Police Department clearly didn't rank high in her estimation. "He can't handle a break-in."

A Cottonwood County Sheriff's Department vehicle was parked in front the house. If we were lucky, it would be Deputy Richard Alvaro's. He was smart and approachable. Although I could see that window closing as he spent more time with Sergeant Shelton and Sheriff Conrad.

Sherman Police Department patrolled within the town limits, while the sheriff's department had responsibility for the rest of the sprawling county. As a matter of practicality, however, whoever had a unit closer responded to calls. The sheriff's department, with more resources, staff, and experience ran most cases more complicated than traffic stops and the milder bar fights.

Mike in his SUV and Diana in the Newsmobile—a station all-wheel drive that was a close relative to a tank—pulled in right behind me.

Diana might have heard the news from the scanner in the Newsmobile, but Mike must have been instantly notified via the newsroom grapevine and come after us.

KWMT now outnumbered law enforcement. I liked those odds.

Faith Lawton came out the front door, pulling her daughter into a hug.

"Jen, you didn't need to come home. I just didn't want you to worry after hearing it on the police scanner. That's why I called."

Why *hadn't* she heard it on the scanner?

Jennifer stiffened, "That damned Thurston Fine."

Ah. Of course. He claimed the scanner disrupted his work routine. In other words, his nap.

"How nice of you to come, Elizabeth. All of you," she amended as Mike and Diana walked up.

"Okay with you if I shoot video, Faith?" Diana asked.

"Not much to see, but you're welcome to come in, all of you. The break-in was through the back, so we're not interfering with the investigation here."

"What did they steal, Mom? Did they trash the house? Vandalism? What about—?"

"No, no, nothing like that. We don't know if anything's been taken. We haven't had a chance to check thoroughly yet. I can tell they went through your room and Adam's and the den. No sign of them in our room. In fact, the officers will be glad you're here to see if anything's missing."

She spoke over a mechanical whine from across the street that made me turn. A woman trimmed evergreens with an electric gadget like my dad used. He always said the best time for this chore was early spring. Next time we talked I'd have to ask if it was better before or after snow.

Faith raised her hand in greeting and the woman responded by waving the hand not holding the trimmer.

"Any idea when it happened, Faith?" Mike asked.

"Couldn't have been long. I left the station, picked up dry cleaning, then swung by the supermarket and bought ice cream for Kent because he likes it with the dinner I've planned for tonight—"

"Lasagna?"

"Yes. With salad."

Jennifer's wistful expression clearly belonged to the lasagna, not the salad.

"Bought the ice cream and..." urged Mike.

"Bought the ice cream and—Oh, my gosh. I left it on the back porch. It'll be soup by now."

Maybe not, since Wyoming's spring weather could double for a freezer.

"Mom." Jennifer gave it the two-syllable pronunciation that made it the verbal equivalent of an eye roll. "Forget the ice cream. You can get more later. What happened when you got home?"

"Parked like usual, then... There it was. It was such a shock to see the back door jimmied. For a second, I thought I must have forgotten to lock the door. I mean, my mind knew I had or why would they jimmy the door, right? But there was still that moment." She touched her forehead. She wasn't quite as calm as she appeared. "I didn't go in, because they say you never should. I called 911 right away. Then I called Kent. He got here first and he wanted to go in, but before he could, the deputy arrived, then Officer Hollister."

The whine of the bush trimmer paused and I turned.

Judging by the pile of clippings, this woman had done a lot already, with a line of evergreens across the front of the ranch house and disappearing around its corners.

"I was so glad Kent wasn't in there with both officers going in with their guns drawn," Faith said from behind me.

When Dad trimmed our bushes to a third of their previous size the spring before I started high school, Mom lamented they looked like they'd been bombed. But Dad was right that they'd bounce back fuller and healthier. It just took until I graduated.

"Are you coming, Elizabeth?"

Faith Lawton was holding the door for me, with the others already inside. "Sorry. Wool-gathering." That sounded better than admitting I'd been reminiscing about bush trimming.

"Did your neighbor see anything?" I asked as I caught up with the others at the far side of the living room.

"The officers already questioned her. Not a thing."

Officer Hollister stood at the kitchen doorway, arms crossed, which with his thin frame still didn't block the opening. It didn't matter because the Lawtons—mother and daughter—plus Mike and Diana were all at the passthrough opening into the kitchen.

Past them I saw that we weren't lucky enough to have Deputy Alvaro. The sheriff's deputy talking with a man who must be Jennifer's father, Kent, was Lloyd Sampson.

From the standpoint of getting him to share information, Sampson might be preferable. The problem was, he generally didn't have a whole lot of information to share.

Diana, at the front of the group at the passthrough, zoomed in on Lloyd's open notebook. A nice shot that wasn't the usual pan of the pried open door.

Rather than trying to peer around, over, or between people, I went to the door, smiled at Hollister, who blushed but didn't move, then looked over his shoulder.

"It's funny, though. Usually they go for doors with glass so they can smash it, reach through to the lock and get in that way. They don't often go for solid doors." Lloyd said with uncharacteristic confidence, "Pretty clear what happened. Pried it open and waltzed right in."

"Evidence will tell," said another voice. "Hey, what are you people doing here?"

I'd gotten what I wished for—Deputy Richard Alvaro—in yet another lesson about the dangers of wishing. Because that question wasn't for his fellow law enforcement officers and presumably not for the Lawtons. That left the representatives of the Fourth Estate.

"All you from the TV station, get out of here."

"Hey, I live here," Jennifer protested.

"Okay, but the rest leave."

"We'll go. See you at my place tonight, Jennifer?" Diana's willingness to leave meant she had enough good video.

"I'll be there."

"THESE BREAK-INS SEEM to be going around."

I looked away from checking out the bush-trimming job to Mike, as we circled from the back of the Lawtons' house—just for a peek from the outside—toward the street. "What do you mean?"

"My back door was forced open while we were in Colorado."

I stopped. "What?"

He took a couple more steps then turned back to me. "Yeah. Spotted it when I swung by home this morning before going to the station."

"And you're just mentioning this now? What did the sheriff's department say?"

"Nothing. I didn't call them. Nothing was taken. I thought maybe kids tried to get the SUV for a joyride, but it didn't look like it had been messed with."

"Was anything taken? Valuables?"

"TV was still there. I would have noticed if that was gone."

"Did you check anything other than the SUV and TV?" His definition of valuables, clearly.

"No."

I nodded toward the Lawton's house. "Go back and tell them—tell Alvaro. Even if nothing was taken, that's too much coincidence for me."

"But why would—?"

"No idea. Just tell him. Get it on record."

In my SUV, I immediately called Diana, told her about Mike's house, and asked if she'd noticed anything at the ranch.

"Not really, though Shadow did go off Sunday night. I figured it was coyotes. I'll be on the lookout."

✧ ✧ ✧ ✧

ARRIVING AT THE station, I realized I'd spent the rest of the drive after hanging up with Diana mentally drafting the story as I'd report it.

Another time, another place, and I'd be making calls, getting the video from Diana, trying to book Alvaro on-camera, calling dibs on the editing bay … the old rush of events.

Even though it wasn't much of a story, except for in Cottonwood County.

Also a waste of time and imagination, since Thurston would handle—in other words, mangle—this story.

Yet when my phone rang, I grabbed it like someone who wanted something urgent to do.

"Ms. Danniher?" A pleasant female voice said in response to my crisp identification. "You probably don't remember me. I'm Ivy Short from the Cottonwood County Public Library?"

I had a vision of a blue sweater and a warm smile. "Oh, yes, Ivy. How are you?"

"I'm well, thank you. And you?"

"Very well."

Was this why she called? To exchange pleasantries? Was I so far outside the rush of events I should be holding up my pinky and putting doilies on my desk?

"I, uh, I was wondering if you might come by the library. There's something… Some, uh, elements I think you might be interested in. And you could, perhaps, help us at the same time."

Not urgent, but at least it was something.

"Would now be a good time?"

"Now would be an excellent time."

✧ ✧ ✧ ✧

"GOT AN INTERVIEW," I mumbled to the assignment editor, who was uninterested in my whereabouts when I stood in front of her and would be even less so when I was out of sight.

The drive to the library was a leisurely progression into Sherman.

The walk from my SUV in the parking lot, across the semicircular drive, and along the sidewalk was a wind tunnel.

I wrestled the first of the building's double glass doors into submission and threw myself inside. I recognized the woman behind the desk as a helpful source from earlier visits here. She smiled and I returned it. Her nametag confirmed Ivy Short.

She said something to a colleague, then gestured for me to alter the angle of my entry and intersect with her, well away from the desk.

Quickly, almost stealthily, she escorted me to a small study room and closed the door.

"I'm so sorry to have dragged you here for no reason. The situation appears to have resolved itself."

That was fast. "That's good news. Would you mind sharing what the situation was?"

"Oh. Well. We have some visitors who, uh, unsettled a patron. You understand, some of our patrons are not much exposed to a broad spectrum of society."

True in some ways, though the longer I lived in Cottonwood County, the more I understood it encompassed quite a broad spectrum. Even if they did mostly wear cowboy boots.

"I thought of you, since you have experience with many kinds of people. And, then, you also have experience with some of the people here in the county. They're coming to know you."

"I'm not sure…"

That pretty much covered it. I wasn't sure what kind of experience with what kind of people, nor what experience with whom and how it might help with what.

"Hiram can get worked up and—"

"Hiram? Hiram Poppinger?" I didn't know which surprised me more, that she thought I could have helped with him or that he came to the library.

"But Mrs. Parens arrived and everything's fine. I'm so sorry I dragged you out needlessly."

Of course everything was fine.

And what *had* been wrong could have been anything from two people wanting to check out the same book to a potential nuclear meltdown, though with Hiram involved, the nuclear meltdown sounded more likely. Still, with Mrs. P on hand no wonder I was no longer needed.

That didn't mean I wasn't going to find out what happened.

"That's fine, Ivy. I'll just say hello to Mrs. Parens before I go. Unless, uh, Hiram...?"

"Don't worry. He's banned from bringing firearms into the library now."

Now. Was it my imagination or did that sound like maybe something happened to prompt that specific ban?

Since my first encounter with Hiram involved firearms, this was not encouraging.

Maybe I'd call Mrs. P later to get the rundown.

"She's in the Cottonwood County History Room talking with all of them."

That stopped my mental retreat.

All of whom?

Oh, hell. I was going to find out what happened, even if Hiram Poppinger was still around.

Chapter Twenty-Six

HE WAS.

Hiram resembles those cartoons of a little old miner from the gold rush days, with overalls, boots, and a long gray beard. Except his beard's of the short and scruffy variety. Also, they're usually portrayed as happy and that's not Hiram. Think of Grumpy the Dwarf's evil twin.

And most of the time Grumpy the Dwarf's evil twin was packing heat.

If he truly was unarmed, it made the library the best place to meet Hiram Poppinger.

Unless a meeting could be avoided completely.

"*You*," he said with disdain when I entered. "Should've known. That's all this needs."

In addition to Hiram, Mrs. P sat with five people I'd never seen before.

"Hiram." Having quelled him with the single, mild word, Mrs. Parens said, "It's lovely to see you, Elizabeth. I'd like to introduce you to my new acquaintances. Cran and Blue—"

These two were siblings, if not twins. Each had a triangle shaved close to the head from temple to crown, a second triangle cut short from the hairline behind the ear to crown, and the rest boy-band short. But their triangles were on opposite sides of their heads.

Both had fine, not quite delicate features, and enviable skin. Both wore black jackets over black shirts over skinny black jeans with black boots—not of the cowboy variety.

They were in their late teens. It was unclear if both were boys, both were girls, or—if there was one of each—which was which. All that was fine. But if their parents had named them Cran and Blue and their last name was Berry, they had a strong case for parental abuse.

"—Sergei—"

This was a square-faced male of maybe thirty with cheekbones sharp enough to stretch his rarely-sees-the-light-of-day pale skin over them. Incongruous dirty blond dreadlocks tumbled untidily over rounded shoulders and down the back of a rumpled blue plaid shirt over baggy jeans and pristine sneakers.

"—Daisy—"

I perked up at this.

"Are you DaisyDukes? Jennifer's friend?"

"I am," she said in a soft, high-pitched voice that sounded like she didn't use it very much.

She was in her mid-to-late twenties, with wispy pale hair covering much of her face, a rounded chin, and a softly curved figure under an unflattering, faded pink prairie dress. Where the others stood out, she blended in. Was that her super power?

"—and Vic."

He wore jeans and a t-shirt with a rude saying on it. This shortest member of the group surely should have been in class in a middle school somewhere, where he'd be the smartest kid in the school, not well liked, and yet, would like everyone even less than they liked him.

But he and the others appeared fine with Mrs. P's company.

"We struck up a conversation and I discovered these young people are among a group of computer experts visiting Sherman at this time," she explained.

Sergei said, "Not computer experts, exactly," in a surprisingly high voice that yet held the gruff intonations of Eastern Europe. Russia? Or a neighbor?

He and Daisy could nearly double as dog whistles.

"Doesn't matter," one of the siblings—Cran? Or Blue?—said, sending Sergei a dark look.

Hackers. That's what the siblings didn't want Sergei to say.

These were some of Jennifer's hacker friends.

"We were explaining to Mrs. Parens that we came to the library to check its internet access," Cran or Blue continued. "We thought we had it covered staying at a B&B. VisageTome is a pit of writhing snakes that give off skunk scent with every machination, so foul that even those who left it are forever besmirched. But—"

Sergei cut across. "But they know how to give good internet. That B&B place has a fine set-up."

Krista Seger's Wild Horses B&B was the only one in town. They must be the booking she'd mentioned Saturday night. And she was the former VisageTome employee being described as forever besmirched and stinky.

"Then why come to the library?"

"Paint." The other sibling said. "They said they're getting ready for the season. Didn't know it would smell. Never heard of No-VOC paint around here? We considered moving to the hotel, but…"

Sergei concluded the thought. "That Buck Rogers Hotel is worthless."

"I believe you mean Roy Rogers," Mrs. Parens said.

"The fast food place?" asked the kid. That middle school he belonged in most likely sat in one of the states around Washington, D.C., a last bastion of Roy Rogers restaurants.

"The restaurant chain was named after a cowboy singer and entertainer, which might remind one of the décor at the Haber House Hotel," Mrs. Parens explained. "Buck Rogers is a fictional hero of adventures in the twenty-fifth century."

Unfazed by this correction, Sergei scoffed, "That place isn't in this century—or the one before—much less in the future."

I didn't sidetrack the conversation to mention its fabulous chocolate pie, though it might soften Sergei's view of the Haber House Hotel. Instead, I asked, "What brings you to Sherman?"

Silence.

Then Hiram piped up again, "They're a modern kind of posse. Came here to drive out the bad guys now that everybody's so namby-pamby. Plain old shotgun would do the job, but can't hardly carry a pop gun these days."

"A gun is good," said Sergei in an East-West meeting of the minds that raised the hairs on the back of my neck. "But to shoot you need to know target. We find the target."

Mrs. Parens clicked her tongue. "Do not talk nonsense and tell Elizabeth why you are here."

"The same Elizabeth...?" DaisyDukes asked.

"Yes. She is a fine reporter—" Scoffing sounds from some of the others nearly overpowered that, but Mrs. P continued confidently. "—as part of a free and active and thoughtful media, which is essential to democracy. In addition, she works with Jennifer at KWMT-TV."

That changed the mood.

Nobody said it, but the unspoken gist was *Oh, well, if she works with Jennifer, then she might be okay.* Though I suspected they still considered reporters, the First Amendment, and all that flowed from the combination as useless.

"J-Bar's the best." The others grunted agreement with the Blue/Cran sibling on the left. "Word went out she needed help. Naturally, we could do a whole lot more with our home setups, but we discussed it and decided it might help having people onsite. We were the ones who could get here fastest. Though that snow delayed us a day."

I was sorely tempted to ask how the kid, Vic, got out of class and on an airplane by himself. I stuck to essentials. "What kind of help?"

"The kind we can give." The Blue/Cran sibling on the right slammed closed that channel of communication.

"Does Jennifer know you're here?"

"No. She's been unhooked. We even tried calling, but—"

"Her house?"

"Yeah. After she didn't answer her phone."

One mystery solved. Why had they hung up? Impatience? Not wanting to talk to strangers? Not a mystery worth tackling, though I suspected a good phone manner wasn't high on this crew's list of accomplishments.

"We were out of town and she had connection issues, then something happened to her phone."

"*Something?*" the kid said with mocking sarcasm worthy of someone considerably older. Say, my age.

"Yes. It wasn't working. But you can call her at the station—"

"No way."

"No."

"Are you kidding?"

"Bad enough the other calls."

"Unh-Unh."

"I like these weirdos," Hiram said. "They're smart enough not to trust any of you people."

Mrs. Parens sent him a look. He dropped his head.

"Elizabeth, would you please call the station and arrange for Jennifer to come here?" she said.

"Good idea," said the chattier of the siblings. "But don't tell her who's here over the phone. Your phone's probably not secure. Anybody could be listening."

What were they? Spies?

I hit the station number Jennifer had programmed in to my phone. She answered.

"Hi, Jennifer. I want to you come meet me at the library. Tell them you're starting lunch."

"It's too early for lunch."

"You're going to take a long lunch. Get Dale to cover."

"A long lunch? Why?"

"Because. It's important."

"*Oh.* Like… Okay." She clearly thought better of revealing too much on her end by asking questions.

Had she learned that from this group? Or from me?

✧   ✧   ✧   ✧

PUBLISHING CLEARINGHOUSE NEVER had a winner as excited as Jennifer was when Mrs. Parens pronounced the names of the other people in that library conference room.

She squealed. They squealed back.

Except Hiram, of course.

It turns out she'd never met any of them in person before.

"What? Not even video chatting?" I asked. If ever there were a group I'd expect to know that skill upside down and sideways, this was it.

"Nah," the kid said with a sneer. "None of us have time to waste on that social stuff. We use our time better."

"We share algos," Blue or Cran said.

"Algorithms," the other filled in with offhand pity for my presumed ignorance.

They were awfully intent on dismissing the human aspect for people who'd just squealed over a first face-to-face.

"That one you sent me last summer, Sergei—"

That's all Jennifer got out before other voices piled in with scoffing comments in a language I didn't speak.

Mrs. P gave them a few more minutes of geek reminiscences, then quietly suggested to Jennifer that it was time to leave for lunch.

"Okay, you guys. We're going to load up and—Oh. How did you rent vehicles? You didn't give your real IDs?" She sounded aghast at the notion.

A few eyerolls answered her.

I appeared to be the odd one out—I was aghast at not using legitimate IDs to rent a vehicle.

Jennifer chuckled and said to the assembly, "Sorry. Don't know what I was thinking to ask that. Okay, load up and we're going to lunch at the café."

An echoing murmur of *café* came from around the room as they accessed navigation on their phones.

In Sherman, they probably could have gone outside and followed the scent of cooking.

"Hey, J-Bar, this woman—Elizabeth—said your phone crashed?" the kid asked.

"Yeah. Really weird. And I haven't had a minute to work on it."

"Hand it over."

She did.

That might have been the most impressive thing I saw that day. Jennifer willingly relinquishing her phone. Without question. To anyone. Much less an escapee middle schooler.

She pulled out a second phone, punched into it, and my phone vibrated.

"Texted you so you have this number."

"To an unsecured phone? Stupid." The kid was starting to get on my nerves.

The criticism flowed right past Jennifer. "This isn't my phone. It's borrowed. But I wasn't texting to an unsecured phone anyway."

That meant—"My phone's secured?" I asked.

"Of course."

I should have known. She'd provided the phone for me. She'd set it up for me.

"Who did you borrow a phone from?" I asked.

"Dale."

So now I could call and text Dale the news aide. And vice versa. Great.

I recovered in time to take Jennifer's arm for a quiet word.

"Call your parents and let them know there's an explanation for the phone calls and hang-ups." I almost said a *simple explanation*, but a glance around deleted that word. "Before lunch."

"But, there's so much to talk about and—"

"*Before* lunch. They're worried. Give them a break."

"All right, all right."

She started to turn away. I held onto her arm. "I know they're your friends, but be circumspect."

"I have to tell them things so they can research. The others—the ones not here—are already doing that."

"You can have them researching. But what we discover is not for public consumption or consumption by your friends." Inspiration hit. I quoted back her words to her mother. "Confidentiality of sources."

Her brewing protest subsided.

"Also, are you sure you want to discuss whatever you're going to discuss in public at the café?"

"Nobody will know what we're talking about," she said.

Good point.

✧ ✧ ✧ ✧

I ASKED MRS. P if she wanted to go to lunch with me. She declined, citing a previous engagement.

To my astonishment, she and Hiram walked out of the library together. From the bit I heard they were headed for the Haber House Hotel's dining room.

"She said she'd go to lunch with him if he behaved himself." Ivy Short had materialized at my side with the answer to my unvoiced question.

Too bad I couldn't turn her into an app that Jennifer could load on my phone as an all-purpose unvoiced question-answerer.

Hmmm.

Scratch that.

Talk about intrusive…

✧ ✧ ✧ ✧

JENNIFER RETURNED FROM her extended lunch with new energy—anger.

"Didn't you have a good time with your friends?"

"What? No. That was great. And they went back to work on the searches so *something*'s getting done while I'm stuck here."

Yes, I got the hint that I wasn't really doing anything. I chose not to respond to it. "Then what's wrong?"

"Some scumbag stole my bag. Can you believe it? Right off the back of my chair."

"You shouldn't hook your purse on the back of a chair."

"In *Sherman*? I should be able to dangle it in front of everybody's nose at the Café and never have it touched. And, of course, it was Hollister from the police department who came again. Worse than useless. All he said—Never mind. The world's going to hell."

She dropped into her chair.

I tactfully did not press about what Hollister said, guessing it had something to do with where she'd left the purse. Maybe Hollister was sharper than I'd thought. "But it was good to see your friends?"

"Yes. It was good to see them all." The anger was gone. "Especially Daisy."

Chapter Twenty-Seven

I CAME OUT of the ladies' room to immediately feel a shift in the newsroom's atmospheric pressure.

A breaking story.

It's like a weather front coming through. One that stirs everyone exposed to it. Even those standing still seemed imbued with movement.

Jennifer was at a desk near Bruce, that day-time producer who was not one of my fans. With him on the phone and turned the other way, I slid in next to her.

"What's going on? Hey. Are you okay?"

"Did you hear? Did you hear?" Under a phone headset, her pale face emphasized fear-widened eyes.

It *felt* like a breaking story, but maybe I had it wrong. Maybe it was personal—

"Your parents—?"

"They're fine. It's not them. There's been a bad accident. On the road between a couple drill rigs. A roustabout's been hurt. Maybe worse."

A roustabout.

I knew of precisely one roustabout, not only in Wyoming, but anywhere. Lance Joudrey. Former boyfriend of, first, Calliope and, more recently, Jennifer. Logic said the chances of it being the solitary one I knew of were slim to none.

Jennifer's face said otherwise.

"Lance?"

"I don't know. They don't have a name."

The phone rang and she clicked to pick up the call about a third of the way through the ring.

"KWMT-TV. Lawton… Yes." She typed into a form. Looking over her shoulder, I saw the name of a road, Sedick Oil, and the words *truck crash*. "Yes. Do you know who? … Oh. Okay. Anything else? … Yeah. I know. When you do—I'll tell him. Thank you."

She turned to me, her eyes still huge, but now with a sheen of tears. "No ID on the victim."

"No conclusions until you have information." I put a hand on her shoulder and felt her breathe and breathe.

She nodded.

"We've re-routed a shooter and reporter to the scene. They should be there soon. I've got to get this to Thurston and—" She jerked her head toward Bruce, still on the phone.

"First, tell me quickly what happened."

"Nobody knows for sure yet. The roustabout was going from one location to another. In an oil company truck." I got the impression that had significance, but she didn't explain and I didn't interrupt to ask. "Maybe he fell asleep or tried to avoid an animal or something, but the pickup went off the road where there's a tight curve—two, actually—between rock walls and he slammed into the side. And then the truck caught fire."

She frowned an accusation at me.

"You said vehicles hardly ever burst into flames the way they do in movies," she said.

"That's true." According to Dex, my FBI lab friend who knows about such things, as well as the metabolism of hummingbirds. "But hardly ever leaves room for it to happen."

Bruce was ending his call. I pressed Jennifer's shoulder again and returned to my desk.

Where I once more was decidedly outside the rush of events.

After two more phone calls, Jennifer stood and jerked her head toward the ladies' room.

This was getting to be a habit.

Of course, I followed her. I also had a quick thankful thought that I hadn't worn the kitten heels today.

She wasn't on the floor this time, though. She spun around when I came in, her arms wrapped around herself, as if for warmth. Or protection.

"You've heard from the crew sent to the accident?"

"*Accident*. Oh, God." She gulped to control her voice, then got out one more word. "Lance."

"I know he works for Sedick, but that doesn't mean—"

"It's what he does—jumping from rig to rig, filling in as they need him. That's what the report said. A roustabout going from one rig to the other in a hurry because there was trouble at the second rig. It's exactly what he does all the time."

"You don't know—"

"In a blue truck. *Blue*. That's what they said. He's the only one who drives that old blue truck. Everybody else uses the new red ones. But because he's the boss' son, he felt he had to take that one. And an *accident?* Another *accident? Really?* I have to get out there. I have to go right now. If you tell Bruce that you need me to go with you, he won't argue with you. He's afraid of you. Just the way he's afraid of Thurston."

I was momentarily pleased to think Bruce was afraid of me. Until she put me on the same level as Thurston.

"Jennifer, we need to find out more before we go running out there. We might find better information at the sheriff's department. Or the hospital. Or—"

"I have to go there. I have to. We're not going to find out anything important except out there."

"We'll find out more if we know more first. I'll do some calling around for groundwork, then—"

The door banged open behind me.

Jennifer looked up and whatever color was left in her face drained. Her mouth formed an O.

"*Lance*."

Chapter Twenty-Eight

SHE STARTED TO sink.

I wedged her against the wall with my arm and shoulder, while turning to look behind me.

I didn't have to turn long, because the young man steamed across the small space and had Jennifer bent over at the waist, head down, like a rag doll.

"Breathe, Jen. Breathe." He gave me an apologetic mini-glance. "She used to do this all the time. I was afraid…"

Was that why I'd found her crumpled on the floor Friday?

When I hadn't been as fast to reach her as this young man.

This very dirty young man.

His hands weren't too bad—either he'd made an effort to clean them or he'd been wearing gloves when he accumulated the grease, oil, dirt, and unspecified grime from his sun-bleached hair down his coverall, and onto his steel-toed work boots.

"Lance," Jennifer said from her head-down pose. Then more strongly, "Let me up."

He didn't release her, but he did let her straighten. "Sorry. I got you dirty, but I was afraid you'd fall."

"You're alive."

"Yeah. It wasn't me in the blue truck. Wallinski took the call and went in my truck because I was under his truck when it came in. It was my turn, but he said he'd take it and I should keep working because I nearly had it. And I did. Maybe two, three minutes after he took off, I got that damned—Sorry. I got the part back in and got it running.

When word came in about the accident, I hightailed it here to let you know it wasn't me."

As he'd talked, I'd studied him, seeing a great deal of his father in the square-faced strength, the attractiveness without being handsome.

"What about your parents?" I asked.

"Dad will know it was Wallinski. Mom won't have heard at all. I knew Jen would hear some, but not enough from working here. I tried calling, but—"

"My phone's not working."

"Not working? I thought you had me blocked or—"

"Blocked—? Never mind that now."

Uh-huh. There was something more to this. Because her tone said never mind it ever, as in, she didn't want it discussed.

Naturally, that made me deeply interested. But I'd have to wait.

"—didn't recognize the number. I can't believe your phone isn't working. You can always figure those things out when nobody else can, get anything working."

"Not this time."

I noticed she didn't fill him in on details of her phone's malfunction.

Did she suspect Lance? And if so, of what?

Surely, if she suspected him of involvement in Calliope's death, she wouldn't have been so desperate when she thought he'd been in the accident.

Unless old habits of caring kicked in despite current suspicion?

"What happened? What on earth happened?" The strain in her voice said she certainly still cared about him.

"I told you. We got a call somebody was needed. I was under the other truck. Wallinski took mine and high-tailed it out. He was on the radio with the other rig, trying to find out if he should stop and get supplies to help them out when he told them there was something weird and then they heard the crash. If it hadn't been for that, if they hadn't known he was coming up on Double Dead Curve, he could have been out there a heck of a lot longer. Maybe bled out. Sorry, Jen."

"I'm not a baby. I'm not going to fall over at the mention of blood.

I've been helping investigate murders."

"I know," he said quietly.

If she heard the words, they didn't stop her flow. "People dying all sorts of horrible ways. I never once fell over. And it's *Jennifer*."

He held up his hands—protesting innocence or warding off blows, impossible to tell.

"Sorry. Sorry, *Jennifer*. Old habit." His hands dropped. He hadn't been smiling, not even an amused glint in his eyes, but now his expression darkened noticeably. "There's something else. The call— the reason Wallinski hurried off to the other rig in my truck? It was fake. There was no emergency. Nobody called for help."

Jennifer frowned at him, then at me. "Not an accident. I *told* you. I *said*—"

Her told-you-so was interrupted by Lance getting whacked in the back by the opening door.

With three of us in here there was no room for the door to open fully.

"Sorry. Sorry," Audrey said from the other side. Then she spotted Lance. "What's he doing in the ladies'—"

I interrupted. "We were just coming out."

I half shoved Lance, encouraging him to squeeze himself around the edge of the door by sitting on the sink. Just before I closed my eyes in anticipation of it collapsing and pulling out a chunk of the wall, he popped free on the other side of the door's edge.

Jennifer wasn't paying any attention to this bathroom version of a clown car. "I feel awful to be glad it's this poor Wallinski guy."

"You're not glad it's him. You're relieved it's not Lance. And either way, you did not make this happen. You had nothing to do with Wallinski getting hurt."

"I was hoping…"

"Even if your hoping had some magical power of life and death— which it doesn't—by the time you were hoping, it was over. C'mon, let's go."

Audrey looked at us with curiosity. But some things demand attention even before satisfaction of curiosity. Not many, but a few.

Lance's exit let the door swing in. I went with it on the outswing, then Audrey followed the next inswing.

Jennifer, the last one out, had a militant look in her eyes. I suspected more I-told-you-sos.

I was saved by Dale loping up to us. He has long legs and KWMT isn't that big, so it only took a couple lopes.

"Jennifer. A report came from Jenks at the scene."

"What did he say?"

But Lance was louder "How's Wallinski? What happened to him? Where is he?"

Dale gave him a sympathetic, yet unfriendly glance. Since Dale was crazy for Jennifer and she had no idea, I understood the unfriendly part of that look stemmed from jealousy. That he still felt sympathy for Lance's concern said a lot for Dale's good heart.

"He's on his way to the hospital. Injuries, but they said probably not life-threatening."

I'd prefer better than "probably not" when combined with "life-threatening," but it was a heck of a lot better than dead.

"And—" He paused for dramatic effect. "Jenks said from the way law enforcement's acting it was no accident. That's why he called—to get more people there and others at the hospital."

"We're going out there," Jennifer declared.

"Oh. I don't think—I mean Bruce is sending staff. I don't think he'd want an aide, even though—"

"We're going. Elizabeth and me." She turned to me. "*Now* will you go?"

The reason I hadn't wanted to go before was her emotional state while fearing Lance was dead. Now, with him fine, the injured person having taken Lance's truck and the fake call pointing toward a set-up, hell, yes, we were going.

"I'll drive," I said. "I can make calls while you look things up."

"I'll need your phone again, Dale."

"Okay, but—"

"I'll drive you," Lance said.

"No—"

He talked over her. "You can both do stuff on your phones or whatever while I drive. You don't need to use his phone. You can have mine. Besides, my truck's got a company decal, so we can get in places you can't."

The last point clinched his argument. She didn't hesitate. "Okay. Let's go."

"I need my jacket."

The other three looked at me like I was nuts. I didn't care. I jogged to my desk scooped up my winter jacket, fully-equipped bag, and my phone.

"But Bruce—" Dale started.

"If Bruce wants to fire me, let him fire me," Jennifer said impatiently.

Dale blanched. "I'll fill in for you. He won't know. He won't ever know."

Chapter Twenty-Nine

I DIDN'T ARGUE about Lance driving.

In addition to his truck having a decal, I did not want him in my SUV.

I should have thought that out more.

That realization came after he spread towels on the backs and seats of the two-thirds of the bench seat not designated for the driver. It probably didn't matter—the inside of the truck looked like everything that came off other vehicles in car washes had been distilled to solids then exploded inside the cabin—but it was a nice gesture.

Heck, I'd had my entire available wardrobe turned to ash a while back, I wouldn't quibble over burning a few more items.

He then put on a baseball cap I wouldn't have used to scoop up manure.

Jennifer didn't appear to notice. Not even with her left side pressed up against his right, while I had the dubious pleasure of trying to avoid contact with the passenger door.

"I thought the guy who got hurt had your truck," I said.

"He did. My company truck. This is mine."

If this was what he'd driven for dates with Jennifer, the breakup was explained in full.

I'm no car snob, thinking a car defines a person's—a guy's—worth as a human being. But I draw the line at an oil slick on wheels.

"I'm going to call base," he announced as we hit the highway—and I do mean hit. Not sure this truck had shock absorbers or springs.

Lance's call to base—set to speaker with his well-greased phone in

an equally grimy holder on the dash—didn't elicit any further information except that the person he talked to wanted to know where the
blankety-blank-blank-blank he was and what was the person on the
other end supposed to tell Lance's father when he blankety-blank-
blank-blank called back and endowed the speaker with yet a new
bodily orifice.

The person on the other end didn't say it quite that way. I para-
phrased.

Lance said he was on his way and he'd see his father at the scene.

"Better you than me," the speaker said, not noticeably appeased.

Lance told him, "Heard that Wallinski is at the hospital. His injuries aren't considered life-threatening."

The person on the other end produced another string of blankety-
blank-blank-blanks that somehow sounded like a prayer of gratitude.

Jennifer groused just once about the state of Lance's phone, not
specifying if she meant the outside or the software. Whichever
bothered her didn't slow her much, because soon she was monitoring
communications between the newsroom and KWMT-TV's people at
the scene, reading aloud pertinent bits.

I had time to listen, because I spent strings of minutes on hold
with the oil company's local office, then the Cottonwood County
Sheriff's Department. When Ferrante finally came on the line, I was
told Shelton, the sheriff, Alvaro, and Sampson were not available, and
there was no way for me to reach them. Since I'd already tried each of
them individually, I believed him.

Then I had an idea.

There was no way for me to reach them.

From my phone.

Barely explaining to Jennifer, I reached across and took Lance's
phone, immediately getting a smear of something across my palm,
despite her previously absorbing most available grime.

I paused. I had one shot at this.

Shelton would have the most information, with everything anyone
found out flowing in to him, but he'd be the most suspicious. Conrad,
as sheriff, had the most power, but would be a step behind on

information trickling up from Shelton, plus, he'd be equally suspicious. Alvaro's information would be narrower, but he was perhaps most open to an appeal to his humanity. Sampson was the most manipulatable ... which is why they allowed him the least amount of information.

But would any of them talk to me once they realized who was calling from Lance's phone.

"If you're not going to use it, give it back." Jennifer demanded.

"I'm waiting for the brilliant idea I just had to gel. Lance, I'll dial. You talk."

"What? To who? What'll I say?"

"Jennifer will whisper to you what to say. And I'll whisper to her."

"Who?" she asked.

"Alvaro."

"I don't know—"

She ended Lance's uncertainty. "You'll do it. Dial, Elizabeth."

"Alvaro" came from the phone. I hadn't even had a chance to return it to the holder.

I held it out toward Lance's mouth.

"Uh, Deputy Alvaro? This is Lance Joudrey."

"Where the hell are you?"

Tut-tut-tut. Deputy Alvaro went for rougher language when he thought it was just another guy listening.

"I'm heading for Double Dead Curve right now."

"Where did you go?"

I whispered to Jennifer, she relayed it.

"I'll tell you when I get there." On his own, Lance added, "What's the word on Wallinski?"

The guy was so genuinely concerned about his co-worker, I could practically hear Alvaro softening.

"He's at the hospital." Lance, wisely, didn't say he already knew that. "No further word since he left here, but the medical people seemed optimistic."

Before that ended, I'd whispered the next question.

"You know it was supposed to be me taking that run? And in that truck?"

It wasn't giving up much to Alvaro and the rest of the sheriff's department. They likely already knew that from oil company employees. Even if, by some stretch, they didn't know yet, Lance would tell them when he got there.

Telling Alvaro now gained Lance brownie points that I hoped would pay off in other information.

"Yeah, we know. That's why we want to talk to you."

"I don't have any enemies," Lance blurted without a prompt. Then he looked at Jennifer for an instant before the road reclaimed his visual attention.

Had that look been because he recognized his goof by not waiting for her whisper?

Or because he connected the word enemies with her somehow?

The latter was not a comfortable question. He thought she was his enemy? Or he knew he was hers?

"We'll go through all that when you get here. How far out are you?"

"Fifteen minutes maybe."

"Park along the road, at the back, then walk in. You can't bring a vehicle in close."

This was not the sort of information I'd hoped for. I started another game of whisper telephone.

"How'd this happen?" Lance asked.

"That's what we're working on, but you know what that stretch of road is like with the double blind curves."

"But everybody knows to honk before you enter and as you're going through it."

I wasn't happy with Lance going off script until Alvaro's answering "Yeah" twanged my antenna.

I leaned across Jennifer to whisper directly.

Lance repeated, "You don't think it's an accident?" But it sounded more like he was asking me than Alvaro.

"Is there somebody else there?" the deputy demanded.

"Here? In my truck? I'm the only one talking to you." The tops of his ears turned pink—where they weren't dirty. Without waiting for a relay, he added, "Why do you think it's not an accident?"

I winced.

Alvaro jumped on that immediately. "Where'd you hear that it wasn't?"

I speed-whispered to Jennifer, not risking the direct route because Alvaro was surely listening closely now. She relayed it as fast.

"Are you saying that it *wasn't*? Guess that rumor going around town's wrong."

It was too delayed, too stilted.

Alvaro breathed into the phone. A not-buying-it breath.

I should have gone for Lloyd Sampson.

After a noticeable pause, Alvaro said, "We'll see you when you get here. Check in with me. If I don't see you first."

That sounded like a threat.

He clicked off.

Chapter Thirty

AS IF MY thought conjured him up, Lloyd Sampson awaited us at the end of the line of parked vehicles along a road where gravel was no more than a long-ago rumor.

"Sergeant Shelton wants to see you," he said to Lance. The message that he did not want to see Jennifer or me came through clearly. "Your dad, too."

Which I took to mean Lance's father wanted to see him. Not that he *didn't* want to see Jennifer and me.

Lloyd sent a look toward the media-associated two-thirds of us. "Your folks are over in an assigned area. You'll see when you get down there. On the right. C'mon, Lance." He gestured as if he'd take the younger man's arm, but didn't touch him.

"No reason I can't walk with them."

Lloyd frowned mightily at this development he had not received instructions about.

When Lance took Jennifer's arm and we started forward, Lloyd followed like a cattle dog who'd forgotten exactly what he was supposed to do, but was sticking close hoping it came back to him.

As late-comers, we'd parked well back, leaving us a considerable walk past law enforcement, oil company, KWMT, and civilian vehicles parked single file along both sides of the road, leaving just enough room for a good driver to maneuver out. That left a center lane unimpeded.

A road sign warned of a single lane ahead.

The center lane and the parked vehicles banked sharply in a right-hand turn.

"This is the start of Double Dead Curve," Lance said. "First of two blind curves for drivers coming either way."

"That's why people honk?" I said.

"Right." He peered ahead. "In case emergency vehicles or something come, we better move over and be ready to get out of the way."

We did so.

Jennifer, I realized, made the shift automatically, squeezed that direction because she was bracketed between Lance and me. She'd paid no attention to our scintillating discourse.

Instead, she frowned at a parked truck as we walked past, for no reason I could see. It had more room in front of it than most of the vehicles, but other than that it was a plain vanilla dark green pickup. Unlike most I'd seen in Cottonwood County, it had no logo, no modifications, no individualized compartments in the back, no stickers on bumper or back window, no scars of usage, no badges of honor of any kind.

Walking on, I realized the reason the curves were blind was they'd been built around the ends of slightly offset bluffs that just missed connecting by the width of the road's narrow and tight S-curve.

Even at walking pace, it was like turning a corner in a maze where the barriers were taller than a two-story house. No hint of what was coming.

Driving, you'd barely see a few seconds ahead.

A dozen more steps and a huge SUV with EMS identifiers on it came into view, parked sideways, effectively blocking the road.

"Huh. Surprised that's here. They must have used an ambulance to take Wallinski out," Lance muttered.

"They could get an ambulance in here?" I asked him.

"Sure. This road's good." He clearly considered pavement optional.

"What is it?" I tipped my head toward the EMS vehicle that made my SUV look like a compact.

"Part of the Wilderness Response Team. They use it as a base for search and rescue. Might not have been sure of the road, so they dispatched it," Lloyd said from behind us, then seemed to regret it as he gruffly added, "Media's over to the right. C'mon, Lance."

The younger man looked at Jennifer. She didn't look back.

I gave Lance the permission he sought. "Isn't that your father over there?" I nodded to a group congregated a few yards from the left side of the EMS vehicle.

He looked, then swung back to us. "I, uh, better go see him. He'll be worried. But I'll drive you back to town when ... when I can."

"Sounds good," I lied. On the other hand, a return trip in that truck couldn't make the transfer of grime worse and he might pick up information here to share on the drive back.

Brady Joudrey spotted Lance and cut through the group of men, heading straight for him.

Lance looked at Jennifer. But I was the one who told him, "Go."

He and his father met halfway.

With no regard for his sports jacket, Brady threw his arms around Lance and held on. His head tipped back like he was giving thanks to the heavens.

The resemblance of their strong-boned square faces seemed even stronger. The father was broader, but maybe an inch shorter, which he'd brag about to friends but never acknowledge to his son if he was anything like a lot of fathers and sons I knew.

"Over that way," Lloyd repeated to Jennifer and me, tipping his head.

I turned. As far from the EMS vehicle as they could be yet still be within the curve that accommodated the first of the bluffs, I spotted four KWMT-TV staffers, a reporter and photographer from the *Independence*, as well as its editor/publisher, Needham Bender, surrounded by police tape.

When I looked back, Lance's father was guiding him toward the group of men, probably all from the oil company.

I'd love to ask them questions, but Lance would have to handle that—for now.

"Let's go see if the folks from the station have anything new."

Jenks, one of KWMT-TV's senior shooters, met us partway. "Hey.

They sent you guys out, too?"

"Uh-huh." A fib didn't count when it saved time. "You're heading back? What did you get?"

"Not back. Over to the oil camp to talk to co-workers about the victim. Just missed anything decent of him. He was already tucked up in the ambulance. Leaving me a pan of his feet and the paramedics fixing to leave. But got some footage of it leaving, then the deputies and oil guys milling around."

"Seeing his feet might be effective, Jenks. Vulnerable."

"I like that, Elizabeth. I'll see if I can persuade Thurston."

"You shot with Shelton's okay?"

"Didn't ask. It's a county road."

Jenks' journalistic instincts had been in a coma and he'd been one of Thurston's adherents when I arrived here. That ended over the summer. He was no Diana, but he'd definitely stepped up his game.

"Got some of the wreck, too. He was lucky he got himself out before the fire got real bad. Truck's pretty burnt up. It's further along the curve. Shot that before they swept us away."

"Good for you."

"Yeah. Shelton's got things shut down tight now. The *Independence* folks might have more, but they're not sharing." He said that with no recrimination. We wouldn't have either.

We swung past the knot of three remaining KWMT employees. They had nothing to add. In fact, Iverton, a reporter, was on the phone with the newsroom discussing whether he should return.

We headed toward the *Independence* group.

Needham came away from the others. A friendly gesture or to keep us from getting too close to his reporter and photographer who might have something juicy?

"Jennifer, I'm real sorry about Calliope. I know how close you two were." He rested a hand on her shoulder in genuine sympathy.

That still didn't mean he wasn't keeping something from us.

"What brings you out here, Elizabeth?" He asked partly to give Jennifer a chance to blink back tears, largely because he suspected something was up.

"Just a mix-up about who was covering for KWMT."

He knew it wasn't true, but nodded anyway.

"Doesn't matter who's here. They're not going to tell us anything," Jennifer said bitterly.

"Welcome to the journalist's lot," Needham said. It was good for her to hear such truths from someone other than me. "Speaking of which, want some coffee? Looks like the only way we're going to get together for coffee today."

He gestured to a mega-sized thermos and a stack of plastic cups.

"From your office?" The *Independence*'s coffee was the best journalism-related coffee I'd ever had.

He confirmed it and I accepted.

It gave us the opportunity to move away from both the KWMT-TV and *Independence* camps for un-overheard conversation.

"Have you picked up anything?" I asked, because sometimes brick walls need to be hit, just for the record.

"Nothing more than your folks." Which meant that if he had, he was saving it for the next edition. "Meant to thank you properly for the call Friday. Real nice of you. You could be even nicer, say by sharing what you turned up from spending the weekend amid Cottonwood County's glittering social scene, then down in Colorado."

"I'm sure you know exactly what turned up—from Leona's reports Saturday and then Sunday's chaser from the charity party at Linda Caswell's, where you undoubtedly learned twenty times more than I did."

"Ten times maybe." He knew my skipping any mention of Colorado meant I wasn't sharing that.

"Modesty doesn't become you, Needham. Anyway, the marathon of events she dragged me to weren't as fluffy as I expected, but I sure do prefer hard news. Less gluttony. And at least you have a hope of finding out something."

"You mean like now and what we're encountering courtesy of Wayne Shelton? They got us over here like they're the cool kids and we're not."

"Or like they're the grownups trusted with all the secrets."

He raised his bushy eyebrows in silent invitation.

I accepted. "Divide and conquer?"

"Mmm-hmm. At least one of us might break through enemy lines."

We wouldn't share information, but we would cooperate to try to break through those lines.

✧ ✧ ✧ ✧

THE DWINDLING NUMBER of officials—law enforcement, oil company, and medical—were on the far side of the big EMS vehicle and three sheriff's department pickups and SUVs. Even dwindled, there were plenty of eyes to spot us.

Needham opted to circle wide to the left around the other official vehicles. That left us the right, which offered less cover.

"We can run," Jennifer said.

"Fast movement is more likely to draw attention. Walk normally, with lots of confidence."

It worked.

Or else no one looked in our direction.

Either way, we reached the masking bulk of the EMS vehicle. A glance in the open back doors showed a mini-command center and medical supplies. Police tape extended from the left door's handle out of sight, heading in the direction of the section Lance had ducked under.

We skirted the right-hand door, then down the side of the vehicle. Before reaching the windshield, where we'd be exposed by the lower hood area, I held out an arm to stop Jennifer.

"Shelton," I mouthed.

He stood alone with his back to us, apparently surveying the wrecked and partially burnt pickup, which the huge EMS vehicle had blocked from sight until now.

We were at the top of one of the Double Dead curves, looking toward where the next curve started.

The pickup faced us. Sort of.

The right front of the truck had attacked the rock wall of the eastern bluff and lost. Badly. The impact had crumpled the engine compartment back into the passenger seat. The door had folded, then been driven deeply into the seat.

A passenger would not have fared well.

If the damage inflicted on the passenger side had been on the driver's side, "probably not life-threatening" would have been "almost certainly life-ending" for Lance's co-worker.

The most visible damage on the driver's side was the cratered windshield and burnt marks reaching up from the engine compartment.

Shelton removed his hat, shook his head, swiped a palm over his hair, then replaced the hat.

Jennifer and I backed up as he turned.

No way to get back to our media pen without being spotted if he came our way, so we might as well stay put.

"If he comes," I whispered, "I'll distract him and you get shots of the truck."

We waited, but he didn't appear around the front of the EMS vehicle.

Just as I was entertaining the concern that he'd show up behind us—it would be just like him—we heard his voice, sounding farther away than the opposite side of the vehicle. "Bender. What the hell are you doing?"

"Trying to do my job despite an obstructionist, power-hungry enemy of the First Amendment named Shelton."

Shelton laughed and called Needham a nasty name in a way that sounded almost … friendly.

But he also ordered Needham to "get out of here."

His voice had become more distant, so with a hand at her back, I urged Jennifer to move forward slowly, along the right front quarter panel of the EMS vehicle.

Still speaking quietly, I said, "Both of us take pictures of the truck."

She wrinkled her nose. "Lance's phone isn't great."

"Still gives us more, just in case."

"Yeah, okay. And I'll forward both batches so we have backups."

We started clicking, creeping forward, but not leaving the masking bulk of the EMS vehicle.

"Broaden out, get a view of the setup." I took my own advice.

Satisfied, I handed my phone to her for forwarding.

Staring at the mangled remains of this blue pickup, a vision of the green one we'd walked past popped back into my head. Why had Jennifer—?

We heard motion at the back of the EMS vehicle.

If we went around the front we'd be exposed to anyone on the opposite side. We retreated, staying tight against its tall side.

Lloyd Sampson's voice came, as if he might be by the back doors.

"...gotta admit it's strange. Out here and that big rock suddenly falls right into the windshield. Worst spot, too, coming around the blind corner. Would've given me a coronary. If it was thrown, seems like that's attempted, right there."

Another voice responded, but I couldn't make out words.

"Well, yeah, I know. Not yet. But sure seems strange. Besides, Shelton said it looks like somebody stood up top and dropped that rock right down on the truck. He told the doc that if this was an accident, he'd eat a plate of spurs."

Accident.

That word kept popping up.

Like it was being crammed down our throats.

Felix Robertson's accidental fall, then Calliope's while trying to help him, now Lance's co-worker ... *oh* ... and a possible one I hadn't connected until this moment.

I listened for the departing footsteps before speaking.

"Jennifer, where did you get those eyedrops you bought Saturday?"

"You need some? Oh. Sorry. They were in my bag. They're gone."

Now that she mentioned it, I could have used them with all the dust here. I repeated, "Where did you buy them?"

"The little gift shop in the museum. You know?"

I knew the Sherman Western Frontier Life Museum. I also knew its gift shop. And the woman behind the counter.

"They've got all kinds of stuff there. And they don't charge an arm and a leg like some gift shops. It's real convenient when you're in that part of town."

A faint footfall was the only warning.

A voice came from around the back corner of the vehicle. "Which is where you two should be. In town. Shopping."

Richard Alvaro.

He had us. He knew it. He enjoyed it. Too much.

"Thought I'd find you two skulking around here," he added.

Jennifer glared. "What are you? Some super tracker or something?"

"No. A super counter. I checked the media group and didn't count you two among its number and since I know you, I didn't think you'd come out here then turned around and left. So, I started looking around. But all I had to do was listen." He was pretty proud of himself.

He'd regret that shopping crack eventually, though.

"And now it's time for you two to go." He extended an arm, gesturing for us to move past him, into the open beyond the end of the EMS vehicle.

"You can't make us go back to that pen. We're journalists," Jennifer protested.

"Not making you go back to that pen. Ordering you to leave a scene controlled by law enforcement."

I said, "We have to wait for Lance Joudrey. He brought us out here."

"Then get him and go."

I started ducking under the tape.

"Hey!"

"You told me to get him."

"Not in there, you don't."

"I can't get him without going in there. Unless you want me to start shouting?"

Alvaro growled like a Shelton-in-training.

Was it wrong to feel that getting that reaction was a small victory?

"What the hell is going on here?" That was accompanied by the original growl of the original Shelton.

"Found these two skulking on the far side of the vehicle. I've ordered them to leave."

"Skulking?" I repeated. "Really?"

I held Alvaro's gaze as a tinge of color came into his lean face. So he wasn't totally hardened.

Shelton on the other hand... "You've been ordered to leave by a deputy. Get out of here."

"We aren't leaving until Lance Joudrey is released."

"Released? He's not—" Alvaro's words shut off as soon as Shelton's side-eye glare hit him.

"He's our ride," I added with a slight smile. A smile, honest. Not a smirk.

Without looking away from me, Shelton shouted, "Sampson. Get Lance Joudrey. Tell him to drive these troublemakers back to town, then come give us his formal statement at the office."

My ears, assaulted by the shout, were grateful he used a slightly lower volume to add, "Now, get out of here. Wait for your ride down the road."

I didn't move immediately, thinking.

"What're you waiti—?" He bit that off, clearly unwilling to give me an opportunity to answer that or any other question. "I told you to go."

I smiled again. Sweetly. Really. "There might be something else."

"Well, you call right in to the tip line if you decide there is."

Smart ass.

"You don't think all this is of interest? Like it might be related? Calliope dies, then this, which easily could have been meant for Lance. In fact, it makes no sense if it *wasn't* directed at him. Then Jennifer getting those calls—"

She twitched beside me, but didn't speak. Yes, I knew and she knew the calls were from her hacker buddies. But Shelton didn't. And it tied her into my argument. Also into the population of people who might be targets of ... whatever was happening.

If that made the sheriff's department more watchful of her, it was worth the fib.

"—and the break-in at her parents'. Did Mike Paycik tell you his back door was forced?"

There was one more possible item, the one I'd thought of shortly before, but that would need confirming to persuade Shelton.

His eyes narrowed, as if he'd followed the progression of my thoughts and didn't think a whole lot of them. "Never heard Mike was pals with these three younger ones."

"If you can't recognize a potential pattern... C'mon, Jennifer, we've got what we need." I touched her arm to start her, then, as a parting shot, looked back and said to Shelton, "Better check out that plain green pickup back a way in the string of parked vehicles. West side."

"*Go.*"

We went.

Chapter Thirty-One

LANCE DIDN'T MAKE eye contact as he got in the driver's seat of his truck.

Jennifer stared at him as he performed a three-point turn with an added degree of difficulty because he avoided looking at her, while she was jammed up against his side.

Then he looked straight ahead as the truck bumped slowly back to the highway.

Jennifer shifted, gaining more maneuvering room for herself by pressing me into the door, then backhanded his bicep.

"What are you up to, Lance?"

"I don't what you're—"

"Forget it."

He glanced past her to me.

"Forget it," I reinforced.

"It's just..." A half-mile of road passed. "Seeing my dad."

"Seeing your dad?" Jennifer repeated with disbelief. "You see him all the time."

"Yeah." Another stretch of road. "I mean, I live there and everything. But lately... Uh, I've been working a lot. And he's always busy—both of them are. I hardly ever see them. So..."

If this guy played poker he should save time and show everyone at the table his cards.

Though why he'd lie about an apparent strain between him and his parents I couldn't guess. It clearly had been forgotten in the moment of reunion, so it hadn't reached the core of their relationship.

On the other hand, the closer the relationship, the bigger any disagreement could seem. It was like the relationship magnified the emotions. As any first responder would tell you about walking into a domestic dispute and the dangers assoc—

Click.

Domestic.

A report filed as a domestic after the sheriff's department responded at a Sedick drill rig.

"The fight out at the rig. The one the sheriff's department responded to. That was between you and your father?"

He said nothing. He didn't need to. His face gave him away.

"Jennifer, when we get back, will you look up who responded to that call? We know it was reported as a domestic. If it was Shelton or Alvaro or one of the other deputies who don't make those mistakes, we'll have good cause to—"

"You don't need to do that. It was me fighting."

"Just you? Fighting usually involves at least two. The public records...." I didn't clue him in that, without charges, there might not be a public record that named the combatants.

"My dad. I was fighting with my dad."

JENNIFER'S MOUTH DROPPED open, but she said nothing.

"Why?"

He dropped his head as he shook it. "Him and my mom, always on me about where I should be, how I should be living, what I should be aiming for." His hands clenched. Ah, not such a purely sweet guy. "Who I should be dating."

"Weren't they satisfied you and Jennifer had broken up?" I asked.

He looked at Jennifer, then didn't seem able to look away.

Until I made the timely observation, *"Road. Truck coming."*

He adjusted the path of his truck back to his side of the middle line, looked at Jennifer again, then back to the road.

I tried to pry more out of him. But he'd clammed up about relations with his parents. And all he'd give us about being at the scene was that he'd heard, seen, and learned, "Nothing."

I ENTERED THE station alone, leaving the other two and their atmosphere of much unspoken in the truck in KWMT-TV's parking lot.

I changed into a studio outfit I kept there, putting my clothes that had contacted Lance's truck in a bag I held at arm's length.

Dale asked if Jennifer was coming back. I said I had no idea. Did that mean a double shift for him?

He shook his head. "Couple more hours is all. I don't mind."

Poor guy really had it bad for Jennifer.

Nobody asked me about my hours. After my weekend with Leona, apparently, I was back to being a newsroom ghost, materializing and dematerializing on my own schedule. Suited me fine.

Returning to my SUV, I noted Lance's truck was gone, presumably with him and Jennifer in it.

Would they talk? If not about their breakup, at least about their shared sorrow over Calliope. Better yet, whatever he'd learned at Double Dead Curve.

Driving home, I spotted one of those greenies license plates and wished Mike had been with me so I could tease him about his invasion paranoia.

At the house, I took a scrubbing shower, put on fresh clothes, then took both the bagged clothes and the studio outfit to the dry cleaners with apologies.

The little woman behind the counter laughed. "Ain't nothing we haven't seen before."

I'd parked in front, but when I came out, I turned right.

And walked to the Sherman Western Frontier Life Museum.

The gift shop had an entry off the sidewalk. That's the one I used—to avoid dashing the momentary hopes of whoever was selling museum tickets today.

I'd hoped there'd be somebody—anybody—behind the counter other than the person I recognized immediately. Vicky Upton.

The recognition was mutual.

The antipathy was on her side. Mostly.

I'd once idly speculated whether brownies she made and sold at the gift shop might be poisoned and decided they weren't—solely because she couldn't have predicted I would come in and buy one. If she could have known for sure, all bets were off.

The brownies were good, but this time I wanted something else I'd previously spotted.

Security cameras. They weren't completely unknown in Sherman— banks and drug stores in particular sported them—but their presence here stuck with me.

I could have gone through the museum hierarchy, but that might have given Vicky Upton time to destroy the footage because I wanted it.

Sound extreme?

Hey, I'd entertained the idea of this woman poisoning a brownie meant for me. Destroying footage to spite me was a lot less of a stretch.

So, I came here first. And intended to stay here, wrestling her away from the security footage if necessary.

Might as well plunge in. I wasn't going to win her over with my charm.

"Vicky, I'd like to see footage from those security cameras from Saturday morning."

"No."

"It's important."

"I don't care what you think is important."

Impasse.

"You're part of the museum, so—"

"I don't have to tell you anything."

On to Step Two.

I pulled out my phone, found the number for the museum curator in my contacts, and tapped it.

"Hi, Clara, this is Elizabeth Margaret Danniher of KWMT-TV. Would you be available to join us in the museum gift shop?"

She paused. Not long. Mentioning the station and "us" when the museum could use all the exposure it could get was like leaving a trail of sugar in front of ants. "I'll be right there."

Vicky Upton and I waited in silence. Hostile silence on her part. Neutral, reasonable, and mature silence on my part.

Clara Atwood pushed in the entry door from the museum, giving each of us a quick, assessing look.

"Thank you for coming, Clara. I'm sure you will recognize it would be to the museum's benefit to help with an inquiry into a possible serious crime by letting me see the security footage from Saturday morning. It does not pertain to the museum directly. But important information might well have been caught by your security cameras. And, as you're probably aware, there are no other cameras that would cover the vital area. The museum's cooperation—or lack of cooperation—would be mentioned in any coverage by KWMT-TV."

She knew I was parsing my words. She knew there might not have been a crime and there might not be any coverage.

Still, the carrot of possible coverage dangled there in front of her.

The museum was a contender to take possession of historic gold coins discovered during one of our earlier inquiries. As the decision slowly made its way through the court system, some grumbled about the museum acting in its self-interest.

What I offered was an opportunity for the museum to show up as a good guy by helping solve a crime. Maybe.

"Something on the street?" she asked.

"Probably. I can't be completely sure. That's why I'd like to see what each camera caught."

"I can't let you see all the footage. There are privacy issues, among others."

At Clara's words, Vicky started to relax into satisfaction.

Then the curator added, "However, I will look myself to see if there's anything significant."

"Clara—"

"I'll review that video tape now. Set it up." Clara left no doubt who was the boss.

She went behind the counter with Vicky, who fiddled with some-thing beneath it.

"What time?" Clara asked.

I gave a range of an hour.

Clara glared.

"Okay, try the twenty minutes in the middle of that range, but if there's nothing there, we'll need to expand."

"We can speed it up," Vicky said.

"Not too much," I warned.

This time I got a double glare.

I stayed on the shop side, but shifted to see a tablet-sized monitor tucked under the countertop. I couldn't see it well, but the speed, while faster than real time, was reasonable.

Vicky Upton stepped back, keeping an eye on me, since I was so close to the register and the brownies she wouldn't have had a chance to poison.

Without pausing the replay, Clara made a note on a pad. She kept watching for several more minutes.

"I'm rewinding. Both of you come around here."

I went by way of the far end of the counter, letting Vicky stay between me and the register and putting us on opposite sides of Clara, with good views of the screen.

"Ready?" Clara started the replay without waiting for confirmation.

She played it at real time.

Here came Jennifer appearing into the frame as she crossed the street toward the gift shop. She looked down at her feet. Was it the tape or did she seem to move slower than usual, dragged by the shock and sorrow of learning of Calliope's death the day before?

Her head came up. Alerted by a sound?

She half turned, but didn't wait to see what was behind her to pick up to a jog.

And then it was there, poking into the frame.

The replay was in shades of gray. The truck's shade didn't conflict with green, but didn't confirm it, either.

Jennifer deked to the right. The truck followed.

She cut sharper to the right. The truck tried to follow again, but its tires couldn't go sideways, while Jennifer could. And did.

She also went backward.

The front fender of the truck skidded past her.

Jennifer dropped out of sight behind it. Even knowing what happened, that she was fine other than scrapes and bruises, I caught my breath.

The truck continued, filled the frame, then moved through.

And there was Jennifer, standing up, brushing at herself, glaring after the truck.

"That truck—" Vicky Upton sucked in a breath.

Long story, but her maternal instincts were why she didn't care for me. Seeing the truck nearly hit Jennifer clearly stirred them.

"Yes, it did." It might have been the first time she and I agreed on anything. "Can you copy that to a flash drive for me? Just that part."

Vicky opened a drawer and handed Clara a thumb drive.

"And keep a copy for the sheriff's department." Both of them looked at me. "Just in case it's needed later."

Chapter Thirty-Two

I SAT IN my car, thinking about loose ends.

So far, that's all we had. A bunch of loose ends.

Or maybe puzzle pieces that didn't go together.

I needed to clear some up or go nuts.

I made a call.

"Zara, this is Elizabeth Margaret Danniher from Sunday night's dinner when we talked about Calliope."

She remembered.

I went for direct. "You shut down the conversation about Calliope's recent dating."

"I didn't—"

"You did. The other girls looked to you and you shut it down. This could be important. Not only to find out what happened to Calliope and why, but possibly to keep other people safe. What do you know about her recent dating?"

"You think there's danger—?"

"I have no reason to think any of you there are in any danger. But people close to Calliope here might be."

There was a pause. When she broke it, her voice was firm. "Calliope and Lance were getting back together. I don't know if you can call it dating, with him there and her here, but the connection had ... mended. She was really serious about him. She thought he was really serious about her. Was he lying?"

"I don't know. Thank you for answering, Zara. What about Felix Robertson or gambling, was there anything there you wanted to—"

"Nothing. I swear. Never heard of him and never heard of Calliope gambling. Didn't even get in on the NCAA basketball bracket."

Interesting she should mention that. Though it was fairly recent and it had been a topic of conversation with all the upsets.

"Okay. Thanks again. I'll—"

"Do you still want the EMT's phone number?"

"Yes, please."

Sure, I had a number for him. But you never know if he might have given her a different one. Never say no to a phone number.

It was the same number.

STILL PARKED ON Cottonwood Avenue, I called Jennifer.

"Did Lance tell you anything about what he heard at Double Dead Curve?"

"No."

"Anything else pertinent?"

"No."

"Do you have a recent photograph of him?"

She didn't answer immediately. Then she said, "You want to see if the Valentines recognize him?"

"Yes." I left it at that.

"I'll send you one."

"Thank you." I heard voices in the background. I thought I recognized one. A surprising one.

"Where are you?"

"Wild,Horses B&B with everybody."

Meaning her hacker friends. Had she had Lance drop her off there? Did he know who they were and what they were up to? "Mind if I stop by?"

"No."

"See you soon, then."

"Okay."

That wasn't enthusiastic, but she did send the photo right away.

✧　✧　✧　✧

"OH, NO, DEAR," Kassandra said.

The Valentines' skills in communicating with their grandchildren made transmission of the photo to them painless.

"That's not who we saw. The one we saw was softer. This young man looks like he works hard, you know? The young man we saw was more … indoors."

Great. How many young men would look more *indoors* than an oil roustabout?

"Kassandra, there was something you didn't tell us yesterday. Something when I asked you about making the decision that you should go down the trailhead. What was it?"

"Oh, no, it wasn't about that. It was… To tell you the truth, we were already talking about me going down to call when we heard him take the old trail. Because that young man … well, he didn't seem like a hiker, you know. As I said, kind of soft. And we figured I could get down to where a call could be made before he did, even with the head start. That's all."

I tried a few more questions, but drew no additional information.

We wrapped up the phone call with their cheerful agreement to talk any time I had something to ask.

If only they had answers, they'd be the perfect sources.

Chapter Thirty-Three

THE WILD HORSES B&B started life as the see-how-well-I'm-doing statement home of a Sherman businessman of more than a century ago.

It had declined drastically before Krista and her husband renovated it into a B&B last fall.

She opened the red front door with paint spattered on her shirt. She waved me in. "Hah. Think about you and here you are."

"Thinking about me?"

"I'm repainting a, uh, certain guest room."

"They all know about it," Jennifer said, as she walked through the hall on the way to the kitchen. "No need to be discreet."

Krista gestured for me to precede her in following Jennifer. "I wish people would stop talking about it."

"Why? People love staying where there was a murder. You should advertise it," Jennifer said.

Krista looked pained. "I'm going to the basement to clean up and try to forget all about it, now that the room's a different color. If you want snacks in addition to the drinks, Jennifer, there's a basket in the cabinet next to the fridge."

Jennifer thanked her and continued taking out glasses and putting them on a tray.

I broke the silence. "The Valentines didn't recognize Lance."

"You thought they would?"

"It needed to be checked."

"He'd never hurt Calliope. Never."

"It needed to be confirmed. You know how it works." She didn't answer, so I tried another tack. "It must be good to spend time with all these friends you've known so long but hadn't met before."

"Yeah."

I probed a bit more. "Or is it hard when you know someone well through the internet, but when you meet them in person, there's still an aspect of being strangers?"

"It's no big deal."

"Daisy seems a bit shy."

"Yeah."

"Is Daisy not what you expected?"

"She's great. All the work she's done, organizing all the information everyone's sending in, I really appreciate that."

"But?"

She looked up quickly, then back down to pouring lemonade into the glasses. "It's not Daisy. It's… I keep thinking how Calliope used to get so angry when we were in school. Said I was choosing imaginary people over her. She made me so mad. I mean, she had Lance, but then she didn't want me to have my friends."

"Then, later, you had Lance," I said gently.

A one-shoulder shrug. "I never really did. He tried. We tried. But…"

"Why would Lance think you'd blocked his calls?"

"How would I know?"

Oh, Jennifer, you have so much to learn about how to avoid talking about what you don't want to talk about.

"You do know. When he said it, I saw it in your face." Actually, heard it in how she responded, but this was more impressive.

"He kept calling after the breakup. I told him to stop. That there wasn't anything to say. But I didn't block him."

I tipped my head, studying her. "However, you did stop answering his calls. Or listening to his messages."

"How did you…? Yeah."

"Why?" Was she afraid of him at some level? Could that explain—?

"He always thought he had to take care of me. He was calling to make sure I was okay."

"Even though you broke up with him."

"Yeah. You'd think that would get through to him."

"Get what through to him?"

"That ... that it was over."

Footsteps sounded in the hallway, announcing Mrs. Parens' arrival. Her voice was the one I'd recognized on the phone, so I wasn't surprised to see her.

"Ah, I came to inquire if you might benefit from assistance, Jennifer, but I see that Elizabeth is here before me."

Which she already knew or she would not have made such uncharacteristic noise on her way in.

"I was just coming back," Jennifer said. She lifted the tray.

"Are you joining us, Elizabeth?" Mrs. P asked.

"Yes, thank you. I'll grab the snacks. It's a pleasant surprise to see you here."

"You are surprised that I took the opportunity to expand my experiences by conversing with those young people about their area of expertise?"

"Not at all. I am impressed they were wise enough to enjoy conversing with you."

"They are interesting and engaging individuals."

"Like Hiram Poppinger?"

"Not at all like Hiram, since they are friends of Jennifer." She never lost her straight face.

In the meeting room I remembered from last fall, Jennifer's friends had equipment strung from end to end. They were all there except Vic.

"I thought computing had gone wireless."

My comment was almost lost in the pouncing on the snacks basket.

But Daisy said in her high, little-girl voice, "We talked about that with Mrs. Parens already. You give up power with wireless."

"That is precisely how Vic explained it to me," agreed Mrs. Parens. "We also have been discussing the need for gender neutral pronouns. Blue and Cran expressed their support for the use of *they*, however I believe they might rethink that, considering the potential confusion from its long-standing use to indicate a plural. The goal of gender neutral pronouns is not to confuse, but to allow greater comprehension and, thus, in the long run, greater accuracy."

"No guarantees on rethinking it, but the interrobang's a good argument for something new. Hah." Blue or Cran pointed at me. "She doesn't know about the interrobang, either."

The precise elevation of Mrs. Parens' brows expressed surprise with a soupçon of disappointment.

To truncate the period of surprised disappointment, I came clean and asked, "What's the interrobang?"

"It's a punctuation mark that combines a question mark and exclamation mark, instead of one after the other," Cran or Blue said. "Cool, huh? I'm gonna add it to our messaging font."

"You all message each other a lot?"

"Sure. We—"

Vic came in, interrupting as he did. "You're right, Jennifer. No virus. Somebody remotely wiped your phone."

"What is the significance of the term wiped in this context?" Mrs. Parens asked.

"Deleted all data," Blue or Cran told her in a low voice, like a mourner at a deathbed.

"How? How could anybody get past my security? You know the security I use, we all use." Her horror was contagious.

Except for the kid.

"It was no super hacker," he said with superior disdain. "They didn't get around or through your security. They disabled it."

"How? Are you saying—They couldn't. Encryption. Password guard. They couldn't—A brute force attack? No. That wouldn't—"

"They didn't need any of that. They had your security question answers."

"How in hell did they get those?"

"Because your friend Calliope had them and that's who broke in to your phone."

"What?"

The kid was about to burst with smugness. "At least, whoever had her phone did. I traced it to her phone. A lot of the rest of her record's wiped—emails, photos, texts, contacts, stuff like that. But she had a few stray files, including one called The Other Two, and that's where I found all your info and the info of somebody else named—"

"Lance." Jennifer said it on a sigh that seemed to deflate her. "Oh, Calliope. I told you and told you…"

"For such a simple approach, it was kind of low-level cunning." That promised to be the start of a long, detailed, arcane explanation from the kid.

Mrs. P saved us.

"Excuse me, Victor. Judging from her expression, Elizabeth has questions about this matter. I would like to hear them, as her questions, at times, can bring a measure of clarity to matters."

I didn't have time to sort out how much the caveats deflated Mrs. P's compliment. "I do have questions. The first is: When? When did this attack on Jennifer's phone start?"

"Friday, early afternoon."

Certainly not Calliope. Yet Calliope's phone.

"Other questions?" came from the giant smugness in the pint-sized body.

"Why?"

"WHY WIPE MY phone?" Jennifer said. "Because Calliope's killer didn't want me to be able to communicate."

"But wiping your phone didn't stop you communicating. You did that using my phone. And Dale's. And the phone at the station. So why disable yours?"

"Maybe we could figure that out by knowing what's gone and if anything's left," said Cran.

"Resuscitate data." Jennifer looked around at the others. "But it's not… It's not what we usually do."

"It's not what we do best." Vic made it an objection. Yet he'd been the one who discovered the problem. Why wasn't he interested in the solution?

The siblings began nodding their opposite triangles.

"It's not. But just because it's not what we do best doesn't mean we can't do some good."

"Well, I'm going to keep working on what J-Bar asked for," Sergei said belligerently.

"That's a good idea," Daisy started. "Really we all shoul—"

"Okay." Left triangles said. Blue. I think. Pretty sure. "You three do that and we'll see what we can do with this in the time we have left."

They picked up the phone and went to one corner of the room. Vic and Sergei turned their backs on us as they occupied two other computers. Daisy gave an apologetic purse to her lips and sat before another machine.

"What are they going to do?" I asked Jennifer.

"Blue and Cran are going to see if there's any data left on my phone. They're going to see if they can connect back to Calliope's phone. They're going to see what there is to see. And we're going to leave them to do it."

She started out, none of them saying good-bye. Mrs. Parens and I followed.

"What did he mean in the time we have left?"

"They're talking about leaving the day after tomorrow. They can't stay here forever." That sounded like a quote. And I wondered if her prickly mood had more to do with her friends leaving than whatever had passed between her and Lance. "They'll keep working from home like the others have, but... I don't know what I'm going to do without them."

"But, Jennifer," I protested, "you're the best—"

"Among the best," she corrected with a modicum of modesty. "But this time I'm more useful with you guys. Because I'm in it. I'm in the center of it."

Chapter Thirty-Four

JENNIFER, WHO HAD acquired her mother's vehicle at some point, had promised to take Mrs. Parens back to O'Hara Hill. We would meet later at Diana's.

That left me nearly a whole hour at the Bunkhouse to make progress on the sprawling stacks of clothes left there since Friday. Well, minus the time spent tending to my dog and throwing a stick for him since I hadn't seen him since my drive-by Sunday.

In other words, I made no progress on the clothes.

✧ ✧ ✧ ✧

"WE HAVE A lot to cover," I said.

"A lot of nothing," Jennifer muttered.

Ignoring that, I said to Mike, "We'll have to keep going while you do the Ten. Sorry, but—"

"I've got Pauly doing the Ten. Thurston only allows sports about two seconds anyway."

Haeburn would not like a stringer doing the sports block, but it was Mike's call.

"No curfew for me, either," Tom said. "Tamantha's at a friend's house. Work sleepover, she called it. Preparing their presentation about the weekend."

"Work sleepover? On a school night? You got bamboozled on that one," Diana said.

"Was sort of afraid of that."

Mike, Jennifer, and I reported about Colorado. I went solo on the

Valentines saying the photo of Lance wasn't their other witness, then Jennifer and I covered the wreck this afternoon.

We looked through the photos we'd both taken and Jennifer had forwarded to all of them, pointing to the likely windshield impact of the rock we'd overheard Lloyd Sampson talking about.

"And Lloyd said Shelton said if that wreck was an accident, he'd eat a plate of spurs," Jennifer finished.

After that long recitation it felt good to end with chuckles, though she didn't join in.

She added details about the break-in at her house she'd learned after Mike, Diana, and I left.

"Looks like Lloyd was right about whoever broke in jimmying the back door and walking in. Richard said they would have been in real fast."

"Richard told you that?" Mike asked.

"Nah. I sat around the corner of the stairs and listened like I used to when my parents talked about Adam and me when we were kids. That passthrough's like a sound amplifier or something, because you can hear every word in the kitchen." Jennifer cut a look toward Tom. "You can't tell Mom and Dad."

He looked at her with a steely expression.

"Okay, okay, I know you wouldn't snitch. Especially not when it has to do with our investigations."

"You're wrong. I would snitch all day every day if it involved your safety."

After a couple beats of letting those words settle, Jennifer nodded. "Okay. Deal."

"I wasn't negotiating."

An eye-roll. But it was brief. "It's weird. The only thing I can find they took of mine was an old phone."

"Which leaves you with how many backups?" She shrugged. I let it go and turned to our hostess. "Okay, Diana, you've been holding out on what you've picked up."

"The financial situations of the Grandishers and the Joudreys are solid as far as the rumor mill knows. Very comfortable. They hobnob at Jackson with other oil execs. Nothing too extravagant, at least by Jackson standards."

"That leaves wiggle room, since Leona said Jackson's New York, LA, and Palm Beach stuck in a blender, then poured on top of an underpinning of Wyoming."

Mike and Tom nodded.

Diana shot a look toward Jennifer. She had more.

"There is talk about the Grandishers' marriage," she said. "It seems to stem from about the time it became clear Owen wasn't going to be promoted out of here. India Grandisher's spent considerably more time since then on trips to brighter lights and bigger towns."

"The implication being that his wife is fed up that he's not going any higher?" Mike asked.

Diana tipped her head. Not committing.

"She's not like that," Jennifer said. "Calliope used to gripe about her mom wanting to know everything in her life, but she wasn't all about glitzy stuff. She wasn't."

None of us argued the point with Jennifer. Not now.

"Let's hear what you found on Felix Robertson," I suggested.

"I don't know why you're so interested in him. He didn't kill Calliope."

In a way, he might have… if Friday's events turned out to be a sequence of tragic accidents.

But with the other incidents, I didn't believe that.

If I ever had.

Patiently, because she was feeling raw and it was amazing she hadn't had more such moments, I said, "The most likely reason a bad guy would kill Calliope is he killed Robertson first and she saw too much. Otherwise, if Calliope was the intended target, we have to believe he killed Robertson because he was in the way. Possible, but not as likely. So, why would he kill Robertson? We have no idea. Yet."

She sighed, then said, "My guys checked the hotels. All the way to Denver. Nobody registered as Felix Robertson. But I did find something. His next of kin was not Angela, the ex-wife."

"Oh?" I tried to keep it casual as my pulse fluttered. If his beneficiary was a middle-school-aged son with great computer skills and no social graces…

"It's his new wife."

"What new wife?" Diana asked.

Jennifer warmed to her account. "He got remarried last year and that's who his next of kin really is. The problem is, he had listed his ex-wife's address as his new wife's home address. Bet the new wife would love that if she knew. It messed up the searches, because we'd ruled out that address as Angela's. That's probably why law enforcement went there."

"How'd you find out?" Mike asked.

"First I had to find *him*. It was when I widened the name searches. Not just Felix Robertson, but variations."

"Found the Civil War general, huh?" Mike said.

"Why would I want a Civil War general?"

"You wouldn't, but remember Elizabeth found—Never mind. How did you find our Felix Robertson?"

"I broadened to *any* Robertson."

I whistled. Searching Felix Robertson was bad enough. I couldn't imagine how many listings the last name without the uncommon first name pulled up.

"I sorted those, eliminating age ranges that didn't apply. I tried Nevada, Utah, Colorado, then Pennsylvania, New Jersey, and Delaware to cover around Philadelphia, but that was still a lot. So, I added gambling to the search."

"Smart."

"Should have been done earlier. I thought I'd passed on to my guys what Elizabeth said about checking the gambler Felix Robertson, but I must not have. Wasted all that time. I know, give myself a break, but, really, all that time… Finally, I found a mention of Rainbow Robertson and when I followed that up, it turned out to be a poker nickname because of a shirt he wore for luck. I tracked that back to an article on a poker blog about big recent wins."

"How did you figure out he was our Felix Robertson?"

"Rainbow Robertson won the same things Felix Robertson did

that were listed in that article in the Vegas newspaper. But the article about Rainbow also gave me his middle initial and *then* I found the record of the wedding. I've sent you the copy of that."

She gave the others the information about his recent gambling prowess.

"And then I went back and started checking hotels for Rainbow Robertson and he stayed in one near Estes Park on Thursday night."

"Good job," Diana said.

Mike talked over her. "Alone? Because if he wasn't, we might have a lead on the Valentines' mystery witness."

"He registered solo, but that's no guarantee he was alone," world-ly-wise Jennifer said. "I could see about getting into the hotel's security system. There might be footage…"

All eyes came to me.

"No." Tempted? Oh, yes, I was tempted. But if I gave permission and Jennifer got caught, Faith Lawton would come after me. Not to mention my own conscience. Besides, we were only a few days in, barely at the beginning, really. We could come back to this if we needed to. "Not now, anyway."

I felt more than saw Tom's frown and quickly added, "Jennifer, will you send us the articles about Felix Robertson? The ones about his big jackpots, the Rainbow ones. Everything you have."

"Sure. I'll do it right now." She typed at her device. Paused, then tapped faster. "They're not here. That's weird. They should be right… I know I saved them to this folder." Now, she typed and tapped furiously. "Geez. Now *this* is acting up, too?"

"Can you find them again?"

"Sure. But—"

"Don't worry about it then. Get them to me later. And start on this new wife. Find out what you can on her."

"I've got a question about this other witness of the Valentines," Mike said, clearly uninterested in technical glitches. "Anybody else notice he didn't say he'd heard anything until the Valentines said they had. Before that he said he didn't have any idea about anything."

"Good point, Mike."

"If he existed at all." Fussing with her keyboard apparently re-stored Jennifer's distrust of the Valentines. Of course, she hadn't had their chocolate chip cookies.

"Why would they make him up?" Mike said.

"As a way to explain the gap between when they arrived at the scene and when she—Kassandra—called 911? A time gap like that would be suspicious. Making up some guy who'd said he'd make the call explains it away," Diana said.

"But we wouldn't know about a gap if they hadn't told us there was one," Mike objected. "There's no time stamp of when they started up the trail, no stopwatch on how long it took them to get there. None of this is tightly timed."

"Maybe they couldn't count on that?" Diana was getting into this. "The old broken watch scenario. The Valentines couldn't get down to the victims safely to make sure there *wasn't* something that pinned down the time of the fall—or falls—whether it was a watch or a gadget, so they covered their tracks."

I fought down my irrational prejudice against the Valentines being murderers.

I knew better. Even seemingly nice chocolate chip cookie bakers could turn out to be murderers.

"It's another possibility. Though to this point, we haven't found any connection between them and either Calliope or Robertson. Neither have the authorities to our knowledge." I held up my index finger to stop Jennifer's looming protest. "But we'll keep looking."

"Great. But when are we going to find something?"

Mike looked at our morose expressions. "I've got one bit of info that'll cheer you up."

"Well?" we demanded when he opted for a dramatic pause.

"Elizabeth's prediction was right about the green pickup at the accident scene. Nobody claimed it. How's that for interesting?"

"I didn't predict that. I just said Shelton should pay attention to the truck." If I'd been forced to make a prediction, I would have guessed one of the oil company people or, I suppose, law enforcement or first responders, would claim it.

"Well, nobody did claim it. From what they can tell, it was rented from the dealership where you got your SUV, Elizabeth. A few years back, they bought half a dozen pickups in that same puke green color. You know the ones." Tom and Diana nodded. "Nobody wanted to buy them, so they turned them into sort of a rental fleet. Folks use them same way I rent that SUV for tougher trips, keeping their own vehicle new for longer.

"Most surprising part of this whole thing is Aunt Gee volunteered that detail to me. She must figure since Elizabeth gave Shelton the tip it wasn't telling me anything I didn't know. Even though Elizabeth didn't fill me in."

"Or anyone else?" Diana's question garnered confirming head shakes from Tom and Jennifer. She faced me. "You knew something about a green pickup truck and didn't tell the rest of us?"

"Only since this afternoon. Besides, I didn't know something. Jennifer did."

"*Me?* I didn't say anything about a pickup."

"No, you didn't. But you gave that green truck a very significant look."

"How could I? I didn't even notice a green pickup."

"Yes, you did. You weren't aware of it at the moment because your conscious mind was focused on the wreck we were about to see, rather than what you remembered."

"Remembered? I have no idea—"

"Wait, Mike has more to say. Spill it," Diana ordered.

"One more detail. That green pickup in the line of vehicles was rented by someone who doesn't exist."

Chapter Thirty-Five

JENNIFER STUMBLED INTO speech first. "Wha—What? There's no way I knew *that*. No way."

Diana turned her mother-of-teenagers look on me. "Explain how you came to the conclusion that Jennifer knew about the truck and its significance."

"By picking up twigs, grass, and leaves everybody else overlooked and making a nest out of them for hatching her eggs," Tom murmured.

It was as good an analogy as any.

I told them about Jennifer's encounter Saturday with a truck. About her—apparently unconscious—reaction to a truck this afternoon. And about my trip to the museum to confirm my leap from those two facts.

"I hoped what I said to Shelton would get him to check it out. If I was wrong, nothing lost." I faced Mike. "Now, what did you mean about it being rented by someone who doesn't exist?"

"Just what I said. The man walked in with apparently valid ID and insurance, had no problem with the office making copies, and walked out with the truck early Saturday morning. When the deputy went to check at the dealership this evening, they discovered there's no such person."

"Even if we knew who he was, why would someone drive out to Double Dead Curve, cause Wallinski's accident, then leave a perfectly good truck and walk miles back to town?" Diana asked. "He must have a confederate who picked him up in another vehicle. But, still, why leave the truck there."

"The guy was worried it had been seen. Had to be ditched," Tom said.

"That's good. Still, Diana's right. Without a confederate, it makes this guy the same one who got Felix Robertson to go for a hike up a mountain, pushed him off, pushed Calliope off, took her phone, hid his face from the Valentines, wiped the phone remotely, then was up bright and early Saturday to rent the truck—practically posing for the cameras at the dealership—and tried to run Jennifer down?" I shook my head. "I think the truck renter is a decoy. I think we're looking for someone else."

"Busy person," Tom said. "Did all that in Colorado, then was here by Saturday morning."

"Leave Colorado by one or two Friday and they're here well before midnight," Mike said.

"Especially without long stops for food," Jennifer slid in.

"You know, that might explain why Jennifer's phone wasn't totally wiped until later. He was occupied with driving," I said. "I wonder, too, if the attempt to hit her Saturday morning was more of an impulse."

"Jennifer, what do you remember about that truck?" Mike asked.

"Nothing. I just remember hearing it coming, getting out of the way, falling, and my hands hurting, then getting up and going into the gift shop for eye drops."

"What about the driver? Was there anyone else in the truck?"

She was shaking her head.

"A color? An impression? Man or woman?" Mike turned to me. "What about on the tape?"

I echoed her with my own head shake. "Not clear enough. I've got the drive."

I handed it to Jennifer, but she passed it on to Diana. "If those files going missing means something's wrong with my device..."

Diane loaded it up. I felt the reaction from the others during the few significant seconds, but Jennifer appeared immune.

"Remember anything after seeing this?" Tom asked her.

She shook her head. "It didn't seem as close as this looks."

Mike sat back, expelling a long breath. Then he slid forward again.

"There's something about that wreck. If somebody set it up and they wanted to kill the driver, how'd they get the worse damage on the passenger side? They should've made it so the driver's side hit the rock wall."

He took a pen and reached for my legal pad. He flipped to a clear page and drew a giant S, which matched the layout I'd seen at Double Dead Curve.

"This is the way that oil company employee was driving, heading out to the connector road to get to that other rig. You see something unexpectedly—"

"Or a rock hits your windshield."

He nodded. "Or a rock hits your windshield. You naturally yank the wheel to the right to avoid it."

"And ram the passenger side into the wall," Tom filled in.

"Exactly. But if they did it a little farther along the S and on the opposite side, the driver would react and steer left—into the wall of the western bluff.

"Let me see that," Diana said. She oriented it so she saw the curves from the same angle Wallinski would have seen them, breathed out through her nose, then said, "Yes."

"Does that mean you think the person who set it up didn't want to kill Lance?" Jennifer demanded.

"Possibly. Or didn't know what they were doing."

She stared at Mike. "Because they don't know how accidents work or because they don't know that stretch of road?"

"Or because they do know that stretch of road and what happened is what was intended to happen," I said.

Tom's gaze flicked to me, then back to Jennifer.

She got it faster than I expected. Because she'd been wondering at some level, too?

"It wasn't Lance. He wouldn't."

✧ ✧ ✧ ✧

I WASN'T GOING to argue. I also wasn't going to agree.

Diana stepped into the tense silence.

"I was thinking, if the guy the Valentines saw on the hiking trail knew Calliope, it would explain why he hid his face. No, that's not right. He hid his face from the Valentines. We don't know what he did before that." She had not been thinking any of this. She was talking off the cuff to ease the atmosphere. "Okay, I get why he might hide his face from the Valentines to avoid being identified later if he killed both—or either—Calliope and Robertson. But why pretend to call for help?"

"It gave him another excuse to keep his head down, mask his face with the hat and putting his arm up." Mike dropped the pad with his sketch to the coffee table.

I contributed to the atmosphere-easing. "That's reasonable."

"It also meant the Valentines didn't pull their phones out right away, because he appeared to have it covered."

"Good, Tom," Diana said.

"But that wouldn't have mattered because there was no service," Mike objected.

"He didn't know that for sure until they told him," Diana said.

"He was a slow learner, because they said he kept punching at the phone even after," Mike said.

"Let's work through this," I said. "Going by the Valentines, we think this guy has Calliope's phone from immediately after she dies. He calls Jennifer, but doesn't really start to attack her phone until later in the day. Possibly because he's driving here."

"Or he didn't realize whatever was on Jennifer's phone was a possible threat until later. Or no cell service." Mike twirled the pen between his fingers. "Why are you frowning, Tom?"

"I was thinking that if it were me, I wouldn't be able to do that stuff to Jennifer's phone until I found somebody else to do it *for* me. That could explain the delay."

"Not everyone's a Luddite like you, Burrell," I said.

"You are," he shot back.

Jennifer giggled. The first one from her since this started.

But then she went completely serious. "You're all missing the point. He did start on my phone right away. Probably right after he called me. That's what slowed it down. But he couldn't get past my security until he found my passwords Calliope kept on her phone and could bypass it."

"That works with the driving theory." I considered a moment. "What about Peter Bray? We don't know his movements Friday or Saturday, just that he was in Colorado on Monday."

"Boy, you really don't like him," Diana said.

"I didn't. But I'm not being arbitrary. Why is he being so obstructionist? Why did he try so hard to avoid us? And then get rid of us so fast?"

"Lazy. And/or out of his depth," Diana said.

"You scared him," Mike added.

I piled on questions. "Why did he refuse Ivan's suggestions to involve the ISB?"

"Lazy. And/or out of his depth," Diana repeated.

"Plus, he was the most likely one to have called Jennifer on Friday."

"It wasn't him. I told you that," Jennifer said. "And why would he kill Calliope?"

"He and Calliope were having an affair. She threatened to tell his wife and he got rid of her," Mike said immediately.

"*Eww.* She would never. Not with that guy."

"She could have threatened him some other way," he insisted. "She knew something that would get him fired. She did all that hiking, maybe she crossed paths with him somehow."

"I don't believe it for a second, but I'll check with the Colorado girls to prove it to you." She made a note.

"What about this EMT?" Tom asked. "Same could go for him. They could have met when she was hiking and it sounds like that would be a more likely romantic pairing."

"But it wasn't *him* on the phone, either," Jennifer said.

"Either of them could have disguised his voice," Mike said. "One of those voice changing apps. They don't all sound like computers or

ET."

She cocked her head, considering. "Maybe. It was kind of stilted, but not like from an app or something changing his voice. It was more the way he talked."

"Like English wasn't his first language?" I flashed on Sergei. But how or why...?

"More like he was thinking through what he was going to say."

"Could someone else have been telling him what to say, like you did with Lance?" Diana asked.

Because the person telling the speaker what to say had a voice Jennifer would recognize?

If I'd been thinking Lance might be in the clear from the apparent attempt on him, this angle put him right back in it. Making today's accident a blind to steer attention away from him.

But the Valentines hadn't recognized him.

But if there were two people involved...

But who would the second one be and why?

Jennifer frowned deeply. "I guess he could have. But how would I tell?"

Chapter Thirty-Six

"WE'RE STUCK," JENNIFER said.

We'd gone round and round on the who, both of a caller and a partner, getting nowhere.

Mike leaned forward. "Start from the beginning again."

"Go over everything again? What good is that going to do?" Jennifer demanded.

Maybe it wouldn't advance our body of knowledge, but it would—or might—distract Jennifer from the discouragement visibly settling on her.

I pushed my hair back. "You're halfway through your shift at KWMT, the phone rings, you identify yourself and…"

Jennifer huffed, but didn't put her heart into it. "And this man's voice says, Jennifer Lawton? I said 'That's me.'" Close enough. "And he said, 'You're friends with Calliope Grandisher?' I said yes and he said, 'I have bad news for you.' And then he told me there'd been an incident and Calliope was dead. From a fall at Rocky Mountain National Park. I… I didn't know what to say. I just got off the phone. I went to the restroom and I called her parents."

"Why call them?" Diana asked.

"I guess I thought they'd tell me it wasn't true. But Mrs. Grandisher was screaming…"

No new information, but something tugged at me. The call itself or…?

"Let's go back to the call," Mike asked. "You didn't talk to him long on the phone. That's not much to go on."

"I told you and Elizabeth in Colorado. Neither of those guys was the voice that called me. I won't ever forget it. Ever."

"If it wasn't Bray or Quentel, then—"

I interrupted Mike. "Wait a minute. Wait a minute."

"I love when she says that," Diana murmured.

"I hate when she says it. It means we've missed something," Mike said.

"It means *I've* missed something." I sat up and grabbed my phone.

"It means we're going to figure out what *we* missed," Diana said calmly.

"Maybe. I hope."

"The question of who called her?" Mike asked.

"No. Another question," I said from the hallway on my way to the guest room.

I CALLED BRAY first.

"I need a minute for one straight-forward question."

"At this hour?"

It wasn't even eleven.

"I can either report you refused to comment on our report of the tragic death of a local young woman raising questions about safety or you can answer a simple question not related in any way to matters of safety."

"Oh, for heaven's sake—" he said in an abbreviated moo. "What?"

"Actually, a couple questions, depending on how you answer the first one. Did you call Jennifer Lawton to inform her of Calliope Grandisher's death?"

She'd said it hadn't been him or Ivan Quentel, but it was the foundation question that needed to be asked. Besides, it might stir the pot if one of them had been involved with a confederate.

"Call who?"

"The young woman who was with us in your office. She also works for KWMT and—"

"Never mind. It doesn't matter who she is, because I didn't call her. I made courtesy calls to the man's wife—" Apparently he still didn't know he'd called the ex-wife." "—and the young woman's parents."

"How did you know how to get in touch with the families?"

"We contacted local law enforcement from their IDs. They made official notification. I followed up with a call expressing condolences."

I bet he really warmed their hearts.

"When?"

"After the release went out."

Saturday.

Yet Jennifer and the Grandishers—according to their niece's online sharing—had calls Friday.

"Do you have her phone? Calliope Grandisher's?"

"All her belongings are being returned to her parents."

"Is the phone among those belongings? Did you ever have her phone?"

"You said one question and I don't see—"

"Check the inventory to see if park officials ever had her phone, then I'll let you go."

He grumbled as he moved around, then pounded a keyboard hard enough that I heard it. "Backpack, wallet, keys, water, power bars, nuts, rain gear, repellant, lotion… No. No phone."

"Thank you, Ranger—"

He hung up on me.

❖ ❖ ❖ ❖

IVAN QUENTEL HAD caller ID, because he answered by asking if we had news.

"No. But I do have more questions. Did you call Jennifer to notify her of Calliope Grandisher's death? Or Calliope's parents?"

"Me? No. I don't call. That's the office. I guess Bray, with everybody else out. Can't imagine he's any good at it. Heather and Scott—the boss and her top assistant, who usually do that job, are really good. But it takes a lot out of them. Glad it's not my job."

"I thought maybe with the connection you seemed to feel with

Calliope…"

"Even if it weren't policy about who calls, I wouldn't."

"But you could have? Using her phone, I mean, to find out who to contact?"

"I never had her phone."

"Oh, I heard you did."

"No. Never. Come to think of it… She didn't have a phone." *That's strange* edged into his voice.

"What about in her car?"

"Didn't see one there, either."

"Ivan, did that strike you as strange? Her not having a phone?"

"*Did* it? At the time? No. Never registered, to tell you the truth. Does it seem a little weird now? Yeah. Most hikers carry them. GPS, for starters. You can never count on coverage, but if you can get it, a phone can be a life-saver. Maybe Bray—?"

"He says there was no phone on the inventory." Hadn't been a hundred percent convinced by that, but I was closer to that figure now.

"I've never heard of one of those inventories being off, so… Tell you what, I'll connect with the other guys on that run and see if anybody saw her phone."

"Thank you, I'd appreciate that. What about Robertson? Did he have a phone?" I should have asked Bray that to get the official version. On the other hand, Ivan was less official, but far more helpful.

"Yeah. Smashed up pretty good with the fall, but he had one. Why the interest in phones?"

I sidestepped. "All the little details that need to be cleared up before we can even think about reporting a story. Somebody asks an innocuous question like, 'Could Robertson have slipped while taking photos with his phone?' or 'Did Calliope try to call for help?' Because if she tried and couldn't get anyone, that might have pushed her to try to help Robertson on her own. And then I realized we didn't know if either had a phone there. That's all. Part of the million little pieces needing to be checked on. Really appreciate your help."

❖   ❖   ❖   ❖

"WELL?" MIKE DEMANDED as soon as I returned to the living room. "Who called her?"

"No idea. Bray and Quentel say it wasn't them. I'm inclined to believe them. Especially since Jennifer says no. Though it's possible Bray used that distinctive, weird mooing sound—"

"Mooing?" Diana repeated.

"*That's* what he reminded me of," Mike said.

"—to disguise his voice by getting someone to focus on that. But you'd think he would have used it for calling Jennifer so he didn't need to assume it from then on. Because he's talked that way each time. But he might not have been thinking that far ahead. We could check with Ranger Attleboro if it's his normal voice. I think she would tell us, because—"

"You said you had another question?" Tom interrupted.

"Yeah. You're right. The question of who called Jennifer might turn out to not be all that important. But Calliope's phone is. Jennifer said whoever called her would have found her through the contacts on Calliope's phone. Vic said Calliope's phone was the gateway to wiping Jennifer's. So where is Calliope's phone? More, specifically, who has it."

After a moment's silence, Tom said, "You think whoever has Calliope's phone was the one who called Jennifer and that will point to whoever—"

I shook my head. "That's going too fast. There could be official reasons for someone to have her phone. Or unofficial but innocent. That's why I called Bray and Quentel. I could see innocent explanations for why either might have her phone. However, both said they did not have it. Both said that to their knowledge, Calliope didn't have a phone with her. That's—"

"No. No, no, no." Jennifer shook her head in case we missed the meaning of the word. "She'd've had her phone with her. Always. And especially up there. She told me for safety, but she also took scads of photos with it. Views and stuff, but also close-ups of plants or wildlife. No way she went hiking without it."

"Elizabeth's not saying Calliope didn't have her phone. She's reporting what those two men said." That unusual support came from Tom. "She's also thinking the two things might be connected—no phone and some guy calling you."

"Look at it this way," I said, "there's a scenario where Bray, Ivan, and the Valentines all told us the truth. That other witness did exist and he came away with Calliope's phone. That means he had Calliope's contacts, he had access in the cloud to get through your security, to mess up your phone. He also had your address."

"And we can't take the risk of not acting like that possibility is a certainty," Tom said. "From now on, we assume this guy exists, knows your connection to Calliope, wants to harm you, Jennifer. You go nowhere alone. You stay with Elizabeth for now, because he doesn't seem to have made that connection. I'll go talk to your folks when we end here."

"We should all turn off our GPS, too. Though you'd think if he's any good at ha—computer stuff, he already has that."

I ignored that last cheerful bit from Mike. "There's something else, Jennifer. I want you to get as much background on Felix Robertson as you can. You, not the others."

"But... Okay."

That went easier than I'd expected. "But no—"

"I know. No hacking."

That drew chuckles and on that eased note, the group broke up for the night.

Chapter Thirty-Seven

JENNIFER LEFT FIRST. She was going to return her mother's car, then I'd pick her up from the Lawtons' house and take her back to my house for another sleepover.

Considering tonight's conversation, indirect routes would be followed.

I considered taking Shadow, but decided a calmer introduction to the new house would be wiser. Poor dog hadn't had a lot of consistency in his life.

Tom started to follow Jennifer out, making good on his promise to go talk to her parents.

With the door open, he let Shadow slip past him, then turned back.

"What about this EMT? Ivan Quentel. We haven't really considered him or—"

A frenzy of barking exploded from outside. A cry, abruptly cut short.

Tom pivoted and was out the door. I was the next closest, barely clearing the open door before Mike caught up.

I saw everything at once under the security lights and a warmer pool of brightness near the porch, taking it all in. No prioritizing, no triage.

A vehicle skidding away, raising a dust spout behind it.

Shadow chasing it.

Diana holding her arms out in a gesture to stay down as she approached Jennifer, who was trying to stand, saying, "I'm okay."

Mike, already there, with his arms around her.

Tom pulling a long gun—shotgun? rifle? The identification didn't come to me immediately—from his truck, barely breaking stride at he ran after the vehicle.

I took the center of the drive, Tom ahead on my left, Shadow well ahead on my right.

Shadow wasn't barking now, running stretched out, cutting the slight curve in the drive, making up ground on the vehicle.

A mini-truck or something else square.

I could hear Jennifer behind me. "I'm okay. I'm okay. Really."

The vehicle swerved.

The driver steered into my dog.

"*Shadow.*"

Shadow feinted to the side and put on his brakes, but the rear end of the vehicle swung, slapping at him.

He went airborne. Then dropped out of sight.

Not high. He didn't go high. I kept telling myself that as I ran toward where he'd disappeared. *He wouldn't have hit the ground real hard. Surely not hard enough to—*

Tom was already past where Shadow had gone down, but on the near side of the drive. He took a shot on the move. Pulled up and took another shot at the retreating vehicle.

I thought I heard Jennifer's voice again, sounding impatient. A good sign.

"Get the tag number," Mike called.

Screw the tag number, I was headed straight for where I'd last seen Shadow.

And then there he was.

Rolling up to his feet on the far side of the ditch, lithe and easy, like he was rolling out of a bed.

And heading after the vehicle again, just as Tom shot again.

"Shadow! Come!" If he got between Tom's gun and that vehicle…

"*Now.*"

He stopped. Swung his head toward me, looking surprised. Bobbed his head once, then headed back to me at a slow trot. Was he favoring his left front leg?

I breathed for what felt like the first time in hours.

"You get back here, too, Burrell," I called for good measure.

No sign of the vehicle slowing, much less turning around, but no sense taking a chance and he was standing out there with no kind of shelter, like Gary Cooper all by himself in *High Noon*.

Burrell didn't respond as quickly as Shadow, who limped/trotted toward me. But after a moment, the human slowly turned and started back.

Shadow had reached me. I dropped to my knees and put my arms around him. A quick hug of his neck, then slowly feeling down his front legs—he yanked back on the left one—his shoulders, his midsection—

"Might not want to go any farther back," Burrell said. "Looks like he hit a pile of cow manure with that roll."

So that's what I smelled.

"No sign of injury back here," Tom said from that end of Shadow.

I stood. "He's favoring his left front leg."

"Might've strained something. We'll let the vet take a look at him."

"Is Shadow okay?" Jennifer asked as we joined her, Mike, and Diana, all standing now. "He's limping."

Dirt smeared one side of her face, then stopped and started in a dotted streak down her left side, presumably because she'd hit the dirt partially rolled up, leaving only some parts exposed.

"We'll get him checked out. What about you, Jenny?" Tom looked at Diana as he asked the question.

"She's shaken, bruised, dirty, no major injuries," the mother of two recapped succinctly.

"Could've been a lot worse if it hadn't been for Shadow," Jennifer said. "That guy grabbed me, but Shadow growled and lunged at him."

"Did he hit you? Throw you to the ground?" Mike asked.

"No. I dropped down. I was trying to get to my knife."

"Knife?" I repeated blankly.

"It's in a holder in the wheel well. Dad got it for Mom, but I couldn't get the darned thing loose."

"Why?"

"That guy was yanking at me."

"I think she meant why your dad put a knife in the wheel well." Tom switched his interpreting skills from Jennifer to me. "It can come in handy on the road. 'Specially if somebody locks you out of your vehicle."

"That's when I was a kid," Jennifer protested.

"Wouldn't a key be more useful?"

"I had the keys. I needed the knife against that guy."

"I meant—Never mind."

"How about if the rest of the discussion waits until we call the sheriff's department and see to Shadow," Diana said.

"I'll see to Shadow," I said. "The rest of you go to the sheriff's department. Get Shelton. No excuses. Don't clean up, Jennifer. Show and tell will have a lot more impact than just tell."

"Anybody get the tag number?"

"It was covered," Tom said. "Dark cloth or painted over."

"By the way, how did you hope to shoot out his tires from that distance?" I asked.

"I didn't."

"Not with a shotgun," Mike said, apparently for my benefit.

Tom lowered his head in agreement. "I hoped to ding up his vehicle enough to add to the identification."

"Did you?"

"Left rear panel. Maybe the back door."

Movement caught my eye and I turned.

Shadow abruptly sat, then went down to his side.

TOM HAD SCOOPED up Shadow and put him in my lap in the passenger seat of his truck.

Mike was taking Jennifer straight to the sheriff's department.

Diana was staying at the ranch. With her shotgun at hand.

"You'll be okay?" I asked her again through the open window as Tom got behind the wheel.

She showed her deep and abiding patience by saying only, "We'll be fine."

"She'll be better than that ass will be if he's stupid enough to come back," Mike said. "Don't worry about the rest of us. Take care of Shadow."

Tom drove at Diana speeds to the vet, who lived by his office.

The vet was calm and reassuring and let us come into the examination room.

I stroked Shadow's head as Tom described what happened—the part involving the dog—and the vet ran experienced hands over him.

"Don't feel anything broken. Most likely bruised. We'll monitor him tonight. If he rests okay, then we'll take X-rays in the morning. Could have reacted to the adrenaline ebbing."

"We have to leave him here tonight?" That felt like lousy thanks for his heroism.

"Yep. Less he moves around the better until we know for sure there's nothing more serious than bruising. Besides, Hezekiah here will keep an eye on him." He nodded to a wizened man who stepped forward at the sound of his name. "And it looks like you should spend the rest of tonight getting some sleep yourself."

Hezekiah slowly extended one hand toward Shadow. My antisocial dog licked it.

Okay. Hezekiah was a good guy.

"I'M TAKING YOU back to Diana's to stay with her and the kids in the house tonight," Tom announced once we returned to his truck.

"No. That—"

"You're not spending the night alone in the house in town."

"If I'm at the ranch, Jennifer will be alone at that house in town."

"She'll go to her parents."

"Even if you could persuade her, there's still the fact someone broke in there today. So far, the only place no one has shown up is that house in town."

"And my ranch."

I wasn't touching that one. Because my focus was on the important issue.

"All that's for later, anyway. Head for the sheriff's department and in the meantime, I'll try to get Mike."

Chapter Thirty-Eight

"WE DO NOT need you here."

That was Sheriff Russ Conrad's greeting to me, beating around the bush as usual.

When I'd called Mike, he'd said they were at the sheriff's department, expecting Shelton and Conrad any second.

Reading between the lines of what he said, I suspected he'd leveraged a combination of his position as hometown sports hero and nephew of Gisella Decker to persuade the dispatcher on duty to get both the sheriff and sergeant to return to the office at this hour.

As Tom and I entered, Mike was finishing with "...hurting Jennifer. Look at her—and it could have been a whole lot worse. And we won't know about the dog until we see how he does through the night."

Even in my current state, I appreciated the fine, dramatic spin he'd put on Shadow's condition without an untrue word.

Then the sheriff spoke and my attention shifted.

"We'll take statements from Jennifer and Tom, as the one who saw the vehicle best. We do not need you all here." Then, focused on me alone, "We do not need you here."

"Was that pickup truck at the accident scene claimed? Was it identified? We have to know that."

Of course, we did know that. But it would be hard to proceed unless Conrad and Shelton acknowledged it. Otherwise we'd get sidetracked in their petty insistence on knowing how we knew things.

"You don't have to know anything. We sure don't have to tell you anything about any details at that scene. Just because you told Sergeant Shelton—"

"Just because *we've* found everything that's been found. Just because we went to Colorado to find things out when you can't be bothered to—"

"There's a little thing called jurisdiction—"

"One of the reasons journalists can be more effective. We go where the news is, not following some imaginary line on a map."

"—and I don't have any in Colorado and—"

"You can *talk* to them—"

"—I won't go poking into their business because I wouldn't want them poking into mine."

"So, while you play nicey-nice, one of your citizens has died, and a murderer could be getting away free."

"You have no evidence—"

"No evidence? All those phone calls to the Lawtons that I know they reported to you. The break-in at their house today. The attempt on Lance Joudrey—"

"You don't know that was intended—"

"—that sent that other poor guy to the hospital. And now, tonight, this attack on Jennifer? Evidence? You haven't *looked* for evidence. Evidence would have to walk into your office, lean over your desk, and take you by the throat before you noticed it."

"Elizabeth—"

I heard Tom's voice from a distance, through a haze of anger and fear.

I leaned over Conrad's desk the way evidence would need to.

"If you don't get on the ball, get the people down in Colorado to actually investigate, you're going to be investigating Jennifer's murder."

Tom put his hand on my back. I was breathing hard enough to break the contact and come back to it, over and over.

"Why would someone try to kill her?" Shelton asked.

"*That's* what we're trying to find out. But what happened tonight means none of the other things that have happened have solved this guy's problem, because he's still trying to hurt Jennifer."

Tom spoke. "If it *is* someone still out there, if it's not coincidences, then they're either incredibly lucky or they know where we are."

Tom's statement snapped everyone's attention to him. I even forgot how angry I was at Conrad.

"You think somebody's been following us?" Mike asked.

"You mean me," Jennifer said. "They've been following me. Oh. With a tracking device? Or…"

She looked at the phone in her hand.

I'd never seen her look at a phone that way. With distrust and wariness. Her usual look was a cross between miners coming into daylight after a cave-in and delight at watching kittens cavort.

Tom said, "Not your phone or they'd know you've been at Elizabeth's. Maybe tracking's not likely, but it's still possible. And that makes it worth taking precautions."

"You didn't have this phone until this morning, Jennifer," I pointed out. "And they didn't follow us to Colorado. At least there was no sign of it."

"The rental," Mike said. "We didn't take my SUV. If they had tracking devices on our vehicles they wouldn't have known."

"Right. They'd have started with Jennifer's address from Calliope's contacts list, but they'd have had trouble because she's been on the outs with her parents so she wasn't borrowing any of their vehicles. But why don't they know she's staying with me?"

"I haven't told anybody, haven't mentioned it anywhere," she said. "I didn't want… You know. It's family stuff."

"And that house isn't on record in your name yet, Elizabeth. No way for anyone to connect it to you," Tom said.

"True for an outsider, but everybody in the county knows the Undlins are inheriting the house and plan to sell it to me."

"Nobody outside of us and the Undlins knew the two of you have been staying there. They'd expect you to still be at Diana's."

"Or," Mike said, "they followed one or several of us out to Diana's tonight and—"

"Stop."

Russ Conrad had a lot of practice barking orders. It effectively reminded all of us of his presence. But was that a hint of displeasure in Shelton's eyes that his superior stopped us?

"You have no evidence of any of this," Conrad continued. "Comes to that, we do have evidence that some of this fairy tale you're weaving is dead wrong. Those phone calls the Lawtons got? All the hang-ups? Those were her friends." His head-tip pointed to Jennifer. "They were too shy—" No trouble picking up his silent added phrase *or too weird.* "—to leave messages."

"It still leaves all the physical and physically threatening actions."

"With no evidence—"

"I *told* you what happened," Jennifer protested.

"There's a vehicle out there with buckshot holes in the left rear panel. Also should be evidence of them covering up the tag."

"If we had a vehicle to look at." Shelton humphed. "Would've helped if somebody saw the driver."

"We were a little busy."

✧   ✧   ✧   ✧

MIKE AND TOM escorted my SUV to the house in Tom's truck, leaving Mike's SUV at the sheriff's department, just in case.

They searched the whole house and checked every door and window. They also informed Jennifer she was back to sleeping upstairs with me, while Mike stayed in the guest room again.

More sheet-changing.

That gave me time to think. Or at least to pick up another piece of this puzzle and look at it long enough to decide it might actually be a puzzle piece.

"This is part of something more." I saw the question coming from both of them and pre-empted it. "I'm not sure exactly what. But, listen. Jennifer had her purse stolen at lunch today at the Sherman Café."

The others looked at her. "You did?" Mike said. "Why didn't you say something before?"

She said, "It's no big deal—"

I said, "There was so much to cover…"

"What happened?" Tom asked.

4444

"Some jerk took it right off the back of my chair. We called the police, but Hollister isn't exactly a crime-fighting master. Besides, I don't see what—"

"That happened *after* the break-in at her parents'. It would make sense if it happened *before*. Somebody wanted her keys to the house. But they went to all the trouble of breaking in by jimmying the back door to avoid being seen by the neighbor trimming bushes—"

"Even if they had my keys from my purse it wouldn't have helped them," Jennifer said. "I lost the key to the back door. I've been meaning to get a copy, but most of the time Mom and Dad let me in. Or, if it's late, I go in the front and go right up to my room without waking them."

"Go back to why it's significant they took her purse after the break-in, Elizabeth," Mike said.

I had to fight to pull together the thoughts again. Being so close to sheets and beds had reminded me exactly how tired I was.

"They break in. Then they take the purse. Then they come after Jennifer tonight. It can only mean one thing. They still haven't found what they're looking for."

DAY SIX

WEDNESDAY

Chapter Thirty-Nine

THEY STILL HAVEN'T found what they're looking for.

It had seemed such a breakthrough last night.

This morning I saw there was one little hitch.

We didn't know what they were looking for.

Details, details.

I had ideas. They just weren't clear and sharp in the unfamiliar light of morning. Even with no bacon, eggs, and coffee aromas to distract me this morning. Mike had said something about leaving first thing.

First, I called for a report on Shadow. He was resting comfortably. The chances of X-rays had dropped but weren't gone completely. They wanted him under observation another twenty-four hours.

I started one idea rolling by calling Linda Caswell from the bathroom to ask a favor.

Linda backed away from the favor. "I... I don't know them all that well..." But she didn't absolutely say no.

Couldn't blame her for not wanting to do this. "It could be important. I can't promise you it is and you shouldn't let them think there's anything significant about it. If you can work it in casually..."

She emitted an unamused laugh. "That's all."

"It could be important," I repeated.

She sighed. "I'll call and let you know if I get anything. Or if I don't."

❖   ❖   ❖   ❖

MIKE HAD LEFT.

Jennifer was eating toast. With hot sauce.

I shuddered and pretended I hadn't seen that.

"Jennifer, what's your neighbor's name? The one who was trimming bushes Tuesday."

"Viv Eckhart."

"I want to talk to her."

"I'll send you her phone number."

"In person. And you're coming with."

She cut me a suspicious look. "Is this about not leaving me alone in the house? Because it's only a few hours before I start my shift and Dale said he'd pick me up and drive me to the station. Besides, I have a lot I could be doing. Daisy messaged me—"

"Yes, it's about not leaving you alone in the house. It's also about wanting your neighbor to talk to me. She knows you. She doesn't know me."

❖   ❖   ❖   ❖

ON THE WAY to Viv Eckhart's, I asked, "You said Daisy messaged you? Have they made any progress with your phone?"

"Yeah, she messaged. No, they haven't made progress on my phone. She sent a rundown of the material they've found." Her features pinched into a frown.

"What's wrong?"

"There's all sorts of stuff on Calliope's parents. And … and Lance. And his parents. It's like they're investigating them."

"We need them to be thorough. It's important to look at everybody," I said gently.

"It's just… I thought… It's like Daisy doesn't understand why I'm not excited about this stuff, why I don't even want to see it. She's been great. They all have. I know they can't stay here forever. I understand why they're talking about leaving tomorrow. And all the work she's done, I really appreciate that. I'd literally be drowned by now if she wasn't going through it."

I bit my lip to not casually mention that she would not have drowned literally. Maybe figuratively, but not literally.

Keeping focus, I nudged, "But?"

"But they'll go, and then where are we?"

Ah. "Not over, if that's what you're thinking. You already said your friends will still help with research. And Mike, Diana, Tom, and I aren't going anywhere. We've hardly even started. It's early days."

Yet I understood some of her concern. There was a sense that things were speeding up. Unfortunately, without a corresponding sense of where they were leading us.

"I know."

Her voice sounded very small.

VIV ECKHART WELCOMED us with offers of tea or coffee.

To Jennifer's disgust, I said yes to tea. To me it was an opportunity to observe this woman and her surroundings, to ease into the grilling portion of the program, which almost always paid off in better information. It was also caffeine.

To Jennifer it was a waste of time.

Viv Eckhart invited us into the kitchen while she made tea. We chatted amiably about her landscaping, including the newly trimmed bushes, the neighborhood, and her years in it.

By the time I was sipping the fragrant, spicy tea, we were both relaxed and Jennifer was twitchy.

"We'd like to ask you a few questions." I hoped by including Jennifer she'd become more engaged.

"About the break-in? Sorry, but the sheriff's department asked if I'd seen anything and I didn't. I really wish I could have helped, because it's terrible what it does to someone's sense of security in their own home. Could it have been kids? A tramp or something? Somebody desperate and not thinking straight?"

"I'm certain the sheriff's department is examining those possibilities. I'm sure you did tell them everything you saw. You were in the perfect position, trimming those bushes, to see anyone coming or going—at least from the front."

"That's exactly it. I could see the front of the house, but not round back where he broke in. I feel terrible I couldn't prevent it and didn't even see anyone to get a description. I told your mom and dad that, Jennifer."

She roused enough to say, "We know you would've helped if you could. There's nothing you can do about not seeing anything."

"What I was wondering about were the bushes," I said. Jennifer made a sound. "That was a lot of bush trimming to accomplish in one day."

"Oh, I didn't do it all yesterday. I'd started the day before."

My pulse tripped. "Did the sheriff's department ask if you noticed anything Monday?"

"No. But…"

I held my breath as she searched her memory.

And released it when she said, "No, I don't remember anything worth noticing from Monday, either."

The possibility that whoever broke in had made a previous trip to check out the house or look for Jennifer had been worth the trip, no matter what Jennifer thought. It just hadn't panned out.

"There was one thing." Viv Eckhart leaned back, perhaps because both Jennifer and I leaned forward quickly. "It wasn't much. And it was Sunday, when I went out to check the ground. It was too soft from the snow to start trimming that day. That's why I pushed it back to Monday, and only did the drier areas that day, leaving most for yester—"

"What happened Sunday?"

"As I said, it wasn't much. I noticed one of those trucks passing twice. I suppose it could have been by more than twice but that's what I saw in the time I was outside. One of those green pickups they rent out."

Chapter Forty

I DROPPED JENNIFER off at the station—with her promises to find those missing articles on Felix Robertson and to stay at KWMT-TV until Mike, Tom, Diana, or I came for her.

Then I went by the vet's for some Shadow therapy. That was therapy for me by seeing him, not for him. Though I did get the tail thunk when he saw me.

Next, I met Needham for our delayed coffee.

We took our cups into his office in the historic part of the nineteenth-century brick building. Glass enclosed the top two-thirds with solid old wood walls below.

"Anything on Calliope's death or what happened yesterday?" he asked.

"Nothing to share. You?"

"Not a thing. So why are you here?"

"Throwing myself on your generosity—" His mouth twitched. "—for background on Sedick Oil. I know it's a subsidiary of Faison-Clafton, with all that entails. But I was thinking more close to home. Leona says you're the one to ask."

He studied me, mentally tracing potential connections to the current news.

He started slowly, "It's in Cottonwood County, but not of Cottonwood County. Folks sometimes say an oil derrick makes good shade for cows. That can mean two things. The derrick's not worth more than offering a bit of shade. Or it's vital because it brings in needed money to support the cattle operation." He raised his hands wide, then let them drop. "All depends on who's looking at it and how. Plus, you ask a rancher, you ask the owner of a town business, you ask one of those executives of Sedick, and you get three different answers. Or six. Or nine."

"Are you telling me there's ranch, oil, and town and they never get together?"

"It's not that clear-cut or neat. They're all tied together. They need each other. They conflict with each other. They fight. They unite."

"Because of the money?"

"No denying that matters, especially in the big picture. In politics and all that. But it's more. It's land. It's tradition. It's progress. It's hope. And it's fear. Some of it justified. And it all goes a long way back."

"Teapot Dome Scandal," I murmured.

He snorted a laugh. "Mrs. Parens, eh? Yeah, then and earlier, too. It's all been mixed together from the start of oil. Water, oil, cows, and women. Trouble, every one of them."

The mischief not quite hidden by his bushy eyebrows confirmed he wanted a rise out of me. I did not oblige.

"Right. How about trouble between Owen Grandisher and Brady Joudrey, fighting for spots on the corporate ladder?"

His brows rose. I chose to think in appreciation of my question. "Suppose you know it was generally considered Grandisher was here filling in his resume to be the next CEO of the parent company and that all stopped?"

"Because of the bribery scandal and trials? But he's still working for the company. Considering the way they fired people, he couldn't have been deeply involved, so what happened?"

He stared ahead. Calculating what and how much of his store of facts he'd share, I suspected.

He clicked his tongue, then confirmed that suspicion. "Wouldn't have been a big story here, anyway, because of what I said before about being *in* the county, but not *of* it. I worked the story some anyway. Never could get enough to run. Maybe you can make something of it.

"Grandisher wasn't directly handing out bribes, but a letter surfaced that showed he had knowledge of involvement of someone above him. He argued against the practice, but in the end, did nothing. When the firing started, some who did similar got booted. He and others didn't."

"Interesting."

"The question has always been where the letter came from. Copies were sent to media, Department of Justice, and police. Anonymously. But with enough to let them squeeze Grandisher into being a witness against the guy above him. Didn't get him fired, but it sure did derail that fast track of his."

"*Could* they have fired him?"

"There'd already been pushback over other firings by then. That one guy won a lawsuit, remember?" I nodded. "Plus, the letter didn't have proof. Nope, they couldn't fire him. Just make his life a living hell for a while, then drop him into career purgatory. Thing is, it became career purgatory for Joudrey, too. He'd been lined up to take over here from Grandisher. You know his wife's from here?" Another nod. "He's not going anywhere. Now he's stuck as number two for the rest of his working days. You know about the families?"

"What about them?"

"Used to be best of friends. More. Close as family. Lived—still live—a couple houses away from each other near the country club. Did everything together, with Calliope and Lance the same year in school and all. The wives best friends, on every committee together. The men worked real well together according to every soul I talked to. Working for the same goal, really. Make Grandisher look good, so he'd move up and out, letting Joudrey into that spot.

"When Grandisher got called down to headquarters in Houston. he thought it was to finalize the next step in his progression to the crown. Instead, he got slapped with the accusations from the letter, saw the steps not only crumble under him but nearly bury him.

"When he came back, first thing, he crossed paths with Joudrey. Quite the confrontation according to my sources. Grandisher accused Joudrey of sending the letter. Came to blows. That changed things for the families, too. The relationships became like a marshmallow burnt on the outside—looked solid, but the insides were goo."

"But… Why would Owen Grandisher think Brady Joudrey sent the letter? Wouldn't Brady have known it would mess up his chances to take over here?"

"Maybe he got impatient. It was tough times all through Faison-Clafton. They weren't promoting anybody until they'd turned them inside out and inspected them with a microscope. That, on top of the general atmosphere wore on folks. Executives, right down through the ranks. Look at incidents of bar fights before, during, and after all that and it's like seeing a mountain ridge rise out of nothing, run along jagged for a couple years, then slide back down to the basin floor. Did do a story on that a couple years back."

"You think Joudrey feared Grandisher wasn't going to be promoted out of his way? Sent the letter in hopes Grandisher would be fired?"

"Could be. Grandisher sure seemed to believe it. Mind you, Joudrey outright denied sending the letter. Didn't like being accused of it, either."

"Thus, the fight."

"Yup."

Certainly explained some of the undercurrents.

I did rough math and figured the letter incident must have been around the time Calliope, Lance, and Jennifer hit high school. In other words, as Calliope and Lance started dating.

Must have been hard on Calliope and Lance to have their parents feuding.

"What about a more recent fight between Lance and his father?"

"Don't know precisely, though the name Grandisher was part of the shouting. Nobody who'd talk to me knew if they meant Owen or Calliope."

Another aspect occurred to me. "Were the accusations in the letter true?"

"Now that would be real interesting to know, wouldn't it? Also, sure would be interesting to know where that letter came from if it wasn't Joudrey."

Chapter Forty-One

WHEN I RETURNED a call that came in during my time with Needham, the voice on the phone was not happy, while trying mightily to hide it under a veneer of politeness.

"Sergeant Shelton would like to know if you can stop by the sheriff's department at your very earliest convenience for a talk."

Ah.

Wayne Shelton could have approached this several ways. He could have demanded I come down there. Worse, he could have had Sheriff Conrad demand I come down there with the anti-cherry on top of having Conrad question me.

He didn't employ any of those approaches because he wanted something from me and knew I didn't take well to being shoved. Especially not after that, uh, discussion with Conrad last night. In fact, he probably had to persuade Conrad to let him handle it this way.

On the other hand, Shelton could have called me himself. Or he could have had Richard Alvaro call me. Better, he could have had Richard come talk to me.

He didn't do any of those because he wanted to keep this official, not on the level of asking a favor. Which he had done a time or two, but never happily.

This time I suspected he wanted more—in other words, everything I knew or thought—about the green truck.

Apparently taking my momentary silence for reluctance, Deputy Ferrante added, "It's important. Could be real important to, uh, a case."

"Tell Sergeant Shelton that I'll be there shortly."

I CHECKED IN with Jennifer and Mike before turning on the SUV.

Jennifer, to be sure we had multiple copies of the museum security camera footage squirreled away. Just in case Shelton and/or Conrad tried to make a footage grab after I told them about the truck trying to hit her Saturday morning.

I didn't see what advantage that would be to them, but if things became heated, I couldn't rule it out, either.

Jennifer already had us covered.

"I also searched for those articles again. Used Thurston's computer and printer."

"But he locks—"

"Everybody knows where he hides his office key. I figured if there's some bug or something attached to *me*—"

"Is that a real thing?"

"No. But if it were and something started to go wrong with his equipment no one would notice because he does so little work. Though if he *did* notice, it would drive him *wild*."

I left her in happy contemplation of that.

Mike informed me his buddy at the dealership checked over his SUV and found no evidence of a tracking device.

I filled him in just in case this *discussion* went sideways and the sheriff's department wanted to extend the pleasure of my company past what I considered pleasurable.

"How long you want me to wait to call James Longbaugh?"

"One hour."

He whistled. "Not very long."

"All the time I'm willing to give them." I had a twitchy feeling things were either heating up or we were settling in for the long haul. I wasn't going to share that with him, because he'd want explanations. Twitchy feelings didn't come with explanations. Besides, I didn't want to devote a hefty stretch of today to Shelton. "Maybe it will teach them to take my cooperation when I offer it."

"You think so?"

"No. If James needs persuading to act for me—"

"I'll get Tom on the job. Good luck."

SHELTON PUT A coffee on the table in front of me and sat.

Since he hadn't asked how I take my coffee, he'd given me the same thing he liked. Warm cream with a hint of coffee.

"I prefer ice water, please."

I didn't say that solely to be difficult. I'd already had my quota of fun with the sheriff's department when Ferrante had, over the sound of his grinding teeth, acceded to my cheery declaration that I'd go on back to find Sergeant Shelton on my own.

The request for water was mostly because I didn't want to wipe out the pleasurable memory of Needham's coffee but was thirsty.

Shelton growled.

Not taking his eyes off me, he shouted, "*Sampson.*"

Lloyd Sampson opened the door. "Sir?"

Shelton said nothing, so I smiled warmly at Lloyd and said, "May I have ice water, please, Deputy? Lots of ice and if you have an extra bottle of water, that would be ideal."

Lloyd glanced at Shelton, didn't receive a countermand, so retreated, leaving the door open.

Shelton and I looked at each other—not a staring contest, we each blinked quite normally—while listening to Lloyd bustling around the break area down the hall.

I was listening, anyway. Shelton might have been trying his hand at mind reading.

Lloyd returned with a large plastic cup brimming with ice and two plastic bottles of water.

"That's perfect, thank you so much." Another smile.

"You're welcome." He returned the smile as he backed out, caught sight of Shelton, stopped smiling, and was out the door in record time, closing it softly behind him.

I sipped the water that fit in the cup around the ice, then poured more so the cubes would chill it.

We sat there maybe another minute.

He was trying to see if I would break and ask what he wanted.

I wasn't breaking.

To his credit, he didn't hold that against me.

When he spoke, it was in his normal tone. Which for him was irritated and unsociable. "How the hell did you know?"

"I can't possibly answer that without knowing what you're referring to."

He grunted. Darned near an admission that I was both right and reasonable. If this went on it would be a sure sign that lions and lambs were about to cozy up together all over the world.

He skipped all the introductory stuff. "That green pickup truck was rented in the name of Vincent Winfield."

"One 'n' or two in Winfield? And any idea who the renter really was?"

He glowered, but answered, "Surveillance tape and folks at the dealership have ID'd the man renting the truck as a drunk known to law enforcement as Chaps, who hangs around at the Alley Bar behind Easley's Garage."

"He wears chaps?"

"No. He calls everybody *chaps*. Didn't look like his normal self at all. Real cleaned up, he was. He rented the truck as Vincent Winnfield—two 'n's'—with perfect ID. Now, how did you know?"

"I didn't know. I suspected."

I used that last word purposefully. He'd once said I had a suspicious mind and that it was my one redeeming quality.

"What made you suspect?" His best question yet.

"What's been happening to Jennifer and her reaction to the truck at the crash site."

"What reaction?"

"She frowned at it."

"Well, that covers everything, doesn't it?"

I returned his glare with one of my own and held my tongue.

He backtracked and echoed my earlier statement as a question,

"What's been happening to Jennifer?"

"We told you last night." In fairness, I added, "Most of it."

"Tell me all of it."

"Her best friend dies in unusual circumstances. She gets a call from somebody telling her about it, but no one official or unofficial you'd think might call will admit to it. And even then, it's downright weird calling a friend so soon after the death or possibly at all. But, okay, forget that you ignored what we said at the beginning. Then her phone goes kaflooey while we're in Colorado—"

"Everybody has phone problems."

"Not Jennifer. Not problems she can't figure out. And then it turns out someone wiped the memory, probably remotely. Add onto that someone trying to run her down Saturday morning—"

"What?"

"Check with the museum staff. They have video of someone— someone driving what looks like that green truck—trying to hit her. Oh, by the way, that truck or one like it was seen going past the Lawtons' house Sunday. Ask the neighbor. Then, the calls to the Lawton house, Jennifer's purse stolen yesterday at lunch at the café, her home broken into, and the attack on her last night. If you can't add those together to—"

"Hold on there. Why would someone want to hurt Jennifer? Or Lance if what happened to Wallinski was meant for him?"

"That's what we've been trying to find out and it's about time you're asking."

And then I knew.

Sitting there across from Shelton, I knew.

It was so obvious. Why the heck hadn't I put the pieces together earlier? He—whoever he was—was after Jennifer's phone.

But—

No. I couldn't think about that now. Shelton might not be a mind reader, but he was an excellent face reader. If he got an inkling, I'd never get out of here.

I stood, taking the cup of ice and the full bottle of water with me.

"I have more questions."

"I have work to do. To try to get answers to the questions you could have been—should have been—asking days ago. But I'll tell you something, Sergeant Shelton. Not that Vincent Winnfield is not the dead man's real name—you know that. But that Vincent is the first name of the character John Travolta plays in the movie *Pulp Fiction* and Winnfield—double 'n'—is the last name of his partner Samuel L. Jackson."

"That so? Never took you for a Quentin Tarantino fan."

"I'm not. *Pulp Fiction* is my ex-husband's favorite film. I saw and heard about it far more than I would have liked."

"Well, a movie review doesn't get me anywhere."

"Not a concrete step forward, no. But it is suggestive."

"How so?"

He might already have known and just wanted me to say it.

Fine with me. I'd give him that much. Especially because I didn't see how it connected to what I knew.

"Those characters killed people as part of their job."

Chapter Forty-Two

"**DIANA, ARE YOU** someplace you can talk?"

I'd driven five blocks away and around two corners from the sheriff's department. Not that I thought Shelton could read my mind or face through buildings, but why take chances?

"Yeah. What's up?"

"I have it."

"Have what?"

"Scratch that. I have one *part* of it. The obvious part. For all I know, though, it's the left ear of a live grizzly."

"You know what's going on?"

"One part of—"

"Got it. Grizzly. But what's the left ear look like?"

"Jennifer's phone. Whoever was behind the break-in, the purse-snatching, the attempts on Jennifer wants her phone."

"Wh—? Oh."

"Exactly. Calliope must have sent her something that has worried the whoever. That's why they wiped the phone."

"But then why aren't they satisfied?"

"That's the problem. It's especially a problem because the most obvious people are Blue and Cran and Daisy and Sergei and Vic."

"I wouldn't say *obvious*," she murmured.

"Because they know about phones. They'd also know how to wipe the phone remotely. They have the skills. Especially because the other top choices don't have those skills—the Grandishers, the Joudreys, the Lawtons—"

"*What?*"

"—and Lance. Well, the Lawtons might be stretching a point, but you get the drift. Oil execs, their wives, and a roustabout. Would they know how to remotely wipe a phone? Would Ivan Quentel? Or Bray? Or the Valentines?"

"You said the Valentines were adept with getting that photo…"

"Big leap. Very big leap. But I suppose it's possible. Bray or Quentel seem more likely, but with what motive? We've found absolutely no connection to Robertson or Calliope. Which reminds me, another call to Angela Robertson might be in order. I sure would like more on her before… Anyway, as I said, the hacker crew members have the skills and they came *here*, which makes them suspect—"

"Friends do go to help friends through difficult times you know, Elizabeth."

"These friends? They aren't exactly social beings. Well, maybe Cran and Blue are some, but that could be a ploy. Besides, look at all Jennifer's hacker friends who aren't here. That's their normal mode. That makes *these* guys suspect in my book. Any of them could have taken her purse. And we don't know for sure that they didn't get here until Sunday. I'd usually ask Jennifer to check the travel records, but there's no way I can ask her to check her friends in her current state, especially since she's farming that sort of work out to these very hackers. So *that's* suspicious, too."

"*But…* I hear a *but* coming."

"A major *but*. They *have* the phone. At least Cran and blue do. They've had it since yesterday before we met at your house. So, what was the attack on Jennifer last night for?"

"They're afraid she's seen whatever it is that's on the phone?"

"I hate to say it, but if that were the case, they've had chances to kill her, including last night. Easier to kill her than try to grab her."

"I can see why you're not telling this to her. Or Tom."

"So then I come back to the non-hackers. But there's no sign they'd have the skills to have wiped the phone."

"Two different people or groups with different goals?"

I groaned. "That would be like trying to put together two jigsaw puzzles with the pieces mixed together."

"Be patient, Elizabeth. It's only been a few days. We are making progress—you're making progress. After all, you have that left ear."

"It's the rest of the grizzly I'm worried about."

✧   ✧   ✧   ✧

MY PHONE RANG.

Thinking it was Diana, preferably with all the answers, I clicked without looking at the number.

"Elspeth Daniels?"

Now I looked.

If I hadn't recognized the 703 area code for Virginia, I probably would have dismissed the call at that point. Instead, I said, "Do you mean Elizabeth Danniher?"

"If you say so. Got your load here. We're about an hour out."

"An hour? *Today*? Here?"

He must hear that sort of panic frequently or, possibly the opposite dismay—*Where* is the truck? *How* many weeks?—because he was unmoved by my questions or tone.

"Yeah."

"But—"

He was also unmoved by my protest.

"Have the driveway and curb in front of the house clear. Any low-hanging branches have to be gone."

"In an hour?"

"Yeah."

"How do you think I can get branches cut in an hour?"

"Hey, if we can't get the truck in, we won't get your stuff out."

I didn't argue. We'd already ticked off one or two of the sixty minutes he'd given me.

"Do you need directions?"

"Not unless you're off the grid. Heard of GPS, lady?" He had one more parting shot. "And we don't do setup."

✧   ✧   ✧   ✧

SET UP? I was far more concerned about take down. Or squeeze in.

How on earth was everything going to fit in that little house? How was I going to transfer what didn't fit into … the garage, I supposed. And what if I put something in the garage that I later wanted in the house or vice versa?

That was the sort of job most people said to use a neighborhood high school boy for. Since most, if not all, of the high school boys I knew in Cottonwood County I'd once suspected of murder or other crimes, that would be a tough order to fill.

But I was getting ahead of myself.

First, I had to get stuff into the garage.

✧   ✧   ✧   ✧

THE GARAGE WAS full.

Neat, orderly, well-labeled, and utterly full.

The few areas not occupied by furniture the previous owner, Renata, must have used to stage clients' houses, held real estate yard signs, reams of paper for fliers, boxes of welcome bunting, and two cases of Girl Scout cookies.

I had one hand on the top case of cookies when my phone rang.

"What?"

"It's Linda."

"Oh. Hi. Sorry for snapping. I just found out the truck with all my things from storage will be here in an hour and whatever the opposite of ready is, that's me."

"Oh, dear."

"Yeah. So, again, sorry for snapping."

"That's okay. Perhaps this will help. I went to the Grandishers' to personally extend my condolences. They had just received a box from the park service with Calliope's belongings in it."

"God." Talk about putting my difficulties into perspective.

"Yes. Her cell phone was not included. They received everything else, but not her cell phone."

✧   ✧   ✧   ✧

STILL STARING AT the floor-to-ceilingness of the garage, I called Dex, my long-time source in the FBI lab.

"Hi, Dex, it's Danny." That nickname started as a way to deflect potential suspicion that he was talking to then-well-known journalist E.M. Danniher. Not that he'd ever reveal information on active cases.

He was probably more discreet than their news releases were. But some in the bureau had knee-jerk reactions to journalists. And Dex wasn't a political animal. Using that nickname protected him.

Now, the powers that be probably would have cared less if he chatted with a reporter from KWMT-TV in Sherman, Wyoming. But the nickname had stuck and spread among my colleagues, friends, and family.

"Where are you?" I asked.

I learned a long time ago not to ask Dex the more standard "What are you up to?" or "How are you doing?" because he'd launch into all the scientific and none of the juicy parts of whatever he was working on.

Besides, lately, he'd been splitting time between the FBI's campus in Quantico, Virginia, and the headquarters building in D.C., so I really did wonder where he was.

"I returned from the Mall eight minutes ago."

We'd been there together a few weeks ago. A few weeks that work a miracle on that wide, mostly open space from the Lincoln Memorial to the Capitol.

The miracle of spring.

For an instant the Mall in spring was so vivid, I could smell the freshening grass and hear the snap of flags in a breeze under a vivid blue sky. I didn't even need the pink explosion of cherry blossoms to vicariously breathe in the exalting essence of new growth.

"It was raining," Dex added. My vision dissolved. "But the squirrels are hungry when it rains, too."

The man spent his lunch feeding squirrels—in D.C. or Virginia—then returned to considering the intricacies of how one human being committed mayhem on another. Whatever kept you sane—or close.

"I'm sure they appreciate it."

"There are a number of ongoing studies on squirrels' physical attributes including dexterity and visual acuity, as well as their social organizations, and deceits in hiding nuts, but I know of no studies that would indicate appreciation among their responses."

"Studies about—?" No. Dex's expansive reading and my question-asking could be a dangerous combination. I was not going down one of his rabbit holes—or in this case, into a squirrel nest. "Dex, what do you know about restoring photos from a phone that's been wiped?"

"It can be attempted. The success rate is variable."

"Do you know anyone—someone reliable and with a good enough reputation to impress law enforcement officials—who could do that as a favor. Right away?"

"No."

"Nobody?"

"That skill is in great demand. The kind of people you specified are working at full capacity for law enforcement. They do not have time for such outside work."

"How about somebody retired?"

"The few among such experts who are of an age to retire have not done so because of the press of demand."

"Okay. Say we needed it for a court case later. Could it be done later? Without cutting the, uh, success rate?"

"Yes. Unless the data has been further compromised subsequent-ly."

Like by a band of hackers.

I said a bad word.

Chapter Forty-Three

"WHAT'S THE MATTER, dear?"

I started and turned from the open garage door to find Iris Undlin, my next-door neighbor, behind me.

I pretended she wouldn't have heard my bad word or abrupt end to the call with Dex, neither of which would bother him in the least.

"The movers are bringing my things from storage in less than an hour and I'd hoped to put them in the garage until I could sort out—" Calliope's death, Jennifer's emotions, my life. "—what to keep. But..."

"An hour? My, my. We'd best get started then. *Zeb*! Oh, and it looks like you have some friends here."

Mike's SUV swooped into my drive and braked hard behind my vehicle. He, Diana, and Jennifer came out simultaneously.

"Linda called and said the movers will be here soon," Diana said.

"Tom's on his way. With reinforcements," Mike added.

I didn't know whether to celebrate or cry. I did neither. I gave orders.

Starting with, "Open those cartons of cookies."

AUNT GEE AND Mrs. Parens had taken over the kitchen. They were organizing as they consolidated to make room for my possessions.

Tom and Mike had moved several bigger pieces from the garage into the back of Tom's truck for a later trip to the storage locker the Undlins kept for the neighborhood yard sale. That was after they stood in the bed of Tom's truck and used the Undlins' loppers on low hanging branches, aided by a rope to bring the branches within reach. It helped that they were both good ropers.

Under Iris' direction, Zeb was using a handcart to move smaller pieces, plus sorting boxes, throwing out real estate-connected ones, adding those they expected would go for the yard sale to the truck, then setting aside others for me to look through later.

Tom and Mike then joined Diana, Jennifer and me inside, stacking and consolidating furniture to make room for more. We'd finished the first floor and were in the master suite.

Diana kept giving me significant looks, but I couldn't talk about the grizzly's left ear in front of Jennifer, not with that left ear most likely belonging to her hacker friends.

"Be sure to leave a path to the bed," Diana reminded us all.

We'd had to redo part of the guest room because we'd forgotten that important point downstairs.

"As long as it's just us up here, tell us what happened at the sheriff's department," Mike said.

I did.

"The guy who rented the truck killed people for a boss in the movie? So who's the truck renter's boss in real life?" Jennifer asked.

"If we knew that, we'd know everything."

Her brows lowered. "What happened to that boss in the movie, the person those characters worked for?"

"Nothing. Well, he gets raped and then he shoots his rapist, but I'm pretty sure he's alive at the end. Take that lamp off the end table and then we can stack the other table upside down on it with the lamp still usable between the legs."

"Some of the guys—" Which for Mike probably meant teammates on the Chicago Bears. "—loved that movie. I never got it. Just seemed like a mess."

"Amen," Diana said.

"Maybe we should watch this movie," Jennifer said. "If there are clues—"

"*Clues* might be overly optimistic. I'm speculating the guy chose that name for Chaps to use from a movie he liked. And maybe—

maybe—it indicates he associated himself somehow with those characters."

"Do you think Shelton will follow up on this *Pulp Fiction* connection?"

"I doubt it. Not their style."

"But they should. They have to," Jennifer said.

She and Mike turned to Diana, silently asking her to persuade the sheriff to pursue this angle.

She shook her head. "We've been here before. I'm not pressuring Russ and he's not interfering with what I find out."

"Well, then maybe Jennifer's right. Maybe we should," Mike said.

"We can add it to the list of things to do later, like another call to Angela, but…" I let it trail off, wondering if I should end the topic here or try to edge closer to the live grizzly. "Those characters were hired killers. But if the person who killed Felix Robertson and Calliope is the same person who's been doing these things to Jennifer, it's almost certainly a DIY killer. And since things have been happening in Sherman, that's a DIY killer who's *here*."

"Here? Like lives here?" Jennifer's voice had gone small.

I understood. I even sympathized. This was her home. Supposedly her safe place. Among people who knew her and, if not loved her, at least felt a connection to her.

But weighed against keeping her safe, I'd willingly sacrifice her believing in all that.

I didn't pull my punch. "It does limit the field."

"What are you thinking, Elizabeth?" Tom asked.

"I'm thinking we need to talk to a number of people. Together would be best. And we have to do it fast."

"Too late," Mike said looking out the front window.

EVEN AS THE movers were bringing wrapped and shrouded pieces in the front—along with multitudes of mystery boxes—I was called out to the garage to decide about gardening tools found against the back wall, now that they'd been revealed by clearing out a single row of boxes.

A figure significantly larger than Zeb was taking down boxes from atop other stacks so Iris could look into them—Lance Joudrey.

He colored a bit when I gaped at him.

"Jen—Jennifer called and said you could use all the help you can get."

"I can. Thank you." Though I suspected he'd come here more because of the olive branch from Jennifer than out of concern for me and my moving issues.

His gaze shifted and I saw Jennifer had followed me out the back of the house.

That alone was a feat, because Mrs. P and Aunt Gee had instituted a rule that empty boxes and all wrapping had to immediately go out the back door. No exceptions.

"Can't impede the flow," Aunt Gee declared. "Impede the flow and everything stops up."

None of the boxes went very far, however, so the backyard was a box obstacle course.

An appropriate metaphor for the relationship Jennifer and Lance might be trying to negotiate.

Iris said, "Zeb, come with me to check Tom's truck so we know if there's room for more to go to storage or we need another truck."

"Later. These tools—"

"Now, Zeb."

They went.

"I forgot to give you the printouts of those papers," Jennifer mumbled, not looking at me or Lance.

I took them from her and folded them into a pocket.

"As long as you're both here, I have a question. Lance, you said you didn't know if Jennifer had blocked your phone—"

"Yeah. Because she wouldn't talk to me about—"

"There was nothing to talk about. You kept wanting to go over and over and over what's already done. What can't—doesn't change because—"

"Whoa. Both of you. Lance, you also said something about maybe she wouldn't recognize your phone number?"

"Huh? Oh. Because I got a new phone and didn't want to pay extra to keep the number."

"Why did you get a new phone?"

"The other one stopped working."

"You broke it? Or...?"

"No. I mean, work's tough on phones, but nothing recent. It just went dead."

Jennifer looked up with heightened interest. "When?"

He looked from her to me and back. "Friday. Friday afternoon."

"Your phone was easier to hack than mine. Do you still have it? It might help Vic reverse engineer—"

"Tossed it."

"That was stupid. We could have—"

"How was I supposed to—?"

"Stop. Both of you." I was too tired, too worried, and too wound up for consideration or tact. "Did you know about your parents' history before you started dating?"

They looked at each other.

Well, at least I'd managed to get them to do that.

"Yeah. But not growing up. We sort of heard a few things, but the pieces didn't fit," she said. He nodded. "Not until we got to know each other through Calliope and started really talking."

"And Calliope ... Well, she asked her mom about it and got more of the story. Gossip we never heard."

"What did you think about that?"

"Not much," he said flatly.

"Yeah. What difference did it make? So they'd dated. They broke up and found other people. No reason to be weird about that."

"Well, my mom was kind of a bitch to your dad, what with dating my dad while she was still going with him."

"It was like a hundred years ago. How can they care anymore?"

Because it doesn't feel like a hundred years when you're living it. No use saying it. They wouldn't believe it until it happened to them.

"Did that have anything to do with you two breaking up?"

Jennifer's face scrunched in disdain. "No way."

"Did it have anything to do with you starting to date?"

"No. That was more…" Lance trailed off and looked away.

Jennifer looked in the opposite direction.

Back to that.

"That was more about Calliope? Because she was in Colorado? Because she was using drugs? Because the two of you missed her and were trying to hold onto her?"

He looked over at Jennifer, who still stared at the garage wall. "Jen wanted to try to figure out a way to help her. To get her into rehab. That's how we started seeing each other. Getting together to talk about that. Jen just wanted to help her."

"Yeah, by dating her boyfriend." Jennifer still had that self-flagellating thing going.

"I wasn't her boyfriend then and I kept asking you out."

Silence.

"So, what happened?" I asked.

Lance answered. "We went out. It was good. Fun. Easy. But Jen broke it off. She was working so much and the things with you and—"

"It wasn't right. You and Calliope, *that* was right."

They looked at each other then. Tears in both their eyes.

My heart broke for them, for their heartbreak, and for the girl who was no longer here to be loved by these two.

"You realized it, too," Jennifer said quietly. "You and Calliope got back together and that's why you and your parents have been fighting."

Needham Bender had said the name Grandisher was mentioned during Lance's fight with his father. Calliope Grandisher sounded like the lead candidate.

"How'd you know Calliope and—?"

"I'm not stupid. And you two always loved each other. Always. I knew that."

"We weren't back together. Not like before. We were talking. Seeing if it would go somewhere. We were going to tell you. But Cal was worried how you'd take it. Felt like she was cutting you out. I tried to tell her you'd moved on. That—" He ducked his head. "—I was the one who took longer to realize you and I were holding onto each other for old time's sake."

How any kid that age could have old times… Okay, Okay, I know. A sure sign of getting old.

"Elizabeth? We need you," Diana called, coming out the back door.

Lance said to Jennifer, "Cal said she was reaching out to you. To reconnect. So, she could really talk to you, make sure you'd be okay before we told anybody else."

"That's why she sent me the email the day before she died?"

My heart dropped to my toes.

Could we have gotten this wrong? Could Calliope have been the primary target all along? Could the motive have something to do with the email she'd sent to Jennifer?

If so, she'd just announced to one of the suspects that she'd seen it, that she knew about it. Even if it was gone from her phone.

No point in trying to pretend Lance hadn't heard all that.

"What email?" I demanded.

Chapter Forty-Four

"JENNIFER, WHY DIDN'T you tell me—us—" I amended to both include Diana, who'd reached us by then, and bring her up to date. "—that you received an email from Calliope the day before she died?"

"It didn't have anything to do with her death. It was personal. Besides, it just says what you all already know. She wanted to talk." Jennifer blinked twice. "That's why I didn't answer. But if I hadn't been a jerk, if I'd answered, we'd probably have talked and talked. Late into the night. Then she might never have gone on that hike and—"

"You can't backtrack all the mights and kick yourself for not following them. You can't." Diana's emphasis echoed with her own experience with loss.

I focused on now. "But you remember this email, right? Can you write down what she said? Everything you can remember."

"Sure. But—"

A bellow came from the house. We all swung around toward it.

"That's why I came out. You've got to rescue the moving men from Aunt Gee," Diana said. "Now."

IN CASE LANCE truly was a threat, I kept Jennifer clamped to my side with an unending string of "Can you help me withs."

But after the moving truck left, I was the victim—and beneficiary—of a conspiracy, led by Mike.

"It's for your own good. You need to get out of here," he said.

"I can't leave." I tried to communicate why with a look, but this was the downside of Jennifer being beside me. "I mean, look at this place."

Boxes and furniture filled the yard, walked up the pathway, and occupied the steps. They were what wouldn't fit in the now bulging house.

"Give folks a little time to sort it out and it will be better. Go with Mike now." Diana held my gaze and added significantly, "I'll keep an eye on things here."

In other words, she'd stick with Jennifer.

"I shouldn't—"

"Yes, you should," Mike said. "You've got a whole crew working and you can't let us starve. C'mon."

He handed me into his SUV. Forcefully. And pulled away.

"This isn't the way to Hamburger Heaven."

"Going to the supermarket. Penny insisted. Said she couldn't get away from work to help, but she could keep us going."

I took the opportunity to tell him about my left ear of the live grizzly and the email Jennifer had received from Calliope.

"You think that's the answer? If she can remember what was in it—?"

He broke off, his head snapped to me, and he jammed on the brakes.

"Holy—uh, crap. I was right. Jennifer *was* the one person who knew the clue and without even knowing it. And someone was trying to get her."

"You often are right. You don't always give yourself credit for it, though."

He grinned, then leaned toward me with a move that echoed both cowboy and lounge lizard. Imagine John Wayne playing the John Travolta role in *Saturday Night Live* ... while sitting in an SUV. "You think I'm too modest?"

I chuckled. I put a hand on his chest to move him back.

He covered it with his hand and held it there.

I wasn't chuckling.

"Mike."

He looked down at me for two beats longer. "Yeah, I know. We're in public."

Did I wish we weren't?

I shook my head at myself. What was the point of wishing? Even more pointless was wondering if I was wishing.

"But, yes, you are too modest. In some ways. You're better at this than you think."

"This? How would you know? You rarely give me a chance."

I felt heat in my cheeks. At my age. Ridiculous. "I'm talking about the inquiries. About putting things together."

"Oh, that. Thanks. I think I'm pretty good, too."

"Not always. You doubt yourself too much. Remember the first night with all this, with all of us at Diana's? You figured out what I was driving at with the news releases and how long after the fatality they came out. But then you looked at Diana and Tom to see if you were right—or to make sure you weren't wrong."

"Huh. I'll have to think about that."

"You do that, cowboy."

He leaned toward me again.

A vehicle behind us tooted politely. We *were* stopped in the middle of a block.

He groaned.

I might have, too.

✧ ✧ ✧ ✧

I WAS DEEPLY touched when we pulled up in front of the Sherman Supermarket and the manager hurried out to begin loading boxes into the SUV.

It looked like Penny had cleared out the deli, the drinks aisle, and the snack aisle. A case of Pepperidge Farm Double Dark Chocolate Milano cookies went carefully into the back seat.

I was arguing with the manager that, of course, I had to pay, when Penny came out. I'd never seen her more than a few feet from her register.

"Penny. You can't—We have to pay."

"Not at all. Haven't seen you since the cookies and pears. Not—"

"Colorado." I edged in.

"—enough to keep you going. Especially not now. Told the boy—" Her term for the manager. "—only way we could help when you do so much. Poor, poor girl. Dying in Colorado. Wouldn't've happened here. Dead's dead, but can't have murderers going free. And you don't. This one this time, eh." She looked Mike up and down. "Sad news. Sad, sad news."

He looked slightly alarmed at being juxtaposed with sad news, but I was pretty sure we'd moved on from Mike.

"Still, connections. Mothers and daughters. Always difficult. Want to stay close when the daughter wants—"

I had no idea what she was talking about.

"I want to thank you—" I tried to shake her hand. She waved me away, turning back toward the store.

"—to be free. Not always the best way. Just get it done. Bye-now. Boy!"

I shook the manager's hand, hurriedly thanking him. He trotted after Penny.

Mike said, "C'mon, let's go. There was ice cream in there. Don't want it to melt."

On the way back, we took Sherman's main street—Cottonwood Avenue—because there's no reason for shortcuts.

I looked. Looked again, then shouted. "Stop. *Stop*."

Mike braked. Not fast enough for me.

I got out while the SUV was still rolling and Mike's "What's going on?" trailed after me as I backtracked.

"Ivan? Ivan Quentel?"

He turned.

It was.

In Sherman, Wyoming.

Chapter Forty-Five

HE CAME BACK toward me with a smile and outstretched hand. I gave him back the same.

Before I could do more, Mike was beside me. If I hadn't been so focused on Quentel, I would have turned around to see how and where Mike left his SUV.

"What are you doing here, Ivan?"

"We came for the services. For Calliope."

"We?"

"The Valentines, too."

"They're here?"

"Not yet. Should be in a few hours. We've been, you know, in contact. They told me about this hotel—" He tipped his head in the direction he'd come from and the Haber House Hotel.

Interesting. The Valentines were familiar with the Haber House Hotel? It wasn't like it was a well-known tourist spot, despite its spectacular chocolate pie.

"—and they had a room there. I got one, too. The place is kind of a trip."

"That's the Haber House Hotel, all right. It's a surprise to see you here, Ivan."

"Yeah, well, the Valentines called after you sent them that photo to see if they could identify the other witness, and then when you called about whether I had Calliope's phone, it got me thinking. We were talking about that and everything and the topic came up of being here for the services. Hadn't ever been to Sherman and there're a number of good hikes west of here, so I, uh, thought I'd do both."

"You didn't say anything about coming last night."

"No. Sort of spur of the moment. Hey, I asked the other guys who were on that run like I told you I would and nobody ever saw Calliope's phone."

I was not surprised. I believed it had been taken by someone—the mystery witness, the Valentines, or Quentel himself—before the other rangers arrived. "Thank you. When did you get here?"

"Little while ago." To be here now, he had to have left far earlier this morning than I'd like. "Drove straight through."

Or, he hadn't been in Estes Park when we talked last night. That was the thing about cell phones. They could be anywhere.

"How do you know about the services?"

"Calliope's friends told me about the VisageTome memorial page. Saw the information there."

"But the viewing's not until tomorrow evening and the funeral the day after."

"Like I said, some trails…"

"The Valentines, too? They're hiking?"

He shrugged. "Don't know." He looked around Cottonwood Avenue. "Maybe some shopping."

Right. They were driving from outside of Denver to shop in Sherman.

"And of course you're not actually hiking, either."

His eyes flickered, but he didn't crumble. "Not yet. Wanted to look around first. You know," he added, oh-so-casually, "There's somebody else staying at the hotel."

Yes, he made me ask. "Who?"

"Peter Bray."

MIKE LEANED CLOSE and said, "Ice cream."

An excellent point. Especially since Ivan showed no sign of being about to bare his soul to me.

At the moment, in fact, he stood before me looking—or trying to look—like a young man with nothing to bare at all.

That didn't come out quite right.

"Sorry, Ivan." I gave him my brightest smile. "We'd love to show you around, but I'm sort of moving in today and a bunch of people are waiting for us. We'll talk real soon."

MIKE AND I told the others about seeing Ivan and his report on the Valentines and Bray showing up. But that's all there was time for.

Between dishing out food and directing the moving operations, I was beyond busy for the next two hours. So were the rest of them, doing the toting and lifting.

Though Diana told me she'd had an opportunity to bring Tom up to speed on the grizzly's left ear and the email.

Splitting guard duty on Jennifer made it less obvious we weren't letting her be alone with Lance.

At the moment, all of us were at the archway that separated the living area from the hallway to the front bedroom and stairs to the master bedroom. A narrow path was all the open space, so it took some negotiating for traffic to pass.

Mike and Jennifer came from the guest room, Tom from behind me, and Diana from the kitchen.

I was caught in the middle. I tried to step back, but there was no-where to go.

I sat down. Hard. On an ottoman covered in packing material, flipping a piece of cardboard up onto my back.

We all laughed, the giddy laugh of nearing exhaustion.

Mike grinned and the corners of Tom's eyes crinkled. I laughed back at both of them and felt warmth in the vicinity of my heart.

I felt protective of Jennifer. I'd accepted Diana as a friend—a good, close friend. I'd opened the door to two more. Separate from the physical attraction, from the kisses I'd shared with each of them. Gentler, wider. Deeper.

I *liked* these guys.

I liked them a lot.

"Better get back to it now that Elizabeth's not in the way," Tom said.

"Yup," Mike agreed.

Tom bent to a box marked "Books—Chicago," which I knew contained hardcovers, including photo rich coffee table editions that each weighed a ton. Yet he hoisted it with smooth power.

I saw it in his legs as he straightened, in his arms and shoulders as he held the box. I wasn't surprised. Logically, I knew ranch work demanded that kind of power as well as honing it. Practically, I knew I'd seen evidence of this power before, including the first time I'd seen him, swinging an ax.

But there was something in the way he moved now that connected to neither logic nor practicality in me.

My heart *ka-thumped*, like someone had walloped a bass drum embedded in it. The reverberations slammed against my ribs and re-echoed across like tidal waves caught in a pond.

Holy smokes.

I knew my recent trip East shook loose emotional cobwebs. Apparently, it also uncorked my long-corked libido.

Too much. Way too much. All at once.

And with so many people around.

I turned away.

Just in time to see Mike herd Jennifer up the stairs ahead of him while he held a chair aloft, the motion drawing his shirt taut against the triangular shape of his back and lifting the shirttail for full-screen viewing of his jeans cupping a memorable derriere.

My breath caught somewhere below my breastbone. Possibly snared by the still sloshing waves pounding in my chest.

I sat back down on the ottoman. Just as hard.

I'd met these two men a year ago. I'd worked with them in various ways, gotten to know them, to respect them, to like them, to be irked by them.

I'd shared kisses—memorable, unsettlingly wonderful kisses—with each of them.

So, clearly, I found both of them attractive.

Attractive?

How about a mega-magnet sucking lightweight iron filings. In two different directions.

✧ ✧ ✧ ✧

"DIZZY?"

Diana's hand was on my shoulder.

"A little, yeah. I … I, uh, guess I stood up too fast after bending over, digging in the box."

She looked at me. Looked up the stairs where Mike had gone, then in the direction Tom had taken.

She turned back and smirked.

"Uh, I better get back to these boxes…"

She ignored that. "A few months ago, I might have bought that. It had been so long since Gary died… But since Russ came into my life, I one hundred percent do not buy that dizzy from a box excuse. I know exactly what you're feeling." She checked up the stairs, down the hall, then back to me. "Sort of."

✧ ✧ ✧ ✧

THE HELPERS DWINDLED. So did the energy.

Aunt Gee, Mrs. Parens, and Lance had eaten something close to a meal, sitting in front of the fireplace on the furniture jammed together like the rows of seats at an airport gate.

With that cleared away, Aunt Gee declared it was time for the other five of us to sit and eat. They even served us. Then Mrs. Parens went up to the master bathroom and Aunt Gee went to the first-floor bathroom to work their magic, while Lance broke down boxes in the back yard so there'd be room for more.

That left the five of us to talk as we ate.

I felt as if I were inside the tornado in *The Wizard of Oz*, with bits, pieces, and whole cows whirling around, jostling against items they'd never otherwise be associated with. Except all these items came from my brain. And this tornado had been spinning for days.

"Remember what Mrs. P was saying about the Teapot Dome Scandal at the cookout, Mike?" I asked.

Diana and Tom made sounds of recognition of a favorite topic of their former teacher. Jennifer said, "The what?"

Mike dropped his voice. "More important, I remembered it when she asked me about it."

"You don't have much to brag about, Paycik," I said. "Remembering all the lurid details about Albert Bacon Fall's Wild West past with murders and posses and Sheriff Pat Garrett, but little of the greatest presidential scandal before Watergate."

Jennifer's interest sharpened. "Murders? But what's the stuff about posses?"

"Elizabeth's revisiting the topic of journalism getting to the truth better than law enforcement, like she told Sheriff Conrad." Mike turned to the others. "She said something similar to Mrs. P because the *Wall Street Journal* broke the story the day before Senator Kendrick's resolution to start investigating the Teapot Dome."

"Hey, would he ever have done anything if the *Journal* hadn't broken the story?"

"No way did you say that to Mrs. P," Diana said. "Kendrick is one of her guys."

"Oh, that house in Sheridan," Jennifer said.

"Trail End House," Diana confirmed. "Always one of our class trips. You should go see it, Elizabeth."

Tom cleared his throat. "Elizabeth should go see it, but haven't we wandered? Did what Mrs. Parens said about the Teapot Dome Scandal connect to what we're looking into?"

"Yeah. Well, maybe."

"That's definitive." Diana reached for another bunch of grapes.

"I was thinking about what she said about how this major scandal, linked by name to Wyoming, actually had little to do with Wyoming."

"Except guys in Wyoming spotted the oil trucks. Sort of like the Watergate guard who spotted the burglars."

"Right." I said it slowly, staring at the wall, my eyes unfocused and my brain spinning around in that tornado. Oddly, I also heard Aunt

Gee's voice talking about impeding the flow.

I pushed my hair back with both hands as if it had actually been wind-tossed. "Okay. Let's step back. Let's look at the big picture."

"What big picture?" Mike grumped.

"Then the other way. The details. What's been a recurring motif in this?"

"Calliope's death." Jennifer.

"Concern about Jennifer." Tom.

"Your moving. Your house." Diana.

"Things not being clear-cut." Mike.

I focused on Mike. "What do you mean?"

"We haven't been sure what we were dealing with. Accident? Suicide? Murder? I mean, a lot of times we know—or have a good idea—of what we're investigating. Plus, other things. Like the calls to the Lawtons. Seemed like they were bad, then they were friends trying to find Jennifer. But now we're not so sure they're friends."

"That's a really good point."

Jennifer objected, "Not so sure? Of course, they're friends. What do you—?"

"Hold off on that, Jennifer. Keep an open mind to what Mike said."

"But—"

"So lack of clarity is your recurring motif?" he asked me.

"No. My recurring motif is phones. That first call. Calliope's phone missing. The unknown witness saying he was calling out for help. Him—or someone—taking Calliope's phone. Jennifer's and Lance's phones being wiped. Jennifer's old phone taken in the break-in."

Diana had taken her phone out and was turning it over in her hand.

Jennifer watched the movement as she said, "And now my laptop's acting up."

"More since those articles went astray?"

Diana swiped her phone, bringing it to life. Thoughtfully, she tapped a key.

"No, but..." Jennifer's voice trailed off, then came back sharply.

"What did those people say?"

I needed more hints. "What people? Say about what?"

"Those people you talked to. The witnesses. The Valentines. What did they say about that guy being on his phone?" She was urgent, impatient.

Frowning—more in confusion than in an effort to remember—I said, "The man had his phone out when they caught sight of him. He was trying to call for help."

"No, no. You said they said something else. That EMT said something, too. Punching. That was it. He was *punching* at it."

"Yeah," Mike said. "Trying to get service, to call out."

Eyes wide, Jennifer looked around "What if he wasn't? Wasn't punching in numbers on the phone, wasn't trying to call out. You'd figure out pretty fast there was no connection *and* they told him, but they said he kept on punching."

"Some people only know one thing to do—call 911—so they just keep trying," Mike said.

"Or," she said with emphasis, "he *never* was trying to call for help. Because, you know what else he could have been doing that would look like he was punching in a number? Deleting photos or emails or whatever."

"Why would he delete his photos then?"

I jolted up. "Jennifer, that's brilliant. Not *his* photos, Mike. He was deleting Calliope's." I sank back. "But her phone's gone, along with what she sent. That's why he wiped your phone and Lance's." If Lance's really was wiped. We only had his word for it. "To get rid of everything. Like the email Calliope sent you Thursday. They're all gone."

"No, they're not."

Chapter Forty-Six

WE ALL GAPED at Jennifer.

That wasn't easy because she'd become a moving target. She climbed over Mike's knees, then Diana's.

Diana spoke first. "Did your friends recover them from your phone?"

"No." Free of the knees, Jennifer straightened and called out, "Mrs. Parens. Where'd you put our purses?"

"They are in the broom closet near the back door," floated back from upstairs.

Jennifer headed for the broom closet.

"What do you mean they're not gone?" I shouted after her.

"Just a minute."

It felt a lot longer before she came back with a brown leather purse. She dug into it, making a sound of triumph as she pulled out a cord. "*Probably* they're not gone," she said.

"Explain," Tom ordered.

"Just a second. Where's a plug?"

"There's one behind that couch. We'll have to move the chairs and—"

"Good heavens," Aunt Gee called from the downstairs bathroom. "Use a plug in the kitchen."

"Got it." Jennifer plugged the cord in, attached a phone that likely was the one her mother had brought to KWMT, then came back to us, perching on a chair arm. "Mom finally dropped off the right charger cord today, along with a purse for me to use. This phone's so old the regular charger doesn't fit. It might take a few minutes, because it's been without power and it's old, but *that*'s the phone Calliope emailed me on. That old phone and my old number. I kept them for backup when I got the new number. That's where I saw the email."

"You're going to have to explain more," Tom said.

"That's the phone I used when Calliope lived here." She gestured toward the kitchen counter. "It uses my old number. That's the one she knew. I saw an email from her on it Thursday. The phone had just enough power left then to ding a notification. I skimmed the email but... Well, I left the phone and went to work and forgot about it. Then, when my new phone was wiped, Mom brought it to the station Tuesday morning."

I raised a triumphant index finger. "Which is why it wasn't there for someone to find during the break-in."

"Yeah. They stole my next-older one."

My pulse picked up. "They must have seen from Calliope's phone that she'd sent you something."

"But Jennifer said there's nothing in the email," Tom said.

Mike jolted up. "I'll bet Calliope sent you something from the trail Friday."

"And when they wiped the new one," I said, "they must have realized there were no messages from Calliope on it, but knew there *should* be. That's why they kept after your phones, trying to find one with the messages."

"You haven't looked at this phone?" Mike asked.

"I told you, Mom forgot—"

"Right. The charging cord. How long is this going to take?"

"It's not like the new ones. It might be a few minutes." She turned to me. "What about those articles, Elizabeth? Were they any help?"

"For Pete's sake. I totally forgot." I dug in my pocket and found them nestled at the bottom with a box cutter. Closed, thank heavens.

Printouts of newspaper photos posted on the internet often have the resolution of mud. These were several steps up. Say, dirty water.

There was Felix Robertson. Smiling. Receiving congratulations. Posing in front of a poker table. Posing with a basketball. Posing with poker players. Posing with a check.

As I looked at each photo, I passed it to Diana, across from me, then she passed it on.

But the second I'd given her the last one, I snatched it back.

"Does anyone have a magnifying glass?"

"Use the one on your phone. You've got that app." Jennifer looked up from passing a sheet to Tom. "Hand it over."

I tamely took my phone from the other pocket—the one without the box cutter—and gave it to her.

In a second and a half, she handed it back with it zooming everything in front of it plus a flashlight app beaming.

"Perfect."

I applied it to the dark corner of that photo.

Looked up.

Then looked back down again.

If...

But...

"I think... No, I'm not going to say it. See what you think."

But Diana, Tom, and Mike didn't know. Jennifer said she couldn't see anything. But she looked even more unhappy.

"We could ask Mrs. P," Mike proposed.

"Let's see what's on Jennifer's old phone first."

She jumped up and retrieved it, looking more hopeful. The cord wouldn't reach to where we were, so she unplugged.

"It won't last long, but... *Yes.* Two messages from Calliope from Friday. It just says *Hiking.* And there are photos..." Her shoulders slumped. "Plants. Dead plants. Snow. A view of mountains through branches. That's it on this one. The next one says. *Still Hiking.* There's a patch of ice. Snow. It's like she's looking down at her feet on the trail. More photos. She has the most ridiculously small feet. Elf feet. This one's... It's a blur..." She looked up. "That's all. There aren't any more."

"Maybe there's another message," Mike tried.

She shook her head.

"May I see?"

She gave me the phone. She'd described the photos accurately—though the plants appeared dormant, not dead. The last one was, indeed, a blur.

Two photos. Neither an answer.

But...

"What is it Elizabeth?" Tom asked.

"The last photo. Jennifer, does it remind you of anything? Look fast, get an impression, not details."

I handed it back, but she shook her head. "It just went out."

She got up to plug the phone in.

"You know," I said slowly. "It might be enough for a bluff. They wouldn't have been so determined to wipe the phones if they hadn't thought the photo endangered them."

"That could work. But doesn't it work better if you know who you're trying to bluff?" Mike asked.

I felt them all looking at me.

"Do you know?" Diana asked.

"It's... scrambled. I can't..." The tornado whipping items around, jostling them together. Historical figures... Disguises... Woody Allen... Phone apps... Bribes... Impeding the flow... Bray's mooing voice... Invasion... A letter... Double Dead Curve and a rock being dropped... A cowboy hat... Rainbow Robertson... The Valentines' chocolate chip cookies...

Or was that last item unrelated?

I slapped my hands on my knees. I swear a cloud of dust rose. "There are so many threads tangled. And with all this—" I arced one arm at the room. "—I can't think straight, much less explain. It's like—"

A knock sounded at the front door.

"*Come in,*" the others chorused without moving. Not the friendliest.

Aunt Gee marched out of the bathroom, saying disapprovingly as she passed us on the way to the door, "No wonder you can't think. Everything's jumbled together. You should sort through your own things first, decide which ones are important, then fill in what you need or want from Renata's. Quit trying to compare. You can't. They're different things entirely."

Jumbled together...

Different things entirely...

The phrases echoed, attracting another phrase I'd spoken earlier... Good heavens, was that just earlier today?

Two jigsaw puzzles with the pieces mixed up...

Or even more than two puzzles?

Three sets of parents, three kids, all tied together. Love. Rivalry. Friendship. Jealousy.

Five hackers, perfectly positioned ... But why?

And the Colorado group. Ivan Quentel, Kassandra and Ralph Valentine, Bray. All here so unexpectedly.

Could that possibly be accidental? Or was somebody doing their best to mix up the pieces of multiple puzzles?

The funnel cloud slowed. Subsided.

The background was misty. Still obscured by the churn. But a few objects in the foreground, those remained intact...

Linda Caswell and Grayson Zane came around the pile of boxes beside the entryway.

"Need help?"

I jumped up. "You've already done so much, but *yes*. First, though, I want to give Aunt Gee a hug. You cleared my mind. Thank you."

She turned rosy with pleasure, hugging me back. "Just common sense."

I noticed she also shot a triumphant look toward Mrs. Parens, who had come downstairs.

"Jennifer, I want you to pull up some of the information you've told us about. But before you do that, there's something more..."

I turned to the newcomers.

"Grayson, Zeb and Iris will tell you what to do out in the garage. On your way out, will you please tell Lance to come in here. Linda, what I need from you is far worse. From you and Jennifer and Lance."

❖ ❖ ❖ ❖

AFTER I'D PERSUADED them, with Tom's backing, to do what needed doing—what I thought needed doing—and sent them off, I tried to gather my thoughts enough to group together pieces of one puzzle.

The second would have to wait. And if a third was involved...

In the background, I heard the voices and sounds of Mrs. Parens and Aunt Gee continuing to work on getting all the stuff crammed into my house sorted out. I hoped we were all successful.

To help my chances of success, I went to Mrs. P and Aunt Gee to ask their help in setting up the second puzzle.

Then I called Shelton.

I explained some. Not nearly as much as he wanted. Even if I could have given him everything he wanted, I wouldn't have.

In the end I had to tell him he wouldn't be allowed in until we were ready and if he didn't co-operate I wouldn't let him in at all.

I was well past the left ear, though dust still obscured chunks. Trouble was, the more of the live grizzly I held onto, the more real and dangerous the parts I didn't have became.

Chapter Forty-Seven

"**READY?**" **TOM ASKED** at the top of the stairs, outside my bedroom.

It was an unconventional spot for this gathering, but the only two places in the house with barely enough room left over from boxes and extra furniture were the bedroom and living room. And the living room would be acquiring its own gathering soon, with Mrs. P and Aunt Gee waiting downstairs to greet the hackers.

Grayson and Linda had opted to join the Undlins, working in the garage thanks to Zeb's floodlights.

At the moment, I wished I could join them.

And not only because there were still cookies out there.

I was about to do what they told lawyers never to do—ask questions I didn't know the answers to. Journalists do it all the time. But seldom as many questions of as many people with as many possible outcomes with such high emotion.

And possibly a big step forward in solving a murder.

Lucky me.

"As ready as I'm going to be," I told Tom.

He held my gaze, gave a single nod, then opened the door.

The Lawtons—Jennifer, Kent, and Faith—sat on one side of the bed, with the other side stacked high with boxes to make room for carefully placed chairs. The Joudreys—Lance, Brady, and Holly—had chairs arcing out from the near end of the bed. The Grandishers—Owen and India—had chairs on the opposite end. Diana sat with them, making their depleted status not quite as glaring.

A solitary chair sat in the opening across from the bed. I took it.

Mike and Tom brought up chairs to either side of me and slightly behind. Like bodyguards.

Not a pleasant thought.

I cleared my throat. Ready for something brilliant, like *Good evening*. Jennifer beat me to it.

"Mom, Dad, I'd like you to officially meet Elizabeth Margaret Danniher. My friend."

I nodded to them, then to the Joudreys and the Grandishers.

"Thank you all for agreeing to come." Owen Grandisher opened his mouth. I kept talking. "I'm going to be blunt in the interest of getting to the truth about Calliope's death in the shortest time possible. I know the desire to get to that truth is the reason you've come."

Again, Owen opened his mouth. Again, I kept talking.

"Mr. and Mrs. Grandisher, I understand you received your daughter's effects. Can you tell us how?"

Owen finally got his opening to talk. "What do you mean how? What difference does it make? And how you think *you're* doing to *get to the truth*, I have no idea."

His wife didn't seem to hear his irritation. She answered me woodenly, "A man delivered the box when he came to offer his condolences."

"Did the man give you his name?"

"Ray. Something like that," Owen Grandisher said.

"Bray," India corrected.

"Ray. Bray. What difference does it make? Can we get on with this—whatever *this* is."

His wife slowly turned her head toward him and, in the same wooden voice asked, "Do you have somewhere to go?"

His stunned silence gave me the opportunity to regain control.

"Thank you, Mrs. Grandisher. Was Calliope's cell phone in the box?"

"No." Something small seemed to spark in her as she repeated, "No. It wasn't."

I already knew that from Linda, but I wanted India to confirm it.

Plus, I'd forgotten to tell the others that item amid today's chaos.

I was aware of looks being passed among Jennifer, Diana, Mike, and Tom. Also of Lance trying to catch Jennifer's gaze.

I plowed ahead.

"You three families have long and intersecting history together. Connections linking one to the other."

I looked from Holly Joudrey to Kent Lawton. "You dated in high school."

Then from Owen Grandisher to Brady Joudrey. "Your career ambitions tied you, making you both rivals and allies of sorts." Grandisher snorted.

Finally, around to each of them. "Your children created another bond. Their friendships. Their love for each other."

The Lawtons and Joudreys looked at their children automatically, then went absolutely still at the recognition that the Grandishers could not, would never again, look at their child.

"Until something broke that connection apart. Abruptly and sharply. What that was—"

"The letter," India Grandisher jerked out.

I was happy to stay quiet, giving this a moment to see what bubbled up.

"You have always blamed me—never having the nerve to say it, but blaming, blaming, blaming," Holly Joudrey said across the open space. Impossible to tell which of the Grandishers she'd aimed that at, but I thought it was India.

"Quiet," Owen Grandisher said.

"Don't talk to my wife that way," Brady Joudrey said.

"I will say it. To her. And to my wife. *Be quiet.* This is—"

India wasn't being quiet. "What's the point? What is the point? Your *career*? It's gone. You'll be here until you retire. And Calliope will not be here. Not ever again."

"The point? The point is that—that viper who pretended to be Calliope's friend did her best to ruin me completely. The fact that I held onto the shreds of a career are no thanks to that one." He jerked his head toward Jennifer.

He blamed *Jennifer*?

That was a curveball.

"You can't—" Kent Lawton started, putting his arm across in front of Jennifer, as if she were a toddler in a vehicle about to crash.

But another voice topped his.

Lance's.

"Tell them, Jen," he said.

She bit at her right thumbnail, all her attention focused on it.

"Jen. What's the point of keeping any of it quiet now? We aren't kids anymore. Calliope—"

"Is dead. She's dead. *Dead.* I know. You don't have to say it. I know."

Her harsh words echoed with such pain that even Owen Grandisher was quieted.

She sucked in a ragged breath.

Her father reached toward her, but she shook her head.

"I have to..." She tucked her thumb inside her fingers, hiding away the ragged nail. Making a fist. "I found it. The letter. Calliope dared me and I got into his computer system—easy—and I found that letter." Her head tipped toward Calliope's father. "It showed he knew before the bribes happened. Knew about all the bribes that got people fired and put in jail."

"*All* the bribes?" he mocked. "No, no, no. Rumors, only rumors about one or two. That's all."

"You made a joke about them."

"And you did what?" All mocking gone, he was furious. "Sell the letter? Or just give it to Joudrey? Or did—"

"I told you I never—"

Grandisher wasn't even looking at Brady Joudrey, now held back by Holly. Grandisher focused on Jennifer.

"—you do it yourself? To make trouble, to try to ruin us. You were supposed to be Calliope's friend. She swore up and down you were. No matter how many times I told her to keep her distance. She couldn't see that your jealousy corroded everything she tried to do for you."

"I was never jealous of Calliope and I didn't send the letter." Her head came up. "I was her friend. I am her friend."

"Oh, come on. What's the point of lying now?"

Her vigorous head-shaking jerked her voice. "I never sent that letter."

"You were always digging into things that don't concern you. Calliope told us how you could do all these things on the computer. Hacking. Who knows what else. Stealing identities or—"

"Hey. Don't accuse my daughter—" Keith started to rise, but stilled when Faith touched his arm.

"I found it," Jennifer said, "but I never sent it."

"Quit lying. You—"

"Owen." India Grandisher's voice was no longer wooden.

"Tell them, Jen," Lance said again. "Tell them all of it."

She looked at him, then back down. "Daisy says—"

"I don't care what she says."

"She's my friend."

"*I'm* your friend. I'll always be your friend. We didn't make it as a couple, but that's because… But I'll always love you, Jen. You have to know that. And I say you've held this too long." He looked around at the parents. "We all knew about the letter. Jen, Cal, and me. All of us." He returned his focus to Jennifer and repeated, "Tell them now."

"I think…" She cleared her throat, glancing up, then back to her fisted hand. "Calliope sent it."

Calliope's mother sucked in with the pain of someone punched in the gut. "No."

Owen Grandisher's face turned red, a pulse in his neck. "You're trying to push this off on *Calliope*? Our dead daughter who can't defend herself. Blaming her for what *you* did. You were always jealous of her because of what she had that you didn't. Always wanting Lance, looking for ways to get her out of your way so you could have him. You led her into drugs and—"

Roars from every direction broke out.

I heard Jennifer's denial. Her parents' outrage. Calliope's parents' anger. Lance's parents' confusion.

What finally broke through was Lance's voice. Aided by standing and shouting down at the six parents.

"*Stop it.*"

They did. Probably from shock.

"Jen didn't lead Calliope into drugs. Nobody did. She did that to herself. She also got herself off them. Don't take that away from her. And don't put that other crap on Jen. Jen found the letter, yeah. But when she showed it to us, Calliope was the one who wanted to send it to the authorities." He looked right at Owen Grandisher. "She said it would serve you right for being such a hypocrite. *Jen* was the one who said no. She didn't do anything wrong. Well, maybe except digging that letter up to start. But Calliope asked her to. Begged her to, because she was sure you'd done something wrong. And if there hadn't been something to find it wouldn't have mattered what poking around Jen did. Besides, she was a kid. We all were. What does it matter if she sent it or—"

"Jennifer didn't send that letter"

"—Calliope did? It—"

"She didn't, either."

In a delayed reaction, Lance gave a double-take. All the other heads had already turned to the quiet speaker.

"I sent it."

It came from Faith Lawton.

"You? *You?* How? No. You couldn't have," Jennifer said. "How would you know—"

"How?" Her bemused smile turned both sharper and softer as she answered her daughter. "You're not the first to ever use a computer in our family. It's not that complicated."

"You—? No. No. That's wrong. Calliope sent the letter. We had a big fight about it. She knew my password and she got into my computer and sent it. I'd showed it to her and she wanted to send it, but I said no. And I told her it was my decision, because I'd found it and she had no right to make the decision. But she did. She *did*. And that's wrong. And I told her that and she... She never said she didn't. She didn't say *anything*."

"I sent it," Faith said. "Not Calliope."

"You... *You* did that to my husband?" Holly Joudrey leaned forward, her hands curled around the ends of the chair's arms, as if for leverage to spring. Lance stepped beside her. Her husband slowly swung his attention from Faith Lawton back to his wife. "*You* kept Grandisher here so Brady could never get away from that boot on his neck?"

"No," Faith said strongly, also leaning forward, confronting the other woman. "I did it to *you*. Because if you'd been willing to leave here, to try somewhere else, he would have gone. You all would have gone. At first, when I read the letter, I thought about it never coming to light and how Grandisher would advance and maybe—maybe Joudrey would, too. Maybe he'd be offered a position so good you'd all go..."

"Mom," Jennifer whispered.

Her mother showed no sign of hearing her. Faith Lawton and Holly Joudrey seemed aware only of each other.

"But then I thought if I sent the letter and Grandisher was ruined, maybe that would take Joudrey down, too. And then you'd go. You'd be so embarrassed, you'd have to go away. Far away. But of course that didn't happen." Her harsh, painful sound brought a sympathetic ache to my throat. "Grandisher will be here forever and so will you and I'll never get my husband back or to have him for the first time."

"*Faith.*"

Nobody moved at Kent Lawton's single word, even seeming not to breathe while we all waited for her to turn to him. "You've always had me. From the first time and every moment since. You. And then the kids. Always. You don't know that?"

Her eyes filled with tears, but she said nothing.

He held out his hand.

Slowly, slowly, she brought hers to meet it and they wrapped around each other.

"God, you're an idiot, Faith," Holly Joudrey said with something far too raw to be amusement. "I've known it since high school. I'd lost Kent to his *buddy* Faith. It was as good as done. Why do you think I went after Brady?"

He made a sound beside her.

She turned to him. "I did, you know. Shamelessly. You never had a chance."

He didn't look displeased by the fact.

Lance blew out a breath. Jennifer looked shaken.

"She didn't send it?"

I had to look around to find who said those words. It was Owen Grandisher. I hadn't recognized his voice. He sounded bewildered, lost.

"She didn't send that letter to make sure we stayed here? She was so angry about leaving. She said she hated Houston. Hated me. She said…"

His wife said, "No, Owen. Calliope did not send the letter."

His strident accusation of Jennifer, of Brady Joudrey, had all been a defense. Against anyone seeing what he believed—that his daughter had betrayed him.

"Calliope… didn't. She didn't do that to me…"

He bent forward, as if in pain.

India put a hand on his back. "No, no, she didn't do that to you."

"My girl, my girl, my girl." He slumped into India, his forehead on her shoulder, the lament continuing. "My girl, my girl, my girl."

Chapter Forty-Eight

"WHEW," DIANA SAID when we huddled at the bottom of the stairway. "That was tough. He thought all this time that Calliope sent the letter? Felt betrayed by her?"

"I did not see that coming," I said.

"Didn't see three quarters of it coming," Mike said. "But what the hell does it tell us?"

"It clears a lot of pieces off the table that were mixed up with the other puzzle's pieces. Now the remaining pattern becomes much clearer."

Mike looked dubious. I had to admit, there was a huge difference between seeing the pattern and actually fitting piece after piece together until it made a whole everyone else could see.

The first round had been all emotion. The rest added in the bare blade of someone willing to murder.

Fun.

"Are you sure?" Diana asked. "You look tired. Both of you."

Jennifer and I looked at each other.

"Your call, Jennifer," I said. "We can let tonight go. Slow down. Try to build this up bit by bit. Or we can bluff now."

She sucked in a breath. "Bluff now."

"Okay."

I looked around at Diana, Mike, and Tom. "C'mon, guys. Confidence."

Before they responded, our group separated to let the Lawtons and Joudreys pass through on their way to the front door. The Grandishers were still at the top of the stairs.

We followed them into the living room, where the five hackers sat squeezed together on one side.

Remembered words rushed into my head.

Faith's words.

Ever since she discovered computers, it's like we'd have to crawl inside the thing to connect with her.

Penny's words.

Mothers and daughters. Always difficult. Want to stay close when the daughter wants to be free. Not always the best way.

If I was right…

But if I was wrong, the pieces might never fit no matter how long and hard we worked.

And if I didn't take the chance, the pieces would be scattered forever.

I spun around. "Wait."

They did. The two couples heading for the front door. And the Grandishers just entering from the hallway, having come downstairs last, needing time for Owen to regain his composure.

Jennifer and the others looked taken aback by this change in script when the play hadn't even started.

"I, uh, I'd like to introduce you all to Jennifer's friends who've offered their internet wizardry during this difficult time. They discovered information for us. Not as much as we might have hoped and Jennifer needed to search herself to find background on the man who fell before Calliope did, Felix Robertson. But we appreciate all they did.

"Meet Blue and Cran. They've been a stabilizing influence on the team. They also volunteered to try to get data from Jennifer's wiped phone. That could have been vital."

Both looked down.

"And this is Sergei. I wondered if he was connected to Felix Robertson. The strong Eastern European accent could be faked, used to hide another accent. Say, a Philadelphia accent. That's where Felix Robertson previously lived."

Surprise washed over everyone in the room. Except Sergei, who seemed confused. "What accent?"

I ignored that. "And this is Vic. He's from the same region as Felix Robertson and he's the right age to have been the son of Felix and his first wife, Angela."

"*Me?*"

"But the person Jennifer's relied on the most has been her best online friend, DaisyDukes."

Daisy put a hand to her throat. "That's so—"

I talked over her soft, high voice. "Which reminds me of a quote from Warren G. Harding."

"*Who?*" Vic said in the same outraged tone.

"Mrs. Parens, will you do the honors? The one about friends."

Ever the teacher, she said, "Warren G. Harding was president of the United States from March 1921 until his sudden death in August 1923. I believe that the quote Elizabeth is referring to is 'I have no trouble with my enemies. But my friends ... they're the ones who keep me walking the floor nights.' "

"That's the quote." I looked at the woman on the couch in the seat closest to the fireplace, hardest to escape from. "And it made me think of you and how difficult you've made it for Jennifer by pretending to be DaisyDukes, by pretending to be her friend when you're really her enemy."

She smiled sadly. "I *am* DaisyDukes. And I am Jennifer's friend."

"The real DaisyDukes is her friend. You're not. You're Nessa Robertson. We've seen the photo, Nessa. The photo Calliope took of you just before you killed her."

Her face went rigid, but her high, light voice was good. "I have no idea who that is, but I am the real DaisyDukes. Jennifer and I have been friends for—"

I'd felt the shock from behind me coalescing into action, I half turned, anticipating the response from one member of the audience.

"You're not DaisyDukes. *I* am."

I'd turned the wrong direction.

I had to turn away from Faith Lawton to see the woman who'd

spoken. Everyone turned with me. Toward the arch leading to the stairs.

Toward India Grandisher.

She said again, "I am DaisyDukes."

Chapter Forty-Nine

IT FIT. DESPITE being a different mother, a different daughter from what I'd believed.

It also changed everything.

The momentum, the possibilities…

It was now or never.

Against the rising voices, I held up a hand.

"Before anybody says more, Kent, would you please open the front door?"

He obliged and Shelton, followed by Robert Alvaro, stepped in. A murmur rose at the sight of their uniforms.

I spun, turning my back on them, to zero in on the target.

Tom's hand came to my elbow, tugging me.

At first, I thought… But, no, he wasn't trying to yank me away, just edging me to a different position.

I gave him a questioning look. He tipped his head toward Shelton and Alvaro, then to the fake DaisyDukes.

Then I had it.

And I could use it.

"Please, everyone, move to one side. We don't want anyone innocent to be in the deputies' line of fire."

Murmurs became gasps. Including one from Nessa Robertson.

"When I said we have the photo, Nessa, I should have said two photos. We also have one from your wedding day to Felix. Were you already thinking about murder then? Is that why you tried to duck out of the photo. But there you are, in a corner of the background. With your groom. And then the one from Friday. Without your groom. The one Calliope Grandisher took, catching you as you pushed Felix to his death."

"I don't know what you're talki—"

"Forget it, Nessa. You think the photo wasn't clear enough? You're wrong. You'd be amazed at what software can do. Because you don't know computers and tech as well as you've tried to pretend these past days, do you? Oh, you know enough to delay and misdirect the searches Jennifer asked you to organize. But it must have been a strain trying to not give yourself away to the others. But she's made mistakes, hasn't she?"

Predictably, Vic was first. "Yes!" Sergei grunted agreement. I could imagine Blue and Cran looking at each other ... but I wasn't turning away from her to check. "Slips. Yes, odd slips," said Blue, I thought.

"This is ridiculous. Tell them, Jennifer—"

For those of us who'd been upstairs it echoed with Lance's impassioned words. But his had been for Jennifer's good. These were not.

"We have the photos. We know who you are. We know what you did." I half turned. "Sergeant Shelton, this is Nessa Robertson, the wife—widow—of Felix Robertson. She was also his step-daughter. You will find records of their marriage under her mother's address." I faced Nessa again. "We thought that was Felix's mistake, but, in fact, your official address was your mother's house until you married her ex. She blamed Felix, but she's not happy with you, either.

"Also, Sergeant Shelton, a couple staying at the Haber House Hotel can identify her as the person they saw at the location from which both her husband and Calliope were pushed to their deaths, though she was dressed to pass as a man then, using loose men's clothing to hide her figure, her hair tucked up, and a big cowboy hat to obscure her face. They should especially recognize her voice. Her real voice, not the one we've heard tonight. Like her mother, she has a naturally low, raspy voice that can pass for a man's.

"Authorities in Colorado will certainly want her held on murder charges."

"Yeah, yeah, you told me all that already or I wouldn't be here.

Deputy Alvaro, take this woman into custody and read her her rights."

"Don't touch me. I don't know what she's talking about. Jennifer. Jennifer, tell them I'm DaisyDukes." The high, light voice was gone. This was like hearing Angela. In a rage. "I came here to help you. Tell them."

Jennifer stood. "She's Nessa Robertson. She murdered my friend and *that's* the voice of the person who called me Friday."

Chapter Fifty

WITH LAW ENFORCEMENT and their prisoner gone, India Grandisher's explanation of how she became DaisyDukes came first.

"It started with wanting to know more about computers. Maybe because Calliope admired what Jennifer could do so much. I don't know anymore. I signed up for a class and then another. Until classes at the community colleges weren't enough. I took classes online. Special intensives in various cities."

So much for rumors of her traveling in search of glitz and bright lights ... unless you counted the glow of a computer screen.

For the first time, she looked toward her husband. He didn't seem to comprehend what was happening.

She turned to Jennifer.

"I... I searched for you online. Joined where you were. Watched and read. At first, I thought maybe I'd find out all the things Calliope wasn't telling me anymore. But you didn't talk about teenage things. You and your friends talked about concepts and skills... I had to work even harder to catch up, to be accepted. I created DaisyDukes. And we became friends." She glanced at the others, but came back to Jennifer. "We have been friends."

I saw Jennifer struggling to take it in. To give her time, maybe to give all of us time, I said, "Nessa took advantage of your understandable absence from online these past days to slip in and become DaisyDukes. I wonder if she blocked you somehow, India. She certainly impeded the flow of information."

I sent Aunt Gee a smile, though she probably didn't understand that her words about boxes had opened my eyes to why we'd hit so many roadblocks with the computer searches.

"I've only started checking," Jennifer said, "but it's clear she kept information from me. Steered us away from Robertson and herself. Slowed us down. It was the perfect spot for her. She had Calliope's phone—"

"I recommend you have Elizabeth start earlier, Jennifer," said Mrs. Parens, "while everyone listens quietly."

The room stilled. Even those she hadn't taught recognized her authority.

"Felix Robertson was a gambler. Nineteen years ago, he married Angela, who had a daughter by her previous marriage, Nessa. Felix and Angela divorced two years ago. Over Nessa? We don't know. But earlier this year, just after Robertson won two million dollars at poker, he married his former step-daughter.

"Tell them about Woody Allen." Mike drew a reproving look from Mrs. P.

"Yes, that was one of the things Angela said about Felix, pointing out that his type of woman and Allen's type were different. It wasn't until a few other pieces came together that I started thinking maybe what prompted her comment was not how they were different, but something they had in common."

"Marrying their ex's daughter," Mike said.

"Exactly. These Robertson newlyweds were barely back from the honeymoon when Felix won another huge jackpot on the NCAA basketball tournament. But he was spending like crazy. And Nessa had been around him long enough growing up as his step-daughter to know money slid through his hands. We don't have proof of the next part, except it makes sense and her actions seem to confirm it.

"She wasn't going to let Felix go through all that money she'd married him for." Had she done more? Had her computer skills helped win the money? I doubt she'd spill that. "The only sure way to keep the money was to kill him. How she came up with a fall at Rocky Mountain National Park..." I raised both hands in a who-knows gesture.

"Internet search," murmured Cran.

Sergei cleared his throat heavily. "Jennifer gave me name from the wedding certificate—Nessa Robertson. It was her maiden name, also. I found she attended college—computer science—at Colorado State in Fort Collins, Colorado."

I nodded at him. "There you have it. She knew the area. And computers, though not at the level you all are. How she persuaded Felix to hike—"

"We can guess," said Blue.

"She had her plan. She pushed Felix to his death. Except she didn't check the trail carefully enough. Calliope Grandisher heard or saw something. There's a point higher on the trail where the curve shows the rock shelf where Felix landed. Did Calliope see him there? Did she see him actually fall?"

"You said the photo showed her pushing him," objected Cran.

"Bluff," Mike said with a grin. "Elizabeth's pretty good at it."

I slid past the matter of Calliope's death. "She had Calliope's phone, probably thought she had things covered. She starts looking at the photos. Then the Valentines arrive—"

"Who?" Kent Lawton asked.

I'd forgotten not everyone knew the whole story. I sketched in the Valentines' role.

"Nessa leaves them, gets to the trailhead and her vehicle. She'd gotten away. She'd deleted the photos from Calliope's phone. But then she saw Calliope had sent photos to Lance's and Jennifer's phones. Lance's phone was easy. If she was smart, she removed the photo first thing. Either way, she wiped the phone quickly. But Jennifer's had many additional levels of security that Nessa kept attacking, trying to get to the photo.

"She was growing concerned. Then she sees communications between Jennifer and her friends. This was her opportunity not only to follow exactly what was happening, but to insert herself so she could divert information. As DaisyDukes, she said she'd join the others coming here. In fact, she drove here Friday, arriving in time to spend several hours in a disreputable bar, scoping out people who might be useful. She stashed her vehicle and made use of it when she pretended to go for long walks. If it's needed, law enforcement will surely find residents who noticed a Colorado plate and unfamiliar car parked on their streets."

I sucked in a breath. I had done exactly that. On the way to the dry cleaners yesterday.

"At the same time, she kept pointing toward associations with Calliope, not Felix. And there was plenty there to keep us tangled up." I didn't look at the three sets of parents.

"But why must she kill him for spending? He could win more," protested Sergei. Who knew he could be so soft-hearted?

"Not with his record. Winning that first money was a major anomaly. Winning the second time was a lightning striking," Vic said. "I sent his gambling resume to—Oh. To Daisy. Or I thought to Daisy."

"While I told her everything," Jennifer said bitterly. "What about Lance? Why go after him when his phone was already dead?"

"*Because* you told her everything, she was sure you hadn't seen the photo, but she couldn't be sure he hadn't. She was careful to never be around him, but, still, it must have worried her. Jennifer, did you repeat that I thought Lance might be hiding something?"

"Oh, yes," came from the remaining hackers.

I felt a wave of protectiveness from the direction of Brady and Holly Joudrey, still standing by the door with the Lawtons.

I continued, "She must have kept thinking she'd be able to leave any second. But Jennifer's multiple phones and not having the old phone with her because she lacked the charging cord—"

"And Shadow."

"—and my heroic dog foiled Nessa. She made mistakes. She must have had transportation to or from the area of Double Dead Curve, so somebody knows something about her movements." Looks all around and head-shakes declared nobody here knew. Perfect job for Shelton's minions. "She went into Jennifer's computer to kill articles Jennifer had found. But the articles going missing focused attention on them." If I hadn't been moving today, I'd have looked at them immediately instead of shoving them in a pocket with a box cutter. "The attack last night—"

Both Lawtons gripped their daughter.

"That's quite enough for tonight," Mrs. Parens said. "Everyone needs a good night's sleep."

DAY SEVEN

THURSDAY

Chapter Fifty-One

SIX OF CALLIOPE'S friends from Colorado arrived for the funeral.
Four from the dinner, including the sponsor, Zara, and the blonde
hiker, Suzanne.

With the B&B full, they stayed at the Haber House Hotel.

The night before the funeral, right after the viewing, we shared
with them, Ivan Quentel, and the Valentines—who had immediately
identified Nessa Robertson as the "young man" on the hiking trail—
chocolate pie, explanations, and tears.

Shelton had filled in gaps.

First, how the person calling herself DaisyDukes got from Double
Dead Curve. She'd left her vehicle nearby early Tuesday—the green
license plate was noticed—expecting the break-in to solve all her
problems and planning to drive back to Colorado immediately after
dealing with Lance.

She'd hiked several miles, then called Krista, saying she'd gotten
lost.

Krista, of course, had no idea she'd transported a murderer, thinking she was providing good customer service. She was taking it hard
that the B&B now had associations with two murders in its first six
months of operation.

She planned to do more painting.

Second, Nessa's green-license-plated vehicle was found several
blocks from the B&B. It had marks from shotgun pellets in the left

rear panel, just where Tom had shot it.

Third, Chaps, the stand-in truck renter Nessa used so she wasn't associated with it, had been located in Cheyenne on a colossal bender. He had no memory of how he'd gotten there, but had a vague recollection of dressing up for a nice lady.

Finally, Nessa was spotted on a security camera in the Estes Park hotel's parking lot. She'd avoided the lobby, but that hadn't been enough.

Sergei pinned down another element.

Because of Nessa's crime, Felix Robertson's estate would go to his son, a middle-schooler with no discernible aptitude for computers.

Earlier in the day, Jennifer packed up her belongings from my guest room and went home.

But I was not alone in the house that night.

I OPENED THE front door to Shadow and Diana.

He nudged my hand in greeting, then stepped into the house, clearly on patrol.

He stopped by the narrow chest that had belonged to my grandfather's grandmother, sniffed audibly at the handles, then all around the three sides he could get to. At the end, he turned and looked at me.

He made a chuffing sound.

"He knows it's yours," Diana said.

"Maybe he can smell the family tree."

To that crack, she said seriously, "He probably can."

"Want some coffee while he's at it? Assuming I can find where Mrs. Parens and Aunt Gee put everything."

I FOUND EVERYTHING I needed to make coffee with little difficulty. The ladies of O'Hara Hill's system made a lot of sense.

Eventually, Shadow returned from his explorations of every room, circled three times, and laid down on the oriental rug I'd added in front of the fireplace with a slight grunt, followed by a long, satisfied sigh.

Diana grinned. "He's home."

I couldn't help smiling back. "I guess we both are."

"Now all you have to do is figure out what to do about Mike and Tom."

DAY EIGHT

FRIDAY

Chapter Fifty-Two

THE GRAVESIDE SERVICE had ended.

Jennifer's parents flanked her, each holding a hand. I suspected they received as much comfort from the contact as they gave.

She held tight to their hands. Until she took a tulip and dropped it on Calliope's casket.

Ivan Quentel had come with the Valentines. Worry had lifted from his broad shoulders.

Now, he appeared to be introducing himself to the Grandishers. India's mouth formed an "Oh." Would knowing he'd been with her daughter just after her death make her feel better or worse? Was he sharing that he'd sensed Calliope's presence?

He turned and the Valentines moved forward. Kassandra grasped both of India's hands in a gesture of condolence.

The mourners trailed toward their vehicles. We joined them. Tom hung back, a sentry outside the encampment of the bereaved. The rest of us reached Mike's SUV, but none of us got in.

Six figures remained beside Calliope's grave.

Lance stood alone. Looking down, toward the casket. He'd arrived with his parents, but while they'd stayed well back, perhaps from tact, he had moved to the front, never looking away from the casket holding Calliope's remains.

Calliope's parents held onto each other.

Jennifer's parents still flanked her. As if realizing the wholeness of

their unit emphasized what was missing in the Grandishers', Kent and
Faith Lawton stepped back, letting Jennifer lead the way to Calliope's
parents.

We heard no words from this distance. There might not have been
words.

They hugged, Owen and India collapsing around Jennifer.

They released her with seeming reluctance. The two sets of parents
embraced then, much more briefly.

India touched Jennifer's arm, said something. Jennifer put her arms
around the woman and hugged. A hug, I suspected, for DaisyDukes.

Finally, the Lawton family turned and started in our direction,
joined by Tom.

As they came toward us, past them I saw the Grandishers and
Lance still at the graveside. Separate, yet united in their grief.

As the Lawtons neared, Faith detached and reached me first.

"Thank you, Elizabeth. Jennifer told us… Well, she filled in
around the edges of what we'd seen ourselves. Thank you for being
suspicious of everyone to make sure our girl was safe."

I met her hand. She used the hold to pull me in for a hug.

We were backing away from each other when Jennifer reached a
hand to me.

Adapting her mother's ploy, I used the hold to turn her.

She resisted. I nodded, trying to tell her it was okay to look.

She turned toward Calliope's grave. Over her shoulder I saw what
she saw. The Grandishers embracing Lance.

Jennifer swung back around, a faint smile beneath new tears.

She pushed at those tears with the fingertips of both hands, then
pulled in a long breath.

"Remember Friday night? When you talked about the truth maybe
not being what I'd want?"

"Uh-huh."

"I wanted to know what really happened. I told myself it was for
Calliope, but *I* needed it. Thank you for what you did. All of you."

She held out her hand, as if all of us could shake it at once.

Instead, Diana, Tom, Mike, and I met in a group hug, with her in the middle.

"There's one more thing." Jennifer looked around at each of us, then a second look at Mike and me. "Remember what Ivan Quentel said at the park? About how he felt her? He was right. She was there. Calliope. With him on that rock ledge. She told me once she was sure she'd die young, but she wouldn't go right away. She knew it. She just knew it. And that's what happened.

"It all makes sense now."

Chapter Fifty-Three

MIKE AND TOM had come over to take more loads from the garage to the community yard sale storage. If this continued, I might someday get my vehicle in the garage.

Then they wrestled a double dresser I wanted upstairs, instead of in the guest room.

Pretty sure I wanted it upstairs.

After that, I asked them both to sit down on the couch. I took a chair opposite them.

Because it was time.

Past time.

"I want us to all know where we stand. I don't think it's a surprise—I mean each of you has indicated... And I feel... I mean..." I sucked in a breath. "I'm just going to say this. I'm interested in more."

Neither of them said a word to help me out.

Maybe I'd rethink this. Maybe I'd forget the whole deal...

I licked my lips and watched their eyes follow the movement and felt an answering response.

Never mind about rethinking and forgetting the whole deal.

On a surge of ... *something* ... I finished with, "I'd like to date you. Both of you. Not together at the same time," I added hurriedly. "One at a time but with the times close together, not one for a stretch, then the other. Oh, hell, I want to see where this—" I waved my hand from Mike to me, then from Tom to me. "—might go. What do you think?"

They looked at me. I looked back.

At last, Tom said, "Okay. Mike?"

"Okay with me. You?"

"Yep."

The End

Thank you for reading Elizabeth, Jennifer and friends' latest adventure!

One of the hallmarks of the Caught Dead in Wyoming series is its deep dive into contemporary Western culture with roots that trace to its earliest settlers. In *Left Hanging,* readers learned along with fresh-off-the-jet Elizabeth about ups and downs of a small-town rodeo circuit. In *Last Ditch,* the murder mystery was muddied by tension over local water rights. For the next mystery, rangeland as well as water must be managed in this rough country—and where there's rules, there's trouble.

In *Reaction Shot,* stolen cattle and some frontier justice have Elizabeth, Tom, Mike, Diana and her team of investigators on the search for truth.

Reaction Shot

Elizabeth, Jennifer, Tom, Mike, Shadow and friends ask if you'll help spread the word about them and the Caught Dead in Wyoming series. You have the power to do that in two quick ways:

Recommend the book and the series to your friends and/or the whole wide world on social media. Shouting from rooftops is particularly appreciated.

Review the book. Take a few minutes to write an honest review and it can make a huge difference. As you likely know, it's the single best way for your fellow readers to find books they'll enjoy, too.

To me—as an author and a reader—the goal is always to find a good author-reader match. By sharing your reading experience through recommendations and reviews, you become a vital matchmaker. ☺

For news about upcoming books, as well as other titles and news, join Patricia McLinn's Readers List and receive her twice-monthly free newsletter.
https://www.patriciamclinn.com/readers-list

Other Caught Dead in Wyoming Mysteries

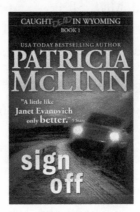

SIGN OFF

Divorce a husband, lose a career ... grapple with a murder.

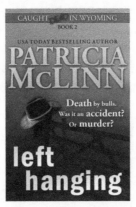

LEFT HANGING

Trampled by bulls—an accident? Elizabeth, Mike and friends must dig into the world of rodeo.

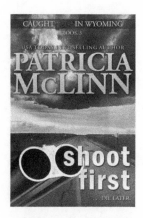

SHOOT FIRST

For Elizabeth, death hits close to home. She and friends must delve into old Wyoming treasures and secrets to save lives.

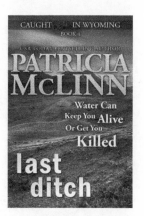

LAST DITCH

KWMT's Elizabeth and Mike search after a man in a wheelchair goes missing in dangerous, desolate country.

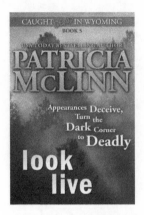

LOOK LIVE

Elizabeth and friends take on misleading murder with help—and hindrance—from intriguing out-of-towners.

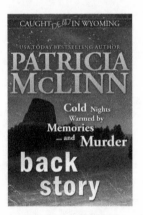

BACK STORY

Murder never dies, but comes back to threaten Elizabeth and team of investigators.

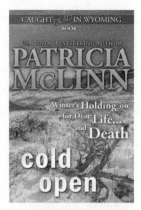

COLD OPEN

Elizabeth's looking for a place of her own becomes an open house for murder.

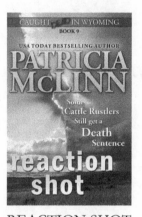

REACTION SHOT

Some cattle rustlers still get a death sentence.

"While the mystery itself is twisty-turny and thoroughly engaging, it's the smart and witty writing that I loved the best."
—*Diane Chamberlain, New York Times bestselling author*

"Colorful characters, intriguing, intelligent mystery, plus the state of Wyoming leaping off every page."
—*Emilie Richards, USA Today bestselling author*

More Mystery by Patricia McLinn

Secret Sleuth series

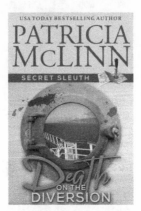

DEATH ON THE DIVERSION

Final resting place? Deck chair

DEATH ON TORRID AVENUE

A new love (canine), an ex-cop and a dog park discovery.

DEATH ON BEGUILING WAY

No zen in sight as Sheila untangles a yoga instructor's murder.

DEATH ON COVERT CIRCLE

Death on the Diversion "is such an enjoyable story, reminiscent of Agatha Christie's style, with a good study of human nature and plenty of humor. Great start to a new series!"

—*5-star review*

Mystery with Romance

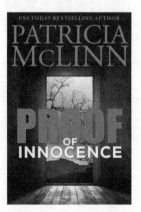

PROOF OF INNOCENCE

She's a prosecutor chasing demons. He's wrestling them. Will they find proof of innocence?

PRICE OF INNOCENCE

She runs a foundation dedicated to forgiveness. He runs down
criminals. If they don't work together, people will die.

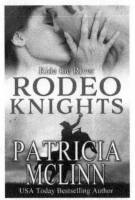

RIDE THE RIVER: RODEO KNIGHTS

Her rodeo cowboy ex is back … as her prime suspect.

Bardville, Wyoming series

A Stranger in the Family
A Stranger to Love
The Rancher Meets His Match

Explore a complete list of all Patricia's books
www.patriciamclinn.com/patricias-books

Or get a printable booklist
patriciamclinn.com/patricias-books/printable-booklist

Patricia's eBookstore (buy digital books online directly from Patricia)
patriciamclinn.com/patricias-books/ebookstore

About the Author

USA Today bestselling author Patricia McLinn spent more than 20 years as an editor at The Washington Post after stints as a sports writer (Rockford, Ill.) and assistant sports editor (Charlotte, N.C.). She received BA and MSJ degrees from Northwestern University.

McLinn is the author of more than 50 published novels, which are cited by readers and reviewers for wit and vivid characterization. Her books include mysteries, romantic suspense, contemporary romance, historical romance and women's fiction. They have topped bestseller lists and won numerous awards.

She has spoken about writing from Melbourne, Australia, to Washington, D.C., including being a guest speaker at the Smithsonian Institution.

Now living in northern Kentucky, McLinn loves to hear from readers through her website, Facebook and Twitter.

Visit with Patricia:

Website: patriciamclinn.com

Facebook: facebook.com/PatriciaMcLinn

Twitter: @PatriciaMcLinn

Pinterest: pinterest.com/patriciamclinn

Instagram: instagram.com/patriciamclinnauthor

ISBN: 978-1-944126-36-0

CPSIA information can be obtained
at www.ICGtesting.com
Printed in the USA
LVHW092259180120
643993LV00002B/57